HMS Expedient

Peter Smalley was born in Melbourne, Australia and hails from a seafaring family. After an early career in advertising he became a screenwriter, broadcaster and novelist. He lives in London with his wife, Clytie.

Praise for HMS Expedient

'A real page-turner, engrossing and enthralling with memorable characters...salute a new master of the sea' *Daily Express*

'Good taut writing...gets Peter Smalley's series off to a flying start' *The Sunday Telegraph*

Also available by Peter Smalley

Port Royal

HMS Expedient

PETER SMALLEY

arrow books

Published in the United Kingdom by Arrow Books in 2006

1 3 5 7 9 10 8 6 4 2

First published in the United Kingdom in 2005 by Century

Arrow Books
The Random House Group Ltd
20 Vauxhall Bridge Road, London SW1V 2SA

Random House Australia (Pty) Limited
20 Alfred Street, Milsons Point, Sydney
New South Wales 2061, Australia

Random House New Zealand Limited
18 Poland Road, Glenfield, Auckland 10, New Zealand

Random House (Pty) Limited
Isle of Houghton, Corner of Boundary Road & Carse O'Gowrie,
Houghton 2198, South Africa

The Random House Group Limited Reg. No. 954009

www.randomhouse.co.uk

A CIP catalogue record for this book
is available from the British Library

Papers used by Random House are natural, recyclable
products made from wood grown in sustainable forests.
The manufacturing processes conform to the environmental
regulations of the country of origin

ISBN 9780099474173 (from Jan 2007)
ISBN 0 09 9474174

Printed and bound in Great Britain by
Cox & Wyman Ltd, Reading, Berkshire

This book is dedicated to my father, who was a naval officer in World War II, and to my father-in-law, who sailed as an ordinary seaman on a four-masted barque.

CONTENTS

ACKNOWLEDGEMENT

I would like to thank the staff of the National Maritime Museum at Greenwich, in particular the staff of the Caird Library, for their unfailingly kind assistance during my research for this novel.

PROLOGUE

An onshore breeze ruffled the riding sea, and made flurries in the wavelets at the beach. Offshore at the Downs a squadron was heaving to, topsails aback, assembling for the run south into the Channel. A stray merchantman, running before, found herself momentarily at odds with these greater ships, with their pennants and ensigns, and came over on the opposite tack to avoid falling on board the flag, His Majesty's ship *Centaur*, seventy-four. The breeze picked up, and became brisk.

On the sand and shingle of the beach a figure stood, sniffing that breeze, and squaring his head to it under his thwart-wise hat. It was the figure of a sailor. His bearing said so, and his squared shoulders, and his feet a little apart; but most of all his long glass, as he focused on the ships.

'What does the fellow think?' he said to himself. 'What does he attempt, when there is fighting ships assembling? Good God, he will certainly—ah, no, he has come over. Well well, he damn' near caused mischief, the fellow.'

He sniffed, and walked on, the glass under his arm, his head a little bent. His head had been bent a little these last days. Commander William Rennie RN—a spare man of middling height, who looked older than his thirty years—was on the beach.

Presently his friend Admiral Bailey joined him there. The admiral was beginning to be stout, and arthritic, but at sixty had not lost his cordiality.

'William, good day to you.'

'Good day to you, Admiral. I was just—I had my eye on the frigate.' Nodding there.

'Yes, I see her. She is the *Heraclea*, thirty-two, I think, twelve-pounder. Young Bainbridge had her at Chesapeake, and after he was killed she went to, to, hmm . . .'

'She was put in Ordinary at the end of the war, and has only now been recommissioned.'

'Who has got her, now?'

'Captain Wrigley, sir.'

'Aye, Wrigley, that is the fellow.' A glance. 'No doubt you are hellishly at work, wondering why you was not favoured, hey?'

'It is not for me to wonder, not at all. We are not at war, and places is limited by circumstance. No no, I simply look to seaward, as a matter in course, and observe what is happening there.'

A gun was fired on the flag, a puff of smoke rushing out from the port before the heartening bang reached the ears of the two observers ashore. The squadron came to the wind, forming in line ahead.

A tear formed in Commander Rennie's eye. He made no attempt to brush it away, but let it fall on his cheek.

'It is a sight,' he said at last.

'Aye.' Quietly.

'I can never see it without I am moved.'

'Nor I.'

And the two sea officers watched the squadron beat away close-hauled, heeling tall into the Channel wind.

Admiral Bailey—Rear-Admiral of the Blue—would never again have a ship under his legs; he was retired on half-pay, and lived widowed here at Deal with no particular difficulties or regrets. A post had been found for him, a duty of inspection once a month of half-forgotten naval stores in a line of shabby old buildings beyond the town: Officer of the Keys. Dutifully, for he was a dutiful officer, Admiral Bailey inspected the stores on the last Friday of each month, walking there and back with the absurd bunch of keys on a great brass ring, usually in the company of his younger friend. And once a year the Navy Board forwarded to his name the sum of one hundred pounds.

'It ain't a thing to boast of,' he had said to Rennie more than once. 'It is a fanciful, purposeless, valueless sort of duty.' Holding up the keys ironically as they walked, shaking his head.

'But it is a duty—an official duty.'

'Aye, no, you are right. Indeed it is a duty, paid for and recorded as such.' A barking laugh. 'But by God, it is a foolish one, looked at in a clear light.'

'The walk is beneficial, though.'

'And the hundred of money, that supplements my pay, and keeps me in wine. Heigh ho, I must not complain.' Jingling the keys. 'I must certainly not complain.'

The admiral was sometimes unthinking in these jaunty self-deprecations, unthinking in that he did not always see that a fellow officer, a much younger man, might feel hard used with no duty to do at all—that he had a right to feel it, that he had been hard used, and that the Lords Commissioners of the Admiralty were shabbily at fault.

Commander Rennie, on the beach, on meagre half-pay, had acquitted himself with distinction at the Battle of the Saints.

———※◆※———

In January 1782, Commander Rennie, Captain Rennie—the title a courtesy rank granted to officers not yet made post, who commanded vessels above a cutter—had been sent in his ship sloop *Mystic*, twenty guns, clear across the Atlantic from Ushant by Admiral Kempenfelt with a message warning Admiral Hood at Antigua, in the Leeward Islands, that a large French convoy of troop ships and supply ships approached, to join the French fleet under Admiral de Grasse at Dominica. De Grasse had taken St Kitts, and now the whole Caribbean was under threat. Hood's chief concern—his only concern—was to save Jamaica, the shining jewel in England's Caribbean crown. Hood's fleet was twenty-one ships of the line, and he was soon joined by his superior Admiral Rodney, with a further fifteen ships, plus a scattering of frigates and fireships. Hood and Rodney conferred, and over the following weeks formed their strategy.

Battle was first joined on the morning of April the 9th, when part of the French fleet sailed between Dominica and a small group of islands to the north, Les Saintes. Both Hood's and Rodney's ships engaged the French, but action was indecisive. Rennie, now temporarily attached to Hood as repeat signals, was kept busy between Hood's flag *Barfleur* and the centre and rear of the line. Firing ceased in the early afternoon.

Overnight on the 11th there was a mishap in the French fleet, and on the morning of the 12th a damaged ship, the *Zele*, was towed out of the line. Four of Hood's ships attacked the *Zele* and her assisting ship. De Grasse, determined to save the *Zele*, advanced to give protection. Rennie stood by in *Mystic*, awaiting orders from Hood in *Barfleur* as battle was joined, the British line in reverse order, steering east-north-east, to leeward of the French line—which was disorderly, with ships missing stays, and lagging astern—steering south-south-west, the wind in the east.

Hood now sent Rennie to inform Admiral Rodney that he intended to try and break through the French line at the van. Rennie caught the wind and fled up to leeward towards *Formidable*, and repeated the message. The quarterdeck acknowledged. And now Rodney made contact to starboard with the sixth ship in the French line, and opened fire. The French to windward, the English to leeward, and the thundering stutter of great guns, smoke, and orange flashes; the lighter, sharper, high-carrying crack-crack of muskets as French marines fired from the tops. Rennie decided:

'We will go about, and rejoin the other squadron to the south!'

At the same moment he gave the command there was a whistling rush, and a twenty-four-pound round shot traversed *Mystic*'s deck, ripping across the hammock cranes and smashing a boat in the waist utterly into splinters. A seaman staggered up the ladder, and along the gangway, clutching his head. Blood streamed through his fingers. He stumbled, reached out his hand to a shroud, and the blood gouted from his head in glossy spurts. No murmur came from him. He turned in slow motion on the lift of the sea, sagged, and went over the side. And now, deep in the waist, the animal groans of wounded men. Rennie, momentarily transfixed, came to himself.

'Put your helm down! We must get out of this right quick, or be smashed and destroyed!'

As *Mystic* came round into the wind, and beat away south-east, Rodney in *Formidable* cut through the French line, turned and cut through to starboard, and Captain Affleck, in Hood's squadron to the south, broke through in the *Bedford*, pounding with broadsides, and the whole French line was thrown absolutely into confusion, telling and fatal.

'I never saw anything like it,' said Rennie in wonder.

'Your face is very bloody, sir.' Young Upsher, his lieutenant. 'You are hurt.'

'What?' Lowering his glass a moment. 'Did you see? We have cut the French line, twice cut it, and have broke through! By God, I have never seen anything like it! Mr Tench!' To the signals midshipman. 'Mr Tench, make to *Barfleur* that we are standing by, awaiting instruction. We cannot go in closer, Mr Upsher, else be made into match-wood, hey? But what an action, by God!'

Grape-shot, wide of its mark in the battle line, cracked overhead in the mizzentop, and a block fell to the deck. More splinters, and falling rope. Rennie stood to the weather rail, glancing anxiously aloft.

'Sir, you are bleeding.'

'Yes, I dare say.' Now looking away to larboard, again raising his glass. 'By God, what a fight. *What* a fight. I never saw anything like it.'

And later, he could not tell quite how many hours later—having repeated signals in a long chase to the north-east—he was close in by Hood's ship. He could not quite recall how *Mystic* had got there. No, he could not say. He was bloody right down the front of his shirt and his britches, he was light-headed, but he would not go below, he would not sit down. He called for a pint of grog, and drank it off.

Barfleur worked in very close, until she was right alongside the French flag, the *Ville de Paris*. A muffled shout, amid the yells and general din, and then *Barfleur*'s side lit up in a glorious flowering of fire, a great wall of flashes, in the instant before the sound crashed over *Mystic*'s deck. The sound was so tremendous it seemed to be carried on a whirlwind, shattering, thudding, trembling in the timbers; shivering up through feet and legs, making the ears sing blackly, and the head spin. The *Ville de Paris* shuddered, and shuddered, and the sea all round her rippled with the shock, with the sheer weight of metal slamming into her. A boiling storm of smoke and burning fragments, the cracking tumble of tangling yards, falling blocks and rigging, unheeded orders shouted, and skin-tightening, horrible screams.

And now, dazed as he was, exhausted as he was, Rennie saw with a terrible clarity the truth of that broadside. Blood began to pour from the French ship's splintered side. It poured and streamed from smashed port cills, from roundshot holes, from scuppers, poured red and glistening down the curve of the side and into the sea, and lay riding there in a long accusing stain.

'Oh, Christ,' murmured Rennie. 'That is men dying, that is their blood streaming away, and their lives lost.'

'You had better go below, sir.' Lieutenant Upsher. 'You are—you are not yourself.'

'Am I not, Mr Upsher? What are those poor wretches? They are not themselves, neither, any more.'

— ⚋✦⚌ —

Afterward, at Port Royal, Rodney had sent for him, and praised him for his bravery as signals in the late action, praised him, but added:

'I fear I cannot admit you to a share in the prizes, Captain Rennie, since you was not properly attached to me, nor to Admiral Hood, neither. To be exact, you was attached to Admiral Kempenfelt, and caught up by circumstance in the battle, after he sent you here. In course, you are disappointed, but it cannot be helped. Fact is fact.'

'Very good, sir.'

'I will do what I can for you in England. Say a word in an ear, and write a letter or two, hm? You apprehend me?'

'Thank you, sir.'

'Yes, I will certainly do what I can. You deserve to be moved up. And now, there is much else I must attend to. Good day to you.'

— ⚋✦⚌ —

And now, in '86, as he walked disconsolately about Deal in the company of his elderly friend, and watched departing squadrons, Rennie was still waiting to be 'moved up', still waiting to be favoured again with his own ship, and had not he every good reason to feel hard used?

He did not know it, but soon—very soon—his long wait was to come to an end.

PART ONE:
REFIT FOR FOREIGN SERVICE

Rooks spoke in the trees as Lieutenant James Hayter RN rode round the foot of the slope, past the church and the lichen-blotched gravestones, and the great oak by the lych-gate. At the corner of the lane he reined in, and smelled the morning air. From above, far above, at the wall of the ruined abbey—in the town of Shaftesbury, in Dorset—the view was unsurpassed in all England. He had stood there earlier on this, his last morning, and drunk it in as if for the first time. The spires of the churches at Stour Magna and Fifehead Last and South Oak, the hedges marching down into the green hollows, the copses on the rises and folds, and the long slope down to Magdalen Row, where the hunt ran on crisp mornings on the promise of the horns. He had thought how he would miss this country, the sweep of it, the soft smoke of the cottage rows, hanging on the air, and the sounds of the birds. And now he reined in, and was thoughtful, looking at the handsome old stone rectory of St John's—so thoughtful that he did not see the Reverend Dr Armitage until that gentleman was at his stirrup.

'Is it James? Yes, it is. Good morning to you.'

'Oh, Rector. Good morning, sir. I was quite lost.'

'Lost? Here?'

'In my head, you know. I'll walk with you to the gate, if I may, sir.'

He dismounted, and they turned the corner and went along by the rectory wall.

'So this is your last day?' said the rector. 'Tell me, d'you go by the turnpike coach?'

'No, by cutter from Weymouth.'

'Weymouth? Ain't that the long way round, though? Would it not be quicker and faster to go by the turnpike coach?'

'Turnpikes are damned expensive. I do beg your pardon, Rector. They are expensive in the extreme, and I am poor. My father has been pleased to let me have Jaunter to ride as far as Winterborne, where I have cousins, and then I make my way with them to Weymouth. *Snipe* is a fast, weatherly little vessel, and we shall arrive at the Nore in no time at all.'

'You will be pleased to go to sea again, I expect?'

'Yes, to get back my sea legs. That is another reason not to go by road. I must get back my sea legs after three years on the beach.'

He did not say that living at home on a lieutenant's half-pay, unable to draw on an allowance which his father, Sir Charles Hayter, would—perversely—condescend to pay only when his son was again possessed of a commission, was a bitter thing. To depend on his father for a roof, and victuals, his pay always held up, was a bitter thing altogether. Had he not to ask permission to ride? His brothers when at home had free run of the stables, yet he must ask leave to ride. Once, when he had taken the bay without asking leave, his father had said as they drank their port:

'I wish you had asked me about Jaunter, you know, James. He was near lame last week, and Padding was fearful when you brought the animal back this afternoon. Sweaty, said Padding. "Lathered under the leather" was his expression, I believe. I wish you had asked me first. Then you could have had Spitzer, or Bramble.'

'I'm sorry. I was in haste, you know, and did not think.'

'In haste?'

'To ride.'

'Ah. Ah. Why, in haste?'

And so forth, it was damned near impossible, under the circumstances, to believe that he was an adult being at all. Had it not been for his mother's delicate understanding, and her willingness to leave a guinea or two under his pillow— Lady Hayter had six hundred a year of her own—he should never have been able to think of himself as other than a piddling boy, a dull and piddling boy, lost in the lanes of Dorset with straw in his hair. As it was he could not pay his tailor, or his bookseller.

'This bill has come to me, James,' his father had said one morning.

'Bill, sir?' In dread.

'Indeed, a bill. From a bookseller fellow in—where is the place? Something Lane, in London. Four pound seven and tenpence. For books!'

'Yes, well, that is my bill, as a matter of fact. If you will just give it to——'

'Your bill, sir?' In mock astonishment.

'Yes. Yes. It is my bill. Now, if you will just——'

'Four pound seven and ten? When you are penniless? You astound me. For *books*!'

James was fastidious about his clothes, and without books in the country he would have run mad. And so his father, who was a bookish man himself, and took care in his own appearance, tortured him in his mildly savage way, and his son grew wild in his thoughts, and bit his tongue so fiercely that more than once he spat blood.

'Do you stay in the cutter?' asked the rector now, as they reached the gate. 'Your commission is in that vessel, at the Nore?'

'Oh no, sir. No, I am to join my ship at Deptford, in London.'

'It is a great many years since I was last in London. What is your ship?'

'She is the *Expedient* frigate, thirty-six.'

'Thirty-six years of age?'

'No, sir, thirty-six guns.'

'Ahh. Like the seventy-four. I have heard of the seventy-four.'

'Well, not entirely. The seventy-four is a two-decker, you know, and a frigate is a single-decker, all her guns on one deck pretty near, except for her quarterdeck and forecastle.'

'Ahh.'

'I am most profoundly relieved to have got this commission.'

'I can see that you are. You sailors like to sail, after all. You are not quite at home on dry land.'

'On the contrary, we are too much at home.'

'Yes, yes, I take your meaning,' said the rector, who didn't. 'Is your father well?'

'He is, thank you, sir.'

'And your dear mother?'

'She is quite well, I thank you. Quite recovered.'

'Recovered?' The rector searched his mind. He found nothing. 'I did not know her ladyship had been ill. I am most distressed to hear it, yet greatly relieved in my distress to hear that she has recovered.'

'From Mrs Halliday's dance at Blandford. She attended with my cousins from Winterborne, it was a great expedition.'

'And her ladyship fell ill there? How very unfortunate.'

'No, sir. My mother flung herself in a whirl of delight into the entertainment, and the conversation, the dinner before, and the supper after. Then quite wore my father out in explication upon her return. She exhausted us all, indeed. But we are all quite recovered.'

'I see that you make fun of me,' chided the rector. 'When d'you depart, James? I mean, at what hour?'

'This morning. My things have already gone to Weymouth. I have only to hack back to Melton directly, say goodbye to my mother and father, and then I must away. It is a longish ride, but costs nothing, and going on by cutter has the further advantage that my friend Cobbett will charge me nothing for my passage. He is permitted to do me this service gratis, you see.'

'I do see, I do indeed. The navy is not the only profession which counts its pennies. Not that I myself, you apprehend me, not that I think constantly of these things myself. Will you come in, James, and drink a glass of sherry? Say that you will, I beg you. A farewell glass.'

'That is kind in you, sir, I will.' And they went in at the gate. The rector's groom took Jaunter's bridle, and James and Dr Armitage walked in under the stone portico, scraped their boots at the door, and went inside.

'Catherine!' called the rector.

James followed Dr Armitage into his library, a tall brown room with brown curtains, a pedestal desk covered in tooled brown leather, and brown leather chairs. For all its brownness it was a pleasant room, and had the easeful odour of hundreds of books and masculine solitude. There was a decanter of excellent sherry, which the rector served in generous glasses.

'Catherine!' he called. 'What has become of my daughter, I wonder? Has she grown timid, all at once? I don't like to ring the bell, you know, when Tabitha is at her duties in the kitchen; it disturbs her, and then she is like to forget an important ingredient, and we shall face disaster at luncheon. Cath——ah, my dear, there you are. Look who has——'

'James!' said Catherine. 'How glad you have made me by coming to say goodbye.' James looked at the lovely young woman who advanced towards him, her fine dark hair, her fine dark eyes, the flush of colour in her cheeks, the gracefulness of her movements—looked at her and felt himself a fool.

'I—I had meant to call yesterday, you know, but I——'

'No doubt you have been very busy, packing your chest.'

'Well, my mother really did all the work, and her maid.'

'Surely a sailor must pack his own things. Is not life at

sea all about self-sufficiency, and being neat and tidy and disciplined?'

'Yes, I suppose so, in a way. The truth is, I had meant to call before this, Miss Armitage.'

'Miss Armitage?'

'Catherine. I had meant to, and——'

'Pffff,' said the rector suddenly. 'I had quite forgot. I must go into the church, my dear, and retrieve something there. A book. Will you excuse me a moment, both of you?'

And when he had gone Catherine said quietly: 'Surely you had not meant to go away without saying goodbye, James?'

'Of course I had not. Look, I am here.'

'Yes, you are here. Now, you are here. But it is like an afterthought. As if you had decided, at the last moment, to ride down the hill and past the house, and perhaps come in— if you saw my father in the lane.'

The truth of this was so acute he could think of nothing to say in reply. He drew breath, held it in his lungs until it burned, and:

'I am here, Catherine,' he said at last, with a guilty sigh. 'You—you said that you was glad.'

'And I am. I am very glad. But I had thought—I had thought you would say something to me before this, about going away. I learned of your commission only by chance. Tabitha was in the town, and saw your mother's maidservant. Could not you—have said something to me?' Her voice was now very soft, very low. Her eyes searched his, and then were turned away, and the delicate curve of her cheek, the soft curled hair at her neck, nearly stopped his heart. He knew that he had wounded her. He knew that he must go away, and not come back for a long time. He knew that she cared for him. He knew too, if he searched his heart, that he cared for her, deeply cared for her—loved her. But in God's name, what was the use? He could not ask this girl to wait for him, could not ask her to be his wife, when marriage for a man in his position was impossible. Indeed, for a woman in her position.

Catherine Armitage had no money of her own—well, fifty pounds a year, left her by an aunt—Dr Armitage had no money to speak of, and could not make a settlement, and James's father would give him nothing, he was a third son.

And yet here he stood, he had come in with the rector, knowing that he would see Catherine, knowing that there would be just such a scene. In fact, had he not ridden down the hill hoping for this encounter exact? And now—should he be honest with her? Should he say to Catherine that there could be no understanding between them, as things were?

'Tell me your thoughts.' Again searching his face.

'Catherine, you know that I am your dearest friend——'

'Friend! I am your friend! How can you say such a thing!'

'Catherine, please. You are more than a friend.'

'Yes? Am I?'

'Oh, good heaven, I love you.' And he took her in his arms, and kissed her. Her tears wet his lips, her arms circled his neck, her fingers touched his hair, and he felt her body against his. This beautiful creature, how could he leave her? This dark-haired, dark-eyed, bewitching creature?

At last they broke their embrace, and looked at each other.

'Catherine, dearest Cathy, I have no right to ask, none at all. But will you wait for me? Say that you will.'

'You know that I will. You have always known it.'

'Yes, I think I have.'

'Ah, mmm, I have found my book,' said Dr Armitage outside the door, and then he came in, that discreet man, and drank his sherry. He did not ask a question, he did not make a remark, but he saw their faces, and was content.

—◄►═►—

'And you do not know, I expect, the length of your absence?' said Sir Charles.

'No, sir. I shall send letters when I am able, but these may be very few, and greatly delayed.'

'No no, I apprehend such things. It is military secrets, and the like. I have served His Majesty myself, don't forget.' He tugged at his waistcoat and drew back his shoulders.

James turned to his mother, and saw the thing he had most feared, feared because it might unman him at the moment of his release: her tears.

'My dear, dearest boy.' She clasped his hands, and he bent to her cheek. The lace of her bodice touched his cheek, and he was aware of how graceful and delicate and feminine she seemed in her brocaded dress and lace bonnet, that she and the close world she represented would soon be lost to him, the world of comfort and softness and understanding, and he felt a pang, a deep pang, and was nearly undone.

His horse stood quiet in the drive, held at the head by rat-faced Padding, a man he did not like. James detached himself gently from his mother's embrace, and put on his hat.

'Goodbye, Father.' They shook hands. His father looked him in the eye, and there was today in his gaze nothing of the irritation and mockery James had sometimes read there; today there was nothing but pride, and fond regard.

'All is settled, all is settled,' said Sir Charles, and gave his son a soft leather purse tied with silk. It was heavy with coin. 'All is settled.'

'Thank you, sir.'

'Tell Fanny I shall write to her,' said his mother, 'and that——'

But the rest was lost to James as he swung up into the saddle in a rush of emotion, waved blindly, nearly dropped the purse, and turned the horse's head towards the gates. Melton House, his father and mother, Padding in his velveteen britches, the row of elms, all fell behind, and the world opened.

As he rode through the late morning, James thought of his encounter with Catherine, thought of his family as they had stood waving in farewell, and was again filled with emotion. He was leaving his home, and his family, and his sweetheart.

For a moment or two he thought that he should have declined his commission, after all, and stayed where he was, safe in Dorset—but only for a moment. Then he shook himself free of thought, dug his heels into Jaunter's flanks, and cantered on to lunch at the inn at Childe Handley.

Birch Cottage at Winterborne lay in a fold of the high hill, overlooking the stream at the bottom of the garden. It was a perfectly presentable, well-built small country house, more than a cottage but not a manor house, square at the front, with a drive down from the road leading to a paved forecourt. The Misses Ibbetson lived there, daughters of Lady Hayter's late sister. Mr Ibbetson, their father, had been dead near ten years, and his wife had died five years ago, leaving the girls to fend for themselves. Mrs Ibbetson had had some money of her own, and this had passed in trust to her daughters, Fanny, Amelia and Anne: three hundred a year, just enough for them to live on and keep up their little house. Their father, who had been inclined to speculate, and to drink to cheer himself through his losses, had left nothing. For several years after his death there had been difficulties about his innumerable debts, until at last a settlement had been reached with his creditors through the family lawyers at Dorchester, necessitating the sale of a parcel of land which had been attached to Birch Cottage as the home farm. Now the girls lived on three or four acres of ground, secluded ground, if not in luxury or great comfort then at least in adequate circumstances. They were noisy, affectionate, quarrelling and exuberant in a way that James found both attractive, and daunting.

In the early evening, after a pleasant ride through the long afternoon, he turned Jaunter's head down the drive, rode down into the paved court and dismounted. The girls came rushing at him from inside the house, attended by dogs of diverse sizes and breeds, all leaping, barking and eager with welcome. James quailed, lifted his leather valise from the saddle, and faced them with a hearty smile.

'Cousins!' he said, clutching the bag as they flung themselves on him. 'Dear Fanny, Amelia, Anne. How glad I am to see——Ouch! Is that a dog, or a wild wolf!'.

'It is only Cerberus. Down Cerbo, you fool!' said Fanny, and tore his bag from James's grasp with great amiability, hefting it before her in both hands. 'You must be very tired after your journey. Do come in and have some grog.'

'Grog?' James looked at her to make sure she was in jest. She was not.

'We have made some grog for you, because we know how sailors like it, and cannot live a day without it.'

'Ha-ha, very good, well.' And he allowed himself to be half-pulled, half-pushed inside to a fire in the drawing-room and a large pewter tankard on the table, with four large tumblers, water tumblers, and a plate of cakes. Fanny poured out a tumbler of the grog, and they watched intently as he raised it.

'Your very good health,' he said, and drank.

Cinnamon and pepper clashed fierily on his tongue and in his throat, and there was the juniper fire of nearly neat gin. He coughed horribly, gasped, put down the glass and tried to smile, and coughed again. Spluttered. Got his handkerchief out of his pocket, brought it to his mouth and spluttered ground peppercorns and cinnamon mud into it. The girls giggled, frowned, giggled again and became concerned. James sneezed, blew his nose, and recovered his breath.

'Perhaps you are unused to grog, cousin, when you have been so long absent from the sea?' ventured Fanny.

'Grog?' croaked James. 'This is not grog.'

'Indeed it is,' said Fanny, glancing at her sisters for support. 'We made it especially for your visit. Four parts gin and one of water, cinnamon, pepper, and vinegar. Grog.'

'Who—who told you that was the recipe for grog?' James coughed again, and dabbed at his streaming eyes.

'Why, it was Mr Brimley, who is our neighbour, and was himself at sea as a young man.'

'Mr Brimley, hey? I should very much like to meet Mr Brimley.'

James later repeated this as they sat at dinner, saying only half in fun that Mr Brimley sounded like a very odd customer.

'Tst, ah, there lies a tale, James. Mr Brimley has gone away for a week, out of the district, and has taken his carriage with him. The carriage he had promised to let us have to go to Weymouth with you. I fear that you must now ride there on your horse, and we must stay here. It is very vexing, and a great shame.' Fanny shook her curls. 'It don't matter to me, but Amelia and Anne had been looking forward to it so.'

'Well, I am glad it don't matter to you, cousin Fanny,' said James with a smile, teasing her.

'Oh, I didn't mean——What I had meant to say——I *did* want to wish you farewell at Weymouth, James.' Then she saw that he was teasing her, and she blushed.

Fanny was pretty in a trim, neatly dressed, energetic sort of way, but she was no beauty. Her sister Amelia was plumper, and plainer. Anne, who had a fancy for a young lieutenant of marines stationed at the fort at Weymouth, was by far the prettiest of the three.

'It is too bad of Mr Brimley,' she said. 'I begin to think he is an odious man.'

'Nonsense, Anne,' said Fanny. 'Has not Mr Brimley allowed you his carriage to go into Weymouth twice in a month?'

'Allowed? Allowed?' said Anne crossly. 'A gentleman would gladly offer, not *allow*.'

'Perhaps he is not a gentleman,' said James lightly, and there followed a vigorous argument over the sillabub as to whether Mr Brimley was or was not a gentlemanlike fellow. With the taste of cinnamon and pepper still clinging to the backs of his teeth, James was secretly glad that he must ride on alone tomorrow. He loved his cousins as a dutiful cousin should, but a few hours together in their company were enough.

It would mean leaving Jaunter with the groom at the Harbour Inn, to bring back to Birch Cottage, where Padding would come for him, but that posed no difficulty. So long as the horse was returned to Melton, Sir Charles would not fret. With these thoughts turning in his mind James was about to refuse a glass of port and go to bed, when Fanny let something slip, which quite knocked him over:

'One day, perhaps quite soon, you will be able to choose your own bedroom, James.'

'Eh?'

'Yes, when you are married.'

'When I am married? My dear Fanny, I am commissioned on foreign service. What on earth d'you mean?'

'You will not always be on foreign service, though. And then no doubt you will take a wife. And then you will come here.'

'Come *here*?' He was aware that they were all looking at him. 'Come *here*?'

'Oh,' said Fanny, and dropped her napkin. 'Oh, I have—— I have said what I oughtn't. Forget I said anything. I have said nothing.'

Fanny avoided his gaze, as did her two sisters. Amelia coughed.

Had they been midshipmen James would have known how to deal with this sort of nonsensical denial, but they were girls, and therefore he did not.

'Fanny?' He regarded her in bewilderment.

'No. No. You must not press me. It is most unfair of you to press me when I have taken wine.'

Fanny had drunk perhaps half a glass of claret. James stared at her, frowning and bemused, and saw by the set of her mouth that he could not press her. He shrugged, sighed, kissed them all good night, and went upstairs.

As he was about to blow out his light there was a knock at his door, and Fanny came in with her candle-holder. She was still fully dressed, and looked troubled. She sat on the chair beside his bed, and in a very roundabout way became confiding:

'You know that I said something about a bedroom just now?'

'Yes, and about my marriage, Fanny.—Well?'

'I did not mean to suggest that you were engaged.' What could she know of Catherine? he wondered. But women always did know these things, somehow.

'No?' he said. 'Then what could you have meant, cousin?' He did not say it harshly.

'I thought that you—must have known, already have known.'

'Ah.—Known what?'

'Oh, dear. It isn't fair that you should be kept in the dark. I have gone this far, and I must go the whole way.'

'Yes, you must.'

She sat forward in the chair and put the candle-holder on the cabinet by the bed. The glow lit her face, making it sharper than was flattering, but her large eyes softened the effect.

'It is an arrangement,' she began.

'Go on.' Gently.

'When the home farm was sold to pay Father's debts, the money was not enough. The creditors began to threaten further proceedings, and the lawyers in Dorchester said we might probably have to sell Birch Cottage. Your father—it was very kind in him, so very kind—your father then made the proposal that he should assume ownership of Birch Cottage in return for settling with the creditors. We should continue to live here, my sisters and I, just as we always had, and our affairs should in future be managed jointly by the trustees, that is the lawyers, and his man of business, Mr Pinkerton. And so it was arranged.' She paused briefly, then: 'There was a condition.'

'Go on.' Again gently.

'Since your eldest brother Charles is to inherit Melton, and your elder brother Nicholas had expressed the wish always to live in London, where he practises the law, your father said that you must have Birch Cottage when you were to be married. I thought that by now he must have told you all about it.'

'But Fanny, where would you go, you and the girls? It is the cruellest nonsense. I could not possibly turn you out of your own house.'

'We are to have one of the cottages at Melton. East Lane Cottage.'

'Well, this is the first I have heard of it. My father has said nothing to me, nothing at all.'

'I assure you, everything I have said is true.'

'Dear Fanny, I don't doubt your word. Thank you for your honesty.'

She kissed him on the cheek, and left him, and he lay back on his pillow with his mind whirling, certain that he would spend the night in sleepless perplexity. In two minutes he was dead to the world.

＊⇥◆⇤＊

A chilly south-westerly gust whipped along the harbour wall at Weymouth as James came down the stone stairs and got into the boat. The coxswain touched his hat, and put out a hand in aid, which James rather brusquely refused; then he nearly stumbled on the aft thwart before taking his seat in the stern. His chest lay stowed between the thwarts amidships.

The sea outside the harbour chopped and heaved, the wavetops whipped off in streams of spray. The sky was grey, and the water had a dull worked pewter sheen under the spray. James braced himself as the midshipman, a boy called Mathers, who couldn't have been more than thirteen, shouted: 'Ship your oars!' then: 'Give way!' and the boat moved out into the harbour, riding a swell that even in here was considerable. At each fall James felt a disturbing weight in the pit of his stomach.

'Lay out with a will, come on there!' yelled the midshipman in his choirboy's voice, and the coxswain steered them inexorably into the troubled water of the harbour mouth. The boat's crew rowed heartily, and James's heart sank as something else rose within him, rose from the pit, and at last was unconquerable. He twisted quickly, bent his head over the side, and lost his rations. Ignominy.

As he came aboard *Snipe* ten minutes later he was in that transitional moment of elation so common to those afflicted by seasickness, the moment between overwhelming bouts of retching.

'James, I am glad to see you, welcome aboard!' said his friend Hansard Cobbett. He had noticed a stain on James's coat, but said nothing. They shook hands, once the brief formalities of the deck had been dispensed with. 'We are going to run before a brisk blow, but you won't mind that, hey?' *Snipe* rolled heavily. For James the moment of elation was ending.

'No, indeed,' he said bravely. 'Oh, God.' And he ran to the lee rail and was wracked once more.

Lieutenant Cobbett watched him with a mixture of sympathy and dismay. If his friend was commissioned for foreign service, and yet could not master his guts in home waters, what was to become of him? But Lieutenant Cobbett was forgetful of what a long period on the beach could do to the stoutest, toughest seaman on his first reacquaintance with his chosen element; Lieutenant Cobbett was used to dashing up and down the coast of England, in the filthiest weather the Channel could produce, under a press of canvas that would have left the captain of a sloop or a frigate stiff with fright. In short, he was not mindful of the cruelty of the sea towards those who have not kept it all the time, and his sympathy and dismay were tinged with hardness of heart.

Snipe made the trip in just two days, in the way that only a flying fast cutter could, in strong but favourable winds. She reached the Nore as the light faded into evening rain on the second day. James, who had wished to be companionable with his old friend to make amusing conversation and renew their former easiness of discourse and spirit, had failed utterly in this intent. Nearly all the trip he had been confined to the cramped little 'great' cabin in prostrated wretchedness, oblivious of what was said to him. And now he was faced, as he thought, with the further hellish difficulty of making his way on the morrow from the anchorage to Chatham, and from Chatham to Gravesend, where he must get himself aboard the Long Ferry for the trip upriver to Deptford. Then Lieutenant Cobbett was able to lift his spirits:

'Did you say the Nore, James?' In answer to a question. 'No, I am not going to remain here at the Nore, thank God. I have business at Chatham.'

'Oh. Then you——'

'I can take you there, all the way in. It is despatches, you know, from Plymouth, from the port admiral, Admiral Liston.'

'Ah.'

'Mind you, we have made excellent time. The papers wasn't expected quite this quick, hey?' He smiled, and tapped his nose.

'What?'

'The truth is, James, these despatches and so forth are not urgent. They are matters of routine, and I said I would convey them to Chatham. They might easily have come by a supply ship, any transport ship, at any time in the next few months, and have been received without remark. I said that I would take them so that I might give you a lift—and so that I might visit a certain young person.'

'At Chatham?'

'Indeed, at Chatham.'

'And, certainly, this person is female.'

'Your brain has not gone the same way as your innards—I am happy.'

'And this person, are you engaged to her?'

'Good heaven, no. I am a dutiful sea officer, busy all the time, and unable even to contemplate such a drastic idea as marriage.'

'Ah. Well.' A nod.

'Christ's blood—do not tell me *you* are engaged, James?'

'No no. No, well. Not exactly quite engaged.'

'How can a man be engaged "not exactly", pray? The thing is true, or it isn't. One cannot fool about with a girl's affections, hey? So which is it? You are to be spliced, or no? Do I know this hapless creature? Have you hidden her? Where does she live, you sly dog?'

Lieutenant Cobbett was a slightly balding, stoutish, sturdy, pleasant-faced young man, not much given to contemplation or reflection. He was not vain, but he had a view of himself that was uncritically complimentary. He had a sense of fun, he liked fun, and the company of girls who liked fun. He led a rigorous life, largely devoid of material comfort, and he knew that he was lucky to have a smart little ship under his legs. A vessel that gave him the opportunity to flit from place to place, that afforded him the responsibilities of command with no grave or pressing attendant weight upon him. He was proud of his seamanship. He would have liked what all sea officers wished for: more action, real fighting action, and prizes. He knew that at present, in the year '86, three years since the end of the War of American Independence and the last great sea actions against the French, there was no hope of such things.

He had got *Snipe* by pure chance. Another officer, a year or two Cobbett's senior, had been offered her; this officer had been struck down by yellow-jack at Port Royal and sent home in a very low condition to recover; he had died. Cobbett's uncle, a semi-retired admiral with connections both at the Admiralty and in Parliament, had put his nephew's name

forward, and the lieutenant had got the command. He liked
to think it was because of his abilities, but in his heart he knew
it was nothing of the kind. He had been favoured.

James knew all these things, and bore his friend no resentment. That he had got a command while still a lieutenant
might have been a source of envy, might have made a rift
between them, had they not been midshipmen together and
formed a bond of friendship unmarked by rivalry or con-
tention; they were brothers, not by blood but of the heart.

In turn Hansard Cobbett was glad that his friend had got
his own commission for what looked like being a wonderful
voyage of at least a year, probably two years, leading to—
what? Glory? The kind of glory which clothed Cook on his
return from his first two voyages? Would Captain Rennie
aspire to such glowing recognition?

'I haven't met Captain Rennie,' said James.

They were standing on the quarterdeck, in spite of the
drizzling mist that was still falling across the Thames Estuary
and in a long curtain out to sea. Lights ashore gleamed
through the mist. They had anchored overnight, since to
attempt the difficult passage into the Medway and Chatham
in darkness was folly. They had come on deck for air, because
the stuffy confinement of the 'great' cabin was intolerable to
James, still suffering as he was from the after-effects of
seasickness; and Cobbett wished to see for himself that his
guns were secured, and that the midshipman taking the watch
was awake.

'Never met him?' said Cobbett in surprise. 'Ain't that
strange, a little? He didn't ask for you, or anything?'

'No, we have no connection at all. I don't think Captain
Rennie had any say in his first, nor do I know why I was
singled out. It cannot have been for any distinction in service.
I spent a year of the late war on convoy, as third in a villainous
old frigate, the *Persistence*, thirty-two, south to St Helena, or
on the West Indies run, you know. Slog. A penniless gunroom, grog and biscuit. My father did not then give me an

allowance, not until the year '83, and within a few months *Persistence* was paid off.'

'Do you go into *Expedient* with any friends from *Persistence*? Who was her first?'

'Scud Whatmore, and her second was a curious fellow, very bald, perhaps three teeth, always laughing at something, name of Badham Rudd. I rather liked him, he had a line in scurrilous fantasy about senior officers. Never saw him again after we paid off. Neither of those gentlemen is to join *Expedient*. I shall have no friends, Han, I fear.'

'Ymm, pity on a long cruise. However, you'll have your books. You was always a great one for print, James.'

'Oh, look, never think I am downcast about this commission. I am glad of it, with all my heart.'

'Good, good, very good. All you need now is to recover your equilibrium, hey?' And he laughed. 'Your sea legs, and your sea stomach.'

'Shut up, Han. I am perfectly well. The air has revived me.'

'It seems like an age, don't it, since we berthed together in *Gargoyle*?'

'It is an age. Half our lives, nearly.'

'And then you gave up the sea for Cambridge.'

'Yes, I did. I had thought of becoming a clergyman, of all things. And then when the American War continued, I very gladly returned to the service.'

'And now we are old men, God save us,' laughed Cobbett. 'I wish we had seen more of each other over the years, but it's too late, we shall soon be dead.'

'What a fool you are, Han. D'you know, I'm feeling uncommonly starved. D'you suppose your steward might be able to——'

'You wish to eat? My dear fellow, only too happy.' He moved to the companion. 'Willard!' he bellowed. 'Supper!' And they went below.

On the Long Ferry from Gravesend, going upriver on the flood, James looked over his commission again. He had seen his chest safely stowed, was a little tired still, and not quite his usual self, and he wished to lift himself by sight of his deliverance from nothinghood.

By the Commissioners for executing the Office of Lord High Admiral of Great Britain and Ireland &c. and of all His Majesty's Plantations &c.

To Lieut. *James Rondo Hayter* hereby appointed Lieutenant of His Majesty's *Frigate* the *Expedient*

By Virtue of the Power and Authority to us given We do hereby constitute and appoint you Lieutenant of His Majesty's *Frigate* the *Expedient* Willing and requiring you forthwith to go on board and take upon you the Charge and Command of Lieutenant in her accordingly: Strictly Charging and Commanding all the Officers and Company belonging to the said *Frigate* subordinate to you to behave themselves jointly and severally in their respective Employments with all due Respect and Obedience unto you their said Lieutenant; And you likewise to observe and execute as well the General printed Instructions as what Orders and Directions you shall from time to time receive from your Captain or any other superior Officers for His Majesty's service. Hereof nor you nor any of you may fail as you will answer the contrary at your peril. And for so doing this shall be your Warrant. Given under our hands and the Seal of the Office of Admiralty this *twentieth day* of *May 1786* in the *Twenty-sixth* Year of His Majesty's Reign

Howe
J. Leveson Gower
C. Brett

By Command of their Lordships
P. Stephens

On the left, the seal. He folded the document with great care, and replaced it in his coat pocket.

There had been trouble for Lieutenant Cobbett after all. When he had gone ashore with James, he had made his duty to Admiral Roper, who had been distinctly unamused. He had required Cobbett to remain standing in the outer office for nearly half an hour, and then had required him to come in. Noticing James, who while anxious to depart for Gravesend had remained out of loyalty to his friend, the admiral required him to come in too.

'Do you serve in *Snipe*, Mr Hayter?'

'No, sir. Lieutenant Cobbett obliged me by giving me passage from Weymouth. I am to report to my ship today, at Deptford.'

'At Deptford? Do you carry despatches there?'

'No, sir. I am newly commissioned in the *Expedient* frigate, lying at Deptford.'

'*Expedient*? I do not know her.'

'She has never before been commissioned, sir. She has lain in Ordinary at Chatham since the end of the late war, and is now refitting for foreign service.'

'Who is your captain?'

'Captain Rennie, sir.' He reached inside his coat. 'I have a letter . . .'

'Yes yes, Mr Hayter, there is always letters.' He returned his blue gaze to Cobbett. 'Now, as to you, sir. As to you, I don't believe that these despatches are anything of the kind.'

'Well, sir, I said I would bring the papers to Chatham, and Admiral Liston said that I might. Accordingly, I have——'

'Tom Liston said that, did he? Lists of tarred twine held? Weight of rope held? Number six canvas, Mr Cobbett? No no, I am not a fool. But I am a man, and was once a young man. I'll wager a guinea—ten guineas—that there is a young female person in the background. Well?'

'I—there—I had hoped, indeed, sir—when I had delivered the papers——'

'Then you had better see her, Mr Cobbett. You had better see her, and then you will report to me in this room at nine o'clock in the forenoon tomorrow. I have a duty for you, sir. A despatch duty, by God, that will more than keep you busy, and make you forget all about your nether parts. Now, as to you, sir,' he looked at James, 'why are you still here?'

'You had not given me leave to go, sir.'

'No, you are quite right. By the by, is your father Sir Charles Hayter, of Melton House?'

'He is, sir.'

'I knew your father, long ago. He and I were rivals for your mother's hand. Well, rivals. Charlie had me beat from "take your marks". Remember me to him when you write to him, will you, and to your mother?'

'I will with pleasure, Admiral.'

'Very good. You must go to Deptford. I do not envy you. It is a place cursed by many a sea officer, including the late Captain Cook.'

'Cursed, sir?'

'Never mind. You will discover my meaning, I assure you.'

And now James did ponder that meaning, as he looked at the letter which had come to Melton shortly after his commission. This official letter informed him that he would be departing on foreign service of long duration, on a voyage of considerable importance in the furtherance of exploration in the far corners of the world's oceans, in particular the Pacifick Ocean.

Admiral Roper had mentioned Cook. Had not Cook, and others before him, ventured far into such remote places? Had he not recorded and charted them? But it was not for newly commissioned lieutenants to question these things. Perhaps *Expedient* would make great new advances in the question of longitude. Chronometers, and the like. A new reckoning of the lunar tables. Who could say? James settled in the not very comfortable seat and dozed as the ferry made steady progress upstream, winding past Greenhithe and Thurrock and the marshes beyond. A stray mallard, his plumage beginning to be dulled by the early summer moult, flew over the ferry, quarking in complaint, dipped low over the flats to the north and was lost against the dun colours of the ground. James nodded forward asleep as the ferry rode a passing swell, and his cockaded hat fell on his knee. He did not wake.

* * *

Captain William Rennie RN woke in his hanging cot with a feeling of apprehension which grew rapidly into gastric unease.

'What have I ate?' he muttered as he swung out of the cot and reached for his piss-pot. The knowledge came to him as he relieved himself that he had eaten nothing but a wedge of cold pie, a small wedge, since breakfast yesterday. The ship's cook had provided him with neither his dinner nor his supper. The cook had provided for no one on board. The cook had been senseless drunk.

'Damn the wretch,' muttered Rennie with a sigh as he shaved himself in his quarter gallery, squinting at his image in the small oval mirror tilted on its wooden stand. The water was cold, and twice he nicked his chin with the slipping blade.

'Damn the thing,' he said both times.

He had no steward, no servant boy. The ship, it had seemed to him when he came aboard yesterday at two bells of the forenoon watch, was a shambles. He had instituted at least a semblance of watches as soon as he had assumed command; these had no real authority because the ship had no people, only her standing officers. He had tried to make other improvements, to little avail. Meals were erratic, to say the least. His sleeping quarters were not ready and he must

sleep in the great cabin. In his quarter gallery the lights were
part boarded up, the consequence of an accident at Chatham,
not yet repaired. Thus he was shaving in demi-gloom.

The day before yesterday he had been at the Admiralty to
meet, at their Lordships' request, late in the afternoon, an
important gentleman from the Royal Society; that gentleman
did not appear. Rennie had been kept waiting in a clerk's
room for two hours, had then inquired, and had been, less
than courteously, he thought, asked to come back on another
day: he would be informed as to the date. He had come down
yesterday at an inconveniently early hour in the wherry,
having breakfasted hastily at his less than adequate overnight
lodgings in the Strand. And now he was irritable, his guts
pained him, and nothing was right. When everything should
have been right, when at last after years of hope-on-hope and
living cheap in rooms at Deal, his uniforms getting thread-
bare and his shoes worn down, when at last he should have
been suffused with good cheer, humming good cheer, at
being made post and given a frigate, a nearly new frigate, he
was reduced instead to—what? Dyspepsia.

'Christ in tears,' he said gloomily; pulled on a shirt and
breeches, dragged on his stockings and hopped back into his
cabin, one shoe on and the other in his hand. At least here it
was light. The morning sun, glancing on the river, was
reflected in dappled patterns here and there through the stern
gallery windows, and gave the cabin a gladdening air. Did he
smell cooking? There was a knock at his door, but before he
could answer the door was opened and Mr Adgett, the ship's
carpenter, came in. He removed his hat. Shavings scattered.

'Your pardon, sir.'

'Yes, Mr Adgett?'

'I've got a list, sir. I have took the liberty, as I say. Now, the
port cills——'

'Before I look at anything I must eat something, Mr
Adgett. Have you had breakfast? Why was I not called? Why
is the bell not rung each——' Just as he spoke six bells

sounded. He stared out of the stern windows in alarm, then looked for his pocket watch. Could it be eleven o'clock? A boat bumped along the side, there was a thudding crash, a yell, and terrible curses. An oar scraped harshly against the ship, and something fell heavily into the river.

'I'll, what I will do, sir, is find you at a more convenient moment.' And Mr Adgett retreated in haste with his list. Rennie sighed again. He had wanted to ask Mr Adgett about the refitting of his sleeping cabin. Sleeping in the great cabin was slovenly, and irksome to him. Damnation.

Nothing had improved. What had seemed at first pleasingly arduous work, the essential and worthwhile labour of refitting, storing, making ready for the sea, now looked like fruitless drudgery, impossible to be managed, a dead weight on his belly and heart.

'This will not do,' he said. 'It will not do.' And he went on deck, downcast and savage.

When James came aboard late in the afternoon, having had a furious argument with the ferryman about his chest, about putting him ashore at Deptford, when that was not a stopping place, &c., &c., and having had a subsequent and almost equally violent confrontation with a waterman about his fee for rowing James out to *Expedient* at her mooring; when at last he came on board he was not in a very amiable temper himself. His chest, parbuckled up from the boat by an artificer who took James's penny with a shrug, lay upended on the deck, tipped as the ship swung a little on the tide, and thudded on its beam in a tangle of rope falls and part wormed rigging. A figure turned at the aft rail, interrupted in staring down over the counter, and strode forward. It was very ill dressed, thought James, and yet it must be the figure of an officer, since it occupied the quarterdeck. Surely—surely it could not be . . .

'Captain Rennie, sir?' James removed his hat, aware that his dress coat, in these circumstances, looked perhaps too fine.

'Are you for *Expedient*, Lieutenant?' Looking at him intently, this coatless figure.

James bowed, and produced his papers. Rennie took the document, but did not notice it.

'I hope to God that you are my first? That you are Mr Hayter?'

'I am, sir. Lieutenant James Hayter, asking your leave to——'

'Thank God you have come at last! I have had no help at all, until now.'

'I am sorry to hear that, sir.' Politely. Far forward a mallet fell with a hollow clatter.

'I have no notion of who will get your dunnage below, Mr Hayter. The ship is at the mercy of the dockyard, and I have no people of my own. Have you had dinner?'

Having been long on land James was still not quite used to the naval idea of dinner in the early afternoon, a meal he would usually call luncheon. But now he said:

'I ate a little cake in the ferry, thank you, sir, at about two o'clock.'

'Well, that might probably be the most substantial meal you will get before tomorrow, I regret to have to tell you.'

'Are we not provisioned, sir?'

'It is all a great muddle, Mr Hayter.' They went below to the great cabin, James glancing uneasily over his shoulder at his chest, which lay where it had fallen. 'My table groans with paper, and little else. The purser, Mr Trent, has absented himself from the ship. Where he has gone, nor why, I do not know. He'd better come back damn quick, or risk his five hundred pound.'

James followed his captain into the great cabin, noting as they passed the sleeping cabin that it was crammed with timber and paint-pots. 'That is where I do not sleep,' said Rennie. 'Heaven knows how you fellows in the gunroom will manage. I inspected the ship a week since, and there was nothing there. No bulkheads, no accommodations of any kind. The whole ship is naked, and there is a further shame: our guns have already been condemned.'

'Our guns *condemned*?' James had begun to form the impression that *Expedient* was so far from being ready for the sea that she might never be got into that condition. He would not let himself address the question of Captain Rennie, who might well be a competent man badly let down by incompetent men.

'In answer to your question,' Rennie pushed papers to one side of the table, 'yes we are provisioned, after a fashion. I have brought with me, and thank God I did, two cases of wine: one of madeira, and one of claret. I had thought to get in my own supplies of food, fresh produce, you know, but I had not reckoned on the curious circumstances of this mooring. From the deck, when you look beyond the yard itself, it is like the countryside. Yet I have been able to purchase not a single egg, not a single chop. I have survived a week on cheese, and diverse pies the cook has been enjoined to produce by the standing officers, when he has not been drunk; their content I have not dared contemplate.' Rennie was enjoying himself. A week of solitude and frustration had made him voluble and inventive, and at first he did not notice James's increasingly dismayed frown.

Captain Rennie continued: 'I have had to deal, in turn, with Mr Ormerod, the Master Shipwright, and a more penny-pinching, grudging man I have never met. With his assistants. With Mr Pontius Booning, the Timber Master, and never was a fellow less aptly named. Mr Clavering, the Master Attendant, who has permitted us this mooring, I have not seen. For all I know he is an amenable, upright, decent, estimable man. For all I know. The artificers are a slovenly-looking, sideways-looking, shifty, dirty, slow, clumsy lot of blackguards, jealous of their rights. They are able to operate by a system of combinations, and I do not like it. I have no authority with them or over them, their work is negligible, they may do as they please. Mr Tangible is tying himself into knots because the rigging crew ignore his instructions, his complaints, his——'

'Mr Tangible is the boatswain?'

'Yes, Tangible. A good man, I think. As to the other standing officers, Mr Adgett has not been what I should call—— Well well, I must not be unfair to him.'

James glanced towards the sleeping cabin. 'He is the carpenter?'

'Just so. The gunner, Mr Wearing, has been ill these last days, confined to his bed. The cook is a drunkard, name of Stamp.'

James was liking it less and less. He was uncomfortable. He was embarrassed. This was not the Royal Navy he had wished to find upon his return to duty. Then he thought: I must do my best with what I find; I must not judge in the first five minutes a man I do not know, nor a ship that might well be weatherly and fast even if, at present, she looks like a whore dishevelled.

'Who is the master, sir?'

'Mr Loftus. Well, that is the name of the man so appointed. I have never seen him yet.'

'He is not here? He is not aboard the ship?'

'No, nor any other member of my supposed complement. I have no steward, no servant boy. I have no clerk, good God. My muster books lie empty. I warned you, Mr Hayter, it is all a very great muddle.'

'Sir, are we not a commissioned ship? Could we not man her ourselves? In the peace there is a dozen men for every berth. I know that at Weymouth, where I took passage to come here, there is fifty men, an hundred, that would come at once. Good Dorset men, that know the sea.'

'Yes, Mr Hayter, no doubt you are right. Sit down, will you?' They sat down, James on a locker at the side, Rennie in his chair. Rennie raised his eyebrows, and his receding hair seemed further to recede as his forehead wrinkled up. His skin was weathered, but not coarse. His eyes were grey, and had in them a hint of disappointed youth, and there was still something of youth in his figure and energy, yet his appearance in the overall was that of an older man. James could not guess his age. Thirty? Forty? The shaving cuts on his chin gave him the look of a man whose life were troubled. For his part Rennie saw a young man, well made and handsome, a little above the middle height, with a full head of dark hair, his facial expression now unhappy. Rennie felt that he had gone too far, had laid too much emphasis upon complaint, and was a little ashamed of himself.

'I beg your pardon, Mr Hayter.'

James was astonished, and for a moment mute.

'I have not made you welcome as I ought.'

'Sir, I assure you——'

'You are shocked by the circumstances of the ship, and by my not very seamanlike acceptance of all that you see. I assure you, it is not resigned acceptance.'

'I did not mean to suggest, by anything that I have said——'

'Not resigned acceptance, and now that you are here, Mr Hayter, I know that I may rely on you to help me. There is a great many things must be done if we are to be ready for the sea in time. Now, let me see your papers, if y'please, and then we'll have a glass of—— I have your commission in my hand.' He looked at the commission, scratched the side of his head, rubbed his nose, pursed his lips, nodded.

'Very good,' he said, and returned the document to James. 'Let us drink a glass of wine, and then we will look at the ship.'

◆━☲◆☲━◆

HMS *Expedient* was a Perseverance class frigate of thirty-six guns, a fifth-rated ship of 869 50/94 tons burthen. She was one hundred and thirty-seven feet long in the lower deck, and one hundred and thirteen feet two and a half inches at the keel; her breadth was thirty-eight feet, and the depth of her hold thirteen feet five inches. Her official complement of officers and men was 258 souls. At present a mere handful of these men was in the ship. Dockyard rigging crews had been aboard, and her upper masts had been fidded, and part of the running rigging rove up. The boatswain, Roman Tangible, lacking even a rudimentary rigging crew of his own, had objected to the dockyard artificers' work, objected so loudly and vehemently that their foreman had ordered the removal of his men with their work less than half-completed. Mr Tangible, not content with this development alone, had himself dismantled much of the rigging, leaving the *Expedient* with the sad appearance James Hayter had noticed when he came on board. She was ported for twenty-six eighteen-pound Armstrong pattern guns on the gundeck, two nine-pound guns and two thirty-two-pound carronades on the forecastle, and two nine-pounders and eight carronades on the quarterdeck; so that although she was officially shown as a thirty-six-gun vessel, her true armament was forty guns, plus what few additional guns her captain might choose to get into her: chasers, swivels, and the like.

But now as she lay moored fore and aft at Deptford there were no guns in *Expedient*. Since her launch in 1782, she had never been a proper ship; in 1783 she had been put in Ordinary at Chatham, the home of frigates, where she had been built, and had never been commissioned until now. Captain Rennie had been in jest when he said that her guns had been condemned, but only in part. Rennie had been informed, though he had yet to see the evidence, that his ship was to be armed with brand-new guns, of a new pattern entirely. He explained this to James as they inspected the ship. On the forward platform of the orlop, holding lanterns, they peered into the hold. The ship had not been stored, and since there were no guns in her either she rode high in the water. But as ever in a wooden ship there was water in the bilges, and the smell of that water.

'When was she last trimmed?' asked James.

'I asked Mr Ormerod that, when we inspected her last week. He said a year ago, according to her books from Chatham, which I have not sighted. There should be no difficulty about it; her pigs was laid in, and her shingle, at Chatham, and I have no reason to suppose anything is faulty.'

'You have not seen her particulars?' James held up his lantern.

'There are a great many things about this commission, Mr Hayter, that have puzzled me, as they puzzle you now.'

'She will need to be a little by the stern, would not you say?'

'Indeed she will. When the Board is content to let me have Mr Loftus I shall discuss that with him. But I'm happy we are of like mind. By God, it is foul here.'

'Ain't that usual, though?' said James lightly as they climbed to the lower deck by the forward ladder.

'It may be usual, but that don't mean I like it. Uncleanness, Mr Hayter, can be the greatest curse of a commission.'

'D'you mean bodily uncleanness, sir?' Again lightly. 'Or impurity of thought?'

'Good God, no. That is the province of chaplains. No, I mean filth. Filth leads to foul air and disease. A diseased ship is entirely useless to the King's service. I shall require the ship's cleanliness to be seen to be their first concern by all officers. I don't mean that we should take out her ballast and boil it, but that we should twice a week wash and smoke between, and wash the deck daily. Any man to be put on the ship's muster books will be required to be clean. By that I mean washed clean in his person, and if his clothing is dirty or verminous he is to be issued with clean clothes from the slop chest *upon that day*.' They had paused amidships on the lower deck, and Rennie peered at James in the lantern glow.

'I see that I astonish you, Mr Hayter.'

'I am not so much astonished, sir, as delighted. My last commission, in the *Persistence* frigate, was—well.'

'Was what?'

'Well, she could not have been described as sweet. She very persistently stank, that is the only word.'

'*Expedient* will never stink while I have her. It is the thing I most abhor, and by God I will pump that bilge reek out of her as soon as we get to sea. No, she will never stink while I have her, Mr Hayter. We are not Frenchmen, after all.'

'Frenchmen, sir?'

'That is why they will always fail against us, in time of war. Their ships are wretched dirty.' They climbed to the upper deck and looked at the gunports, the lids lifted open. 'And of course our gunnery is better. I must see about our new guns, and discover whether or no we shall need to alter the ports to accommodate them. By the by,' he added, 'I didn't mean that navy chaplains—what I said just now—that *they* have impure thoughts.'

James kept his face straight as they went forward to look at the gammoning of the bowsprit.

'She was brought partway here jury-rigged,' said Rennie, 'then towed into her mooring. Towed like a hulk, a very abominable thing for one of His Majesty's ships.'

Was he in jest? thought James. He could not tell. Rennie was a curious man, but then were not all captains singular and curious in their own way? They were of the ship, but set apart in a way that no other man on board could ever be, apart from the rest. It was no wonder that captains were singular men; the only surprise was that more of them did not go mad in their isolation. When they had looked at the ship, James asked if he might go into the maintop.

'By all means, Mr Hayter.' He looked aloft, and sighed. 'It has not been done, even now,' he muttered.

'Sir?'

'I want cross catharpings in the standing rigging. I said so to Tangible, but he is at such odds with the damned dockyard riggers that nothing is amenable to them any more.'

'Would you allow me to ask about this, sir, tomorrow?'

'Ask Tangible?'

'Mr Tangible, and the rigging gang foreman.'

'By all means, by all and every means.' Rennie sniffed in a breath, paused, then: 'Since we are the only officers in the ship, and you have nowhere else to go, will you eat supper with me, Mr Hayter?'

'I should be honoured, sir.'

At supper Rennie became expansive over the cold pie, opened a second bottle of claret, and allowed that although *Expedient* was as yet in thoroughly disreputable shape, things might be able to be improved upon in the not far distant future. Soon, however, he qualified this remark:

'My chief concern is to get my muster books filled,' he said. 'I must also have my officers. Well, I have you, Mr Hayter. But my second, Mr Makepeace, is delayed, and my third, Mr Longman, has broke his leg in a riding accident at Kibworth, and cannot join us. Who is to be his replacement? I do not know. Who are *Expedient*'s midshipmen? I do not know. Her standing officers do not care for Deptford, having lain so long at Chatham, and are not disposed to work. When are we to get our scientific instruments aboard? I do not know. When are we to have our new guns, and what pattern are they? Don't know that, neither.'

'Scientific instruments, sir?'

'Aye. Yes. We are to be a scientifical commission, Mr Hayter, in adjunct to our duties of exploration. That is why there is such interest in us at the Royal Society.'

'From Banks?'

'Well, Banks, I do not know that. There is another fellow wishes to see me. Sir Robert Greer.'

'Greer . . .'

'You have heard of him, no doubt?'

'No, sir, I confess—no.'

'Mm. Well well, he is a very high fellow, so I am informed, and I must meet him. There is another man I must meet, too, a scientifical—Baragwanath. Certainly you have heard of him?'

'I—I have not, sir, no.'

'Indeed? He has invented a most ingenious machine to measure the force and direction of the wind. An enamameter, I believe.'

'Perhaps an anemometer? The Greek for wind—*anemos*?'

'Ah, yes. Yes. Anemometer. You know Greek? You read it?'

'With Portlock at Cambridge. He drank too much, but he was a very admirable tutor.'

'Ah, yes, Portlock . . . Who is Portlock?'

'On Herodotus and the Muses he was peerless. Demosthenes, too.'

'Ah, yes.' Clearing his throat. 'Those fellows, yes.'

'I will admit that I did not read long, since I decided quite soon that I was unsuited to the profession I had thought to follow. But an undergraduate life was capital fun while it lasted. Was you never at university, sir?'

'I was not, I was not. Unless you call the sea itself a college, and middy's books. Falconer's book, you know.'

'Yes, the sea bible. Well, I suppose knowing another name for the wind is neither here nor there, according to Falconer.'

'There is no harm in knowing, Mr Hayter. That's what poetry is, hey? Knowing prettier names for things, and getting them all rove up?'

'Yes, I suppose so.'

'Rove up handsome?'

'Yes.' What else could he do but agree?

'Mmm-mmm:

> There is a tide in the affairs of men,
> Which, taken at the flood, leads on to fortune,
> Omitted, all the voyage of their life
> Is bound in shallows and in miseries.
> On such a full sea are we now afloat,
> And we must take the current when it serves,
> Or lose our ventures.'

'Our present circumstances could not be more handsomely described, sir.' Surprised.

'They could not, I think.' Rennie rubbed his nose, and cleared his throat. 'I may not know very much about our commission, but I sense that——Well well, I shall go no further. What I can provide is wine. Push your glass, Mr Hayter.'

They drank their wine, and after a minute or two Rennie sniffed and leaned forward.

'Listen, Mr Hayter. I do know something about our guns, after all. Just now, when I said I did not, that was an affectation, you know.'

'Well, sir, I—I guessed that perhaps it was.'

'A sea officer frets at delay, don't he? I hate delay.'

'I knew it must be that.'

'Good. Good. The thing is, a fellow at Woolwich, the assistant inspector of artillery, name of Waterfield, Alexander Waterfield, has designed an entirely new pattern of gun. What is more, we are to have new powder for it.'

'That is a relief, even in the peace. Restored powder ain't the same thing, no matter what the Ordnance——'

'Mm-mm-mm,' Rennie shook his head, swallowing wine. 'No no, a new *kind* of powder.' He put down his glass. 'Another fellow at Woolwich, he and Waterfield together have invented it, and we are to carry it to sea for the first time. Neither our guns, nor our powder, have ever before been tried at sea.'

'So—we are an experiment, then? *Expedient* is to be a scientific experiment?'

'Just so.'

'I thought we were to go into the Pacifick Ocean, to explore there, and that we would keep the sea a year or more.'

'We shall keep the sea a year and more.' Rennie drank off his glass, and refilled it, and beckoned James to send his glass across the table. 'Let me show you my instructions.' He pushed the wine aside, found a packet, opened it and spread a document on the table with a flourish. He sat back in his chair, slightly flushed. James pulled the document to him, and read:

Whereas we have appointed you Captain of His Majesty's *Frigate Expedient*, now at Chatham, and intend that you shall command her during the present intended voyage of Exploration into the remote corners of the Pacifick Ocean, in search of suitable Anchorages and places of Haven for His Majesty's Ships in such times of Conflict which may in future ensue, involving His Majesty's fleets, where said Ships may water, wood, repair, and re-victual so far as may be practicable; and whereas we have ordered the said *Frigate* to be refitted and stored at Deptford for Foreign Service, manned with 258 Officers and men (agreeable to the scheme attached hereof) and victualled to Twelve months of all species of Provisions (allocated at whole allowance agreeable with the said scheme attached) except Beer, of which she is to have only a proportion for one month, and to be supplied with Spirits in lieu of the remainder; you are hereby required and directed to use the utmost despatch in getting her ready for the sea accordingly, and then falling down to Woolwich, take in her guns and gunners' stores at that place and proceed to Portsmouth for further orders.

Given to *Captain William Rennie RN* under our hands:

And underneath, the date, and signatures, and the seal.

James pushed the document back across the table.

'The only thing that genuinely puzzles me, sir, is why we are not refitting at Chatham.'

'Yes, I had thought the same thing. It is to do with the proximity of Deptford to the Admiralty itself, d'you see. Their Lordships wish me to be close at hand.'

'The other thing—I know I said there was only one—but the other thing that puzzles me is why we are being sent only to the Pacifick. Surely Cook has explored there, nearly everywhere there? Not to say Byron, Wallis, Anson—a host of men before.'

'It has sometimes struck me, in observing their Lordships' actions, that the fate of mere sea officers is to be kept blindfolded, and that even if our blindfolds was permitted to be taken off, we should still be in the dark. However, Mr Hayter, I am honoured to have command of *Expedient*, and I shall do my duty as ordered.'

'Of course, sir. I did not mean——'

'Will I tell you my idea of a commission? I like to stand on the quarterdeck, loose the foretopsail, bring her to the wind, and put to sea. I like to know my course, and keep to it. I like to know exactly what I am doing, and why I am doing it.' Rennie swallowed some wine, and sniffed.

'With respect, sir, since I hope we are talking frankly, we are said to be a direct, forthright, plain-speaking service, are we not? And yet——'

'Yes, and yet?'

'Is there not a great deal of port and scheming behind?'

For a moment James thought he had made a terrible mistake, that he had ventured far beyond what was wise in so short an acquaintance with his commanding officer. Rennie sat silent, then drew in a long breath through his nose, and put down his glass.

'I could not have put it better. Port wine and scheming.' He smiled and frowned at the same time. 'We must do our best to clear the fumes, hey?'

⁂

On the morrow, having for the first time in many years slept in a hammock, slung in the naked gunroom, James found the carpenter and the boatswain at their breakfast, and required them to meet him on the forecastle in fifteen minutes. He was dressed now for work, and the two warrant officers saw that here was a man who meant business. To all intents and purposes James might have been a seaman, except that his working clothes, although old and worn, were better made. He wore no hat, but had tied a kerchief, a dark blue cotton kerchief, round his head.

'He looks like a pirate, for Christ's sake,' said Mr Tangible, as James went up the ladder.

'No piratical him, no bloody corsair. He wants things done correct. Not before time, as I say. Not before time.'

They found James waiting at the forecastle. 'Mr Tangible, Mr Adgett. Look aft, will you?' They looked aft, dutifully. 'Now look aloft, if you will.' They did that, too. 'Will you tell me what you see?'

'His Majesty's frigate *Expedient*, sir.'

'Is that what you see, Mr Tangible?'

'The river, sir?' ventured Mr Adgett. He did not like this kind of thing. It was always unsettling.

'What we all see, if we look careful, is a fucking disgrace,' said James almost gently. 'Hey?'

'I see what you mean, sir,' said Mr Tangible. 'It's the rigging, ain't it?'

'It is everything,' said James. 'At present we have no complement, no people of our own to aid us. However, that need not deter us from doing our work. Our work is to render *Expedient* into her proper condition as a fighting ship, in which we may all be proud to serve the King. You will now come with me, and we will go over the ship. Mr Adgett, you will write down everything we notice that is in need of attention. No doubt the yard has made its own assessment, but it is very well to have our own. Then we can be sure that nothing has been left in the hands of that old villain Mr Luck-By-Chance. When we have done that, I am going ashore, where I shall seek and find the Master Shipwright, the Timber Master, and the foreman rigger. If it takes me all the day I shall find them, and we shall then begin the refitting of the ship. That has not yet even been attempted to be commenced. All that has happened is that she has been towed up from Chatham, and left lying in a state of lamentable and barbarous undress. You there!'

An artificer with a clay pipe in his mouth paused and looked at James with a frown. He pointed at himself and raised his eyebrows.

'Yes, you! Throw that pipe over the side!'

'I don't know who you are, mate, nor who you fink you are. But I smoke if I please, see.'

'Throw the pipe over the side, or I will throw your arse there! D'you hear me!'

'Now, look. You can't——'

James moved towards him with such concentrated purpose that the artificer lost his nerve and flung the pipe away.

'Thank you,' said James. 'You might tell the others that I will not have smoking on the deck. Neither on the deck, nor anywhere in the ship. A fire is the last thing we can afford.'

'As you like. I don't mind.' A surly acceptance.

'We will begin, if you please,' said James to the warrant officers, and he strode aft into the waist. Mr Adgett looked at Mr Tangible with a sharp little sideways jerk of his head, and they followed. Their days of pissing in the wind, and farting away the hours, and being looked down at by the dockyard men with insolence and contempt, were over and done, thank God.

─━═━─

Captain Rennie had been called away early to the Admiralty on a matter of urgent business, otherwise James would never have taken so entirely upon himself this attempt to bring order and system into the refurbishment of the ship. Certainly his captain had given him leave to speak to the boatswain, and the riggers' foreman, about the poor tangle of cordage that had been rove up and left to shame *Expedient* as her running rigging. He had no real authority beyond that simple acquiescence. With the captain out of the ship, however, did not the Admiralty Instructions give him leave to supervise and oversee? Well, he thought that they did. He would proceed, and take the consequences. Rennie now seemed to him to be a commanding officer anxious to do his best. It was not Rennie's fault that he had no crew.

'He might have made a better attempt at finding men, though,' James said to himself.

'Beg pardon, sir?' Mr Adgett said behind him.

'Eh?'

'I thought I heard you speak, sir.'

'No no, I was clearing my wind. Hold the light up, Mr Tangible, will you? I want to look—— Good God, was that a rat, or a great dog?'

'A rat, sir.'

'We must do something about that, Mr Adgett, or her timbers will be eaten through.'

'They do get into what provisions we has, sir, that is very true. I don't know they will eat timber.'

'Rats will eat anything. In my last commission they ate—— Well, I won't pursue it.'

They moved aft in the reeking darkness.

At the Admiralty Captain Rennie was again informed, by the Third Secretary Mr Soames, that Sir Robert Greer, who had agreed to meet Rennie there, had again alas been delayed; would it be convenient for Captain Rennie to pass the night in London and return to the Admiralty on the morrow?

'You mean, I am to spend another night out of my ship? If Sir Robert is not here today, how am I to know that he will condescend to appear tomorrow? Hey, Mr Soames?'

'Captain, I understand your anxieties.' Placatingly. 'They are perfectly understandable, and I assure you that their Lordships are cognizant of them, and sympathetic to your

desire, your most natural and commendable desire to return
to your ship, the, the——'

'*Expedient* frigate.'

'*Expedient*, to complete her repairing.'

'Refitting.'

'Refitting. To complete it, at the earliest opportunity.
However, with your indulgence, Captain, your kind indulgence, the meeting may be effected tomorrow afternoon.'

Mr Soames's coat was nearly black, and that black was
nearly rusty. The material certainly shone like metal here and
there, at the elbows, and in the back. The buttons were worn
dull. His linen by contrast was crisp and fresh, and he was
cleanly, pinkly shaven. A hint of astringent cologne water
wafted from him, from the lace at his cuff, and the fine
fabricked kerchief that nestled there. The buckles of his shoes
were worn, but the leather gleamed. His wig was powdered,
and his facial expression below it was full of patience and
goodwill, but there was something implacable about Mr
Soames, about his calm and understanding language, and
Rennie saw that he must accede.

'Very well.'

'That is most kind in you, Captain. Have you somewhere
to sleep when you are in London?'

'I must go to an hotel. Well, it is more a lodging-house. In
the Strand.'

'Ah. Yes.—Will you permit me to make a suggestion?'

'Certainly.'

'A Mrs Peebles keeps rooms in Bedford Street, a most
agreeable house, not more than ten or a dozen rooms, quiet
and comfortable and an excellent dining-room. Her charges
is very modest. You might very probably like it there, I think.'

'Thank you, Mr Soames. I am in your debt.' He bowed.

'By all means say my name to Mrs Peebles as you go in.'

'Thank you, I will.'

'At three o'clock tomorrow, then. Good day to you.' He
shook Rennie's hand with every appearance of affability and

friendship, and yet there lingered about him an air of inexorable detachment; it seemed to drift out from him in the dry, austere fragrance of his cologne.

—◄✦►—

Sir Robert Greer was dressed in a very black coat, black breeches, and severe white stockings. His black shoes gleamed under small square silver buckles. His black cane was silver-topped, his pocket snuffbox was silver, everything about him was subdued, but grand. His face was ashen pale, his eyes deep black. His voice—dry, almost hushed—had a deep resonance, and could not have come from anything but powerful self-conviction, from power itself.

The truth of that power was in the fact that for their meeting they had the Admiralty boardroom to themselves. Rennie had never before been in here. It was not an enormous room, but it was beautifully proportioned, and everywhere was evidence of its purpose. On the wall at one end, in a grand arch, was the cocked arrow of the wind telltale, attached to a device on the roof. On the wall above the ornate fireplace hung, one above the other, a dozen large furled charts, the charts of all the oceans. Above the long central table hung bell-pulls, all at one height. From this table, at this table, were directed all the ships of His Majesty's fleets, across the globe.

They did not sit down. Sir Robert did not suggest it, in fact he had the appearance of a man who was about to be called away, at any minute, to a far more important place. The Royal Society? wondered Rennie. Perhaps there was a matter of great moment waiting on his attention there.

'We are very pleased that you are to aid us, Captain Rennie.'

'The Royal Society, Sir Robert?'

'All of us, all of us. Will you take a biscuit? Certainly, you know the value of the observations we would wish you to make in our behalf. Their value, let me iterate, could not be higher. And that is why—let us walk to the end of the room—that is why I cannot emphasize enough the need for discretion in dealings. You apprehend me? Say nothing to anyone of your crew——'

'At present I have no crew, Sir Robert, no people.'

'They will be well chosen for you, I am in no doubt—every one of them. I know that to be so. However, we rely on *you* to carry these matters to fruition, to conclusion. They must follow *you* in this.'

'Well, yes, sir. After all, I am in command.'

'Indeed, indeed—*obedience*.'

'Naturally, I must have confidence in my officers. Command is a chain. The chain of command.'

'Confidence?' Sharply.

'They must trust me. And I must trust them. That is how a ship is worked, Sir Robert.'

'Yes, certainly. Forgive me. I meant only . . .'

'Only . . .?'

'I meant—that we trust *you*.'

That half an hour was the most unsettling experience of all the unsettling experiences Rennie had lately suffered. Sir Robert had retrieved his hat and cane from a chair, shaken Rennie by the hand, and hurried away—leaving him with the deep, certain, disquieting opinion that Sir Robert had not told him the whole truth. That men like Sir Robert never dealt in the whole truth, not if they could help it, Royal Society or no. Was Sir Robert in fact connected to the Royal Society at all? Rennie did not know. He did not know, and it made him uneasy.

When Captain Rennie returned to Deptford he found that all but the standing rigging had been dismantled and the upper masts sent down. Mr Tangible, with a mixture of satisfaction and disgruntlement, informed him that the ship had been granted, unexpectedly granted, since Rennie had requested it

on the first day of the commission and had been refused, a
two-tide dry docking so that *Expedient*'s copper might be
examined. This was to happen on the following day. There
were now no artificers in the ship.

'Where is Mr Hayter?'

'He is ashore in the dockyard, sir. There is a person below,
sir, waiting on your presence.'

Rennie went below and found the person, a reed-thin
young man with delicate features and long, delicate hands.
He was waiting at the door of the great cabin.

'Who are you, sir?'

'My name is Dobie, Alan Dobie, and I——'

'Very good. Perhaps you will like to take off your hat, Mr
Dobie.'

Dobie took off his hat, fumbled in the pocket of his green
coat, dropped his hat, retrieved it, and produced a letter. He
was not at his ease. Rennie took the letter and went into the
cabin. The young man followed him in there, and waited
while the letter was quickly read through.

'Lord Gillingham?' said Rennie, putting the letter on the
table.

'He—his lordship thought—that you might require a
person to assist with your books. A man of business, as it
were, in a way.'

'Man of business? I regret to have to tell you, Mr Dobie,
that the only man of business in this ship, in any ship, is the
purser. My purser, though I confess I have never seen him
yet, is one Mr Trent. I am not, I fear, acquainted with his
lordship. Further, I fear his lordship does not understand the
practice of the Royal Navy in the appointment of pursers.
That is done by the Navy Board, you know, by warrant.'

'I am sure Lord Gillingham did not mean that you, that I—
indeed I am not a purser, no.'

'Have you any experience of naval life, Mr Dobie, any
experience of the sea?'

'No, sir.'

'Then forgive my being blunt. I cannot help you.'

'I am a friend of Lieutenant Royce.'

'Ah, that is the connection. I did not quite follow it in the——' Rennie took up the letter and glanced through it again. 'Yes, Lieutenant Royce. Who is Lieutenant Royce? I don't know him, neither.'

'Why, he is—he is to be your third lieutenant, sir. Taking Lieutenant Longman's place, who has broke his leg.'

'Is he, indeed? How d'you know that, Mr Dobie.'

'I—I had thought he would be already aboard the ship when I came here this morning.'

'Did you, indeed?' Rennie was beginning to be angry. Then he saw that the young man was not at fault, that he was merely trying to get himself a situation, and could not be blamed. If he knew Lieutenant Royce, it was certainly through Royce's influential connection with Lord Gillingham that he had got this letter of recommendation from his lordship, who in turn probably knew Admiral Somebody or Sir Whatnot Otherfellow, which was how Royce had got his commission. It was the way of things, the way of the world. He could not help Mr Dobie, however, who knew nothing of the sea. Then a thought came to him.

'Mr Dobie, I am in no doubt that you can read and write, and please do not be offended when I ask: are you an educated man?'

'I think I might say that yes, I am educated, sir. I would not claim to be a scholar, but——'

'But could you, can you, teach boys?'

'I have already done so, sir. At home in Norfolk, at a—well, it was in truth a dame school.'

'No matter, you have taught boys. Excellent. Now. Can you write down accurately what I say? What I mean is, can you write letters? Make lists? Are you able to manage such things as these, Mr Dobie?'

'Oh, yes, sir. My uncle was a shopkeeper, and I have made a great many lists for him, and wrote all his letters, since he could not write himself. Alas, he died three month since——'

'Did he, did he? Very sad. And now you are without employment. Well well, if you can make *lists*, Mr Dobie, and write letters, and teach boys, I shall make an exception in your case, and put you on the ship's books as clerk and schoolmaster.'

'Thank you, sir. Thank you, indeed.' He held his hat, turned it. 'Who—who am I to teach, sir, in a ship?'

'Barbarians, Mr Dobie. Barbarians, that must be made civilized if they are to proceed in the King's service.'

He heard a shout, and the bumping of a boat as it came alongside.

Expedient rode tethered, the tide swirling and sucking at her cables, and Captain Paxton came uninvited, unannounced aboard, puffing up the side from his gig in a very choleric condition. He made no ceremony of removing his hat, made no gesture at all, but stamped aft towards the great cabin. Mr Dobie, emerging from the great cabin, was pushed aside as if he had been a stool, or a hat stand, and Captain Paxton strode in to confront Rennie, who had half risen in surprise from his chair at the table.

'What the devil d'y'mean by shoving me aside, sir?' demanded Captain Paxton. 'What right have you got, in your first command, to get athwart my hawse in your bloody fucking little frigate?'

'I—I am at a loss——'

'D'you know who I am?'

'No, sir, I do not.'

'I am Paxton, the *Obelisk* seventy-four, and you have took my place.'

'If I have, Captain Paxton, it was inadvertent, I assure——'

'Be quiet, sir. I am the senior officer present, and I will have an answer from you, if you please, right quick.'

Rennie began to see that he was not after all at a disadvantage. Captain Paxton had come uninvited aboard his ship, and had been uncivil to him in his own cabin. Further, Captain Paxton had required him to provide an answer to an impertinent question, and at the same instant to be quiet.

'Will you take a glass of wine, Captain Paxton?'

'What? What say?'

'I can offer you a fair-to-middling madeira, lately bottled, or a good ordinary claret.'

'Are you a wine merchant, sir, to talk to me in this fucking ridiculous way?'

Rennie had had enough.

'With respect, Captain Paxton, you have forgot that you are not in your own ship. I am doing my best to be hospitable, and to behave in a gentlemanlike manner—an *officerlike* manner. Now. Will you take a glass of wine with me?'

Captain Paxton put down his hat and blew out his cheeks. He was in undress coat, rather old and shabby, his wig was unpowdered, and he was very red in the face. He cleared his throat, stared distractedly out of the stern gallery windows, and recovered himself.

'You are right. I have spoke hasty. I apologize, Captain Rennie. Madeira will do very well, if you are still inclined to give me some?' He took his glass, and said: 'Your health, and damn the French.'

'Are we at war again?'

'I am inclined always to damn the French, war or no war. I see no reason not to. Your health.'

'Your health. And by the by, *Expedient* is not my first command. That was the *Mystic* sloop, twenty, at the Saints, you know.'

'Was you at the Saints? What a fool I am.'

'How can I be of service to you?' They sat down.

It was the two-tide dry docking. Rennie, since he had only just returned to his ship, had been quite unaware until now that Captain Paxton's ship, the *Obelisk*, had been given the opportunity of a two-week dry docking, arranged with a view to the spring tides, at Deptford, no other yard having been able to take her; quite unaware that *Expedient* had effectively ruined Paxton's arrangements, that he would lose at least a month when *Expedient* took his ship's place in the only available dry dock, for a damned piddling two-tide in-and-out.

'I have had to bring her up from the Nore, for the love of Christ. Will I ever get her down again, now? If the next spring tides ain't full, I may be here two month or more. A year.'

'Had I been kept informed, sir, I should have spoke up,' said Rennie.

'No no, nothing you could've done, not your fault. It is the dockyards. Deptford, in particular. In the ordinary way I should never come near the place. Every man in it is a parasitical rogue and a pestilential dog. The King's service never had a greater enemy than Deptford Yard.'

'Then may God help us both,' said Rennie mildly. He thought it best to be mild.

'They should all be taken out, every one of them, hanged, their heads cut off, and their brains burned in the fires of hell.'

'Then how should we refit?'

'Our ships would be the better for it. Ships not built or repaired or refitted in this damned abysmal den of scoundrels would be better in every particular.'

He drank off his glass, and sighed.

'Commanding a guardship is a miserable thing for a sea officer, Captain Rennie. Yes, we are in the peace, I know it, and I must be thankful that I am not on the beach, left on the beach permanent, to rot. But what I cannot understand is: why was I given her in this condition? There is a hundred and more ships of the line in Ordinary, yet I am given a seventy-four with rotten timbers. She is rotted right through. Why was I given her? Perhaps it is a penance. I am to pay a penance. Why? Hey? What have I done? I do not know. It is a very miserable sort of commission, even in the peace.'

Captain Rennie pushed the bottle, and Captain Paxton refilled his glass.

⊶ ≕✦≔ ⊷

James was still in his working clothes, the kerchief tied round his head, as he made his way through the hazards of timber, tools, horse benches and the like which festooned the side of the dry dock, where a seventy-four lay shored. Artificers pushed past him, heedless of this seaman wandering in their world. He was making his way to the rigging house, where he hoped to find the foreman of the rigging crew assigned to *Expedient*. Yesterday he had searched for the Master Shipwright, had been to his office in the large block to the left of the dock, had even made his way to his house, but had not been able to find him.

'Mr Ormerod, you are wanting, is it?' a clerk had said, when James returned to the office. 'Oh, no. No, I shouldn't think you will find him, no.'

'Why not? This is his place of work, is it not?'

'When he is here. He is a great one for going about from slip to slip, and calling in at various places in the yard. It is a very large expanse of ground.'

'Where might I find the Timber Master, Mr Booning?'

'Mr Booning. Mr Booning. Yes. You might look for him any number of places. The carpenter's shop, which I know he visited yesterday, over past the smith's shop, at the corner of the gate yard. Or the mast house, which is—well, that is a long walk, at the far end of the yard, by the great mast pond. Or he may've gone to the sawpits, over beyond the block-makers' shop.'

'Yes, I see. You are saying to me that I had better not bother.'

'Oh, no. No, I should never do that. I am trying to assist. What you must apprehend is the size of the yard. A dockyard is a very considerable enterprise, employing many hundreds

of men. Even if we was only to consider the storerooms, leave
alone the——'

But by then James had left this clerk in his office, and gone
looking for himself.

And now as he walked, looking for the rigging house and
the sail loft, with the clatter of the yard all round him, the stink
of dung from the wagon horses hauling timber, cordage,
casks, the acrid waft of tar, and the resin scent of sawn timber,
he closed his senses to these roiling things and thought of
Catherine. A picture of her came so suddenly into his mind
that he drew in a sharp breath, and stopped in mid-step. She
was there in his head, not as he had last seen her, but as he had
first seen her, turning with a pail of water in her hand, in the
rectory garden, turning to see who had come with her father
into the garden, and her hair gathered up from her slender
neck; her dark eyes; her mouth, slightly open in surprise; her
astonishing beauty. It had made him stop in mid-step then,
just as it had again now. He felt his eyes prick, and his heart
beating in his breast. And caught himself, brought himself
back into the bright day. Gabled buildings confronted him, he
smelled the river, and heard the ringing crack of mallets.

'What a damn fool I must've looked just now,' he said to
himself. 'Standing there staring at nothing, like a half-grown
boy.'

But Catherine was not nothing, was very far from nothing.
She was in his heart.

'Are you looking for me, sir?' said a grating voice. 'I have
heard you was.'

James turned and saw a man who could only be Mr
Ormerod. His demeanour said he was, and his hat, and his
blue coat, and the lists tied with twine in a leather folder
under his arm.

'Mr Ormerod?'

'The same. And you are . . . ?'

'Lieutenant Hayter, HM *Expedient* frigate, presently
moored——'

'Oh yes, ah yes. *Expedient*. Yes. I have had many and many a complaint about that ship, sir. My artificers do not care for her. They do not care about her. They say she is a troublesome refit in all distinctions, with troublesome standing officers, and no work satisfactory.'

'I think we had better discuss these things, Mr Ormerod, don't you? Captain Rennie has no wish to remain at Deptford longer than can be minimally helped. You do not wish us to remain here indefinitely, neither. We are a commissioned ship, refitting for foreign service, and we need your help to get us to sea. May we agree on that, at least?'

'We may agree, sir, on whatever you like. What I cannot do, however, Mr Hayter, is work miracles with men that have got it in their minds that their work is scorned aboard your vessel. I have their combinations to contend with, do not forget that.'

'Combinations? Mr Ormerod, you know as well as I do that combinations have been outlawed.'

'Ah, yes, so they have, sir. But what is outlawed, and what is fact—nnnn—two separate things, sir, two quite separate things.'

'Then we must discover between us how we may effect a return to good sense, hey?'

'Very well, sir, I like the sound of that. Only it must not involve extraneous cost. It must not add monies to the calculation. I know sea officers. One minute you have agreed the cost of their refit, and two minutes later five hundred pound has been added here, and five hundred there. Nnnn, that will not do, Mr Hayter.'

'I do not wish to add a single shilling, if you do not.' He brought his list from his pocket.

'Then let us discuss it in my office, by all means, over a splash of something and a biscuit.'

In his office Mr Ormerod laid out for James a vast document, headed:

The Progress of Works at His Majesty's Deptford Dockyard
the Week Past

A perplexing array of columns, sub-columns and annotations lay under this heading. Mr Ormerod's broad finger found *HM Expedient frigate*, traced across the columns the progress of work undertaken—the nature of the repair/refit; the time when taken in hand; the number of artificers employed; what part completed of sails, rigging, cables, boats: &c., &c.—and at length tapped significantly at the final column: *When may be Ready*.

'Now,' he said, in his peculiar grating voice, 'she is to have her copper looked at, we know that.'

'Yes.'

'Captain Paxton ain't pleased by that, but no matter. When her copper has been passed fit, which I know it will be—it was not my preference to have it examined, but the Board's—we shall then be able to——'

'Who is Captain Paxton?'

'Ah yes, well. Well, Mr Hayter, the least said about that, nnnn? That is the edicts of the Board, from the higher places occupied by such as Sir Charles.'

'Sir Charles?'

'Sir Charles Middleton, Controller. A very definite and uncompromising Scotch gentleman.'

'Ah. I see.' James did not see, but he settled to the discussion with determination and patience, and tried not to think of Catherine, as Mr Ormerod chewed biscuits heavily and swept their fragments off the broad table.

><+==+><

'Rotted through,' said Captain Paxton. 'Why give me a rotten ship?'

'None of us knows,' said Rennie.

'Eh?'

'We none of us know these things.' A swallow of wine. 'It is not our privilege to know the minds of, of—of others.'

'Couldn't-have-put-it-finer.'

'It is just—dockyards, I expect.'

'It is an unpalatable thing, a shameful thing, to command a guardship.' He put down his empty glass. 'It is the last command I should choose, were the choosing in my choosing.'

Rennie pushed the bottle. It was their second bottle. They refilled their glasses.

'Guardships, hey?'

'Damnation to all such things, sir. And to all dockyards. Your health.'

On the morning following this health-giving encounter Rennie was in the wherry, falling down to Woolwich with some few of the Deptford Dockyard officers, who were all talking very loudly about things Rennie felt sure were of such little moment that it was wicked in them, infernally wicked, that they should discuss them at all. He felt like saying so, but that thought caused him pain. Any thought, about anything; any movement, sudden or effortful; any activity of any kind caused him pain. He felt that the morning, the wherry, the world itself was painful, and that these damned chattering fools ought properly to understand, and desist. His sweaty pallor, his sickly scowl, his slumping posture did not deter them, however, and the brief journey was misery to him.

Rennie was going to Woolwich, to the Ordnance Depot, to meet Mr Alexander Waterfield, the assistant inspector of artillery, and Mr Truscott Dearman, of Dearman & Co., who would introduce him to, and demonstrate, their new pattern naval gun. It was an important occasion, and Rennie knew it. An important one, and a secret one. The letter of instruction which had come from the Ordnance Board enjoined him to vouchsafe no hint of his purpose in going to Woolwich to anyone. Well, he had told Lieutenant Hayter, there it was. What else could he have done? Hayter was his second-in-command, and needed to know all such things. He felt that he could trust Lieutenant Hayter. Hayter was a good fellow. A little superior in his manner and dress, but that was inevitable in the son of a landed family. Rennie's head swam with these reflections, and his belly swam horribly in turn.

The wherry came to Woolwich Dockyard, and put the dockyard officers ashore.

'Now, sir,' said the wherryman, in his knitted hat. 'You is for Galleons Reach, is it?'

'I—I am,' said Rennie, deathly pale.

'Are you ill, sir?'

'No no. I—I am quite well.'

'I could put you ashore here, if you'd like, where you might rest yourself, if——'

'No no, let us get *on*,' said Rennie harshly, and his head boiled and split under his hat. He fell back against the rail, and clutched at his head, knocking off his hat. The wherryman retrieved it and gently returned it.

'Just as you like, sir,' he said.

They came smoothly to Galleons Reach, and Rennie went ashore at the gun wharf. He stumbled as he did, and had to clutch forward at the greasy tide-green timbers of the wharf on the rise of the vessel. He nearly fell. A hand steadied him, and when he found himself on his two legs on the wharf he looked round into the steady gaze of a young man in a brown coat.

'Mr Waterfield?'

'No, sir. I am his clerk, Joseph Miller. I am to bring you to the Burrow, where Mr Waterfield is preparing the demonstration.'

'Very good, Mr Miller. How?'

'Sir?'

'How are we to proceed, Mr Miller? Walk? Ride? Carriage?'

'We are to walk, sir. It ain't far.'

They walked perhaps a quarter of a mile, past the depot buildings, along a cobbled lane with a high brick wall, and into a long, broad field, with earthen embankments. This place lay at a level below that of the surrounds, and was concealed by the wall, and by the embankments, which were raised to a greater height at the far end, a distance of some hundreds of yards. There was an air of peace, of tranquillity. A low wooden building lay immediately below the wall, and Joseph Miller led Rennie there.

Inside, bending over a trestle table covered in detailed drawings, were two men, coatless, concentrated, the younger with his hair falling forward into his eyes. The older man had a square, lined face, which looked unwelcoming, thought Rennie. His wig sat squarely on his head, and he was square in the shoulders. He looked up from the drawings, and nodded to Rennie. The younger man turned, pushed back his hair impatiently, and came forward with hand outheld.

'Captain Rennie? So very glad you are here, sir. It is a great pleasure to meet the man who will take our new gun to sea. I am Alexander Waterfield, and this is Mr Dearman.'

'Delighted,' said Rennie, who felt nothing of the kind. He shook their hands, however, and endeavoured to be an enthusiast for the morning's work.

'Will you look at our working drawings?' continued Waterfield. 'Perhaps you will explain them better than I, Trus.' And he stepped aside to allow Dearman room at the table beside Rennie.

'As you know already, I'm sure, Captain Rennie, this is an entirely new gun, a new pattern. Mr Waterfield has designed it, and we—that is, my company—have made it. We have only cast eighteen-pounders as yet, but we hope to make guns in all sizes if this one suits.' He pulled a drawing forward and caught the edges with little brass weights. 'First, it is shorter than your standard naval gun, and lighter.'

'The Armstrong gun,' said Rennie. Leaning forward made him feel faint.

'Yes, the Armstrong is nine foot, in your standard eighteen-pounder. It weighs a very great deal, forty-two hundredweight. Our gun weighs thirty-two hundredweight, and is seven foot eleven inches.'

'Good heaven,' said Rennie, alarmed. 'How can such a light, short, unsubstantial piece carry the charge of powder for an eighteen-pound ball?'

'Ah, that is the beauty of our gun, sir: the new powder Mr Waterfield and I have invented. The charge may be reduced to one quarter of the weight of shot. It will work equally well with round-, grape-, bar-, canister-, and cone-shot.'

'Reduced allowance?' Rennie's head was again swimming. 'First reduced, or second?'

'Neither, sir. This is full allowance. First and second reduced is similarly equated. What is more, and this is the greatest beauty of all.' He held up a finger.

'The greatest beauty of all,' echoed Waterfield.

'The shot will travel a greater distance, in all cases, with greater accuracy.'

'Greater distance, hey?' said Rennie with a quick nod which he instantly regretted. He rubbed his forehead. 'Yes, very good. Mr Dearman, you said something just now, I believe. You said "cone-shot". Did I hear you right?'

'You did, indeed. Cone-shot is our new projectile, which we have developed for the new gun.'

'I don't think I have ever heard of the notion of cone-shot.'

'Let me show you,' said Waterfield. They followed him out of the hut, and round to the far side, where a gun stood on its carriage, with tackles, on a square of timber decking, prepared and secured with spikes for the occasion. Lying by the cannon were boxes of cartridge, and boxes of shot. One box was filled with strange elongated objects, cylindrical in shape, with a coned head culminating in a near point at the top. Handspikes, a sponge-rammer, and buckets of water and sand all lay arranged. Rennie noted that there was a large metal loop at the top of the button on the cascable of the gun, through which the breech rope passed. The gun was shorter and slightly stouter in the first and second reinforces than the Armstrong guns Rennie was familiar with. A flintlock with a lanyard was fixed above the vent. On the muzzle ring was a raised sight.

Waterfield tapped the box of cone-shot with the toe of his boot.

'This is our eighteen-pound cone-shot, Captain Rennie. We have designed it for use with a grooved barrel. This gun has such a barrel, and we would like you to take four examples with——'

'Grooved barrel, Mr Waterfield?'

'Indeed, sir. It is a new idea, not entirely our own, which the American colonists had begun to develop in the late war. They had no funds to realize their idea in the metal. From the chamber to the muzzle the barrel has six grooves and lands, which——'

'You mean, it is like a rifle?'

'Exactly so, Captain Rennie, you have grasped that notion at once. Bravo.'

'Good heaven, man, a rifle must be aimed. Aimed with great accuracy. That is impossible in gunnery at sea. Quite impossible.' Why had he spoken so forcefully? Lord, his head.

'Perhaps if you will allow us to demonstrate,' said Dearman. 'You will see a line of targets on the far embankment.' He pointed. Rennie saw the targets and was about to nod, thought better of it, and instead raised his hand in acknowledgement.

'Gun crew!' shouted Waterfield, and Rennie flinched. From behind an abutment appeared half a dozen apprentices, who hurried forward and assumed their positions at the tackles. Waterfield crouched behind the gun, closed one eye and peered along the top of the gun, lining up the flintlock with the front sight. 'Ready!' he shouted, and pulled the lanyard. There was a flash at the vent, a belch of flames at the muzzle and a shattering concussion. The gun ran back on its trucked carriage as Waterfield nimbly moved clear. The middle target on the embankment disappeared in a great spout of earth. Rennie's ears sang horribly, his brains seemed to bulge in his head, he lurched, stumbled, and measured his length on the hard ground.

'A bull, I think!' shouted Waterfield.

'Aye! Yes!' shouted Dearman. 'A very fair demonstration, hey, Captain Rennie?'

Rennie came to himself, and found Waterfield peering down at him in concern. 'Are you all right, sir?'

'Ah,' managed Rennie. He tried to lift himself up. 'I fear that I—I was not quite set when you fired.'

'I am very sorry indeed, sir. Let me help you.' He and Dearman got Rennie to his feet, and Waterfield produced a flask. 'You had better have some brandy, sir.' And Rennie shuddered.

─────＊─≡◆≡─＊─────

Expedient came out of the dry dock, having had her copper examined and passed fit, and was returned to her mooring, and her place was taken in the dock by the *Obelisk*, seventy-four. Now two seventy-fours lay end to end in the dock, stripped of their rigging and with their sides shored up, and Captain Paxton removed himself to a nearby inn, and sent word to his wife at Rochester to join him, lest he die of futility. Spring tides would govern his life for weeks and months ahead.

Captain Rennie, when he had rid himself of his madeira-induced sufferings, waxed enthusiastic about the new Waterfield guns to his first lieutenant, who had in turn reached a *modus operandi* with Mr Ormerod, which Rennie and his standing officers between them had been unable to do.

Mr Loftus, the master, made his appearance, and on the same day the purser, Mr Trent, came aboard. Rennie saw them in turn, Mr Loftus first. Bernard Loftus was a man not tall but above middle height, quite spare, with an intelligent face and a capable demeanour. He had not presented himself before this, he explained, because his papers had been sent for perusal by the Board at Trinity House, and that body had required him to be available to them for interview for upwards of ten days; he had submitted, but was unhappy; he had wished to join his ship as soon as she had been commissioned, but could not until Trinity House, &c., &c.

'Never mind, Mr Loftus, it was not your fault, and you are here now.'

'Thank you, sir. Ready to do my duty.'

'Very good. As soon as we begin storing, Mr Loftus, those duties will begin in earnest. Have you had experience of frigates?'

'Yes, sir. As you will see in my papers, I have been master in *Alarum*, thirty-two, and in the *Melanie*, twenty-eight.'

Rennie glanced through the papers again, examined the warrant, freshly written, and felt that he had got a good man.

'Yes, very good.—Stern.'

'Beg pardon, sir?'

'I will like her a little by the stern, Mr Loftus, I think.'

Mr Loftus allowed himself to smile. 'I am glad, sir. That is my preference. By the stern a little, and as few blocks in our rigging as may be achieved.'

'Spare bowers, if you can wheedle them out of the yard.'

'And spare bowers, sir.'

'Very good. Ask Mr Trent to step in, will you?' And a moment after, Mr Trent did come in.

'Mr Trent,' said Rennie. 'Why was you not here, sir, in the ship, when I took command?'

'I was kept away against my will.' Mr Trent was portly, and indignant, and Rennie's first impression of him was that he was neither stupid, nor more than usually self-exculpatory.

'Against your will? Was you under arrest?'

'Indeed I was not, although I might as well have been put

into Clink. I was obliged by the Board to undergo an examination of my affairs, of my affairs and my character, such as I have never before known. I was made, my associates and I was made, to produce the whole of our five hundred pound. The whole of it! When I have given nothing but honourable service, always fair in slops, tobacco, everything. No long lists of this and that spoiled. Yet I might as well have been the greatest thief and blackguard alive!—I beg your pardon, sir.'

'I am very sorry you have been put to this test, Mr Trent. It is most unusual.' He glanced through Mr Trent's papers. There was nothing amiss, no blemish against his name. Because *Expedient* had never been commissioned he had not been one of her standing officers at Chatham, but had come from another ship recently paid off, a convoy frigate. 'Most unusual, but not without precedent, however. It is the unfortunate lot of pursers that the Royal Navy likes to call you to account from time to time. Hard on you, Mr Trent, very hard, but it means that you come to *Expedient* with the best possible recommendation: a shining good name. That cannot be anything but an advantage to us both, hey?'

'Well, sir—put like that, I suppose it is.' Doubtfully.

'Of course it is, Mr Trent. We are all new in the ship, she is a new ship, and I mean to make her a proud commission, and an honourable one.'

'Aye, sir. Very well. I am obliged to you for your confidence in me.'

'We must all have confidence in each other, Mr Trent. I must sign your books, after all, in good faith.'

'Indeed, sir, indeed.' His indignation had passed. It had been partly assumed, of course, and Rennie knew this; but Mr Trent struck him as a man who would rather avoid trouble if he could, and that suited Rennie at all points.

Men had now begun to trickle into the ship, in twos and threes, a few at a time. Some came down in the wherry from the wharves upstream, others from downstream. Most of them were experienced seamen, and had their papers in good order. None of these papers appeared to be forgeries, a rare thing among men who would often sell their papers cheap in lieu of pay held up, and produce crudely scrawled substitutes in order to get themselves entered in the muster books of a ship newly commissioned. There were not among them, either, the usual misfits and miscreants, grinning and servile one moment, grudging and troublesome the next. These men, all of these men, were right seamen, if James was any judge. As he entered them in the books, and asked each man to sign his name, or make his mark, he did judge them in the way all sea officers must learn to judge men, and understand them.

'How did you learn of this commission, Fenton?'

'A word, sir, passed on.'

'By whom?'

'A mate of mine, sir.'

'A shipmate? From the,' glancing down, 'from *Sentinel*?'

'No, sir. Most of my shipmates from *Sentinel* has gone into Indiamen, sir, or scattered to the four winds.'

'I see. So, how did this mate of yours, how did he hear of this commission?'

'Such things is known up and down the river pretty quick, sir, ain't they?'

'Yes, I suppose so.'

There were many such exchanges. James could not put his finger on what was odd about this, what was decidedly odd, but he was aware of a nagging feeling in the pit of his stomach. It was as if all of these men had been gathered by an invisible hand. There was scarcely a landman or an idler among them.

In *Expedient*, as in any ship of war, only a relatively small part of the full complement would be made up of men experienced and skilled enough to be called able, and of these only the youngest and most agile would be topmen, those who went aloft in the rigging, stood out on the footropes of the spars, and handed and reefed the sails in all weathers. These were the men who had now signed on, and again as if by design the next batch of men who came to be entered were the ordinary seamen. James's chief concern of many concerns and duties as the refit continued, and stores were got into the ship, was to produce an adequate and efficient system of divisions, watches, stations and quarters. He consulted with his captain, and soon the ship's books were nearly filled. The marines came aboard, and their officer, Lieutenant Raker. Boys appeared, ship's boys, servants; and at last *Expedient*'s allocation of six midshipmen. The landmen and idlers came. The ship filled up.

Mr Adgett and his newly acquired mate were kept tremendously busy. The officers' cabins had to be fitted, not with canvas bulkheads, but timber; the captain's sleeping cabin was made a matter of priority; furniture in the shape of tables, stools, benches; and partitions for storerooms, wooden cages for the beasts that would soon be brought into the ship; all these things were required to be made, and made quickly and well.

Expedient's canvas had to be got in, and stored in the sailroom; her timber stores, her stores of nails, of Stockholm tar, her cables, anchors, and rope. Her boats had to be prepared, and hoisted in. Mr Adgett became more and more attached to his own plans and notions.

'As I say, sir,' he explained to Rennie, 'she is well found. At Chatham we was very hostile to deterration, very hostile to decay. Mr Mantell and me—he is the assistant master there— we looked after her month on month, we nurtured her, and she is sound, and yet——'

'Yes, Mr Adgett? Please be brief, I am pressed this morning.'

'Well, sir, as I say, it is her knees. Hanging knees, as you know, is how it has always been done. But there is a new method, which is foreign, as I say, but sound. It is bolted plates. Now then——'

'Does hanging knees impede her working, Mr Adgett?'

'As I say, I do not know that, sir. However, as we are refitting, seriously refitting, why don't we please and flatter her with something new?'

'Refit, yes, Mr Adgett. Rebuild her, no. Mr Ormerod, as Lieutenant Hayter will like to tell you, will not like the proposal to be made that more timber is to be got into her.'

'Oh no, sir. As I say, this will *save* us timber, and flatter her, too.'

'How?'

'Because the plates is iron, sir. Less timber is used in each of her knees, whereas before they was all grown, as I say.'

'We must consider whether or no to pay her this compliment, Mr Adgett. Will not the present knees have to be removed, and the others fitted? Well well, I have answered my own question. Do not interfere with her knees, Mr Adgett, lest ye be arrested for criminal conversation.'

The spirit of experiment, fuelled by rumour, had begun to spread through the ship, and soon would penetrate every hole and corner and bemuse every man; he would have to snuff it out, or be faced with an anarchy of invention.

His second and third lieutenants at last presented themselves, Mr Makepeace in the forenoon, Mr Royce very late in the evening.

'Who is that? What the devil is going on?' demanded Rennie, as a scuffle occurred outside his door. Voices were raised. Something fell and splintered. Rennie pulled open the door, and found the marine on duty grappling with a young man in civilian dress of a flashy cut, and flashy boots. His hair was tangled in his face. There was the smell of drink. Glass fragments lay scattered.

'That will do!' said Rennie. The struggle ceased, and the

young man straightened his coat, pushed back his hair, and said:

'I have the honour to present my compliments to you, sir. I am Lieutenant Royce, requesting permission to come aboard.'

'You are already on board, Mr Royce. All right,' he nodded to the marine, who touched his hat and bent to pick up his fallen musket. 'Go in there, sir,' he said to Royce, and pointed.

Royce went in, and Rennie followed.

'Let me see your commission.'

'Fact is, I must apologize, sir. My papers have unaccountably become . . . they are mislaid. My dunnage has altogether gone missing. I daresay it is still ashore. I did order it put in the boat, but the fellow was only interested in his payment. I can only assume——'

'Mr Royce.'

'I know I have not made a good impression upon you. The fact is, I was delayed. There——'

'Mr *Royce*.'

'I was late getting to this infernal place. It is in the middle of nothing at all, and I——'

'*Silence!*'

Lieutenant Royce stopped talking and focused his eyes on his captain. The effort made him frown. Rennie regarded him with utter loathing. His plum coat was of a flamboyant cut, his waistcoat was made of some damned glittering cloth, his boots were preposterous in their glossy disregard for decorum and sense.

'You are drunk, Mr Royce. You are improperly dressed. You have no papers. You are *late*.'

'The fact is——'

'The fact is that you are a disgrace to His Majesty's service.' He shook his head as Royce tried to interrupt. 'Do not continue, sir, with a defence which can only make your position *worse*. Go to your cabin, and stay there until I send for you.'

'I—fact is, don't know where my cabin——'

'Then discover it, sir, damn quick, or you will spend the night at the mast head.'

'Very well. Very good.' Royce bowed stiffly, looked for his hat, did not find it, and left the cabin. The smell of brandy lingered on the air. Rennie reflected that he had no power to send a commissioned officer to the mast head, but that to say it, ferociously say it, had made him feel better about this first and most unsatisfactory encounter with his junior lieutenant.

The ship's boats were ready, and were hoisted in. Rennie had taken the precaution of having the boats' bottoms painted thickly with whitelead, as a preservative measure. All manner of boats, rafts, hoys and other craft continually came to the ship, or were about her at the mooring. The victualling stores came steadily into the ship, and Mr Loftus supervised the storing of the hold, from the ground tier up.

'We must conclude the business of watches and divisions later,' said Rennie on a hot morning. 'I am called again to the Admiralty.'

'I think I may be able to manage the listing of divisions, sir, in your absence.' James was now confident in his work, and was steadily getting to know all of the people.

'Very well. However, I must choose my own coxswain and boat's crew myself. That is a matter of the first importance, which I cannot delegate nor neglect. I must do it as soon as I return.'

'Will you be away overnight, sir?'

'I expect so. Meeting persons at the Admiralty is always a detaining experience. It don't seem to matter who it is, he will keep you waiting there, in a chair, in a side room, the fellow, hour by hour.'

The truth was, he did not mind going upstream. He would stay again at Mrs Peebles's house in Bedford Street, where he would be made welcome, and be given an excellent dinner.

Mrs Peebles herself was an admirable woman, and her daughter Lucy was remarkably pretty.

'I will give you the same room, Captain Rennie, if you like.'

'Yes, indeed, I should like that very much, if you please.'

'Will you come back here for your dinner, sir, or will you eat it elsewhere?'

'I shall certainly make every effort to eat it here, Mrs Peebles.'

But he did not eat his dinner in Bedford Street. The Third Secretary, Mr Soames, had other plans for him.

'Their Lordships are anxious that you should meet the Assistant Astronomer Royal, Mr Lawrence. I have taken the liberty of arranging a dinner.' The same waft of cologne water.

'Oh. Ah. I had already made my own arrangements. Would it not have been easier and more convenient for Mr Lawrence to have met me at Greenwich? I take it he lives at Greenwich?'

'He does, Captain Rennie. However, their Lordships are of the opinion that you should meet him in London, in an easeful atmosphere, at dinner.'

Mr Lawrence at dinner—in a private room at a private club in Jermyn Street—was equally doubtful about the occasion and the circumstances which had given rise to it.

'You wish to take a reflecting telescope to the South Seas, Captain Rennie?'

'To the Pacifick Ocean, yes. So I am informed.'

'You are informed——? For what purpose do you carry it there?'

'Well, I dare say it is to observe the stars, you know. Venus, I expect.'

'Venus is one of the planets.' Tartly.

'No doubt, between you, you will arrive at a wise pattern of observation,' Soames interposed smoothly. 'The purpose of this meeting, gentlemen, this dinner, was to acquaint you one with the other, so that when you come to your joint perusal of the instrument you will find yourselves jointly at your ease, in an atmosphere of discretion.'

Rennie was on his third glass of wine. 'Good heaven, Soames, you make it sound like a tryst at a bawdy house.' He laughed at his own joke, then understood that neither Soames nor Lawrence had seen it. 'Ah. Mm. Very excellent claret, Soames. You do us proud tonight.'

'Your health.' Soames smiled only with his mouth, and merely raised his glass. 'The instrument is bespoke of Mr Lang, and is presently at his house at Long Acre, and will be transported from there to Greenwich next week. It was thought,' he added, putting down his full glass, 'that the other instruments might as well be sent there at the same time. The brass sextants, bespoke of Mr Lumsden, and a barometer bespoke of him also. A thermometer. And the two chronometers bespoke of Plenitude Tyndale, late apprenticed to Mr Arnold. These, I am told, vie with Kendall's copies of Harrison for precision.'

'I—I have heard of Harrison,' said Rennie. 'The other names I do not know.'

'Are there not further instruments?' said Lawrence. 'I was informed——'

'Scientifical called Baragwanath has a wind instrument, I know that,' said Rennie. 'And there is a new patented logship, and sounding-devices. A theodolite. Will they all be sent to Greenwich?'

'I believe—all but the anemometer,' said Lawrence with a slight frown. Why was he vexed? wondered Rennie. They were eating duck, with a sweet berry sauce. What the devil had Lawrence to complain of? A good dinner, and a superlative wine? Then he must be extraordinary hard to please, the fellow. Or perhaps his work was disagreeable to him? It must be that.

'It is an inconvenience to the Royal Observatory to receive all these disparate things,' said Soames, as if reading Rennie's mind. 'However, their Lordships have decided that it should be so, for reasons of disguise. The gentlemen of whom this diverse collection is bespoke believe that they make them for the Observatory alone, as examples of the finest instruments available in the world. What could be more fitting? What more appropriate home could they have?'

'Why not the Royal Society?' said Lawrence. 'What has the Royal Observatory to do with theodolites, sir, and sounding-leads? How may these things assist us in our observations of the heavens?'

'All these things, Mr Lawrence, go into Captain Rennie's ship on a voyage of exploration. A voyage of the greatest significance to the Royal Navy, and to the nation. To the future of the nation. Maskelyne knows it, and has given his consent. As his deputy——'

'I merely ask,' said Lawrence. 'It is not our business at the Royal Observatory to thwart the advance of navigational methods, nor to hinder His Majesty's fleets.'

Very prettily put, thought Rennie, and he did not mean one word of it, the grudging bugger.

'In any case, the inconvenience is brief,' continued Mr Soames. 'You will greatly oblige their Lordships by storing the instruments at Greenwich until Captain Rennie's departure, and by showing him, in the brief interregnum, how to make use of the telescope.'

'I am amazed, I confess, that Captain Rennie himself is to make the planetary observations,' said Lawrence, again with that petulant frown. 'Would it not be more sensible and practical to send a scientific observer, a person with experience of telescopes, to undertake this work?'

Ahah, thought Rennie, so now we come to his true complaint. He thinks I am a buffoon, that all sailors are buffoons. 'Do you volunteer yourself for our little cruise?' he asked Lawrence politely.

'I, Captain Rennie? I? My duties hold me at Greenwich, and I——'

'It is quite out of the question, quite out of the question,' said Soames.

'Surely, on Cook's voyage to observe Venus, there was scientificals aboard?' asked Rennie innocently. 'Trained astronomicals?'

'I could not possibly accompany you,' said Lawrence, getting pale.

'It is out of the question,' repeated Soames. He smiled again, only with his mouth, his eyes flat with reserve. 'Captain Rennie, as a sea officer of long service, knows how to use all manner of instruments. It requires only his close attention to your instruction over one evening for him to become proficient.'

'As you wish,' said Lawrence, relieved. 'I am more than happy.' But his frown remained.

The evening had not been a great social success, reflected Rennie as he walked back to Bedford Street. He could not like Lawrence, and Mr Lawrence could not like him, and there it was. Soames had offered him a lift, but he had preferred the night air, and the chance of brisk exercise.

'I must caution you that there are footpads,' warned Soames. 'You may be attacked.'

'I am wearing my sword,' said Rennie. 'I have not forgot how to use it, neither.'

He had hoped to catch sight of Lucy Peebles on his return to her mother's rooms, but all had gone to bed save the night porter, who let him in, smelled drink, and lit a candle to guide the gentleman upstairs.

＊＊＊＊＊＊＊

Deptford, and the river busy with ships, boats, hoys. The smell of the river distinct in the summer airlessness. *Expedient* nearly ready now; her rigging complete, to the satisfaction of her captain, and her boatswain Mr Tangible; her storing complete, to the satisfaction of Mr Trent, and Mr Loftus the master. Rennie's cross catharpings there in the shrouds, and his ship a little by the stern. When her guns were taken in she would have to be retrimmed, but for now Rennie was content. He stood now on the quarterdeck with James, looking aloft. He moved to the breast rail at the break of the quarterdeck, and rested his knee against one of the hanging buckets.

'The smell of the tide is an extraordinary thing, Mr Hayter.'

'How so, sir?'

'It is always the same; it is a lowering smell.'

'It is pronounced, you mean?'

'No. It is the smell of departure, and absence. It is the smell, before the fact, of far away.'

'Ah.'

'Have you never heard a distant church-bell, rising and falling on the morning air?'

'Often, yes.'

'It is like that, do not you find?'

'The tide, sir?'

'That tidal smell, of the mud, of the sea beyond, of all the world far away—is like the country church-bell. Very near, yet very far. It speaks to a man's heart.'

'Evocative things, indeed,' James said quietly, and thought then of Catherine. 'Intimate and evocative things.' A look sideways, briefly returned.

'Just so, Mr Hayter.' Rennie sighed, and leaned forward a little. 'I had many ideas when we began to refit, to improve the ship, which I have had to discard. Colonial ideas of frigates, which I have heard I cannot remember where. The decking over of the waist, or much of it, and greater barricades on the forecastle, and cutting bridle ports under the catheads, and so forth.'

'You was thinking of these things for *Expedient*, sir?'

'Yes, at first, since we were to be an experimental ship. Yet on reflection I knew that it would impede us. Mr Ormerod would say: "Captain Rennie, oh. Oh, Captain Rennie, dear oh dear. Nnnn. No sir, no sir, if. If, sir, we are to complete, we must have a care for detail agreed, and for timber. What am I to do about timber, Captain Rennie, nnnn?" And we should be here at Christmas, disputing.'

'You carry him off admirably well, sir. It is his voice.'

'Well well, he's an admirable fellow in his way, I expect. I could not tax him.'

'Surely bridle ports is not taxing, though? Why shouldn't we have them, if they answer?'

'I might have prevailed, since it would not be getting more timber in, only cutting it out. But we had enough trouble over the porting for the carronades, and I could not tax him. I had thought of bow chasers, too. Only I knew the Ordnance Board would say where did I expect them to find yet more guns, when I am to have the luxury of Mr Waterfield's new guns as it is?'

'I am sure they would not, sir. We are an experiment, after all.'

'I expect I could say that, even at this late hour. "Gentlemen, we are an experiment, an unique experiment." Indeed, I might well say that, when we fall down to Woolwich. Yes, what is it?'

'Mr Adgett is very—he is very agitated, sir,' said the boy at the waist ladder. 'He asks, would the lieutenant come at once, please, sir?'

'Oh Lord, I had forgot Mr Adgett. He had been promised another hand for his crew, and complained that he had not been accommodated. I said I would investigate, and it went clean out of my head. With your permission, sir.' He left Rennie and followed the boy into the waist. When he returned, Rennie had gone ashore. The last caulkers were going into their boat, watched by the sergeant of marines.

James reflected on the preceding days and weeks. At times he had nearly despaired of the organization of the ship's people, since so many men seemed qualified to fill responsible positions. Few of the men knew each other, and rivalry for status was acute among the topmen, in particular, who all wished to be rated petty officer. Fights broke out in the lower deck, and Rennie had assembled the ship's company, and read them the Articles of War. When he had finished, and had put the book under his arm, he waited a long moment, then:

'While ever I have this ship under my legs, and under my command, I think she is the finest ship in the Royal Navy. You, therefore, are the finest seamen in the Royal Navy. We do not yet know each other well, you and I, but we are going to, right soon. You have all been rated, every man, by the first lieutenant and myself. I expect you to live up to those ratings. I have placed my trust in you as seamen, and you must trust me in turn. That is fair. That is right. From now on, I want no indiscipline, no ill will, no envy, and I will tell you why. Because we are all now proud to call ourselves Expedients.— How are we called?'

A ragged murmur.

'I am a little deaf, today. Let me hear you again. How are we called?'

'Expedients!'

James had been impressed by this simple, straightforward device. It had worked. The fighting ceased, and the ship settled down. There were the usual cases of drunkenness, certainly, which no ship—no matter how virtuous—could wholly avoid, but little else that could be called a punishable offence. Rennie had dealt with them leniently.

Rennie was out of the ship overnight, at Greenwich. In the morning he brought back with him Mr Lang's reflecting telescope, packed deep in cotton waste in its own crate, which was stowed securely in the hold, on the topmost tier. Other instruments were brought aboard and taken to the great cabin, or given into the safekeeping of Mr Loftus: the new logship, the new sounding equipment, &c., &c.; a beautifully made theodolite had been added, and two very fine Dollond terrestrial glasses. As yet there was no sign of either Mr Baragwanath, or his anemometer.

Rennie was dismissive of his experience at Greenwich.

'I had some brief business at the hospital, where I consulted a disciple of Dr Lind's about anti-scorbutics, then I climbed the hill from the park to the Observatory. By God, that is harder than going aloft. I had to pause halfway up, and then when I reached the gate Mr Lawrence became over-solicitous. He enjoined me to sit on a low chair inside the door of Flamsteed House, and "get back your breath, you are very waxy in the face". I think he was trying to imply that I was like a vapourish miss, ready to fall down in a faint, the fellow. I do not like him.'

'Was it instructive, sir?'

'Instructive? Mmff.—Yes, it was instructive. Over-instructive is the definition, I think. He attempted to belittle me in the matter of lenses. As if I could not tell the difference between a simple inverting lens, and a reflective arrangement of lenses and mirrors. I told him that as a competent sea officer I was perfectly aware how to use an Hadley's. He further attempted to make me small by comparing me unfavourably with Dalrymple as a scientifical. "Was you insistent upon Venus, Captain? I must tell you that there is no further transit for ninety year. That is, if you was set on Venus." I told him square: "Mr Bloody Lawrence—well, I left out the expletive—Mr Lawrence, I do not know what I am to observe until I receive my final orders." However, I was much taken with the great observation room at the top of the house, a beautiful room. And Lawrence did give me a perfectly pleasant supper, with passable wine. I must not condemn him in that, the fellow.'

'You wished to choose your boat's crew, sir. You asked me to remind you of it—again remind you of it, sir.'

'You are quite right, I had forgot. Or rather, I had let it drift. I know it is pressing, but there is so many damned things. I had better do it now, before——'

'Boat alongside!'

It was Mr Baragwanath, with his anemometer, and the

matter of Rennie's coxswain and boat's crew was again put aside. Rennie took Mr Baragwanath, a tall, stooping, anxious man, below to the great cabin. The instrument was brought there, as its maker hovered, and placed with great care on the decking canvas. There was a long, weighted arm, and a kind of windmill, and a system of tackles on a central tower, and other more intricate machinery.

'It is a development of Smeaton's principles, also investigated by a gentleman in Leicestershire, with whom I correspond. However, it is entirely my own work in manufacture.'

'It is a—a very considerable machine,' observed Rennie. 'Will you take a glass of wine, Mr Baragwanath?'

'Wine? Oh no, no thank you. No.'

'A biscuit? Some cake?'

'No no, I thank you, no. My doctor.' He did not elaborate. Soon, anxiously, he departed.

On the morrow *Expedient* slipped her moorings and fell down to Galleons Reach on the ebb to take in her guns and powder.

Rennie was considerably eased by their departure from Deptford. As the broad block of the storehouse and the gables of the sheds and boathouses fell astern, he felt himself free of irksomeness. The drear day-by-day complications of administration, of dealing with so many officials and their underlings: the Clerk of the Check; the Master Attendant; the Clerk of the Survey; the Master Shipwright; the Timber Master; the Master Boatbuilder—a bewildering doubling and trebling up of officers, and their Byzantine powers and duties—had exhausted him in spirit if not in limb. Yet his difficulties were far from over. His ailing gunner Mr Wearing had at last worn out, and died. He had no surgeon. His junior lieutenant Mr Royce he would gladly have seen returned, wearing his deplorable civilian clothes and his insufferable sneer, to Lord Gillingham. Mr Royce, sober, was worse even than Mr Royce, drunk. Makepeace, his second, was a quiet, intelligent young man, and would be all right. And certainly he was very lucky in having James Hayter, a man he could not now do without. If he was honest, if he examined his conscience, had not Mr Hayter been his saviour in the damned dockyard? Had he not made things right with Ormerod? Well, he had. And had he not been tenacious, steadfast and even-handed in his organization of the people into watches, divisions, stations and quarters? Indeed without him Rennie knew that he would have been forever in the muddle in which the commission had been begun.

'Find Mr Hayter,' he said now to the boy who was on call at his door. 'Tell him I wish to see him.' Then when the boy had gone he thought that the message would sound abrupt, and perhaps discourteous. He would have to be careful about such things. On long foreign service it was vital that there should be amiability between himself and his officers. He thought of Mr Royce, and excepted him from this rule. He did not mind if Mr Royce thought him hard; he hoped that he would.

James came to the great cabin.

'You wished to see me, sir?'

'Yes, Mr Hayter. It is high time I chose my boat's crew, and my coxswain. We will do it now, if you please.'

'You wish me to assist you, sir?' James was surprised. Surely this was a matter for the captain alone?

'In the ordinary way I should just go about it—in the ordinary way, you know. But I have been busy, insupportably busy these last days, at the Admiralty, and Greenwich and so forth, and I do not yet know the men. You, however, have had time to look at every man, and place him in the ship. I should value your advice, Mr Hayter.'

'Then certainly I will give it, sir, and gladly.'

'Very good. Let us begin with the coxswain.' They began to make a list of names.

*

They anchored in the stream at Galleons Reach, fore and aft, and Rennie went ashore. Mr Waterfield was on hand. Mr Dearman had gone home to Rotherham, to his foundry, his work completed.

'You understand the marking of the powder casks, Captain Rennie?'

'Full, first, and second reduced, yes.'

'Indeed no, indeed no,' said Waterfield with some asperity. 'That applies only to your standard issue, sir. The new powder, which we want you to compare with the old, is marked in red.'

'I see. I see. My difficulty, Mr Waterfield, is that I have no gunner at present.'

'No *gunner*?' Waterfield stared at him in dismay, and took off his hat.

'Our gunner has died, I regret to say. And I have no——'

'*Died?*'

Again James was asked to help. Again, gladly, he did help. He supervised the getting of the guns into the ship, an unusual procedure for a frigate here at Woolwich, since the guns would ordinarily have been sent to one of the official ordnance wharves at Chatham, or Portsmouth, or Plymouth. He listened carefully to Alexander Waterfield, and made notes of all he said.

'I must confide in you, Hayter, since your captain has delegated to you the management of the guns and powder, for the moment. This was all supposed to have been conducted simply, and with the utmost discretion, however—however, it cannot be helped that you have no gunner aboard.'

'Forgive me, Waterfield, but I don't understand why there is all this furtiveness. We are a frigate taking in her new guns. Yes, it is a new pattern, and we are to have new powder. But we are at home in England, far up the Thames from any enemy, and so far as I know we are not at war at present, anyway. Unless you know different?'

'The difficulty is, the difficulty is, as I have been most particularly asked to stress, that there is always spies.'

'Spies? In the peace? Spying for whom?'

'Lieutenant, surely you are not so naïve as to think we will never have an enemy again?'

'Of course I am not. Perhaps I might well hope for an enemy, as a sea officer. But you must know that a ship is damn near an open book. All your people here have seen the guns hoisted into *Expedient*. Every man on board will see them every day. How are these guns to be reckoned a secret? You cannot stop the mouths of seamen, you know, when they go ashore.'

'Yes. Well. I must not speak out of turn. And now I will like to explain the marking of the new powder casks, as opposed to your standard issue. It is most important that they should be stored separately in your magazine, and separately in cartridge in the filling-room.'

'Very good. Why?'

'Because the new powder is much more powerful. A full-charge weight of standard powder, were the same weight mistakenly used in a cartridge of the new powder, would burst the gun.'

'Good God.'

'It is the charcoal. A barrel of powder is sixty-seven and a half pounds saltpetre, nine pounds sulphur, and thirteen and a half pounds charcoal. Our new method of producing charcoal is to burn it in cylinders. This gives it a far greater strength, so that the whole of the mixture, corned large, considerably reduces the weight of the charge required, to a quarter the weight of shot. All charcoal cylinder casks are accordingly marked red. Red.'

'Now I am clear,' James nodded, making a note. He was beginning to like Waterfield.

'The advantages are many. It is also much more durable, we think, Dearman and I. In the one-pound tests it has passed with flying colours. Properly kept at sea, our powder should never spoil, even on the longest voyage. But that is your task, Hayter. You must prove it so.'

'We will do our best.' He smiled, and they shook hands.

The getting of the guns into *Expedient* had been a complicated and time-consuming business, involving the use of the Woolwich sheer hulk, much ingenious rigging of tackles, and tarpaulins as shields against prying eyes. The tarpaulins had at first amused James, then when they got in the way of the work he was irritated, and finally he hated them as a fruitless, foolish, schoolboy measure, designed only to hinder practical men.

It had been decided that the powder should come into the ship on the following day, and Alexander Waterfield came out from the wharf in the hoy, in the company of a short, sturdy man with a thatch of iron-grey hair and a bow-legged walk. With uncanny good timing he had joined the ship at just the moment he was needed; he was William Storey, the new gunner, with his freshly written warrant in his hand. Waterfield also had a document, an official letter authorizing him, indeed requiring him, to see the arrangements for the storing of the powder for himself, and to give what assistance and advice he deemed fitting.

Captain Rennie, glad that soon his ship would weigh and proceed, and be gone from this confining river into the open sea, was welcoming.

'There is no need for letters, my dear Waterfield. You are welcome aboard, indeed. By all means, the powder. By all means, Mr Storey will go below with you. You are acquainted? You have met in the hoy, no doubt.'

'We are old friends,' said Waterfield.

'Eh?'

'Yes, sir. I join the ship entirely due to Mr Waterfield's kindness, sir. He has most obligingly put my name forward in the right quarters, rapid arrangements was made, and here I am.'

'Oh. Well. Very good, I am glad. You will like to show him our magazine, the filling-room, and so forth. You know where everything is?'

'I shall find it, sir, I shall find it.'

Rennie himself was very busy: with the master as they discussed how the ship was to be retrimmed with all her guns and powder taken in; with the purser Mr Trent; and with his need, his now exigent need, for a surgeon. Mr Wearing had died in the ship, without proper medical attention of any kind. No one of the people, nor the officers, had had any real idea of the depth and severity of his illness, and he had quietly declined, lying in his tiny cabin, declined and faded down, and died. This had disturbed the people. They were unhappy that there was no doctor on board. What if any one of them was to fall ill? What would become of him, now, with no skilled man to attend?

Rennie had made known his need for a surgeon more than once, and nothing had happened. No word came from the Sick and Wounded Board, nor from the Navy Board itself. Surely it was not beyond these gentlemen to provide a single surgeon for an important commission? Rennie had begun to see *Expedient* in this light, had begun to regard this commission as very probably one of the most important such ventures conducted since the death of Cook. He could not in conscience proceed without a surgeon, could he, for God's sake? However, no surgeon would come to the ship as she lay at Galleons Reach. He must weigh, bring her down to the sea, and make sail for Portsmouth. At Portsmouth, where he would receive his detailed final instructions, he would make it his business to supply the ship with a competent medical man, and allay the fears of his crew.

'Boy!'

―――✠―――

Spithead, and the ship moored. Moored at a position far from the harbour and the Hard, with part of the Channel fleet assembling to the west. A cutter—not Hansard Cobbett's—had come dashing to *Expedient* as she approached and made her signals, and had delivered a written message. The message required Captain Rennie to anchor and remain at this distant station, and to grant no shore leave under any circumstances, until further notice. His boat's crew were to remain at all times with the boat when he, or any of his officers, came ashore. Would Captain Rennie, at his earliest convenience, wait upon Mr Soames at the Marine Hotel near the Hard?

'This is queer. It is rum.' Rennie showed the letter to James. 'It is official, and yet it ain't, quite. Why don't the port admiral send for me——? Soames? Here in Portsmouth?'

'He is the gentleman with whom you have had dealings at the Admiralty?'

'He is. I had thought that here I should be free of him, and all men like him, and that I would call on the admiral, receive from him my final instructions, and put to sea right quick.'

'Perhaps it's as well we lie here a day or two, sir. For Mr Dobie's sake.'

'Dobie? He has been of no use to me at all. He is the least of my concern.'

Alan Dobie had been horribly seasick all the way from the Nore to St Helen's Road, and he was still sick. A thin young man, he had grown thinner, and all who saw him were shaken, and feared for his life. His pallor, his glassy stare, his crimson dark lips, his hair stuck to his head in a clammy sheen of sweat, all spoke directly to his condition. He could eat nothing. Broth made him vomit within moments of its swallowing. He was reduced, tremulous, exhausted. Rennie's apparently callous attitude was quite usual at sea, but it shocked James all the same. That the ship lacked a surgeon could only mean the end for Dobie, unless:

'He ought really to be put ashore, don't you think, sir?'

'Ashore? You saw the message, Mr Hayter. No one of my people may go ashore until further notice.'

'He will die if he don't go ashore,' said James quietly, gravely. 'The Haslar Hospital is where he belongs, surely?'

Rennie drew in a breath through his nose, his lips pressed shut. He looked away to larboard, at the hospital buildings on the Gosport headland, beyond Monkton Fort.

'If he is no better tomorrow, he shall go there. We must give him the chance to recover in the calmer waters here. I must go ashore. You will inform the crew by divisions that all leave is stopped. Tell Mr Loftus that I wish them to have a double issue of grog at supper, with my compliments. We have made good time on our first run, and the ship has been properly worked. I wish them to feel rewarded, and also to cheer them even as they are confined.'

'Very good, sir.'

'On second thought, it might be useful for you to come with me in the cutter. I would like your opinion of Mr Soames, your considered view of him, and what he is about. I would value it. Will the ship be safe, d'you think, left in Mr Makepeace's hands?'

'I have no doubt of that, sir. He is a very capable and conscientious officer.'

'Yes. Yes. Were it a matter of leaving *Expedient* in the hands of Mr Royce, I should expect to lose her within the hour, with all hands.'

'Mr Makepeace will keep her safe, sir.'

'Yes. I speak frankly to you about Mr Royce because I am half persuaded to put him ashore. He is inimical to the ship. He don't know his duties. He is unseamanlike, ungentleman-like, unofficerlike, crass, foolish, opinionated, and ill-looking. He is unbearable altogether, the fellow.'

James was silent.

'Well well, I cannot put him ashore, I expect. I must endure him until we make Tenerife. I can get rid of him there—fever, a spasm, madness, anything will answer as excuse.'

'We will not find another lieutenant at Tenerife though, will we, sir?'

'I had already thought, if he shows well, and I believe he will, to bring the master's mate Mr Symington up to acting third.'

'He is very young.'

'I have not made up my mind, by no means.'

Ten minutes later they were in the cutter, dashing for the Hard. They had put on dress coats, Rennie's very new, the gold lace gleaming, on the assumption—Captain Rennie's assumption—that Soames would give them dinner, and that they would sleep out of the ship.

'I do not need anybody's permission to sleep out of her overnight, when we are not at war.'

'I wonder—I am not sure—but does that same rule apply to me, sir?'

'Pish posh, we are dutiful officers attending to urgent official business ashore. I hope that Soames will give us a good dinner. The pies Stamp makes are damned dull.'

'At least he is now sober and industrious. It is a near miraculous transformation.'

'Not miraculous enough for me. I want my own cook in the ship. I must find a man here, at Portsmouth, and put him on the books.'

The cutter's boat brought them in to the Hard, and they went ashore.

~ ※ ~

The passage to Portsmouth, of a few days only, had been hard on Mr Dobie, and not a very great deal had been accomplished in the ship. Her guns had not been fired, by the wish of their Lordships. There had been exercising of the great guns, to make each man in each guncrew familiar with his place and duty at quarters, but no more. Some few basic manoeuvres of handling and sailing had been accomplished with success—wearing, tacking, heaving to—in order to shake down the crew at stations. Aside from minor faults, inevitable in any ship putting to sea for the first time, *Expedient* had answered well, and her people had answered well. The jollyboat, loose at one davit, had nearly been lost in a brief squall off the Downs, and had sustained some damage. A stunsail boom had been damaged. The maintopmast back-stays would have to be tightened. Rennie was not unhappy, except with his third lieutenant. It was a further mark against Mr Royce that he had not once inquired after his supposed friend, the hapless Dobic; had not looked in on him, nor expressed the smallest sympathy for his plight. It was almost as if he did not know Dobie, or, if he did, that he wished keenly he did not. Captain Rennie had expressed this view to James, and James in turn had thought the captain hard on both Royce and Dobie. To have said dismissively that Dobie had been of no use to him at all was very unjust in the captain. Dobie, before they had put to sea, had been of infinite use. He had drafted letters, made lists, written out the quarter bills for posting round the ship, &c., &c. He had certainly earned his grog and biscuit. But Rennie under sail—like so many sea officers—was inclined to discount anything which did not relate directly to the sailing of his ship, and poor Dobie, in the captain's head, was pushed down and down in significance until he was almost lost, excepting as a mark against Mr Royce. Royce, in his turn, was undoubtedly a young fool, but James had not detected in him any viciousness of character, nor any other damning fault; no fault in truth which could not be eradicated by an assumption of discipline.

They came to the Marine Hotel, and found Soames waiting for them, not with sherry and a private room, and three courses ordered, but with a carriage.

'Is the lieutenant to join us, Captain Rennie?' Soames had a silver-headed cane in his hand, which he beat into the palm of his other hand, and Rennie briefly, absurdly, wondered if Soames meant to strike him, or his lieutenant, or perhaps both of them. He certainly looked very put out.

'Indeed he is, Mr Soames.' And he made the introductions. Mr Soames looked very severely at James, nodded once, and they went into the street and got into the carriage.

'I thought that I had made it plain in my letter, Captain Rennie. I thought that I had. You were to present yourself to me alone.'

Rennie chose not to take offence, but to confuse the issue: 'I had pondered that, I confess. It is usual for a ship's captain, when first going ashore, to present his compliments to the port admiral, you know.'

'I meant, I meant to me. Yourself to me, *alone*. In the *singular*.'

'Ah.' Rennie fell silent, straight-backed. James, seated opposite, kept his face as rigidly blank as a marine's at sentry, and effortfully did not laugh. The carriage rumbled over the cobbles.

'It is a very great inconvenience that you have burdened me with another party. This was, it is, an occasion for the highest discretion.'

'Yes, well, you may be sure that Mr Hayter is very discreet, Soames. Where do you take us? We are to eat dinner there, I hope?'

'We go to Kingshill House, beyond the village.'

'Is that very far? We don't keep land hours at sea. Your dinner is our supper, eaten long since.'

'No more than two mile.' Mr Soames put his fine fabricked handkerchief to his nose, revived himself with cologne water, and thus composed addressed his guests: 'Gentlemen, I beg your pardon if I was a trifle—a trifle brusque just now. Will I tell you why we go out of town? Kingshill House is empty. That is, the owner is away in Scotland. It is secluded, and lies in its own grounds. No one will see us coming, nor going. Nor will we be overheard in anything.'

Rennie and James listened politely, exchanged a brief look, were mystified.

'Are there no servants in the house?' asked James.

'Eh? Servants?'

'If we are to eat dinner, surely there are servants in the house?—To serve it, you know.'

'Oh, that is what you meant.' Soames left this remark in the air.

They came to the house by a long drive, curving through trees in the fading light. The house was large, in the Palladian manner, and both Rennie and James were impressed. Urns stood within the pillared porch, and there were broad shallow steps. Soames dismissed the carriage with an instruction to the coachman to return at a certain hour, and took his guests inside. In spite of the warmth of the summer evening outside, the interior was chill, the air almost dank. Soames lit a candle as they ventured beyond the broad marble floor of the entrance hall, and led them into a shuttered room through a tall panelled door. A table, a small oval gate-legged dining-table, stood in the centre of the room, with three places laid. There were three fine mahogany chairs, with pierced vase backs, and another chair by the door, and no other furniture. The polished wooden floor was bare of rugs, and their footfalls echoed. On the walls hung three or four paintings, and over the mantel a full-length portrait of a very handsome woman in early middle life, in a wide hat and a blue silk dress with much lace at the sleeves.

'That is Lady Kenton, our absent hostess,' murmured Soames with a discreet wave at the portrait.

'By Gainsborough, I think—or is it Zoffany?' said James.

'By Gainsborough, indeed.'

'My mother was once nearly painted by Gainsborough, at Bath. Nearly, but not quite. She was taking the waters there, staying with cousins, and was took ill—perhaps it was the waters—and the commission was cancelled.'

'A misfortune,' said Mr Soames.

'My father thought not, I fear. He was perfectly content to have saved his hundred guineas.'

Mr Soames did not quite care for that sentiment. He put

down the candle-holder, lit a second, and said: 'I must see about another place setting.' He disappeared.

'Another setting?' said Rennie, further mystified.

'Yes, I see.' James held up the light. 'I was not expected. You were to have dined with Mr Soames and another, sir. Now we are four.'

Voices echoed in the broad hallway, and footsteps approached in slapping concord. More candles glowed in the doorway, and Mr Soames returned, stood aside, and:

'Captain Rennie,' said Sir Robert Greer.

'Sir Robert?' Astonished.

Sir Robert shrugged off a very black cloak and laid it on the chair by the door with his black and silver stick. He came forward.

'I had no notion that we would meet again,' said Rennie. He had not forgotten James at his side, and Sir Robert had noticed him at once.

'We are four?' he said sharply to Soames.

Rennie was equal to this. 'I asked Lieutenant Hayter to come with me tonight to assist me as my second-in-command, Sir Robert. We must trust and assist each other in all circumstances. That is our duty, d'y'see, as officers in His Majesty's service.'

Soames stepped forward and made the formal introductions. James met Sir Robert's hard black gaze with a polite smile and a bow. 'Am honoured, sir.'

'Well, you are here, it is done, and no use asking you to wait elsewhere. There is nowhere in the house where you might, it is empty. Where do you sleep?' he asked, turning to Rennie.

'At the Marine Hotel, I expect.'

'You have engaged rooms?'

'Not quite, not yet, we have not had——'

'Do not do so, if you please. When we are finished here, return to your ship.'

'Sir Robert, with respect, I do not think it is your place to tell me where I may lay my head.'

Sir Robert drew in a breath, and his eyes were very black as he looked at Rennie, but he held himself in, and replied in a pleasant, calm, pre-prandial voice. 'Forgive me, Captain Rennie, for presuming to give you direction. Allow me to put it in the form of a request. Pray do not return to the Marine Hotel tonight, as a favour to me. Will you go to your ship, instead? As a kindness?'

Rennie did not see that this request was much better than the first, but felt all the same that he could not refuse it. It did not make him happy, but he bowed silently, and obeyed. Sir Robert nodded in the way of men who do always get their own way, and regard it as a matter of right. He even smiled a little, to show that he was not entirely graceless.

'And now, Soames, I think we are ready for a glass of sherry,' he said.

Soames rang a silver bell, and presently a footman appeared with a decanter and glasses on a tray, which he put on the table. He did not pour the sherry, but retreated at once, and closed the door.

'He is my own man,' said Sir Robert. 'Deaf, dumb and blind.'

Another chair was brought into that echoing room, now beginning to be chill, and they ate their dinner—three simple courses and a single bottle of wine, served by Sir Robert's footman—at not quite breakneck speed. Mr Soames then produced from a leather fold Rennie's final instructions. They were in two separate parts, the second double-sealed.

'This second document is to be regarded by you as secret,' said Sir Robert, touching his napkin to his thin lips. The wine had added no hint of colour to his ashen pallor.

'I am under Secret Instructions, then?' Rennie's frown spoke his puzzlement. 'Sir Robert, I do not understand. What is your authority in these matters?'

'My authority?' The deep vibrant voice had a querulous edge.

'Forgive my bluntness. I had thought you was attached, in

a high capacity, to the Royal Society. What business has the Royal Society in the giving of their Lordships' instructions to a commissioned officer?'

'I have the honour of attachment, as you put it, in many and several places, Captain Rennie. You may take my word on it that their Lordships are fully acquainted with my presence here tonight, as Mr Soames will confirm to you. Eh, Soames?' Without looking at him.

'Indeed that is so, Sir Robert.'

A nod. 'You are to open the first part of your instructions immediately upon returning to your ship. The second packet is to be kept sealed—*sealed*—until you have doubled Cape Horn. *On no account* is that packet to be opened until you have sailed beyond that place, and into the Pacifick Ocean. *On no account* are these instructions to leave your possession. I hope that I am quite plain?' His deep eyes bored into Rennie's steady, puzzled gaze.

'I am clear, Sir Robert, that I must not break the seal on the second packet,' he said, 'and I am clear on nothing else.'

'That's as well, that's as well. All will be made clear in due course. All you need do is follow everything to the letter.' Sir Robert rose, and let his napkin fall on the chair. His footman appeared at the door, and lifted his master's cloak.

'Gentlemen, I cannot offer you a lift, as I must go swiftly elsewhere. Your own carriage comes to fetch you, no doubt. Good night to you.'

He pulled the cloak round him, took up his stick, and was gone in a ripple of black cloth. The sound of his carriage, wheels and hooves retreating on the gravel. Silence. Rennie drank off the mouthful of claret in his glass.

'That is certainly the oddest damned dinner I have ever sat down to,' he said.

'Sir Robert is not a man to waste his words,' conceded Mr Soames. His fingers broke a water biscuit, but he did not eat it. He glanced at his pocket watch, holding it up to the candlelight. Rennie turned over the packets in his hands, and he examined the seals. They were, indeed, Admiralty seals. 'Our carriage, alas, is not due for an hour,' said Soames.

'Perhaps we could walk?' suggested Rennie. 'It is only two mile, and I should like to stretch my legs.'

'I should like to walk,' agreed James.

'Gentlemen, gentlemen,' said Soames, 'it is very dark. How will you see your way? You do not know the way, in fact.'

'We will take a light,' announced Rennie, rising from his chair.

'A candle, in the open air? No no, let us wait. It is only an hour.'

'Surely there is a lantern or two in a great house? Mr Hayter and I will discover them, and be on our way. You had better come with us, Soames, and get some exercise. Country air, hey?'

'Indeed, country air,' echoed James.

'Night air, night air,' said Mr Soames, shaking his head. 'I shall wait for the carriage. You would do well to follow my example, I warn you.'

Rennie was not in the mood to be warned, or directed, or in any way to be told what to do any more. He put the packets of instructions inside his coat, and buttoned the pocket. He buckled on his sword, and put on his hat. Mr Soames saw that he was not to be heeded, and was vexed. Had he not aided Captain Rennie in London, had he not been kind to him about hotels, and dinners? He was vexed, and Rennie saw that he was, and did not care.

James found a pair of lanterns, lighted them, and the two officers set off down the drive.

As they walked through the darkness, having found the narrow road to Portsmouth through the little village of Kingshill, Rennie and James talked freely.

'Tell me your reckoning of Soames, will you?' Rennie asked.

'He is a lonely man at present, that is clear. But probably he is a lonely man altogether. He is caught between his sense of position, and his comparative lack of it, and must maintain his dignity by effortful reserve.'

'But a man of probity?'

'Oh, yes. Certainly that.'

They came to a fork in the road, and James held up his light to a signpost. In the stillness, the deep stillness, an owl gave its ghostly shriek. The sign was indistinct, but James was sure they should take the right fork.

'I hope you are right,' said Rennie as they walked on that road. He could smell rain on the air, and the night was growing cold. 'What is your estimation of Sir Robert?'

'Ah. There, sir, I cannot tell you anything.'

'Why not? You was at the dinner. You saw and heard him.'

'Yes, I was. And he gave nothing away, nothing of himself. He is at the heart of the club, is he not?'

'Club?—What club?'

'The port and scheming club, sir, behind the closed door.'

'Oh. Yes. Yes. He is the secretary, I am in no doubt.'

And they walked on until they reached the further dwellings of the town, and glimmers of light. Flashes beyond Portsdown Hill, followed by long rumbling concussions, and the iron smell of rain, made them quicken their step.

'Will I tell you what I think?' said Rennie, as they neared the Marine Hotel along the cobbled streets. 'I think that to make the attempt to reach the ship tonight, in the coming storm, is folly.'

'You mean—that we should sleep at the hotel, sir?'

'You apprehend me, Mr Hayter, in the wink of an eye. I gave Sir Robert an undertaking to return to my ship, but I did so under duress, against my better judgement. I am damned if I am going to be told how to lead my life by the secretary of a very wretched club, hey?'

'I am with you all the way, sir.'

'Good. Very good.' They went in at the entrance of the hotel. 'There is no absolute need for us to turn in at once, is there, d'y'think? Unless you are exhausted by walking?'

'I am envigorated by walking, sir.'

'Envigorated is just the word. Envigorated, and in need of refreshment.'

They engaged rooms, and ordered a bottle of wine, which they drank in a quiet parlour.

Rennie was all for calling for a second bottle, but James had drunk just enough to know that were they to drink another bottle they would both be drunk, and not enough to allow him to be reckless of the consequences. There was much to do on the morrow.

'I find the walking has tired me after all,' he yawned. 'I must climb the stairs.'

'I shall be——I shall come up directly,' said Rennie, and lingered over his glass. The maid who had brought their wine was in the far doorway. He beckoned to her, made what he thought was a discreet suggestion, and was—not unkindly—rebuffed. He was briefly and bitterly disgruntled; briefly contemplated drinking a second bottle by himself; told himself not to be ten kinds of damn fool, and went to bed.

Hours later—he was not sure how many hours—he woke to hear the softest of footfalls by his bed, and to sense movement there in the darkness. Was it? Could it be?

'Dora?' he called quietly, and sat up. 'Have you come to me?' He turned back the covers and reached out a hand. 'Where are y——'

An arm curled round his throat, and tightened fiercely. Rennie struggled, gripped the arm, lashed out with one leg, the other caught in the covers. The arm at his throat tightened further, and Rennie saw flashes and whirlings of light before him, felt his strength slipping. He kicked out as hard as he could, and felt his toe catch something and heard a gasp. He flailed out, trying to reach for the candle-holder on the cabinet by his bed. The candle-holder crashed to the floor. The grip at his throat loosened slightly, and Rennie forced out a bellow—

'Murder! Murder!'

—before the arm jerked tight, nearly snapping his neck, and his strength failed absolutely. He felt himself sagging. His head sang blackly. At the edge of things he heard a chair fall, and the ripping of cloth.

He woke to find James bending over him. There was light, candlelight, and his throat hurt like the devil. He had a piercing headache. He felt sick.

'They escaped, I'm afraid, sir. I think I winged one of them with my sword, but I am not certain.'

'How many were they?' Rennie's voice was strained, and weak.

'Two, I think. I heard your shout and came at once, but I had no light, and could see little. They have torn your coat, but I think they have gone away empty-handed. Your purse is there on the cabinet, untouched.'

Rennie turned his head painfully, saw the purse, sighed. Then struggled to reach under his pillow, scrabbled there in terrible fear—and found the packets.

'Thank God they did not take my instructions,' he husked. 'Thank God.'

'You think they . . .? What could they want with your instructions, sir?'

'I do not know—I do not know.'

'Will you drink some water?' He held a glass.

Rennie drank some water, and gripped James's arm as he turned away to put down the glass. 'I am indebted to you, Mr Hayter. I must thank you for saving my life.'

After breakfast Rennie sat in a chair in his room, waiting for his coat to be mended by the maid. Presently James came in and joined him.

'I have asked whether or no anything was seen or heard in the night. Evidently nothing was noticed. How they got in is a mystery, since the front door was locked, all the doors were locked at midnight.'

'Perhaps they got in before then, and concealed themselves.'

'At any rate, I was discreet. I asked only in a general way, you know.'

'Very good. Thank you.'

'With your permission, sir, I shall just go down and settle our account.'

'No no,' Rennie reached for his purse, 'I must not allow you to——'

'Sir, I think you have been taxed quite enough in one night.' And he went downstairs.

Rennie settled in his chair. His head ached still, and his throat was sore, but he had eaten his breakfast and was beginning to feel better. As soon as his coat was sewn together, he would—

A heavy tread in the passage, and his door was rattled, and banged open. Rennie leapt up, and as he turned to face the door his sword was in his hand.

'Come on then, damn you!' he shouted, and was astonished by gold lace, and gold buttons, and powdered wig.

'Captain Rennie,' said Admiral Bamphlett, 'have you gone mad, sir?'

The port admiral was accompanied by the Master Attendant, who also looked shocked and disapproving. Rennie sheathed his sword, and was apologetic.

'Had I known it was you, sir—gentlemen—I should have, I should have, mm. How may I be of service to you?'

'Not only have you not made your duty to me, sir,' said Admiral Bamphlett gravely, 'you have spent the night in this hotel, against direct order, in very apparent debauch.'

'In deb——I must contradict you, sir——'

'Contradict? Contradict? You were not alone, neither. There was another officer with you. A fellow miscreant.'

'Miscreant? That is too much. That is too——'

'It ain't near enough, sir.' The admiral had not raised his voice, but his voice was very hard. 'As if there is nothing for me to do, nothing for Mr Hemmings to do, when the Channel Fleet is assembling. Who are you, a private ship, to give yourself airs, graces, and damned whore's favours in hotels?'

'Admiral Bamphlett, sir, do not continue——' Rennie had gone pale with anger, and was on the point of saying something very rash, when James appeared at the door.

'Was you looking for me, sir?' He came forward, his hat under his arm, and bowed. He was properly dressed, he was shaved, no fault could be found with his appearance, or his manner.

'If you are Lieutenant Hayter. Is that who you are?'

'I am, sir.'

'Yes. I am informed that both of you spent the night in this place, in consort with——'

'Here is your coat mended, sir,' said the maid, coming straight in at the open door with Rennie's coat neatly sewn back together, brushed and pressed. She stopped in mid-step and blushed, as four heads turned.

'Yes, there is the evidence,' said Admiral Bamphlett, looking at her.

'Aye,' said Mr Hemmings, not altogether disapproving; the maid was very pretty.

'Thank you very much indeed for your promptness, knowing the officer was indisposed,' said James kindly, and gave her a coin. She withdrew wordlessly, and James laid the coat carefully at the end of the bed, giving himself a moment to think. He turned.

'Captain Rennie and I, caught in the storm, unable to find transport, unable to find a boat at the Hard late at night, damned wet, you know, and the captain ill, there was nothing to do but come here,' said James in a reasonable, affable, dutiful tone, glancing from time to time at Rennie. 'Thank God we secured rooms, else we should have spent the night very wretched and miserable. Captain Rennie was struck a blow on the head by a falling branch as the storm advanced, was felled himself indeed, and his coat torn. Are you quite well now, sir?' Turning again to Rennie, who gave a startled but brave smile. 'I had thought to summon a physician, then remembered that we must call on you this morning, sir.' A bow to Admiral Bamphlett. 'Which we could not do last evening, summoned to attend at Kingshill as we were, without a moment's delay.'

'Ah. Hah. Ah.' Admiral Bamphlett was not in the least convinced, but could not very well say that he was not, unless he wished to appear churlish, callous and indifferent to the suffering of a fellow officer.

'So you see, sir——'

'Yes, yes, Mr Hayter, I do see, thank you. When you are quite recovered, Captain Rennie, from your night's misfortune, perhaps you will favour me with a call in person. Come on, Hemmings, we must not overcrowd the sickroom, hey?' And he gave the Master Attendant a terrible smile, which said: 'I am not hoodwinked by this bloody nonsense, but I cannot very well call two sea officers liars to their faces.' He strode from the room with Mr Hemmings in his wake.

'Again I find myself in your debt,' said Rennie presently. 'Was it wise, d'y'think, to invent all that dishwater about a falling branch?'

'I apologize, sir, for inventing anything at all—but I did not think it wise to say anything about the attempt to rob you.'

'No. No, you are right. Certainly it was Soames that informed on us, the fellow. Because we left him alone in that empty house, no doubt. He was aggrieved.'

'Perhaps there was ghosts.'

'Hah!' laughed Rennie, and grimaced as his throat pained him. 'He was well served if there was.'

'On second thought, how could Soames have known we came to this hotel?' said James now. 'The admiral said he had been "informed". How could Soames have informed him?'

'Unless he came here later himself, in his carriage, and saw us drinking our wine.'

'Yes. Yes, that must be it.—But it don't explain the attempt to rob you, sir.'

'Could we have been followed from Kingshill? Followed by footpads?'

'Very odd footpads, then. That would not take a purse in plain view.'

'The room was in darkness. However, I do not think they wanted my money. They wanted something in my coat, that was in fact under my pillow. My instructions.'

James stood looking down from the window into the street below. Horses passed nodding, clopping, drays passed, wagons, in a slow jingle of harness and clattering of wheels; people crossed, stepping over and round scored piles of dung on the cobbles. The rain had cleared overnight, but puddles lay here and there between the stones, gleaming in the sunlight, splashed through by hooves. A girl lifted the hem of her dress as she stepped out. It was a busy scene, but tranquil and untroubled and usual.

'What d'you suppose is in those instructions, sir, which would make it worth the effort of trying to steal them?'

'It is spies.'

'Eh?'

'That is the only feasible explanation.'

James was about to expostulate, gently but firmly expostulate, until he remembered Alexander Waterfield, at Woolwich: 'Lieutenant, surely you are not so naïve as to think we will never have an enemy again?' And remembered that all shore leave had been stopped for *Expedient*, that she lay at a mooring far from they Hard and the inns of the town. Remembered Sir Robert and his black gaze, his '*on no account*'—and thought that very probably his captain was right.

'We had better make our duty to the port admiral, and get back to the ship,' said Rennie, and he stood up and put on his coat.

───◆═══◆───

Admiral Bamphlett had been more forgiving than they had expected when Rennie and James made their call on him. He told them that he had received a despatch about them from the Admiralty.

'I do not know why you are so singled out for favour, Captain Rennie,' he had said. 'A private ship, sent on foreign service in search of—what? I ask myself. Harbours? Anchorages? And yet you are crammed with instruments of science. Who is your astronomical? Where is your mechanical man, or men? And where is your Banks, hey?'

'There is no such person aboard, sir.'

'No?—No? How very odd. A scientific voyage, with no scientificals.'

He spoke briefly of Lady Kenton, who owned Kingshill House, by way of showing that he was an urbane man, not confined to naval things. And also by way of—as he thought—subtly pumping these two officers.

'Yes, she had a husband, you know, who died. Then she brought a fellow there who purported to be an artist. He said he was, and she said so, and he painted there all the time, anything and everything. Lady Kenton was much disposed to praise him, and to gain him advantage among her acquaintance, commissions and so forth. I have seen some of these paintings for myself.'

'I think we may have seen one or two of them. Did you think them very good, sir?'

'Indeed, I did not. They were damned bad. The kind of thing done with a Claude glass, you know, and a dainty box of pigments. He was the sort of man—well, man—who is like to sit in a box at Ranelagh Gardens, talking pretty to silken ladies.'

This conversation gained the admiral no advantage, no intelligence as to what the dinner at Kingshill had meant, and presently he let them go. In fact, he lent them his own launch to bring them back to *Expedient*, to show that he was magnanimous, and wished them well.

When they came on board it was with some ceremony, a

sharp lookout having been kept by Lieutenant Makepeace all the morning.

'How is Dobie?' James asked him as soon as the formalities had been dispensed with.

'He is a great deal better. He has eaten, and drunk, and asked to see Mr Royce.'

'And did Royce oblige him?'

'Well, I don't know that he did. I mean, I don't know that he did not, neither. I have not been very much below.'

'Good God, you don't mean that you kept the deck all night, and all the morning, too?'

'Well, I—that is, I thought that with the captain out of the ship on urgent business, and you also, Hayter, that it was just as well.'

Makepeace looked tired, but not in the least resentful, and James was heartened that his opinion of him as thoroughly reliable and conscientious was confirmed. He went below to look in on Dobie, who was for the present occupying the surgeon's quarters, until a surgeon could be found. Dobie was better, distinctly better, but he was not yet well. His colour was still ghastly, and his hair plastered sweatily to his skull; he looked half-drowned. While James was there a boy came clambering down the ladder and said that the captain wished to see him in his cabin.

'We are to put to sea at once.' Rennie waved the despatch given him by Admiral Bamphlett, and gestured at his opened instructions, which lay on the table. 'How in God's name am I to do that, Mr Hayter, when we have no surgeon, and I have no cook?'

James thought, but did not say, that the sooner they were clear of Portsmouth, and meetings with high officials, and hotels, and spies in the night, the sooner they got down to the business of making sail and harnessing the wind, the sure eternal things, the better they should be.

— ⟡ —

At three bells in the afternoon watch, just as Rennie was eating—with resignation eating—his indifferent dinner, he heard a hail, and other sounds, and presently a message was brought to him that a cutter had come out to them. Rennie had already decided that he must weigh and proceed, else give grave offence by not following his instructions and the final despatch strictly. Signals had already been exchanged with the flag of the Channel Fleet, questions and answers, and he did not relish the possibility of having to repair to the flag to explain himself. Fleet admirals were disinclined to accept anything which did not accord with their own notions of what stray frigates might be required to do in the interests of the fleet, and Rennie had been required not to divulge information. It might be very awkward for him if he did not weigh right quick, but still he had no medical man, in spite of something Admiral Bamphlett had said about seeing what he could do. Nor had he his new cook, but must live and make do with stodgy Stamp.

He heard the cutter's boat bump as it came alongside, and he went on deck.

Admiral Bamphlett, knowing *Expedient*'s difficulty, had made it his business to find them a surgeon, since in his opinion a ship could not undertake such a long foreign commission without one. And now he came aboard, this addition to the complement, in a great hurry, and to the great amazement of every man on deck. His name was Thomas Wing, and he had never before been to sea. He had had to assemble himself, his chests and equipment, at the last moment. Yesterday he had been an apprentice to Dr Stroud at the Haslar Hospital, and although he did not have an official warrant from the Navy Board, Dr Stroud had provided him with a kind of certificate, saying that he was 'proficient in all surgical, medical, apothecarial and dietary matters pertaining to the care of seamen in His Majesty's service at sea'. Yet he had never been to sea. He was twenty-four years of age, and alone; there was no man qualified to be his mate aboard. *Expedient* had been fortunate until now in having suffered few illnesses, and as yet no broken bones. Other than in Mr Dobie, who was a case of simple if severe seasickness, the lack of a surgeon had not been deeply felt. But Rennie knew, as he watched the head of what could only be his new surgeon appear at the gangway port, that having him aboard, occupying a particular place in the ship and being available there, would make the people easier in their minds.

Thomas Wing was not an educated man, excepting what he had learned at Dr Stroud's side at the Haslar. He had come to the hospital as a porter, a human beast of burden, ten years ago. His work obliged him to wash out the wards, to take out the soiled bedlinen, sodden with vomit, blood, faeces, the stinking sheets of dying men, and burn them in the bricked yard at the rear, or carry them to the laundry if they were considered recoverable. The work was arduous and dirty, and moiled about with every sound of pain and suffering: groans, sighs, despairing cries, coughing and retching, and the rattling breath, like sea-sucked stones, of men's last moments. He had come to Dr Stroud's attention when he had asked one morning if he might clean and sharpen the instruments after surgical procedures. Until then Stroud had scarcely been aware of him, except in periphery as the figure that gathered up the bloodied cloths at the conclusion of things. Dr Stroud, ever alert to precocity for its uncommon-ness in the bloody profession he followed, took the boy at his word, and allowed him his chance with the instruments. Thomas Wing had flown high in that opportunity; had cleaned down the instruments—amputating saw, bone nip-pers, catling, bistouries, forceps, tenaculum—from a busy morning of procedures, cleaned them of blood, pus, bone and sinew, and sharpened them with the oiled stone, wiped them again and laid them out in neat and shining array.

'You have an interest in tools?' Dr Stroud had inquired.

'Instruments I like, sir. Instruments that is precise and fine.

But not tools very greatly, such as carpenter's tools, no, sir. And I have looked at the labels on the bottles in the dispensary, and learned them all by heart.'

'Indeed?' He had then asked a series of questions, obscuring these labels, and sometimes pouring out a little of the contents of the bottles into a glass, or on a square of paper, and asking the scientific name of each sample. In each case Thomas Wing had answered correctly, and Dr Stroud had determined to apprentice the boy, and bring him on. However, there was an impediment. The boy was very small, and he did not grow. In consequence he appeared always to be younger than his years. Although he was strong and durable, and inured to the sufferings of others from his time spent as a porter, he would never grow as tall as a man, and the Navy Board would not consider him. Only Dr Stroud considered him, and valued him, and had regarded him for several years as his right hand. Admiral Bamphlett was a friend of Stroud, and knew Thomas Wing—had indeed been successfully treated by him for painful boils. Wing had told the admiral often that his greatest wish was to go to sea. No chance of this had yet occurred, until now. On the departure of Captain Rennie and his first lieutenant from his office, Admiral Bamphlett had sent immediate word to Gosport, urging the greatest haste if Mr Wing wished to join the Royal Navy. Reluctantly, very reluctantly, Dr Stroud had given his apprentice his blessing, and the certificate; and now here he came through the gangway and into the ship. Rennie heard a gasp, and frowned; a snigger of amusement, then scoffing laughter. The head of the young man came no higher, there was no young man's body under it. Into the waist came a man waist-low. A boy man.

In the great cabin Rennie examined the document Dr Stroud had given his apprentice. To make it more impressing and official he had written it out on a square of parchment, and fixed a large hospital seal below.

'I have the greatest regard for Dr Stroud,' said Rennie. 'His work with Lind on anti-scorbutics has saved many lives, and his notions of personal cleanliness and clean air accord entirely with my own. However—however—this ain't a warrant, Mr Wing.' Taking up the certificate. 'I must have a warrant from the Board, d'y'see, to put you on my books as surgeon. If we was at Port Royal, or the Rock, you know, some such paper as this might suffice, but at Portsmouth, in home waters—alas.'

Thomas Wing was silent, looking down at the decking canvas.

'However, I don't see why I should not rate you as surgeon's mate.'

Wing lifted his head, as his heart lifted within him.

'It ain't regular, it ain't usual, since there is no surgeon for you to assist. Never mind. If all Dr Stroud says of you in his certificate is true, we shall not require a surgeon, for we shall have you, Mr Wing.'

'I—I am very horribly in your debt, sir. Most horribly, I am.'

'Yes, well well. Tell me that again when we are beating into a storm off Finisterre, will you, Mr Wing? When bones are broke, heads are broke, and everything is spilled between decks, including guts, tell me that again, hey?' Rennie was disposed to be cheerful. 'Boy! Find the master's mate Mr Symington, and tell him I am placing our surgeon in his hands. He is to find him a cabin. Belay that. He is to take him to the surgeon's quarters, which Mr Dobie must vacate. Then find Mr Adgett directly, and ask him to come and see me. We must build a little hole somewhere below for Mr Dobie, and he must have a hanging cot. Mr Symington will see about your dunnage, Mr Wing. I must ask you to excuse me, there is much to do. Mr Hayter!'

'Sir?' Attending.

'We will get under weigh in one glass, if you please.'

'Very good, sir. However, I fear—that may be unachievable.'

'Unachiev——What the devil d'y'mean?'

'I certainly mean no offence, sir. We have just received a signal from the flag. Mr Pankridge!' The signals midshipman approached, and took off his hat, clutching awkwardly at his book.

'Well?' said Rennie. He dreaded what he would hear.

'If you please, sir: "Captain to repair aboard the flag, immediate."'

'Oh God,' said Rennie. 'Oh God.' His dread entirely justified. 'Very well, acknowledge.' And when the midshipman had gone: 'I had better have the launch. What a damned nuisance. What can I tell Admiral Hollister? Nothing. He will ask: "What is the meaning of your red ensign?" And I shall tell him: "I am under direct orders of the Admiralty." "What orders, pray?" "I may not tell you, sir." Oh God.'

'Shall I come with you, sir?'

'I should like that, but it cannot be justified. I had better go alone.' Gloomily.

'Very good, sir.'

'No no, damnation, we *are* a private ship, and we *are* under direct orders. We may do as we please, within bounds. Those bounds include, I think, my reporting to the admiral in the company of my second-in-command. By all means, let us go together. I should welcome your support.'

'Very good, sir,' said James. He went on deck. 'Boatswain! Mr Tangible, we will prepare to hoist out the launch. Mr Trembath!' Another midshipman. 'Assist Mr Pankridge with the signal halyards. He is about to inform the flag that we are ready to open fire, for God's sake.'

Fifteen minutes later, and Rennie and James were in the launch, with double-banked oars, proceeding on a choppy, uncomfortable swell to the flag. The coxswain, Randall South, asked his opinion, gave it: there was weather coming, he could feel it in his water, heavy weather. Both Rennie and James were sure he was right. Spray flew back from the blades. Gusts and flurries dashed across the waves, dulling them on the lift, and capping the crests with white. The flag, maintopsail aback, rode large and black against the sky, and as they came under the lee, out of the wind, James was aware of how mighty she seemed, His Majesty's *Vanquish*, one hundred, compared with their single-decked ship, of how great and high was the wall of wood that towered above them.

'Boat, ahoy! Who are you?'

'*Expedient!*' shouted James though his trumpet.

'Come aboard!'

'D'y'need anything, Captain Rennie?' asked Admiral Hollister. He was a short, rather stooping man, whose posture belied his great vigour. His eyes were an astonishing pale, pale blue.

'Sir?' Rennie raised his eyebrows.

'Do not hang back, sir, in your hour of need, if such it is.'

'I do not—I do not think there is, thank you, sir.' At a loss. At a loss in the very real grandeur of the admiral's quarters, the long gleaming table, the elegant chairs, the silks hung in the sleeping-cabin. The glasses and decanters, and the wine cooler resting on the deck by the lockers. The sound, in the muted background, of dishes being carefully stacked, and the jingle of silver. A faint flush in the admiral's cheeks said that he had had a good dinner.

'I had intended, as a matter of courtesy, to ask you to dine, Captain Rennie, since you are to leave us. However, you was ashore. So I must restrict myself to solicitude in anything you may need before your departure.'

'It is most kind in you, sir, but I——'

'Can't think of a single requirement? Let me send a case or two of wine back with you in your launch. Should be most happy.'

'You are very kind, sir.—What may I do for you?'

'Do for me, Captain Rennie? Good heaven, I don't know. It is you that is going to the end of the earth, sir, alone, God help you—or so I have heard.'

'Have you, sir? Ah.' Politely.

'Since you press me, Captain Rennie, since you press me, there is one very small thing.'

Rennie raised his eyebrows, politely obliging.

'I have in my ship a man in need of the experience of very long foreign service. He is of no particular use to me, or to my officers. He might well be of great use to you, I expect. He is a medical man, a surgeon.'

'A surgeon.'

'I see that I engage your interest. Very good. I had also heard that you was in need of such a man, in need of a surgeon, and this is a perfect opportunity for me to do you a service.'

'Surely you cannot spare your own surgeon, sir?' Rennie was beginning to be suspicious. 'I would not care to deprive——'

'Pish pish, Captain Rennie. There is no question of depriving. Mr Lancing is—well, he is not a supernumerary exact, since he has his warrant, but I do not want him. That is, that is, I have no *need* of him. My own doctor, who was indisposed, has recovered, and I want him with me. Mr Lancing should be got as far away from home waters as is practicable.'

Rennie liked the sound of this less and less. Clearly the said Mr Lancing was a very great handicap to the admiral, who while endeavouring to appear obliging had not been able to conceal his real object: to palm Lancing off.

'As a matter in fact, sir, I have just now, today, acquired my own surgeon. His dunnage is even now being stowed. It was most kind in you to suggest Mr Lancing, to make me the offer, but——'

'You do not apprehend me, Captain Rennie.' The admiral's demeanour had changed. His very pale eyes had turned ice cold, ice hard. His stoop had become almost malignant. 'You will oblige me by taking the fellow off my hands.'

'I—well, sir, I do not——'

'Eh? You do not mean to tell me that you *decline*?'

To answer in the affirmative to that was more than Rennie dared risk. With a very unwilling heart, and a bow of acquiescence, he capitulated. 'Your wishes must be paramount, Admiral Hollister, in all things.'

'Eh?'

'I will take him.'

'Am obliged, am obliged. Let us make that three cases of wine, hey?'

And so the thing was done, and Mr Lancing went back with them in the launch to *Expedient*, on a rising sea, with three cases of wine secured amidships under the thwarts. James had been able to play no part in the transaction, having been required to wait on the quarterdeck in the wind. Now, in his boat cloak in the stern, he looked at their passenger. His face was slate grey, and his eyes bloodshot. There wafted from him, as he coughed, an odour so foul that James had to turn his head away. The hand reaching out to the gunwale, the steadying hand, was unsteady in the intervening time, it trembled. The other hand, clutching his cloak round him, was nearly blue. James thought that they had got a very bad bargain, no matter how good the wine.

Rennie was silent all the way. In his mind was the single despairing thought: Why did I not ask the admiral if he might spare me one of his cooks, for Christ's sake?

PART TWO: SOUTH

Expedient at sea, three days out of Portsmouth, beating into a strong Atlantic westerly, tack on tack close-hauled under double-reefed topsails. The ship was pitching more than Rennie or her master Mr Loftus would have liked, and rolling more too, in the swell which the wind had pushed before it. Heavy going, and the upper masts always under stress, even with tightened backstays. There had been mishaps in the forecastle, and a cold meal or two. One of the chicken coops had come loose and tipped over in a heavy sea, and the birds had been lost. Nothing had shifted in the hold, and there was not a worrying quantity of water in the well, but enough to worry Mr Adgett, who in turn was determined to worry Rennie. This was the ship's first real test, and a newly refitted ship was almost certain—was certain—to open her seams here and there, and let the sea in. On the first night Rennie had ordered the guns doubly secured, lashed up and bowsed taut. He had wished to establish a routine of exercising the great guns, so that when he came to begin the long programme of tests required of him in his instructions the guncrews might be proficient. In the prevailing weather he had deemed this unwise. There would be plenty of time for gunnery in the weeks and months ahead.

There had been injuries, inevitable injuries. Two gashed arms, a dislocated shoulder, and a suspected broken leg. The broken leg was a serious business, and that was where the real trouble with Mr Lancing had begun. His warrant gave him seniority over Thomas Wing, and right of occupation of the surgeon's quarters, which Wing had in turn to vacate, having himself just displaced Mr Dobie. Lancing had not been patient or obliging in this, but had made known his intentions by presenting himself in the cabin, and ordering Wing out, in so foul-mouthed and foul-breathed a way that Wing was much cast down.

The difficulty might have been no greater than that—unpleasant as it was—had not Thomas Wing soon discovered that the surgeon was ignorant of many of the basic treatments for injuries and maladies, ignorant of cleanliness, ignorant of drugs and potions; ignorant in ways that would have shocked and dismayed Dr Stroud, and certainly shocked his erstwhile apprentice.

'Ought—ought not the limb to be splinted?' he inquired, in the case of the broken leg.

'What? What? Who says it is broken, anyway? I do not know that, for certain.'

'Surely you have examined him?'

'I have looked at him. He will not let me touch him, or get near to him, the wretch. It is his affair. If it becomes gangrenous, off it will come, chop. And then he may live, or he may die.'

His breath was so foul that Wing had to clench his teeth and stiffen himself in order not to gag.

'Will you allow me to examine him?'

'What makes you think he will let you come near him, eh? Mr Bloody Miracle? When he whines like a dog and cringes like one? Eh? Hhhhhhh, you are green, Mr Wing. You don't know seamen.'

Thomas Wing turned his head away, and swallowed. Christ in tears, the stench. He recovered enough to say: 'I should like to try, if you will permit it. I do know seamen, you see, I have treated them very often.'

'Ahhh. Hahhh. He knows seamen, does he? Listen, this is your first ship, hm?'

'Yes, but——'

'Then do not presume, Mr Dwarfling, to teach me my trade. You may fetch and carry for me, and assist me in wiping away blood. In all other things, you will stay clear. Do you have me?'

So Wing had waited until the surgeon had gone to the gunroom for his supper. He had visited the seaman, who lay not in the sickbay, for there was no proper sickbay yet in *Expedient*, but in his hammock, slung far forward on the larboard side of the lower deck, to give him a little more room. He was groaning and sighing, and clearly very low. Wing had discovered his name from the sicklist, and came to him, holding a lantern, and lurching with the roll.

'George? George Fenton?'

'Who's that? I won't have that butcher near me. Stand off, or you'll feel my knife.' This last, meant to sound fierce, sounded merely desperate, and nearly breathless.

'Do you mean Mr Lancing? I am not Lancing.'

'We knows about him.' The words fading down into his pain. 'That sodding death's doorman.'

'I am Thomas Wing, late of Haslar Hospital. I am come to relieve your pain, and to set your leg.' Something in his voice was trustworthy, or gentle, or certain, or perhaps all three. The seaman stopped trying to be fierce, and tears poured down his cheeks.

'You won't hurt me, will you, mate? Oh, Christ.'

'I will not. I will take away your pain.'

And fifteen minutes later, having dosed the patient liberally with alcoholic tincture of opium, and with great swiftness and certainty examined the break, determined that it was a clean fracture and had not broken the skin, he straightened the limb and locked it with a length of timber, secured up and down with bandages.

'Do you feel anything, now?'

'Only when you clapped on to it just now, then I felt it. Not no more. You did not—you did not cut it off?'

'I did not. Rest easy now. I will come back presently, and look at you again.'

'We all knows about him, the other one.' His voice was intoxicated, but lucid, and calm. 'Boat's crew heard it from the Vanquishes.'

'Rest now, George.'

'The admiral wished to punish him, see. He give old Holly a potion that near tore out his guts. Poisoned old Holly, the bugger. Poisoned others, too. And tried to cut them.'

'Yes, well—you must rest.' He was again acutely aware of the ship's rolling as he went aft.

In the gunroom there was consternation. Lancing stank, and the assembled ship's officers, by now more or less used to each other, found this new addition to their number very disagreeable. He looked horrible, and he smelled horrible, and his hand—the hand to which they would be obliged to turn in bodily distress—shook and clutched like a claw at dish and spoon and glass. His odour was evil enough, but what in God's name could be the cause of his dreadful colour, and those palsied fingers? What abhorrent disease had him in its grasp?

Makepeace, who was the officer of the watch, was soon joined on the quarterdeck by the master. 'I had better be on deck,' he said. 'I had better be on hand.' He looked aloft, and looked at the binnacle compass, and breathed the wind into his nose. 'The air is a little close below. I will keep you company, Mr Makepeace, while we are beating into this wind.'

Through the second dogwatch, as the wind moderated a little and the reefs were shaken out of the topsails, and the forecourse and a headsail set, Thomas Wing kept watch over his patient, forward in the lower deck. His stomach was empty, and he felt rather ill himself, but he kept his vigil, far into the middle watch too, with the rows of hammocks behind him, and the ship heaving under him, far into the night—five, six, seven bells—and his patient slept deeply, occasionally muttering, occasionally twitching, but he did not wake. He did not wake, and that was a good thing, and at last at eight bells Wing crept away, below to the orlop and his temporary berth, very cramped and uncomfortable, where he fell into exhausted senselessness.

He woke only when the hands were piped to breakfast. He had not heard the deck washed, or hammocks piped up, or any of the great activity of a ship rousing herself to a new day. He was aware, as he woke in the glimmering darkness, his lantern by his side, that the weather had eased and that the ship no longer heaved and lurched. Here, below the waterline, it was as nearly peaceful as he could hope for. His life at the hospital had been in no way luxurious, or restful, or idle, but life at sea—so long anticipated, so many years longed for as the great opportunity—was not what he had expected. Yes, he had heard seamen describe it, had heard their tales of storms, of fever, of short rations and brutal petty officers, but nothing had entered his imagination that was remotely near the truth of shipboard life. It was more unpleasant, and more confining, and infinitely stranger than anything he had ever before understood. The arrangements for living, working, sleeping, and eating were confusing enough, but it was the design and structure of all places below and between that bewildered him. The ship was dark, and the air was poor. The heads, which he was obliged to use since he now had no proper quarters, were dismaying—indeed, in a heavy sea, quite terrifying. He was constipated, and he could eat little. Yet he must be mindful of his obligations. His work was to heal and succour, and he must do it no matter what.

The surgeon, when he discovered what Wing had done with George Fenton's broken leg, was at first astonished, then outraged, then vengeful. He found his subordinate, and confronted him: 'How came you to truss him up like that? How did you contrive to do it? Who assisted you?'

'No one.'

'Well, that is a lie. You could not have managed it alone. Therefore——'

'If you please, I made him peaceful with a drug, and straightened his leg from the end of the hammock——'

'Who did? *You?* Hhhhh, do not make mock. You have not the strength of a water-fly.'

'If you please, I am very strong, in fact. And I am fast and quick and swift. I straightened his leg quick so that I could brace it with the splint, and tie it up.'

'Indeed? *Did* you? Then you are a damn fool. D'y'think that he'll live, now? Fffsss, he will perish. Gangrene and death. That is what you have done for him. You have done for him, you dwarfling villain.'

Thomas Wing felt tears start at his ducts, tears of rage. He clenched his hands at his sides, bit his tongue so that it would not leap bold and fierce, and stood still, his head bowed.

'Nothing to say, hey? Found wanting, hey? You bat's-squeak, do not presume to undertake any further cases. You will not attend this man any more, d'y'hear? Leave him to me to untruss, you have done him quite enough harm.'

'If you please——' Raising his head.

'Well?'

'I—I am sorry that I have offended you. I wished merely to relieve his suffering. Will you not allow him to lie quiet a few more hours, when he has endured such pain?'

'Lie quiet? It is you that has caused him to suffer, and now you want him to rot!'

'No, no, no, I do not. Of course you must attend him as you see fit, but——'

'As I see fit! As I see fit! I am the qualified man!' Lancing clutched at his chest, coughed violently, and had to steady himself with a hand raised to the deckhead. Wing averted his face, and waited until the paroxysm was abated.

'At any rate, I do not—I cannot look at him now,' said Lancing. 'There is—there is lists I must make, potions from the chest and the like—in my quarters.' He turned, stumbling a little, coughed heavily again, and was gone.

Wing went at once to Fenton's side, and looked at his patient. He was peaceful, and there was no sign of gangrene.

'I must protect you, George Fenton.' A whisper. 'I cannot let that man near to you, I must keep him away at all cost.'

But how was he to do it?

His answer came by good luck, or rather the ill luck of Mr Trent, the purser. 'Mr Wing, could I have a word with you.' Meeting him in the waist. They stood a little aside.

'Yes, Mr Trent?'

'I have—mmm. That is, I am afflicted with a—hmm.'

'Afflicted, Mr Trent? With what?'

Leaning close, hushed. 'I have a boil on my arse, Mr Wing. Hmm. It—it pains me something severe. Very severe. I cannot sit down with ease.'

'Then you had better see the surgeon, sir, had you not?'

'The surgeon! Him!'

'Mr Lancing, yes.' He thought, but did not say, that Lancing was well named in this case.

'Jesu Christ. God in heaven. You think I would visit that fellow? Come come, now, Mr Wing. I will like you to treat me. You have a gentle hand, so I hear. You know how to accomplish the healing of such things as boils. Please, now, say you will attend to mine, will you?'

'I am very sorry, Mr Trent, but I may not do so. The surgeon has forbade me to treat anyone. He is the qualified man. You must go to him.'

'Forbidden you? Why?'

'He has not confidence in me. There is nothing I can do.' A regretful frown, a reluctant shrug.

'This will not do,' muttered Mr Trent. 'It bloody well will not do. I must see about this.' He went aft, and made it known that he wished to see the captain.

Presently Captain Rennie sent for Thomas Wing.

'Well well, Mr Wing, I hope that you are settling in, and that you have not found your situation too arduous, or too difficult?'

'Well—no, sir.'

The captain turned his head to one side a little. 'You have something to tell me, Mr Wing?'

'I—no, sir.'

'I hear that you have become reluctant to treat minor ailments. Boils, as an instance. Ain't that very remiss in you, Mr Wing? It is your duty, is it not?'

'I—I am forbidden to treat anyone in the ship, sir.'

'Forbidden? By whose authority, forbidden?'

'Why—the surgeon himself, sir.'

'I see. And if, say, I had a carbuncle myself. And if I asked you to treat it—what then?'

'I—I cannot say, sir. That is—I would wish to treat you, sir.'

'Then you may treat Mr Trent.' Tapping the table once with his fingers. 'Say nothing of this to the surgeon. It is a matter between you and me—and of course the purser, it is his arse, after all.'

'Thank you, sir.—What will become of George Fenton?'

'Eh?'

'One of the seamen, that I was tending. I straightened his broke leg, and bound it with a splint. It is healing well—but I am forbidden to treat him further, for fear of gangrene.'

'Do you fear gangrene, Mr Wing?' Sharply.

'No, sir.'

'Is there any sign of gangrene?'

'No, sir.'

A tap on the table. Another. 'Very well, Mr Wing. You may be confident that a solution to this damned nonsense—to this difficulty—will be found. And now I will not detain you. Mr Trent awaits you with eagerness, I am in no doubt.' A nod, a grim little smile.

For a day or two, to the relief of the other officers, Mr Lancing did not appear in the gunroom, but remained in his own quarters. His duties—all of his duties—were undertaken in his absence by Thomas Wing. Then one morning as Wing came aft on the lower deck Lancing sprang at him out of the darkness.

'I know what you have done, you poisonous manikin.' Softly, the reek of his breath huffing round Wing's face. He grabbed Wing's arm, dug in his claw fingers, and held him.

'I have done nothing but my work! My work and my duty!'

'Your work? *Your* work? You have usurped me, you wretched little villain. It is *my work*! *My work*, damn you!' A half-breathed cough. Another.

Wing wrenched himself free, staggered on the roll, and stood away, fearful but defiant.

'You damned shrimp! You dwarfling! What right have you got to steal potions from the chest! Yes, I saw you! Creeping and skulking like a pickpocket!'

Wing's fear drained from him, and was replaced by a sudden savage anger. 'What right have I got! Whose chest is it, whose drugs and instruments, that you have taken for your own? They are mine, given me by Dr Stroud! Mine!'

'Pfff! Such things is in the ship for the use of the surgeon. Do not claim them, you——'

'I do claim them. I claim them because I am able to use them to best advantage. I have attended men who were in pain, and relieved that pain. I have given a man with a broke leg the chance of recovery and life. I have done my work well!'

'Be careful what you say! Be very careful that you do not accuse me of incompetence! I can have you charged! I can have you broken!' He coughed heavily.

'I accuse you of nothing.'

'*What*, dwarf?' Mishearing. '*What* did you say? You have the impudence to——' Lancing began to tremble violently. He clutched at a silver flask in his coat, sucked it twice, then again, and thrust it away in his pocket. He drew a breath, staggered—and again he coughed. The spasm shook and shook him, and his slate face was tinged with a purplish blue. His stinking breath wafted round him like a miasma.

'You are unwell,' said Wing. 'You are consumptive.'

'I am perfectly'—cough—'perfectly well.' Again he fumbled for the flask, sucked from it, and held it clutched in his shaking hand.

'If you try to go on like this, pulling at that flask and pretending you are hale, you will place your own life at risk.'

'It is nothing, I tell you, nothing—hhhhh—nothing.' The flask dropped from his hand, and fell with a dull clatter on the deck. And now Lancing dropped, dropped to his knees, clutched at his throat, and slumped forward on the deck. A dark froth of blood spilled from him, and moved in a widening pool with the movement of the ship.

Thomas Wing knelt beside him, and took up his clawed hand, felt for a pulse, could not detect it, and put his fingers now to the neck of the fallen man, and felt there. The pulse had ceased, and the blood escaping from his sagging mouth now diminished. Lancing was dead.

Wing found his way to the upper deck, and to the captain's cabin. The marine sentry at the door made him wait, and then the captain called him in.

'Well, Mr Wing, I hear that Mr Trent is quite himself again—Is that blood on your stockings, and on your britches?'

'It is the surgeon's blood, sir.'

'The surgeon's? Has he injured himself?'

'He is dead.'

'Dead? Good God. What has happened? Was it a knife?'

'No, sir. I believe that he was mortally ill when he joined the ship at Portsmouth. I believe that he has died of consumption.'

'Consumption. Yes. He certainly smelled like a dead man, even while he lived. Do not think me over-harsh, Mr Wing, I hope he did not suffer, the fellow.'

'He coughed, and he bled in the lungs, and fell dead. It was very quick.'

'I am glad. I am glad. However, I do not want a dead man

lying in the ship. We must have him sewn in his shroud, and put over the side. Boy!' He gave the order for the sailmaker.

The ship's complement stood assembled in the waist, and the solemn words—the timeless washing of the sea adding to their solemnity—rose and fell in those cadences which captains adopt when they are reading aloud:

'We therefore commit his body to the deep, to be turned into corruption, looking for the resurrection of the body—when the Sea shall give up her dead—and the life of the world to come, through our Lord Jesus Christ; who at his coming shall change our vile body, that it may be like his glorious body, according to the mighty working, whereby he is able to subdue all things to himself.'

The drumroll ceased, the calls sounded. The board was tilted, and the surgeon's corpse, roundshot sewn into the foot of the shroud, plummeted into the sea. A brief splash, and the white shape sank from view in a trail of bubbles. The sea lifted against the ship, and the ship rode, sails aback.

Captain Rennie put on his hat. 'We will get under way, Mr Hayter, if you please, and set t'gan'sails.'

The silver speaking trumpet, glinting in the sun. 'Hands to make sail!' The calls.

The ship, hove to for the burial ceremony as a mark of respect for a gunroom officer, began to heel as yards were braced round. The course plotted for her by Mr Loftus days before was now being followed with more success, in these more moderate airs. They were long out of sight now of the English coast. The heavy weather had delayed them, and Rennie had earlier wondered if it might not be necessary for him to put into Plymouth and wait out the blow. He had put that thought from him, had pressed on, and now on this fairer day he thought that they might still make Tenerife within a month. His orders were specific: Tenerife was to be their only port of call on the voyage south. They were not to stop at any place on the coast of South America, but to sail clear down to Cape Horn, double it, and beat west into the Pacifick before he broke the seals on his second, canvas-bound packet of instructions, and discovered what he must do—or make the attempt to do—in the remote regions of that ocean.

'We will think about royals, if this wind holds steady,' he said, looking aloft.

James exchanged a glance with Mr Loftus. 'And if the wind rises again, sir?' he asked the captain.

'We shall still have royals in our minds, Mr Hayter, before the hands are piped to supper. We are not inclined to be bullied by our servant the wind, hey? And now I must write a letter about our late surgeon, the fellow, while his unfortunate departure is fresh in my head.'

＊＊＊

Thomas Wing had resumed his rightful position as surgeon, and reoccupied the surgeon's quarters. His dispensary, his chest and instruments, were all by him again, and although his quarters were cramped by the standards of the Haslar, and smelly, at least they were his alone. He must think about an assistant, or a plurality of assistance. He had been used, under Dr Stroud, to having the comfort of all the doctor's own assistants at hand, five or six trained men, knowledgeable in all matters of procedure, cleanliness and swiftness. From Dr Stroud he had learned all his skills, the principal among them speed in surgery. If a man was to survive what could never be less than brutal and barbarous, it must be done to him with swiftness; and able assistance in procedure was essential to its success.

He attended to the men who had been injured. The two

gashed arms had festered under the attentions of the late surgeon, and Wing now applied salves, and redressed the wounds. His neatness and certainty of hand impressed the seamen; and by now all the lower deck knew how George Fenton had been rescued.

'For a bantam he is mighty,' they said. 'And gentler than a woman, look.'

'But not soft, mind.'

George Fenton improved, and was greatly cheered when he became certain that he would not lose his leg. The captain, on his rounds of inspection, stopped to ask him how he did.

'I am mending, sir, thank you. Willing to return to duty.'

'Good, yes, well well. We must keep you off your legs a day or two yet, hey?'

As they passed on he said to James: 'Mr Wing tells me he cannot walk except with a limp after this. His days as topman are over. He was in the maintop, was he not, under Gurrall?'

'Yes, sir.'

'I will like to let Gurrall as top captain choose his replacement. Allow Tangible to think he has made the choice, however. Let it be managed so.'

'Very good, sir.'

'Fenton will join the forecastlemen. He is too good a man to waste.'

James nearly said something about waisters, but thought better of it. It was the sort of thing Lieutenant Royce might have said, and then laughed too loud.

'It is time I gave dinners,' said Rennie, as they climbed the ladder to the upper deck. 'Tomorrow I will give a dinner, I think. Mr Hayter, will you join me?'

'Should be honoured, sir.'

'Very good. And I should like to get to know the midshipmen. And I must have Wing at table, too. That will make a good dinner, I think.—Excepting the fact I have no damned cook.'

'Perhaps Stamp can be started into excelling himself, sir.'

'Good God, never start him, he will poison us all. He must be persuaded, Mr Hayter, like an horse to water.'

That image—of the moon-faced Stamp being led by a bridle to a trough—made James laugh. The dinner itself began solemnly.

'Mr Symington, Mr Pankridge, Mr Trembath, Mr Drummond, Mr Neill, Mr Rogers,' Rennie greeted the midshipmen assembled in their blue coats in the great cabin. 'You are welcome.'

They sat down, the youths waiting silently until the captain had sat himself before they drew back their chairs. James had been delayed with the master, who had brought to his attention an apparent attempt to damage the azimuth compass. Thomas Wing had been delayed by an accident in the forecastle: one of the cook's mates had sustained a severe burn.

The six youths sat still, their hair brushed and their faces washed clean, waiting for the feast. Rennie cleared his throat. It was damned awkward his lieutenant not being on hand to help him. What should he say to these youngsters? What had his captain said to him when he was a middy, sitting mute at his first dinner in the cabin? At last he said, to the boy sitting on his left, in what he thought was a kindly tone:

'Mr Trembath, a glass of wine?'

'Oh, thank you, sir, but no, I will not.'

'Will not?' Taken aback.

'That is, I am not accustomed to drink wine, sir.'

'Well well, you must grow accustomed, Mr Trembath, hey? It will not serve, you know, to drink nothing but water, like a Calvinist.'

'My mother is a strict Presbyterian, sir, and has made me swear—that is, to promise——'

'I should not wish to gainsay your mother, Mr Trembath, but we are at sea, and your mother ain't here. Now. Will you take a glass of wine, sir? Or do you insist upon water?'

The boy looked momentarily as if he might be defiant, as

if he might make what Rennie had only meant as a gesture of friendship into a contest of wills. At that moment Thomas Wing made his appearance, and his apologies.

'Is all well now, in the galley?' inquired the captain.

'The man is burned, he is scalded, but he will live.'

'You did not, I expect, notice the progress of our dinner, Mr Wing?'

'I did not, sir.'

'No no, certainly not, you was busy.—Steward!—A glass of wine, Mr Wing?'

'Thank you, sir. I do not drink wine.'

'Do not drink——Perhaps you will like grog, then?'

'Thank you, no.'

'You don't mean to tell me that you never drink any alcohol at all?'

'That is so, sir. I think that, in my work, it is advisable to be always sober.'

'Good God, a man who takes a glass or two of wine ain't necessarily a drunkard, Mr Wing.' Rennie was growing incensed, and checked himself. This would not do, at his own table.

'Will anyone join me in a glass of wine?' he asked the table, and contrived to smile.

'I will, sir.'

'I will, sir.'

'Indeed, sir, with pleasure.'

Glasses were filled, and they drank to the health of the King, and then to each other's health, and to the success of their commission. Their first course at last arrived, a nearly untasting broth. It displeased Rennie that this should be the beginning of his first formal dinner in the ship, and he sank once more into silence. From which he was rescued by the appearance of his first lieutenant, as the soup plates were being removed.

'I am very sorry to have missed the first course,' said James, as he sat down. Rennie noticed that his coat was smudged here and there, and that his hands had been hastily and not very well washed, a very unusual appearance, in this officer, of personal grime. It did not displease Rennie so much as surprise him.

Two of the remaining chickens had been killed to provide the main course, but since they were nine at table Rennie felt that this was not enough to sustain his guests, and he was disappointed again in that he felt he was entertaining them poorly and meagrely. Certainly he was not a rich man, but he did not wish to be seen or thought of as a damned cheese-paring, niggardly fellow, neither. The steward attempted to pile more on Rennie's plate than on those of his guests, and Rennie angrily directed him to 'feed up these young fellows, that are my guests, and never mind me at all'.

At the far end of the table James noticed the captain's displeasure, and thought that very probably it had been caused by his late arrival and disreputable appearance. He had dressed for the great cabin with some care, then at the last moment the trouble with the compass had surfaced, and after he and Mr Loftus had examined the instrument James had thought it prudent to examine the other instruments stored in the hold, in case they had been tampered with. He had looked at the anemometer, the theodolite, and the reflecting telescope, each in its protective encasing, and had found nothing amiss. The compass had been damaged, the sighting ring and wire sights knocked askew and broken. It might have been done accidentally, but to James—and to Loftus—it looked deliberate. Fortunately Mr Loftus had a spare compass, and James had seen it installed before he came below to eat.

When the cheese had been removed and the midshipmen had taken their leave, and Wing had gone to attend his scalding case, Rennie asked James to stay behind and drink another glass of port.

'I must apologize for my appearance, sir. It is not at all how I would wish to answer an invitation to dine.'

'Nothing at all, nothing at all. I did not notice hardly. At any rate, the meal was damned bad.'

'The reason I was late, sir—I went into the hold.' He described the damage to the compass, and his examination of the other instruments.

'It was probably an accident. You did well, however, to go into the hold. Tell me, is it foul there, still?'

'In the usual way, yes, it smells.'

'Then tomorrow we will pump ship. Today, at four bells of the afternoon watch, we will exercise the great guns.'

'Very good, sir. With the new powder? If so, I shall need to let Mr Storey know, so that he may load cartridge.'

'Has he not done so?'

'We have not yet broached any red casks at all, sir.'

'Then we will use ordinary powder, three rounds, then change to the new powder. The grooved guns are those here in the cabin, and those right forrard, are they not?'

'Yes, sir. Number one starboard and larboard, and number thirteen starboard and larboard.'

Rennie pointed. 'Are these guns loaded with cone-shot?'

'Since we have not yet used the charcoal cylinder powder, I think not, sir.'

'Then how are they loaded, Mr Hayter?'

'I—I confess, I do not know, sir.'

'Well well, we must discover that damn quick. We are a man-of-war, on the open sea. Suppose we was to find ourselves engaging one of His Majesty's enemies, hey? Bloody fools we should look, tompions out, with no powder in our guns, and no shot, neither.'

'With your permission, sir, I shall see about this at once.' Rising.

'No no, Mr Hayter, finish your wine. I did not mean to bite off your head. What is your opinion of this wine, by the by?'

'It is very good. Excellent, in fact.'

'Ain't it, though? I wonder what Admiral Holly would think of his bargain now. His pestilential palmed-off surgeon

an hundred fathom down, and his wine in our glasses.' Rennie
laughed heartily.

— ◆ —

Four bells.

'Mr Tangible, we will clear the ship for action. Beat to
quarters!'

A surge of activity through the ship as the calls sounded
and the drumroll rattled across the decks. The crash and
clatter of bulkheads, the pelting of feet, dismayed looks
exchanged as buckets hastily snatched up were dropped and
spilled. Curses. Frantic minutes until each man was at his
place, the nets rigged, and everything ready.

'Silence!'

The only sounds the wind in the rigging, the creaking of
timbers, and the washing of the sea.

'Cast loose your guns!'

Muzzle lashings made fast, lashing tackles loosened,
sponges down, crows and handspikes laid out ready. The
cartridge boxes and the shot on hand.

'Level your guns!'

Breeches raised, and quoins adjusted on beds.

'Out tompions!'

The plugs removed from the gun mouths. An air of
tension, of expectation, the length of the upper deck. Today
the carronades, which comprised all the guns of the quarterdeck and forecastle, the original specification of nine-
pounders having been abandoned, today the carronades
would not be fired. Rennie's aim was to test only the new
Waterfield guns.

'Run out your guns!'

The heavy rumbling of the trucks, the breeching ropes and
tackle falls hauled. The shouts of gun captains.

Rennie stood impassive on the quarterdeck, waiting,
waiting. Gulls hung on the wind at the level of the main yard,

keeping pace with the running ship. The sea slid along the wales and washed astern.

'Prime!'

Cartridges pierced down the vents with priming wires, gun captains forward with their horns, and the guns primed with fine grain.

'Point your guns!'

Handspikes and crows, the guns sighted, today a formality since there was no target. The gun captains crouching with the lanyards.

'Starboard broadside, on the lift—*FIRE!*'

Tremendous thudding bangs, a rippling concussion which shook the whole ship, and smoke filled the deck, puffed in great ballooning clouds from the ports. The whistling of shot. The gulls wheeling away in alarm. Distant splashes.

'Worm and sponge!'

And so the exercise proceeded, three broadsides were fired, starboard and larboard, and the guns were now loaded with 'red' cartridge. A moment of confusion at the number one starboard gun, at 'Load with cartridge', then in the rush to keep up the moment lost, ignored, put behind, and the sequence continued: 'Load with shot, and wad your shot', 'Ram home', 'Run out', &c., until the last command, the command to fire, and in the din which followed a different sound, a hollow WHOOMP, the pinging clang of metal fragments—and screams.

Running feet, shouts, more screams, terrible and desperate, and a midshipman's face appeared, white with shock. His mouth opened, and he stood blinking up at the quarterdeck.

'What is it, Mr Pankridge? Speak!'

'Number one starboard gun has—has exploded, sir.'

'Thank you.' As calmly as possible. 'How many hurt?'

'I—I don't know, sir. There is a great deal of blood.'

'Find out how many is injured, if you please. Belay that. Where is Mr Royce?'

'I don't know, sir. I did not see him after the explosion.'

'Very well, Mr Pankridge. I will come with you. Mr Loftus! We will heave to.'

James was already at the gun, and had taken charge. Rennie joined him, followed by the white-faced Pankridge. Their feet slipped on the bloody deck. The scene was horrible in the extreme. The port cill had been smashed, and had sent splinters flying. The gun had burst at the breech, the metal of the cascable and first reinforce bent out like curled paper. The second reinforce and trunnions lay imbedded in the deck timbers; the remainder of the gun, the chase and muzzle, had been flung forward into the sea. The carriage was shattered, the breeching rope and tackles lay soaked in blood. All round the gun, and behind it, were parts of men. The gun captain and two men on either side of him had been blown to pieces. With horror Rennie saw three fingers imbedded in the ship's side, under a tackle ring. Other men lay groaning, whimpering and screaming on the deck. One man's guts had been scooped from him, and lay in a glistening slaughterhouse lump by a shot rack, his body flung on its back, trailing cords of intestine. The smell was overwhelming, a sickening reek of blood, faeces, burnt powder and smashed wood.

'Oh, sir—oh, sir, I cannot look any more.' Poor Pankridge was panting like a terrified animal.

'Go below, Mr Pankridge, and find the surgeon. Jump now!'

But Thomas Wing was there, now. He knelt by a man who was convulsing, his clothes blown off, and only the remnants clinging to his wrists and ankles. His side had been split, and his left leg smashed. Wing knew at once that he could not save his life, only save him from agony. With swift, neat movements he tipped back the man's head, prised open his mouth, and poured something down his throat. The man coughed, gasped, trembled as Wing held him, then grew still. Wing laid him on the deck, and moved to another man, who lay moaning on his side, his legs drawn up.

When Wing had done all he could on deck, James helped to carry the injured men below, then returned to the upper deck, his shirt, stockings and breeches stiffening with blood, his face set.

'We will not throw the remains of the gun into the sea,' said Rennie. 'We must discover why it burst.' He was very shaken, but endeavoured to be calm and practical.

'I know very well why it burst, sir.'

'Indeed? How?'

'I will stake my warrant it was because the cartridge was overfilled. The full weight for standard coarse was used in a cartridge of red powder, sir.'

'Surely strict instructions was given. How could such a damned foolish mistake be made?'

'We must worm out all the larboard guns, and replace all cartridge presently filled in the magazine. We must discover who loaded them. With your permission, sir.'

'Very well, Mr Hayter. Do all that is necessary, then report to me. Do not think me hard, but you must not waste any powder that can be saved. You have me? Let us retrieve something from this bloody and terrible day.'

James was occupied through the remainder of the afternoon watch, and through the two dogwatches, investigating, determining, making arrangements. He made detailed drawings of the burst gun, and of all the damage, before he allowed Mr Adgett and his crew to effect repairs. He made a list of all the dead men, and the injured men. Three men had been killed outright, and two more had subsequently died; all the remainder of the eleven-man crew had suffered injury, and two of them were not expected to live. He examined Mr Storey closely, and his filling assistants, even the cook Mr Stamp, who had occupied the light room. Mr Storey, earnest and sad, but firm, swore that no cartridge had been overfilled—he had checked each cartridge himself before sending it up. James questioned the powder monkey, but the boy could tell him nothing. He had been near the gun when it exploded, one of his eardrums had burst, and he was still trembling with fear. James let him be.

James missed his supper, yet he did not notice it. His clothes were bloody and stiff, his hands were filthy with blood and other fluids, dried on his skin. Hunger did not trouble him. He had the deck in the first watch, and having cleaned himself up, and changed his clothes, he wrote out all he had discovered in a neat hand, and took the pages—torn from his notebook—to the captain, and went on deck. The whole watch he was silent on the quarterdeck, looking aloft at the mizzen t'gan'sail, and occasionally pacing. He felt dulled to the bone. The night air did not revive his spirits, or sharpen his appetite. He was tired, but not sleepy—the opposite of that.

At eight bells of the first watch he was relieved by Royce. 'Where was you after the gun burst?' James asked him.

'Oh, I was helping to get the wounded below, you know.'

'Eh? I never saw you.'

'Well, I—I dare say, in the confusion, you know—there was tremendous confusion.'

'Yes, there was.' And he gave the course, and the speed of the ship at the last glass, and went below. As he came down the ladder he was called by the captain into the great cabin.

'I have looked through your lists and so forth, Mr Hayter, and your account of all that happened. You have been admirably thorough, and I must commend you for it.' Rennie was still fully dressed, and the remains of his supper—his uneaten supper—lay on the table.

'I fear I could not discover anything wrong, sir. I was mistaken about the cartridge.'

'That ain't your fault. We do not know what happened, except the gun blew up. It is nobody's fault.' He stared distractedly at the cold plates on the table. 'I sent the steward to bed. I should go to bed myself, yet I would not sleep, I think.' He tapped the table with his fingertips, drew in a breath, came to a decision. 'For the moment the grooved guns are not to be fired. Again, for the moment, we will not use the new powder in any of our guns. Only standard coarse grain is to be loaded, until we know more.'

'Very good, sir.'

'First reduced. Belay that. Second reduced. I think that is safest, and wisest. You agree?'

'Second reduced, certainly, sir.'

'It is not the time to celebrate, it has been a very wretched day for *Expedient*, and it is late, but will you join me in a glass of grog, Mr Hayter? To lift our spirits?'

'That is kind in you, sir. It would be most welcome. I have felt low all the watch.'

'Have you ever experienced a major sea action, Mr Hayter?'

There was now a jug of three-water grog on the table between them, and James felt the benefit of the rum as it thawed out his guts, and rose like a balm into his head.

'No, sir. Only two small actions against corsairs, on convoy duty off the African coast. We was obliged to beat them off on both occasions. They are very light vessels, lateen-rigged, and very fast. It is surprising how quick they may tack, and wear away. Their armament is light, and they don't rely on it. Their aim is to board one of your merchantmen by stealth, kill the officers and take command, and send their own vessel away in full view, which engages the attention of the escort. Since many convoys employ only one escort ship, a small frigate, or a ship sloop, the escort cannot be everywhere at once. However, on both occasions, I am happy to say, we succeeded in damaging the corsair, and retaking his prize.'

'That was well done.'

'Have you seen action, sir?'

'Well, I have. I was at the Saints.'

'In '82? How I should like to have been there. I should like to hear your own account, sir, very much. Which fleet, Admiral Hood's, or Admiral Rodney's?'

'I was not officially attached to either. I had been with

Kempenfelt, as repeat signals, at Ushant in December '81. I was then in command of the *Mystic* sloop, twenty, and Kempenfelt sent me across the Atlantic to warn Hood that a large French convoy had escaped and was bound for the Caribbean. I was fortunate to make fast passage, and reported to Hood off Antigua, and Rodney came there with his fleet, and the two combined. I was assigned to carry messages between the flags, Hood in *Barfleur*, and Rodney in *Formidable*.'

'How many sail of the line?'

'The combined fleets made thirty-six sail of the line, and a scattering of frigates and sloops such as my own. The French had thirty-four, I think.'

Rennie pulled sheets of paper to him, and found a pencil. He began to sketch the action, and to speak of it in great detail. James stood up and came round the table to stand at his side, the better to see. His respect and liking for Rennie increased by the moment.

'At sunset on the 11th of April, Rodney disengaged, and stood to the south, and overnight gained the wind.'

He sketched the positions of the fleets, and the direction of the wind, and described how on the 12th the battle was again joined, and brought to conclusion.

'I reveal nothing secret when I say that Hood and Rodney did not like each other. Hood tried to circumvent Rodney's instructions throughout the battle, you know. He greatly resented the fact that Rodney was the senior flag officer, but Rodney made him obedient. Hood always said afterward that Rodney allowed too many French ships to escape. And they both liked to take the credit for closing the enemy to leeward, and thus preventing his escape, and for twice cutting his line. That was the decisive moment; de Grasse could not then recover, he was lost.' He paused, and took a long swallow of grog, and sighed.

'At the end it was very horrible. The *Ville de Paris* took a frightful broadside from *Barfleur*, that killed sixty men outright. Her decks bled, that is the only way to describe it.

Blood poured from the scuppers, as if the ship herself was dying of her wounds. I shall never forget it. Never.'

And now James knew why Rennie had called him into the cabin, and asked him to share a jug of grog. The business of the gun had reminded him of a dreadful scene, had recalled it in all its horror and abomination, and had so exercised his mind that he could not rest.

'Afterward, at Port Royal, Rodney asked for me, and told me—I have had occasion to recall his words pretty exact—he told me that I might rely on him, given my service to the fleet in the late action, to aid me in moving up. He said that he would certainly see that I was made post, and given a frigate. He could do no more for me, he said, he could not admit me to a share in the prizes, since I was not officially attached to him, but had only been sent with a message from Kempenfelt. But he would help me in moving up. He would write letters, and say something about me in the right quarters.'

'Did he honour his promise?'

'Well well—I cannot say that he did. At any rate, not so that it made any difference to me. If he did, it did not signify. I was on the beach three years, nearly four, until *Expedient*.'

'That don't reflect very well on Rodney.'

'However, it is possible that he simply forgot, you know. Clean forgot, in the hubbub of his return to England to great acclaim, a peerage and two thousand a year, and so forth.'

'Yes, for preserving the nation's sugar trade.'

Rennie held up a finger. 'Is it not possible, in fairness to Lord Rodney, that when this voyage was first conjectured, perhaps he heard of it? Perhaps was even party to it, in one distinction or another, I do not know—and when he heard of it, he remembered me, and put my name forward. I like to think so.'

James did not think this at all likely, but he did not say it. He did not like to say that Lord Rodney had very probably forgotten Rennie entirely, and knew nothing at all about *Expedient*. What he did say:

'Almost certainly, I should think. Yes, that is likely what happened.'

'No doubt your own commission came to you by a similar connection.'

'Oh no, I think not, sir. I had no glory in the late war. No sea actions, except those corsairs. Not even worth a letter.'

'Your captain wrote no account of these actions?' Rennie was amazed. 'Damned bad practice. Forgive me, I did not mean to malign a man I do not know, under whom you have served.'

'It was bad. The whole commission was conducted in a grudging, time-serving, reluctant spirit. I was ashamed of it, to say the truth.'

'It was not your fault, Mr Hayter.'

'Oh, but it was. My own feelings were poor. Poor and unworthy. It was because there was no hope of prizes, you see. Our work was to prevent prizes from being taken. We could not profit from it.'

'There is no shame in wanting prizes. Do not think of it. Push your glass instead.'

'I have drunk my fill, I think, sir. I must turn in, with your permission.'

James woke to the sound of shouting, and stirred himself, swinging out of his hanging cot and removing his nightshirt. His head was clear, in spite of the midnight grog, and he was acutely aware of his emptiness. He had eaten nothing since the middle of yesterday.

'Where away!' Lieutenant Makepeace's voice. Then a more distant voice, a midshipman's.

'One sail of ship, on the larboard quarter!'

James scrambled into his clothes, took up his glass, and went on deck. 'D'y'mind if I have a look, Tom?' he asked Makepeace, who was attending to the logline, and the glass.

'Jump up, by all means.'

James climbed into the mizzentop, his glass firmly gripped,

braced himself, and found the sail in the lens. He focused, and tried to make out detail. Square-rigged, three masts, her hull just below the line of the horizon. No pennant or ensign that he could see. A merchantman?

'What is she, Mr Rogers?' he called to the midshipman perched above him in the crosstrees. 'Can you make her out?'

Jonathon Rogers was the only midshipman possessed of his own glass, given him by an indulgent elder brother.

'She flies no colours, sir, that I can see.'

'We are in accord.' James descended to the quarterdeck. He did not slide down a backstay, as he had so often done as a midshipman, but went sedately down by the ratlines, careful of his glass, a fine long Dollond, the objective and ocular two feet apart in an octagonal casing.

'What ship is she, Mr Hayter?' The captain appeared from the companion in his shirt, his nightcap still on his head. James was momentarily disconcerted by the eccentric appearance of his commanding officer, but was careful of his face.

'Mr Rogers and I agree that she wears no colours. A square-rigged ship, certainly.'

'A merchant ship, no doubt.'

'Very likely, sir. Except——'

'Yes? Well?'

'I wonder only how she has caught us up?'

'Why is the deck not being washed?' Rennie peered forward in the slanting early sunlight.

'If you recall, sir, after the—after yesterday's accident, when the decks was washed then, you said that they would not be required to be washed again today.'

'Ah, just so, I did. Thank you, Mr Hayter. Today we will pump ship. And I must go and see the injured men, later. Mr Rogers!' Calling up. 'Keep your eye on that sail the next glass, if you please, and let the deck know her progress.'

'Very good, sir.'

'Mr Makepeace, note it in the log.' He rubbed his face, and

was about to scratch his head when he felt the nightcap there, and snatched it off. 'I am damned hungry, Mr Hayter. What is your own appetite?'

'Acute, sir, I confess.'

'My steward will give us eggs, if there is a chicken left in the ship. Will you join me?'

'Thank you, sir, I will.'

'What speed do we make, Mr Makepeace?' Glancing aloft.

'Eight knots, sir.'

The steward was able to produce eggs, and bacon, and strong tea. James would have preferred coffee, or chocolate, but kept those tastes to himself, since Rennie made his own preference very plain.

'I am a tea man, always a tea man. It is an expense, and many people are addicted to the coffee bean as a substitute, but for myself there can be no substitute. As a lifter of the heart in the morning it is unrivalled.'

'Some say that beer is——'

'Not at breakfast, surely?' Mildly amused. 'Speaking only for myself, you know.'

'The French are not averse to wine at the beginning of the day. Or cognac, with their coffee.'

'Ah, well, yes. The French.' Crunching bacon, and spilling yoke over his lip.

'Have you travelled in France, sir?'

'No no, not widely. They build excellent frigates, I do know that. Well, when I say excellent, I mean there is grace in the lines, certainly, and they dash about very smart. What I wonder is, are they lasting ships? Are they sturdy sea-boats, hey?'

James made this polite small talk, but in his head there were graver things. The bursting of the gun had probably been no more than a freakish accident, but what if there was something more to it than that? The broken compass drifted in there, and came alongside the wrecked gun. And far in the distance, keeping pace with them now, that unknown ship.

No merchant ship should be able to make eight knots, in these airs, and run with a frigate. Should he write down his thoughts? he wondered. Then he thought of writing letters, of writing to his father, and to Catherine. They had exchanged letters while the ship was at Deptford; hers much longer than his, and he determined to write more fully to her from Tenerife, and send the letter back in a merchantman, or another man-of-war should one be at anchor there.

'Will you drink another cup?'

'Thank you, no, sir. I must write up my log for yesterday, before my watch.'

'Yes. Yes. So must I write it all up. It ain't a thing I look forward to doing. I think we had better have the burial service at noon, before the hands are piped to their dinner. Let us give our dead a decent farewell, and get it over and done with.'

'Very good, sir.'

The brief social interlude of the meal was over, and both men regretted it, in a way. Although neither of them acknowledged it with any word, each privately felt that the other was becoming his friend.

The bilges were pumped, and at the captain's insistence the lower deck was washed with a dilution of vinegar, and smoked. This was greatly resented by Thomas Wing, who had prepared and rigged a makeshift sickbay forward on the larboard side, with canvas screens and a little more room for each man in his hammock. While the deck was washing he had had to have the injured men carried into the orlop. And yet he could not be angry with the captain for long. Hygiene was vital. Also, since the beginning of the commission Rennie had insisted on sauerkraut and portable soup as anti-scorbutics in the people's diet. Not all of the ship's complement appreciated this concern for their health. What they wanted, and saw as their inalienable right, was boiled salt beef, boiled salt pork, pease, plenty of biscuit, oatmeal, and cheese. And their twice-daily allowance of beer, or grog.

Anything else was an interference with the custom and tradition of the lower deck messes, and was not to be countenanced. Wing knew, as Stroud and Lind knew, and Cook had proved, that anti-scorbutics ought properly to be carried in all His Majesty's ships. The difficulty was to persuade seamen of this, when they regarded sauerkraut as that damned oxenfood, adulterated by farmyard piss, and portable soup as boiled glue. What good was piss and glue to toiling seamen, for Christ's sake?

'If you ingest these things, you will never get scurvy.'

'Says who? If I drink the goat's piss, that runs from the animal pen, will I go to heaven? I will stay with beer, thank you kindly, and burn in hell ha-ha-ha.'

'That ain't logic, Jacob Gurrall. I have never asked you to drink urine, have I?'

'No, Doctor, I was tickling your rib. Don't take it wrong.'

'What am I to say to the captain, if you come down trembling and stinking with scurvy, and unable to do your duty? What am I to say to him, when he discovers that you have poured the cabbage and the soup away in the head? Am I to tell him that I knew all along what you was doing?'

'I am hale, look. Feel my arm. Is that withered, Doctor?'

'No, it ain't, not yet. You must have seen scurvy, have you not?'

'Yes, we all know what it is. An affliction that rises from the bilges in heavy weather. It is a fever, like. You cannot help it, if the ship is beating to windward many days, you must take your chance like any seaman, and hope you don't fall ill.'

'But that is bloody nonsense! It has nothing to do with the bilges! Scurvy is a preventable disease, altogether!'

The nearly imperceptible shrug, and the closing of the face. The touch of the fingers to the forehead, in apparent submission, behind which was implacable determination not to submit. The suspicion too that although these strong young men liked their surgeon, and trusted him in all questions of physical injury, when it came down to it they

were men and saw him merely as a gifted boy, a manikin with
healing hands.

He knew that if he went to Rennie and told him the lower
deck was ignoring his dietary instructions, and Rennie then
took disciplinary action, he knew that the seamen would
never trust him again, would resent him and turn from him.
He would have to find a way of inducing them to accept anti-
scorbutics without resentment. Could it be managed by
stealth? he wondered. Could anti-scorbutics be introduced
into their meals without their knowledge? He must find a
way, or face numerous cases of scurvy as they bore south, and
the commission lengthened.

Just after the burial service, when the splashing of six weighted
shrouds had freed the ship of its burden of gloom, and the
hands had been piped to dinner, the lookout called down that
the other ship was still there, hull down on the quarter.

'Mr Loftus,' Rennie turned to him, 'will you go into the
top, and tell me what you make of her? Take my long glass.'

Mr Loftus, relieved of his duty this day of taking the
midshipmen through their noon sightings, willingly went
into the mizzentop, and looked at the distant sail. He said
nothing from there, but descended to the deck.

'Well?' At once Rennie saw something in his face, and
asked him to step to the aft rail, so that they might be private.
'You are concerned, Mr Loftus, I think.'

'I am, sir, a little.' Returning the glass.

'Do not be mysterious. What is it?'

'That ship has the look of a frigate to me, sir. The way she
lies close-hauled.'

'A frigate? But she wears no colours. Why should not a
frigate wear her colours?'

'That I could not say, sir. It is very odd.'

'It is damned peculiar. It cannot be an English frigate, at
any rate. It must be foreign. French, or Spanish, or colonial.
But why no colours, in the peace?'

'A privateer?'

'A letter of marque? No no, that don't make sense in the peace, neither.'

'A pirate, then?'

'I think that is unlikely, Mr Loftus. A pirate would never challenge one of the King's ships on the open sea.'

'He has not challenged us, sir. Only followed, at a safe distance.'

'Was I not under orders to proceed south I would wear, chase him down right quick, and demand to know his business, the impertinent villain. He can only be a villain, to behave in this way.'

'We might crowd on sail, sir, and see if he responds.'

'Let us do so, Mr Loftus, when the hands have eaten their dinner. I am going below to look in at the injured men.' And as he passed the helmsmen at the wheel he called out in a cheerful voice, to show the deck that all was well: 'Weather helm, full and bye, keep her steady, now!' And he went on to the companion, his glass under his arm.

＊━━◆━━＊

The wind swung round as they headed further south, and *Expedient* began to run before a steady north-easterly, with the ship Rennie now thought of as their sinister shadow always there astern.

From the crosstrees Jonathon Rogers spied out her lines early in the morning, as her hull emerged from the sea, and pronounced her definitely a frigate. Rennie went aloft himself, fighting a lifelong difficulty about heights. He had conquered the difficulty in earlier service, of necessity, but three years on the beach—never higher than the top of a stair—had left him vulnerable to his atavistic fears, and he had to force himself into the shrouds, hauling himself up without his glass into the top, then again up the topmast shrouds into the crosstrees, where he clung blind.

'Are you quite well, sir?' inquired Rogers anxiously.

'Nothing, it is nothing.' Rennie cleared his throat. 'A headache.' He stood in the crosstrees, and Rogers made him room. The ship, running with the wind on her larboard quarter, under a full set of sail, the ship heeled steady, but the narrowness of the deck beneath, and the line of the wake lacing and curling in on itself, and disappearing into the broad vast blue, were like things in a crystal-clear dream, born of malady, and Rennie stared fascinated. He made himself speak:

'Will you lend me your glass, Mr Rogers? I have forgot my own.'

'Gladly, sir. She is just hull up, in near direct line astern.'

He handed Rennie the glass, and the captain braced himself further, hooking an arm round a tarred topgallant shroud, and focused the lens. There could be no doubt about it, the vessel in pursuit, sharp there in magnification, the sea flickering and glittering in a thousand foreshortened waves between, the vessel was a frigate. A frigate thirty-six, like *Expedient*. He could just make out, on the lift, the yellow paint emphasizing the line of black ports. She was under nearly identical canvas to *Expedient*'s own, neither gaining nor falling off, but keeping station, keeping pace.

He lowered the glass. 'What is his purpose?' he wondered aloud. 'What does he want?'

'She is a frigate is she not, sir?'

'Indeed, she is. Your glass, Mr Rogers, and thank you.'

'Oh, thank you, sir.'

'I—I will make my way down.'

And half blindly, with terrible care, he groped his way down to the top, then forcing himself he swung into the futtock shrouds, over the precipice, above the height-diminished haven of the deck, climbed out hanging and trembling, at last engaged his feet in the lower shroud ratlines and knew that he was saved.

'Are you quite well, sir?' asked Lieutenant Royce on the quarterdeck.

'What d'y'mean, Mr Royce?' Harshly.

'I—I thought you looked a trifle waxy, sir.'

'*Waxy?* Who are you to use a damned presumptive word like waxy, sir?'

'I beg your pardon, sir.'

'What is your course?'

'I—it is——'

'Come come. Answer my question promptly, if you please. What is your exact course? What is your speed? How does she lie? Where are your glass-by-glass notations, hey? Show them to me.' And so forth, more savagely than Mr Royce's simple and well-intentioned question could possibly have warranted. Rennie did not like Royce, could not make any allowance for him, could not apprehend in him any hint or possibility of nor for improvement. He knew he was hard on his junior lieutenant, and it gave him satisfaction. If someone in authority was not hard on lax young men in the service, what was to become of them? What was to become of the service?

They ran all day before, and then the wind changed again, with Finisterre away to the east, and a storm blew in out of the Atlantic, one of those thundery, maladroit, swirling, flashing tumults of weather, throwing up shrieking gusts and blustery uncertain interludes, and all hands were called to take in sail, to reduce and reduce the chance of the ship being knocked down in the sea. Mr Dobie was again reduced himself, to miserable heaving in his box of a cabin, while anything that was not bowsed taut broke free and fell, and rolled about. Spillages slid and frothed, the animals in the pens and cages set up a collective bleating, shouted curses flew aft, and the sea smashed into spray, and streamed in sluicing runnels along the deck.

Rennie kept the deck, bundled in his oilskin, an old disreputable hat jammed on his skull, with the master at his side. The weather helmsman was relieved each glass, his mate on the lee relieved also, and *Expedient*—pitching and

shuddering, her timbers groaning, and her rigging sighing—
came ploughing through.

At dawn the storm blew itself out, the wind righted itself,
and came round on the quarter, and the ship lay true and free.
James inspected the damage with Roman Tangible.

'We was lucky, I reckon.' The boatswain, stoutly. 'Nothing
very bad. Nothing altogether bad.'

'It is not altogether good, however. Blocks flew about when
the wind struck, and I don't like the foretopsail yard.' Peering
up.

'Aye, it is sprung. It must be sent down, and replaced.'

'Where is our shadow?' said Rennie, on the quarterdeck.
'Is our shadow with us still?'

The horizon scanned. No sign of a ship, no sign of a sail.
Repairs begun, and the routine of the ship resumed.
Hammocks up, in the nettings. The deck washed. The
captain below, to gather on his table the lists of damages,
breakages and minor losses; and to drink a quart of tea. He
sent for his first lieutenant.

'We must get Mr Baragwanath's ana—ama—his wind
device, we must get it aloft.'

'Very good, sir. I should think a simple whip purchase——'

'Good heaven, no. No no, it must be carried, Mr Hayter.
It is an instrument of the greatest delicacy. It must be sent up
by hand, into the top.'

'You mean—carried through the rigging, sir?'

'Yes. Yes. Baragwanath was most particular. He made me
promise to take the greatest care.'

'Might I suggest that if we was to send it up by a burton
tackle purchase, that would answer——'

'No no no. I see what you mean, I see entirely what you
propose, but it will not do. A crew of the steadiest men is to
hand it up, and secure it. It is a scientific device, d'y'see. We
are a scientifical commission, and we must do our duty
accordingly, with every care for the very exacting observations required of us.'

'Very good, sir.—Who will make the observations? Mr Loftus?'

'Certainly. Certainly.'

'And the midshipmen?'

'No no no. In least, not at first. Good God, you know what middies are. Clumsy, precipitate and foolish. They might break the machine. Think what a disgrace that would make of us.'

'I will see that it is done. And if the wind should swing round again——'

'Then it must be brought down, sent down at once, and stowed.'

To James these instructions seemed to pose a contradiction, but since he did not perfectly understand the working of the anemometer he kept that opinion to himself. If the thing was so delicate it could not be left to measure any wind that was not fair and steady, it was not his place to wonder aloud at its usefulness.

He supervised the getting of the instrument into the foretop. Rennie had wanted it put into the mizzentop, at first, but was then persuaded that the foretop should be tried out as a suitable platform. James stood anxiously on the forecastle as the machine—very bulky and awkward—was handed up through the rigging by a team of topmen.

'Handsomely—handsomely, there,' he said more than once, as the machine teetered, even in the firm grasp of these able hands, and made itself difficult in being turned, and managed, and lifted clear of falls and blocks, and into the not very great area of the top, there to be placed on the decking. It became clear, as James came himself into the top, that there was not going to be room—in the open tent of shrouds and stays—for the great arm of the machine, with its windmill at one extreme, and weight at the other, to be properly employed. As the hands attempted to turn the large triangular base he said: 'Avast, there. Leave it be, just as it is. I must consult the captain's opinion.' James descended.

'What the fucking hell is this thingumbob?'

'Don't look at me, mate.'

'I know. It is for measuring the wind, see.'

'What, your farts?'

'Ha-ha-ha.'

The topmen did not have a high regard for Mr Baragwanath's patented device. James returned, heaving himself up the futtock shrouds into the top, and shook his head.

'We must return it to the deck, I am sorry to say, and place it—well, I must find a suitable position. Very well, clap on, and—heave. Handsomely! Never forget it is delicate, like a young virgin, with all her parts intact.' And he allowed himself a smile as the seamen laughed.

Late at night in the great cabin, as was becoming a custom with them, Rennie and his first lieutenant reviewed the ship's day on a semi-informal footing, and drank a glass of wine.

'I will want to institute a daily pattern of observations when we have cleared Tenerife. I know the wind machine is not wholly grasped as to how it may be of use to us, but that is something we must endeavour to overcome. Very likely we shall find the same thing with the new logship, and the sounding devices. We must persist. Science is not a thing to be entertained and understood in an afternoon, hey?'

'We have all the commission before us.'

'Well, yes, so we have. But it don't do to be complacent at sea. You never know what is going to happen, and we must get as much done as we can. The same thing is true of gunnery. I have talked to Storey, he is a sound man, and he thinks we may proceed without fear of further mishap, so long as we are careful. At second reduced allowance of powder, and the grooved guns excluded from service, we must proceed, or lose all capability as a man-of-war, to say nothing of our duty to test and evaluate these new guns in all conditions.'

'Before or after Tenerife, sir?'

'Oh, before, certainly. Tomorrow.'

'Tomorrow was to have been a washing day, sir.'

'Yes, I had forgot. Damn. Well well, the day after. Things cannot be permitted to slide. That is how a ship gets slovenly, and careless, and dirty.'

'Even on a washing day, sir?'

'Yes yes, very well, you chide me justly, hm-hm. Tell me—do not think me pushing—but I wonder if you will permit me to call you James?'

'Nothing would give me greater pleasure, sir. It is not at all pushing. I should be very happy.'

'Good, very good, I had hoped that's what you would say. It is sometimes difficult, often difficult for a captain to have any sort of friendly conversation with anyone in the ship, you know. I value these occasions, James.'

'So do I, sir.'

The slight awkwardness of newly assumed intimacy passed, and they were relaxed together over their wine. Each was aware that something important had happened, that a bond had been established, a valuable bond, but being Englishmen they did not mark it openly, or rejoice in it, but quietly drank their wine and were privately very pleased.

·—·=◆≡·—·

Santa Cruz, Tenerife, in very warm weather. The sun shone, the air was balmy, and the calm of the anchorage, with the mountains behind, was easeful after an intermittently rough passage. *Expedient* was three weeks out of Portsmouth, and Rennie determined that they should take in as much in the way of fresh provisions as might practicably be stored. However, he had a difficult and unwelcome duty: he must inform the ship's complement that there was to be no shore leave in this usually welcoming Spanish port.

'I know it is irksome, I know it, but my instructions are

plain. Only the boats' crews may leave the ship, to take in the provisions, and our water. Certainly that need not apply to the officers. You and Makepeace and Mr Loftus may go ashore as you please.'

'And Mr Royce, sir?'

'Ha, Mr Royce. If I could I should *put* him ashore, and bring up young Symington.'

James was silent.

'However, I have decided I cannot. Yes, he may go ashore.'

'The midshipmen?'

'An anchor watch must be maintained. And I don't know that allowing the middies to go larking about the town is at all wise. I must go ashore myself, naturally, and pay my respects to the governor, and so forth, and see the port agent. Mr Trent must go, to make the purchases. Mr Wing must go with him.'

'The surgeon?' Puzzled.

'He must make his report to the authorities that we are free of smallpox. And he is to find and buy as many lemons as he can. And onions. The people don't like portable soup, and they don't like sauerkraut. Well, they may have lemon juice and onions instead, and fresh meat. We must bring more killing beasts in, and chickens, if they are to be had. And wine. The beer is nearly gone, I think. I will like to give our crew wine, and fresh provisions, for so long as may be possible after we weigh. There will be time enough as we proceed south for grog and biscuit.'

'Where do we call before Cape Horn, sir?'

'We will make no landfall after this, until we are in the Pacifick.'

'We do not call at Rio de Janeiro?'

'No.'

The barge and the launch were hoisted out, and the shore party embarked. Santa Cruz was an orderly little town, thought Rennie as his boat's crew gave way with a will. It was as well that it was not to be invaded by the rapacious intentions of a man-of-war's crew. As they landed he gave strict instructions—iterated strict instructions, already issued —that no man was to leave either boat excepting to do his duty of fetching and carrying.

James saw and was heartened by the presence of three British merchant ships. His letter to Catherine would go in one of them. God, but it was hot in his coat and hat. He would have been happier in shirt and britches, bare-headed. Or perhaps a broad light straw sun hat. But Rennie was determined on making a show of smartness, and he and James were in their dress coats—dress coats, in shimmering heat— and cockaded hats, swords buckled. Astern lay a ship full of discontent, and resentment. This resentment would linger, James knew, and he did not like it. All his careful work of encouraging the men to trust him, and respect him, would be undone by their confinement to the ship.

Jacob Gurrall had already asked him a question. 'Is it true, sir, that we are to have no shore liberty?'

'The captain will address the people as to that.'

'But—you know it, sir. You could tell us.'

'I may not pre-empt the captain in anything, you know that. Do not ask what I cannot answer.'

'So it's true.'

'I have said nothing.'

A very glum look, and a perfunctory touch of the fingers to the forehead.

James went with Rennie to the governor's residence, above the fort, on an eminence overlooking the harbour. Terraced vineyards stretched away up the slopes behind. The governor was very courteous, and very grand. Tall, beautifully dressed —cool, in his light clothes—and not quite condescending, he made them welcome without ever allowing them to forget that here a British ship of war was merely another vessel among many which called there, and anchored there, and took in wine. He gave them wine.

'I should like to salute you, sir, as we depart.' Rennie was very stiff, very correct. 'May I know how many guns you will be inclined to fire yourself?'

'How many guns, Captain Rennie?'

'What number of cannon, sir, yes. So that I may not exceed, nor under-number them.'

'Ah. Ah.' Having known at once what was meant. 'Ah, yes. If I may suggest? Fire all of your guns, and then I will endeavour to match them.'

'All?—Well, I—that is forty, sir. Surely you will not ask that I fire forty guns in salute?'

'Just as you like, Captain Rennie. I am at my ease, entirely.'

'Thank you, sir.'

'Certainly, please ask the port agent for whatever you require. He is at your disposal, gentlemen. And——'

'Thank you, indeed, Excellency.' Bowing.

'And I should be honoured if you will dine with me here, this evening.'

Afterward, in the town, Rennie said to James: 'He may be a very fine fellow, and all that, but I did not like his foolery about the salute. That was damned ill-considered.'

'You may care to reflect, sir, that this is a very dull place, far from anything civilized, and the governor must grow very bored. We must forgive him his sense of fun, surely.'

'But, good heaven, it amounts to an insult to the King.'

'No more to our own King than to his, eh?'

Rennie unbent, and laughed. 'You have the knack of seeing the absurd side of every question, James. A happy knack. The fellow had me in a muddle, you know, I felt I had missed stays. We will give him thirteen, and he may fire whatever damned guns he pleases.'

'It was kind in him to ask us to dine, don't you think so?'

'Indeed, indeed it was.' Conceding with a nod. 'Let us hope he will give us a splendid dinner. It will be the last decent meal we shall get in a twelvemonth, after all.'

The governor did give them a splendid dinner. He gave them six courses, and three wines. He sent them back to the harbour in his carriage. Rennie's barge was there, gently riding in the shallows, thole pins up; but the coxswain and crew were not.

'Is that my boat, James?' Peering at it. 'No no, it ain't. Where the devil is my boat?'

'That is the boat, sir, I think. I do not know where——'

'Don't like to contradict you. Must tell you, not my boat. No crew, hey?'

'No. No. Where have they got to? That is the question.— *Expedients! Expedients!*'

'Good God, you will wake the whole town. This is a church-going, moderate, quiet kind of place, James. We must be on our best behaviour, to show the Spanish we are gentlemen.'

Distantly, on the night air, the sound of singing.

'If you will like to wait here, sir, I think I may be able to find your boat's crew.'

'Find them? The boat ain't here. I thought you was hailing the ship.'

Rennie was persuaded to sit on the harbour wall, while James walked a little way along the harbour front to a *taverna*, where he found the boat's crew, and the coxswain, Randall South.

'We was just about to return, sir. We was just taking a very little refreshment, to keep out the night chill, sir, to revive ourself in the chill.' Swaying.

'Chill? Chill? It is warm. We are in African latitudes, for God's sake.' He counted the men at the low table, in the dim light. 'Where is the rest of them? There are only five men here.'

At last James gathered the men together, two of them nearly insensible, and herded them back to the boat. Captain Rennie had disappeared. James found him asleep on the aft thwart, and the boat was rowed—after a fashion rowed—out to the mooring. It was not hoisted in, but left to ride with the ship, tethered to a stunsail boom. James assisted Rennie up the side, and then to his cabin.

'I am perfectly capable. I am perfectly capable in all capacities.'

'Shall you need your steward, sir, to help you to bed?'

'What'n'earth d'y'mean, "help me to bed"? Hey?—I am entirely capable.—Where is my piss-pot?'

'In the quarter gallery, I expect, sir.'

'Ah. Mm. Thank you. Thank you, indeed. I may perhaps write a letter or two before I retire. Or—I may not.'

On the following day, as more fresh victualling stores came into the ship, Mr Adgett requested permission to have the ship heeled so that he might repair a small but troublesome leak in the larboard bow timbers. The starboard guns were run out to cant the ship, at the same time as the launch, filled with water casks, came alongside. Tackles had been lowered, and the first casks slung when James, hungover, saw what was about to happen as he came on deck.

'Avast, there, in the boat!'

'What is the matter?' asked Lieutenant Royce crossly; he had the deck.

'The matter is, Mr Royce, that with her starboard guns run out, and water casks hoisting in on that side, you will weigh her down below the line, with her ports open.'

Royce looked over the side, and made his own assessment. He shook his head. 'You are quite mistaken, I think. There is no possibility of such a thing. I should have noticed at once.'

'Have you no memory of the *Royal George*, sunk at Spithead with all hands, in exactly similar circumstances?'

'I was not there, and I have no memory of it exact, therefore. Was you there yourself, Hayter?'

'Mr Adgett!'

'Yes, sir?' In the boat at the bow, with his crew, and tools, about to prise up copper sheathing.

'Wait a moment, if you please.' To Lieutenant Royce. 'You may be sanguine in the matter of losing the ship, and drowning every man in her, but I am not. I will take the remainder of the watch, and you had better go ashore and stay there for the moment.'

'Go ashore? Why?'

'Because I require you to do so. And you had better thank God that I am not the captain that has caught you out in such folly.'

'Look here, Hayter,' glancing round, and lowering his voice to a heated whisper, 'I think you are being most unjust. As if I cannot see the ship through one watch! As if I cannot judge a few damned casks of water by weight! As if I——'

'*Mr Royce!* What the bloody hell d'y'mean by taking in water, sir, while the ship is heeled for repair, and her guns run *out!*' Rennie stood furiously at the break of the quarterdeck, leaning over the rail.

'I have already taken——' began James.

'I did not ask you a question, Mr Hayter. I asked Mr Royce a question.—Well?'

'The boat has been—it has—I was quite aware, and took all necessary meas——'

'Go below, sir, until I send for you.'

'But, sir, I assure——'

'*Do as you're told, sir!*'

At eight bells of the afternoon watch, Royce sent word to James that he wished to see him in the great cabin.

'I am sorry that you had to take Royce's watch, James. The damned young fool is a burden to the ship. At any rate, I thought that we might eat supper, if you——'

'That is kind in you, sir, but the gunroom is having a supper ashore.'

'Ashore?'

'It is to honour Mr Wing, who has been asked to join our mess. Mr Makepeace, as secretary, proposed it, and we were all happy to say yes. I think you will agree that the surgeon has been a valuable asset to the ship.'

'Certainly, certainly. Could not you have had this supper aboard, just as well?'

'Well, since we are free to go ashore—are we not?—it seems handsome to honour Mr Wing with a last supper ashore before we weigh.'

'Oh, yes. You are free to come and go. Well well, I shall not keep you from your feast.'

James could see that the captain was quite out of temper. Later, as he stepped into the pinnace with the other gunroom officers, he regretted his own feelings of irritation. It was perfectly natural in these officers not to have included Rennie in what was after all entirely a gunroom matter, just as it was perfectly natural in Rennie to have wished to be included, and to feel left out.

'I am glad I am not clever,' said Royce as the girl brought another jug of wine. His face in the candlelight was flushed and sweaty. The room had a low ceiling, and the air was very warm. They had all eaten and drunk a great deal.

'I am damned glad I am not at all clever,' repeated Royce.

'In what way, glad?' James asked him, puzzled rather than censorious. 'How can a man not merely acknowledge his lack of intelligence, but rejoice in it?'

'I do not mean that I am not intelligent, Hayter, good God. I hope that I am intelligent. I mean, what I meant, was that I would wish never to be *acute*. Never to be acutely *knowing*.'

'Ah, that.' James poured wine.

'It isn't the same thing at all—as not being *intelligent*. You see?'

'I see that you do not wish to be thought ill-mannered.'

'No no. I do not mean that at all. Naturally, no man wishes to be thought insolent, or ungentlemanlike. But he ought not, neither, to be seen as too quick, too sharp, too damned *clever*. D'y'see?'

'Yes, certainly. A glass of wine, Mr Wing.'

'Thank you, I do not drink wine.'

'Forgive me, you did say so before. Never mind, we all salute you, Mr Wing. Welcome to our mess.'

'Welcome!'

'Welcome to our surgeon!'

———— ✦❉✦ ————

North-north-east of the Cape Verde Islands, 18 degrees 27 minutes north, 22 degrees 54 minutes west, with the wind still on the quarter, the ship steady and fast and weatherly, her main course part brailed up. The deck hailed. A sail astern.

'Where away?'

The first lieutenant into the rigging, climbing hand and foot. His glass focused. And there was the sail. The same sail, the same ship, neither gaining nor falling off. Flying no colours.

Rennie, on the quarterdeck, as James made his report: 'You are certain?'

'There can be no doubt, sir.'

'Very well. I deplore loss of time, but I cannot endure this any longer. We will go about, beat to windward, and meet him. When we are on the heading, Mr Hayter, I will like to see Mr Storey.'

'Stand by to go about!' The calls. The main course loosed full, and tacks, sheets and bowlines hauled through. The helm to windward. 'Helm's a-lee!' The jibs flapping. Sheets let go. The ship through the eye, and James shouted, 'Main-sail haul!' The yards braced round, and loss of steerage way. The anxious moment as the ship came round and 'Sail and haul!' was called. Tacks, braces and sheets trimmed, and the weather helmsman, feeling her under his hands, and under his legs, brought her just so, and no more, staring aloft to make sure. The quartermaster satisfied. James satisfied. The sea washing along the lee wales, and spray flying back across the deck and through the lower rigging as the bow dipped, and rose, and she found her feet.

'How the devil has he found us, the villain?' Rennie, feet braced apart.

'Perhaps it is by pure chance, sir.'

'Eh? We lost him in that storm, weeks since—and he finds us by chance?'

'Might not he have made for Funchal, sir, having suffered damage, as we suffered damage ourselves? Funchal was nearer. Then while we was at Santa Cruz he was repairing, then he put to sea once more, and made good southing time.'

'If he did he is a damned good seaman. To have done what you suppose he must have flown across the sea.'

'The ship is there, sir.'

'Aye, so she is. Mr Storey, our guns are loaded with roundshot and second reduced?'

'Yes, sir. All excepting the grooved guns, which was left unloaded as you instructed.'

'Just so. Now, very probably we will not fire our guns at all, excepting a signal gun. However, the ship that pursues us wears no colours, and that makes me suspicious of piracy, or blackguardly purpose of some kind, and we must be prepared—in case there is an attempt to attack us. Should we need to open fire—and I most certainly do not wish it—but should we need to, I will like my second broadside to be chain. Chain, Mr Storey. I mean to disable our opponent, destroy his rigging and disable him—and leave him to limp away crippled.'

'We could worm, and re-load with chain for our first broadside, sir, if you wish.'

'No, thank you. Should we need to open fire I have a notion to rake his stern with ball. Then I mean to smash his rigging with chain. That is, that is, should we be forced to do it. I hope that we may not.'

'All cartridge to be second reduced standard?'

'Just so, Mr Storey. We cannot risk anything more potent when we are not yet sure why the grooved number one burst.'

'The frigate is now in full sight, sir, hull up.' James lowered his glass.

'And she makes steadily for us, don't she?' Rennie with his

glass to his eye. He lowered the glass, glanced aloft, and said: 'Could it be that she has a message for us, d'y'think? That all along her captain has merely been trying to catch us up with a message? A despatch?'

'I doubt that, sir. Had she a despatch, particular to us, she would have known—her captain would—that we was bound for Tenerife, and thus followed us in. In any case, she would be wearing colours. She would be plainly one of the King's ships, with ensign and pennant.'

'Just so, Mr Hayter, we are of one mind. I thought simply that I had better make sure we was, since within the hour we may have to defend ourselves.'

'What ship is she?' mused James.

'That is a puzzle we will solve directly, one way or t'other. Hold her steady! Keep your luff!'

Minutes passed. Rennie trod the quarterdeck alone, at the lee rail, then: 'Mr Hayter.'

'Sir?' Joining him.

'We will clear the ship for action, if y'please.'

'Very good, sir. Beat to quarters! Clear the decks for action!' The calls. The rolling drum. Thudding feet.

'We will pass to windward, hail her, and identify ourselves. We will ask her to identify herself. If there is no response, I will remove my hat. As soon as I take it off, the crews at the carronades are to jump into the shrouds, and when I wave my hat—so—they are to sing out loudly: "*God save King George!*"'

'Very good, sir.' Closely attending. 'And then . . . ?'

'You are then to lead them in three cheers. At the third "huzzay" they are to jump down to their guns directly.'

'. . . Directly. Very good, sir. Do you mean to fire on the ship, directly?'

'I do not. I mean to defend my ship—*if* we are fired upon first, and only then. I shall certainly regard *that* as the opening of hostilities by her captain. Should he fire on us, we will pass astern of him and rake him, come about and loose a battery of chain.'

'And then—we will run alongside and board?' James wished to be absolutely certain of his duty.

'No. No no. I don't want the fellow's sword, or anything of that kind. If I have to I will disable his ship, so he cannot follow me any more. We are not at war, so there is no question of taking her as a prize. No no, we will defend ourselves, and then resume our course. I do not mean to lose any more time than is absolutely needful.'

'You do not wish to know what ship she is, and who sent her? Why she has followed us?'

'Yes yes—yes, we must do our best to discover that, certainly. But I want no boarding parties, no hand-to-hand fighting.'

The two ships converged on the rolling swell, the long blue-green Atlantic swell. When the logship was wound off astern the line was as clearly defined beneath the water as in the air above.

'How does she lie?' Rennie to the weather helmsman, and glancing aloft.

'She wants to point up, sir.'

'Very good. Hold her so, just so.'

Expedient beating into the wind, the mysterious frigate running before. As they came nearer *Expedient* came over on the other tack, to pass to windward well within range of the other ship's guns—which had been run out. Rennie was taking a risk, but he wished to give the other captain every opportunity to identify his ship. England was not at war. The two ships came abreast, the flagless frigate very graceful, her port strakes yellow, her side black, everything taut and trim. Rennie raised his speaking trumpet.

'*What ship are you?*'

Silence.

'*I am His Majesty's frigate*, Expedient—*What ship are you?*'

Silence. The *Expedient*s could see men on her deck, and in the tops, but these men did not respond, nor did the blue-coated figures on her quarterdeck. Abruptly her helm was put over, and she bore quickly away. There did not seem to have been any order given, any shouted command; the crew simply acted in unison as if by a prearranged signal, and their ship began to put a wide distance of water between herself and *Expedient*. Her lines were handsome, and she was well handled, the move swiftly and neatly managed. And on her transom—a blank.

'Mr Hayter, we will give her a gun.' The plan to wave his hat abandoned.

The gun fired, and the shot whistled harmlessly away and made a distant splash. No answering gun from the other frigate. Rennie grimaced, paced, raised his glass—and came to his decision:

'We will go about, and give chase.'

The manoeuvre rather clumsily completed, and a little time lost. Rennie growing fractious now on his quarterdeck.

'Come on, come on, *braces*!'—pointing—'What is that dangling block! Jump now, jump! Sheet that home! He is getting *away* from us!—Mr Loftus!'

'Sir?' Close at hand.

'How much can I risk? I don't want to spring my topmasts or my yards, but I must overhaul that vexing bloody bugger, and make him explain himself.'

A hurried discussion as to royals, and stunsails. James watching the frigate in his glass. An urgency now, throughout the ship, the urgency of the predator focusing upon the fleeing prey.

Easily, gracefully, inexorably, the mystery frigate slipped further ahead, and the combined efforts of Rennie, and Mr Loftus, and the crew of *Expedient*, were not enough. Rennie fretted, sighed, exhorted, threw down his hat—and stood away alone at the rail, furious and savage. But it was no good. The mystery frigate, the blank-named, mysterious, shadowing stylish stranger, heeling a little with the wind, outran them, and slipped hull down into the far distance.

'Should we resume our true course, sir, and pipe the hands to supper?' James, at last.

'What? What?'

'I beg your pardon, sir. I should not have spoke.'

The captain's simmering anger and disgruntlement—in the face of his lieutenant's polite and perfectly reasonable suggestion—flared abruptly, and as abruptly died. He knew it was not the fault of his people that *Expedient* was outclassed; she was the slower ship, and nothing to be done. The hands deserved their supper, they had done everything asked of them with a will.

'Very well, Mr Hayter. We will stand down, and resume our course, and then the hands may go to their supper.'

The calls, and tired seaman to their stations, in the tops, and at the falls, and just as *Expedient* came to her original heading—

'Deck! De-e-e-e-ck! Sail of ship, on the starboard quarter!'

'It cannot be!' Rennie, staring aft, in momentary bewilderment. 'He has outrun us, only to resume the chase as *pursuer*? It ain't possible!'

'No, sir, it ain't.' James, peering through his glass. 'That is another ship, altogether.'

The lookout: 'Three masts, and a full press! Hull up!'

'Another ship? What ship?' Rennie levelled his own glass. 'I will not be *dogged*.'

James, polite and in a reasoning tone: 'Ships are free to sail in these waters, are they not, sir? It is another ship, that is all—'

'*All*, Mr Hayter? *All*? After what has happened today?' Rennie strode to the wheel, staring aloft. 'Will that damned man aloft tell me what ship she is, for the love of Christ! Mizzen lookout, there!'

'She is—she has the look of a small frigate, sir, or a ship sloop!'

'Colours? What colours does she wear?'

'None to be seen, sir!' Anxious to please. 'No colours at all!'

All Rennie's anger and frustration boiled up again: 'God damn the bloody wretch! I will not be harried, slunk at, and fucked up the arse by every rat-infested, sly-sailing, pox-riddled pirate in Christendom! He had better make his obedience, by God! He had better have an explanation, the damned blackguard! *Stand by to go about!*'

'Surely this second ship is not to blame for the actions of the frigate, sir——' began James, in the same reasonable tone. And took the full brunt of Rennie's pent-up fury:

'Did I ask for your opinion, sir! Did I ask for your studious damned appraisal! I did *not!* *I did not!*'

Lurching as the ship heeled. Regaining his balance. 'Mr Tangible! You will start any man that does not jump! Jump, I say! Mr Loftus, you will . . . *That man, there!*' Pushing furiously past James, pointing a rigid finger. '*What is he about, wandering like a cunt-struck curate across a fucking meadow!*'

'That is Mr Dobie, sir.'

'Then he is to go below! *Go below, sir! Get your damned idler's arse off my deck!*'

Appalled, Alan Dobie scurried to the ladder, and was knocked heavily down it by a seaman hauling full weight on a fall.

Rennie gave all the commands himself, and James was obliged to stand silently at his side, apparently unneeded on the quarterdeck, as *Expedient*, yards angling, braces, sheets and tacks hauling, swooped and plunged and came round on the reverse heading. James was obliged to admit, silently and willingly admit, that Rennie handled her well. Furious as he was, intemperately furious, the captain was a fine seaman, who knew exactly what he was doing, and did it with whip-cracking precision. Soon *Expedient* was running into range of the second ship. Rennie's signals had been ignored, or if not ignored imperfectly understood. In the wind, and the sun, with signal flags snapping and blacking on the halyard against the glare, that was not in itself remarkable or unusual.

'Mr Hayter!'

'Sir?'

'We will give this bugger a gun, if y'please. We will then pass to windward, and——'

'She is heaving to, sir! And she is making a signal!'

The ship had indeed lost way, had put her topsails aback, and lay quietly riding on the swell. She was a clean-lined little ship sloop, a quarterdeck frigate in miniature, ported for sixteen guns. Weather stunsails were taking in, and her signal halyard said she wished to speak. But—

'Where is his colours, for God's sake?' grumbled Rennie. 'Like the other ship, he don't identify himself. Why not? Why not, hey? He had better be very contrite in explication, by Christ.' Raising his speaking trumpet:

'*What ship are you!*'

She was the *Larkspur*, a hired vessel, her captain Commander Boddington RN. She carried despatches, brought in her jolly-boat. There had been a serious fire aboard, and her colours, mending, had been burned, along with much of her number six canvas. It had been touch and go, Boddington told Rennie, his eyes red-rimmed, his face grimed and unshaven, and they had consequently lost nearly two days, and had not yet had the opportunity to make new colours—his sailmaker had died of burns. He was very sorry to have had to approach without proper decorum, &c., &c.

Rennie's anger had entirely disappeared. 'Had I known of your difficulty, Captain Boddington'—careful to use the courtesy rank—'I should not have come rushing at you like the hounds of hell. Are there injured aboard, other men injured, or burned? I should be happy to put my surgeon in a boat——'

'I have my own surgeon, sir, thank you. All is in hand.'

'Good, very good. Allow me to refill your glass. And now—you said there were some despatches, I believe?'

Boddington gave him a canvas-bound packet. Rennie was about to cut it open with his penknife, when something made Boddington frown, rub his face and frown.

'You will excuse me, sir, but as you are sailing incognito—'

'Am I?' A nod, a smile. 'Well, yes, in a way . . .'

'As a formality, you understand, I must just ask who you are.'

Rennie paused, penknife in hand, still smiling, but puzzled. 'Surely you know what ship this is?'

'I—I do not, sir. Not formally, until I am told. Will you oblige me by——'

'Rest easy, my dear Boddington, rest easy. You have come aboard *Expedient*, never fear, and I am Captain Rennie.'

'*Expedient!* Then I am in error! We could not see your transom, and I have made the most grievous error. I—I fear I must ask for the despatches back, if you please, sir. I am very sorry.'

Rennie was thoroughly bemused, and unhappy. However, he could do nothing but acquiesce, under the circumstances. 'By all means. Here is the packet.' An awkward pause. 'Will you tell me who they are for? If not *Expedient*, which ship do you seek?'

'I may not tell you that, sir. My orders—I may not divulge anything—I am very sorry indeed.'

'I see—I see.' Rennie was even more unhappy. 'You do not, I expect, know the contents of these despatches?'

'I do not, sir.'

'Certainly they are for another frigate, else you could not have mistook us for that ship. Hey, Boddington?'

Boddington in his turn was unhappy. He was much discomfited, felt himself foolish and at a loss. Rennie looked at him, observed him. His height made him seem even thinner than he was, and his arms were sticks. His coat was of a good cut, but had seen better days—or perhaps it had been damaged by smoke in the fire aboard his ship. He held his glass nervously, drank it off, and then held up his head.

'Well, sir, d'y'seek another frigate?' repeated Rennie. 'Which frigate? Who is her captain?'

'I regret that I am unable to say anything.' Resolutely.

'Hm. I see. Then what are your instructions, in this hired vessel? What is your commission? Surely it cannot be to carry papers, and nothing else?'

'Captain Rennie, I wish with all my heart that I was able to tell you what you wish to know, but it is not within my power. I regret—deeply regret—that I have caused you this inconvenience——'

'No, no, no.' Rennie waved his hand, relenting. 'No, Captain Boddington, none of this is your fault. You have had your tribulations aboard, and it was a quite natural mistake to take me for another frigate. You have your duty to do, and I shall not hinder you. Now—you are sure that I can give you no medical assistance? No? Will you drink another glass of wine, or stay and dine? Say that you will dine with me, I beg you.'

'Thank you, sir, but I must return to my ship, and get under way at once.'

'Very good, Captain Boddington, just as you like.' They went on deck. And Rennie pointed, mischievously pointed, and said:

'You will find her there, sir, on that heading. I should crack on, if I was you. Her captain is a very nimble fellow.'

Astonished. 'You have *seen* her?'

'Yes, certainly, I have seen her. And even if her captain and I have never been introduced, I *feel* that I know him—I *feel* that I do.' And smiling grimly he watched Boddington go down the ladder and into *Larkspur*'s boat. James stood on the quarterdeck, uncertain of his captain's temper as Rennie came aft.

'We will wear if you please, Mr Hayter,' he said, 'and resume our duty.'

'Very good, sir.—Did you learn anything from our visitor?'

'I learned nothing, excepting that the very vexatious club we both of us distrust has long arms, and the longest are those of Sir Robert Greer, the fellow. His pen wrote those despatches, and his fingers bound up the packet, I am in no doubt. Only I cannot prove it.'

'Then—the despatches was not for us, after all?'

'They was not.—Boy!—Find Mr Dobie, and ask him to see me in my cabin directly. Belay that. Ask him if he will do me the kindness of coming to the great cabin, at his convenience.'

'Mr Dobie, thank you for attending so promptly. A glass of something? Or do you prefer tea?'

'I—that is—nothing, thank you, sir.'

'Hm. Well well.—This is awkward.'

'Have I done something further to offend——' Apprehensively.

'No no, no no, not at all. As a matter in fact, Mr Dobie, I have offended you, I think.'

'Offended *me*?'

'I said things on deck of which—of which in truth I am thoroughly ashamed. You are not rated idler, you are rated clerk and schoolmaster. I am sorry that I belittled you before the watch. I hope that you will accept my apology.'

Dumbfounded, tongue-tied, at last: 'I am honoured—I have the honour—honour to accept, sir. Thank you.'

———— ⊷≣◈≣⊶ ————

'Relieved?' Rennie raised his eyebrows.

'I know it is shameful, a little, but I was—I am.' James, a shrug, a smile.

'Because we did not go into action this day?'

'Aye, certainly that—and because now, in least, we know she is an English ship, and cannot mean us any harm. I confess that I do not wish to come to harm, on this commission.'

'Well then I will admit that I am relieved myself. As you say, she can only be an English ship, and to have fired on her would have been folly, and murder. Not that he didn't give us every reason to challenge him, the fellow. Boddington, in least, had reason not to identify himself. His ship took fire, and he was unable. The other fellow—well, it don't sit easy with me, James, to be dogged by a resolute stranger on the high seas. It ain't good manners.'

'Perhaps, in truth, he was not dogging us. I wonder if you have considered that possibility, sir.'

'Eh? Of course he was dogging us, James, good God. Sir Robert Greer has sent him to do it.'

'We cannot know that for certain, surely? Is it not perfectly possible, indeed probable, that another one of His Majesty's ships, in the vastness of the sea, simply wished to keep company with us, for a day or two? Perhaps, like us, she is commissioned on foreign service, to carry out an important task for their Lordships, and for reasons unknown to us—of necessity unknown to us—she has been instructed to proceed in anonymity. Could not the despatches carried by Bodding-ton in probable be concerned only with that commission—and nothing whatever to do with us? Further, nothing at all to do with Sir Robert Greer?'

The ship creaked, and the wine in the heavy-bottomed decanter canted gently with the lift. Rennie sniffed, and grunted, glanced at his companion across the table and was disposed to disagree, and argue with him, and then did not. He pushed his glass between his hands on the table, and did not. Instead he contented himself with: 'Mm, well, you may possibly be right. I don't concede entire, you know, I do not strike my colours, but you may be right. Let us hope that you are, James.—I should have liked to frighten him a little, all the same, the impertinent rogue. I should have liked to send a ball or two singing past his head.'

James allowed his thoughts to return to a private world, a tender world. He had written a long letter to Catherine, and sent it by one of the merchant ships from Santa Cruz, the *Gertrude*, eight hundred tons, bound for London with spices and wine. He had taken the letter himself in the jollyboat. The master of the *Getrude*, Captain Denton, had asked James in the town if he might be of service, and—as James knew—

had wished to be asked to dine in *Expedient*. No such invitation had been forthcoming, and James had wondered, as he asked leave from the boat to come aboard, if he might not be frostily received. Captain Denton could not have been more amiable. He had agreed to take James's letter, and all other letters from *Expedient*. There were no others.

'No other letters, Lieutenant Hayter? Has no other officer aboard a wife?'

'We are a bachelor ship, I think.'

A bachelor ship, indeed, reflected James. No man in the gunroom was married, and so far as he knew the captain was not. Was that a melancholy thing, or a sensible thing? It was neither, he said to himself, it was merely fact. He could hope for no reply to his letter, indeed had said to Catherine that she should not endeavour to reply, as he would almost certainly never receive it, given the nature of the commission. Then he scored through the word 'almost'. In his letter he had tried to be expressive of his love for her without being flowery—of all things he wished never to be flowery. Yes, he wished to be sincere, and heartfeeling, and honest with her, and gentle, but he disliked floweriness in a man, in manly utterance it was out of place. He wrote:

Dearest Cathy, you know that I love you, and will always love you, with all my heart. I have asked you to wait for me, and now I will make the proposal that I should have made at our last meeting. Will you be my wife? My darling, nothing in the world would give me greater joy. When I am come home from this commission, I may reasonably hope for advancement.

(He knew nothing of the kind, but felt that his fervent wish justified his saying so.)

My father, upon my marriage, will give me Birch Cottage at Winterborne, a fine, pleasant little house in which we shall be very happy. In the very unlikely event of my advancement in the service being delayed, this need be no impediment at all to our union, since living simply in the country may be managed on very little income. Dearest, you are ever in my thoughts . . .

And now, as he thought of the letter, he regretted it. Not for its perhaps rather plain—though heartfelt—expression, but for its content altogether. What kind of married life could he and Cathy lead on a lieutenant's half-pay, and her small inheritance? How could they be very happy on an hundred a year? There could be no horses, absolutely no carriage, no luxuries or comforts. When children came, as they certainly would, what then? Well, he might have to resign. Resign his commission, and go into the merchant service. Heaven, what tedium, in a slow Indiaman—

'Do not you think so, James?'

'I'm sorry, sir, I was lost.'

'I said: we must proceed with our experiments and observations, with the logship, and the wind-o-meter. And we must establish a more rigorous and regular exercising of the great guns. That of all things. We must work up our gunnery, and try the new powder again. We cannot evade that responsibility.'

'In the carronades? Or the Waterfields?'

'In all of our guns. We cannot shrink from it in any more. We are not timid girls, after all. We are sea officers, and we must do our duty as instructed. Hey?'

'I think that I'd better confer more closely with Mr Storey before we use red cartridge in the Waterfields, sir. I am not so fearful about the carronades. They are after all cast as guns of immense strength, meant to pound with a heavy weight of ball. Yet even they may be at risk if the powder is inherently dangerous.'

'Eh? *Inherently* dangerous?'

'Suppose that, through some fault of manufacture—in corning, say—this new charcoal cylinder powder is unstable. That far from being more lasting and durable at sea, it is inclined to be precarious in bulk.'

'Good God. You think so?'

'I do not think so. I suggest it only as something we must consider. Good men was killed.'

'There is no need of reminding me, James.—Very well, you and Storey consult, then bring me your conclusions as to probable risk, and so forth. Please not to be very long. I must have your report as soon as you are able to make it.'

'Very good, sir.'

'However, that need not impede the observations with the wind measure. At the same time, we must bring up the new logship, and see whether or no it tells our speed better than our present logline.—I think the chronometers have been a success.'

'Undoubtedly, they have. Mr Tyndale is to be congratulated.'

'Just so. Tenerife came up exactly where it should have been, at exactly the time predicted. "Deck! Land!" exactly at the moment we was waiting for it. I never had a chronometer aboard before this. Lunar tables was the thing. Well, we still carry the book, must carry it. But what a damned inconvenient thing the lunars make, hey? Hour upon hour of slog.'

'Terrible slog.' The decanter pushed.

As they bore south towards the equator the weather grew progressively steamier, and the ship was again pumped to rid it of the smell Rennie called 'that foulsome bilge reek', and washed and smoked between. The fresh provisions dwindled, and were gone, and sauerkraut and portable soup made their unwelcome reappearance.

James deliberately delayed his report on the red powder, aware that he could not procrastinate for ever; and concentrated instead on the other observations which seemed to have become his personal responsibility, even if Mr Loftus was often at his side.

James, and Bernard Loftus, and the midshipmen, struggled to make observations with the anemometer on the forecastle. At first—when the efficacy of its installation in the top was found wanting—Rennie had had it secured on the quarter-deck. When this proved inconvenient to all concerned, not last the afterguard in pulling their weight on the falls, Rennie had had the thing removed to the forecastle. There it was no more convenient to the forecastlemen, but since Rennie did not tread the forecastle, he did not care about the impediment to the men there as they strove to step clear of 'that fucking poxy windmill' on the canting deck.

James reported to the captain that the machine was quite ingenious as an instrument of wind measurement, but would operate correctly in only the most untaxing conditions, since it required to be balanced, perfectly balanced, on a flat surface.

'The wooden sails spin faster as the wind increases, slower as it decreases, and the tackles, with the pulley blocks, haul up the weight within the central pillar, to marked levels. Thus the wind is recorded at varying strengths, on a scale of one to twenty.'

'Varying strengths, I have you, yes.' Rennie blew through pursed lips, puffing his cheeks. Was he being facetious? wondered James. Was there a note of scepticism?

'However——'

'Ah, there is always an however, in science.'

'However, the instrument cannot be relied upon to show the strength of the wind, excepting when the ship is not heeling to starboard or larboard, but is more and less on an even keel.'

'Which it ain't, very often.' Nodding.

'Which it ain't, very often.'

'Then the machine is no good to us. Strike it, and send it below.'

'Very good, sir.'

'At least, we'll stow it for the moment. We will very probably make use of it again, make further observations and so forth, when we make landfall in the Pacifick. It may be of use to their Lordships to know the wind velocities on this or that remote island.'

'Perhaps, if there was a counterbalancing device, it might be made to work——'

'It is plain that Mr Baragwanath never went to sea in his life. I am only sorry now that he talked me into taking the thing into my ship. Good heaven, the more I think of it, the sillier it is. When I want to know what the wind does, what strength it blows, I turn my face to it. Then I look aloft, and see what spread of canvas I may deploy, and feel under my legs how the ship lies. A scale of wind? Christ's blood, James. What gullible halfwit boys they take us for.'

The anemometer was removed from the forecastle, and never brought again on deck.

⚡

The gunroom having elevated Mr Wing, whom they now called 'Doctor'—whom the whole ship now called 'Doctor'—it was proposed that Mr Dobie should be asked to join them also.

'After all, we have plenty of decent wine, since Tenerife. Why should he not share it with us?'

'Perhaps he don't drink wine, Tom, like the doctor.'

'I never thought of that. But he is a pleasant fellow, don't you think so? It is a pity he must eat with the mids, when he is their schoolmaster.'

'Why? Does he rate higher than a mid?' Royce, sourly.

'I thought he was your friend, Royce. Shall we put it to the vote?'

The proposal was adopted, against the single negative voice of the third lieutenant—who apparently did not rank his friend his social equal—and Mr Dobie joined the gun-room mess.

On the morning after his welcoming dinner, Mr Dobie was required by the captain to attend the first trial of the new logship, in order to write down all the figures, and such comments as might be made in passing. The trial was a disaster.

The new device was known as Mr Hetton Barkworth's Patented Perpetual Log, and was a large wooden cylinder, with an internal brass rotator, and indicating mechanical dials. The aim of the trial was to test the device for one hour behind the ship, then four hours—the length of one watch—then twenty-four hours. It was to trail on a line astern at a distance sufficient for it not to be disturbed by the ship's wake. Rennie thought privately—he did not say it on the quarterdeck—that the traditional wooden logship, operating with its spindle and knotted line, and an accurate half-minute glass, with observations made each half-hour, was as good a means as any of telling the speed of the ship, and calculating the distance travelled between one noonday and the next.

The perpetual log was lowered into the sea from a boat towed astern, and the group of observers at the rail, including the captain, the first lieutenant, the master, the schoolmaster, and the two midshipmen of the watch, observed the line pull taut, then slacken, then pull taut again in a repetitive rhythm.

'It don't look right to me,' said Rennie.

'Should we continue with the usual knotted line, each glass, sir?'

'Yes, yes certainly. That, in the least, is reliable.'

At one hour the perpetual log was hauled into the boat, and found to be hopelessly jammed. Seaweed had slipped inside the cylinder and caught in the rotator, and the indicating dials had become fixed together and bent out of shape. Running repairs were effected, and the device again lowered with care from the boat. Ten minutes later the line gave a jerk, tautened in a snap of spray, and slackened. When the line was hauled inboard the wooden cylinder had vanished.

'Captain Rennie announced to all within earshot: "The d****d thing has betrayed us. What a f*****g miracle it will be, in this scientifical ship, if we do not lose or destroy each one of our b****y experimental machines, like scatter-brained f*****g hens, for G*d's sake,"' wrote Dobie in his notebook. 'Mr Barkworth's machine is evidently and irre-trievably lost, alas. The Captain was most particularly vexed, & rounded upon Mr Rogers and Mr Pankridge very severe, when the loss could not in fairness be ascribed to them, nor to anyone.' He scored through this last, and waited with his pen.

'What have you wrote, Mr Dobie?'

'I—I have wrote the bare facts, sir.'

'Aye, well, they are naked facts, stark naked and a damned disgrace to the ship. Mr Loftus.'

'Sir?'

'Is there another one of the cylinders, or was that the sole example?'

'I fear it was the sole example, sir.'

'Enter it in the log, if you please, Mr Loftus. Hell and damnation!'

The master did not dare ask if he should record this curse, and they all went to their dinner looking suitably glum.

'I have wrote a letter about it to the Admiralty,' Rennie said later to James. 'Like all the letters on this commission it must wait until we return before I may send it. I sent no letters from Santa Cruz, as you know. My instructions are clear, and that was the reason I forbade all private letters from being despatched, either by officers, or the lower deck.'

'Then—then I am at fault, I fear. I did send a letter, and I——'

'No no, James, I was quite at ease in the matter of your own letter. It was one of a particularly intimate nature, I think. To a young lady, no?'

'It was. And I thank you for permitting me to ignore the injunction.'

'Well well, there was nothing in it that could be interpreted as official information—hey?'

'No, indeed. It was all—all of a personal and private nature.'

'Just so. In which case, should it fall into the wrong hands, it is a love letter, of no possible interest excepting to yourself, and the young lady.'

'The wrong hands?'

'Should your merchant ship—the *Gertrude*?—should the *Gertrude* be intercepted, you know.'

'Intercepted, sir. By whom?'

'A ship, let us say, like that frigate. You look surprised. I have not forgot that damned frigate, not at all. And almost certainly, I think, she has not forgot us, neither.'

'You think she will reappear?'

'I do.'

'Then—forgive me—how could the frigate intercept the *Gertrude*, that is going to England, and follow us at the same time?'

'The other ship, then. Captain Boddington, in *Larkspur*. You are doubtful. You are doubtful. No matter. Listen, you may have noticed that my enthusiasm for science has waned a little?'

'In view of what has happened with the instruments——'

'No no, never think I would shirk a difficult exercise, a difficult test. I do not mean that at all. No, my argument is this:' leaning forward, 'suppose their Lordships devised a plan to make fools of us, at sea?'

'Make—fools of us, sir?'

'I haven't gone mad, James, never fear. Suppose they had devised a scheme of the most burdensome science, the most complicated investigation and exercise—much of it certain to go wrong—and gave us new guns, not fully proved, with a new and perhaps unconfident gunpowder. Hey? To *test us*, James.'

'Ah—mm—test us?'

Impatiently: 'To observe our response. To see how we might cope, on a long commission. I am more than ever convinced of it, the longer I think on it. To test our *zeal*. That was their real purpose. That is why they have sent that frigate, and Boddington, too. It is all the one plan, James!'

James said nothing for a few moments, and pretended to busy himself with a biscuit, and his glass, and brushing something off the sleeve of his coat, &c., but Rennie was by no means taken in. He saw that James in fact thought his conclusion absurd, quite wildly absurd, and was attempting—without evident success—to find the way to say so without offence.

At last Rennie said: 'Well well, I see that I have not convinced you, James. Perhaps I made too fanciful an assumption about their Lordships' intentions, after all.'

'Well, sir, I confess—your understanding of their plan did seem to me——'

'Come come, James. You are a sea officer. Speak plain.'

'Very well, sir. I was not of the same view.'

'Ha-ha—ha-ha-ha—very diplomatic in you, James, very judicious. You do think I am mad, in short. Stark mad.'

'I thought—for a moment I thought—that it was I who had taken leave of——'

'Ha-ha-ha—oh dear—I have not laughed aloud since God knows how long—ha-ha-ha—I have took myself too serious by half, all the commission. And now it is time to see things clearly, get my thoughts rove up, and plot my course.'

'I am glad, sir.'

'We have had, as may be, more than our share of bad luck. We must not, however, grow despondent, nor sink into lunacy. The ship is sound, and weatherly, we are well provisioned, and we have lost very little time. We are not only a scientifical ship, we are principally a ship of exploration. All, nearly all, of our work lies ahead of us. Our task is to aid their Lordships, and His Majesty's fleets, as instructed, by discovering places of refuge in the Pacifick Ocean.'

'I am happy to raise my glass to that, sir.'

'Just so.—But I have not forgot that frigate, James.'

* * *

South and south, in greater and greater heat. The glass turned, and noon declared, the observations making their latitude:

'Mr Symington?'

'Four degrees and 29 minutes north, sir.'

And according to their chronometers, the longitude was 22 degrees 15 minutes west. Although, under the regulations, the ship's officers were still obliged to calculate longitude by lunar distance, Rennie was relying with increasing confidence on the chronometers.

'Very good. I will make the service short today, since the sun is hot. Mr Hayter, when we are finished here I will inspect by divisions and inspect the ship as quick as may be practicable. Nobody wishes to stand long in the sun before his dinner.'

He read from the Book of Common Prayer. Afterward, he read the Articles of War. The assembled men stood still, but they were sweating, and they were not attentive excepting in the careful blankness of their faces.

'Why in God's name we persist in this damned rambling nonsense I cannot comprehend,' said James, but not aloud.

At dinner in the gunroom, the marine officer Lieutenant Raker—a lean, dark, severe-looking officer with a half-hidden and half-wicked sense of humour—said something to James:

'You looked black as thunder at prayers, Hayter. Is it toothache?'

'Eh? Did I?'

'Savage, altogether. Or is it costiveness?'

'It is neither toothache, nor arse ache, thankee.'

'What then? Some other nether ache, hey? Or shouldn't a fellow ask?'

'Ask away, by all means. I was reflecting on the Articles, you know.'

'What, they ain't severe enough, you reckon?'

'Good heaven, no. They are so absurdly severe that they are pretty well nonsense.'

'Too severe? Ah.—Though to say so is treason, pretty well, hm?'

'Pish posh. Read the Articles through, some time. They are fierce, and terrible, and ridiculously equivocal. Most captains know what to do about punishment, without once referring to them. Watch the faces of the people, as they are read. They do not listen to a single word. The quarterdeck don't listen, neither. The whole thirty-six Articles is more or less dish-water, and humbug.'

'You will be hanged, you know, Hayter.'

'Then I had better fortify myself with wine. Will you join me, Raker?'

'Gladly. May your death be quick, and your soul purged of heresy. Amen.'

Exercising of the great guns was now a daily routine, but no gun had been fired using the new charcoal cylinder powder since the accident with the grooved gun. James had deliberately delayed his report to the captain.

'I don't know how we may conduct any more suitable tests of the powder, without we test it in the guns,' said Mr Storey. 'In our little tests on the forecastle we have confirmed that the powder burns rapid and consistent, an even flash over the iron plate we laid out. Yes? I don't know what else to suggest, I do not.'

A man in the sickbay—one of the injured guncrew, now recovering from burns, and a leg wound—asked to see the first lieutenant.

'Yes, Norris? You wished to see me? How do you get on?'

'I am coming along fair, thankee, sir. I will never get no admiring eye from the girls no more, but I will live.'

'Looks is not all, hey? A man is more than his looks.—
Well?'

'I think we loaded two cartridge, sir.'

'What?'

'The cartridge box was dropped, sir, in the rush, and a man
fell. It was thought—I fear it was—that we had not loaded
yet, since we had not rammed. So a second cartridge was
loaded.'

'Are you sure? You are certain?'

'No, sir. I am not. I was tackles, and I cannot be certain.
There was smoke, and hurry up from the other captains, and
water had spilled. Howsomever, there is a picture in my head
of a second cartridge, when the box was lifted up. I see it
being loaded, and rammed. Then—then I don't remember
nothing after.'

'Good, very good. Well done. Lie back now, Norris, will
you?—Doctor.'

'I am here.'

'Doctor, will you mop his forehead a little. It is damned hot
here.' And aside: 'Is there nothing can be done about his face?
The poor fellow fears he will never bed another girl.'

'That is the last thing with which he should concern
himself at present.' Standing a little away with James. 'He is
lucky still to breathe, and——'

'Seamen like to breathe, Doctor, but they also like to cut a
dash with the ladies. Please to see if something cannot be
done for his scars. Will you?' Turning to leave.

'Very well.—Lieutenant, before you go aloft——'

'On deck. Yes? What is it?'

'I was thinking of breathing, in a wider sense. You know
that wind machine?'

'The anemometer?' Glancing at the ladder, impatiently
attending.

'The same. If it is no longer required, I should like to rig it
here, in the sick bay. I should also like to ask Mr Adgett to cut
a small port in the side of the ship, here.' Pointing. 'This

would allow the air to come in. I should then be able to push the air, by means of the windmill, over the faces of the sick men, and so relieve them.'

'Cut a new port?' Doubtfully. 'I should have to ask the captain, and I do not think——'

'If you will like to leave the captain to me, I will undertake to persuade him. All I ask from you, sir, is your kindness in allowing me to have the machine.'

'I have no objection, none. But again, you know, the captain must be asked, not to say Mr Loftus, who has charge of the instruments aboard.' Stepping away.

'I wished only to establish the correct protocol—is that the word?—for going about it.'

'I will do what I can for you, Doctor.—Norris, thank you for your honesty. You have helped me very greatly. I wish you speedy recovery.'

And James went straight to see the captain with his good news.

'Well well, I have heard of double shotting, but double cartridge, that is altogether new. You had this from Norris? He is in your division?'

'No, sir, Tom Makepeace's division.'

'I wonder why he said nothing before this, to Mr Makepeace, or any officer——'

'He was gravely injured. He still cannot walk unaided. His head took a frightful burn, and most of his hair was scorched off.'

'Then it may be that he has dreamed the whole thing, in his delirium. Yes, I remember Norris, now. He never responded to any question when I saw the sick men. He lay mute.'

'If you will like to speak to him yourself, sir, I'm certain he will say——'

'No no, James, I don't doubt what he says is sincere. But double cartridge, you know, is a damn near impossible mistake.'

'It would explain the explosion—absolutely explain it.'

'What does Storey say?'

'I have not yet told him.'

'Eh?'

'I thought it my duty to report it to you, sir, at once.'

'Very good, but I will like to hear what my gunner says, before we make any decision. Boy!' And as they waited: 'God in heaven it is hot. We will lie becalmed soon, I fear. I don't like these equatorial latitudes, James. We lose time, and everything in the ship sinks into laxity and exhaustion, and— Ah, Mr Storey.'

When he had heard the account, the gunner said: 'That is the answer, thank God, thank God. I beg your pardon, sir. It don't seem quite right to thank the Almighty for a terrible circumstance, but at last we know what happened, and that is a mercy to us all. I need no longer fear for my guns, nor my powder.'

'Our guns, Mr Storey.' Gently. 'And our powder, you know. We are all Expedients.'

The full firing exercises began again, this time with a target, and charcoal cylinder powder. A square of number six canvas, painted with a black roundel, was stretched on a frame and mounted on a makeshift raft, and allowed to drift astern to a distance of four hundred yards from the ship. The ship then came about to bring the guns to bear. At first no ball hit the sail. Shot splashed round and beyond the raft in erupting spume. Powder smoke floated just above the surface of the sea, reflected in the glassy water. Rennie allowed the target to drift a further two hundred yards from the ship.

'Surely not further, sir——' Mr Loftus, conning the ship.

'Eh?'

'Well, if we cannot hit the target at a quarter of a mile——'

'Let us see what our new powder can do. It is supposed to make the guns more accurate over a greater distance than standard issue coarse grain. I want to know the truth of that, or the contrary.'

'Point your guns!—*Fire!*'

The thudding, rippling concussion of a broadside of guns, the whistling rush of ball-shot flying across the sea at a thousand feet per second, and six hundred yards out the target disappeared in a fountain of spray. Smoke boiled, silently drifting. When the spray had settled there was nothing left of the sail or raft but floating tatters.

'Hah!' Rennie, his glass focused. 'Well well!' The glass lowered. 'I begin to see what Waterfield has given us in these guns, and what his new powder may do. Excellent. Excellent. Mr Adgett!—Where the devil has he got to?—I want another raft, quick, with a sail mounted and painted. We will send it out to half a mile. And this time—Mr Rogers, find the gunner and ask him to come and see me directly—this time I think we may include the grooved guns.'

'With cone-shot, sir?' Storey panted a few minutes later, having climbed to the quarterdeck from the magazine.

'Naturally, with cone. How else may they be fired, except with cone?'

The raft rapidly constructed, the painted canvas rigged, the whole set adrift as the ship at first wore away, then came about to bring the larboard guns to bear.

'Point your guns!—*FIRE!*'

Again the rippling concussion and the shuddering deck, the whistling shot and boiling smoke. And again the target disappeared in spray, and lay as flotsam when the spray fell. Running feet. The face of Mr Royce, the blackened face.

'Number one larboard gun has burst, sir!'

'Good God.—Good God.—What injuries?'

'The cascable and reinforces have held, sir. The shot jammed in the muzzle. Only Hamble is hurt a little, when the truck went over his foot. The metal has bulged, but not shattered, and powder vented in the cracks. We are all intact, sir—only very black.'

'Very good, Mr Royce, thank you. Return to your section.—*Cease firing! Cease firing!*—Mr Hayter!'

James came running to the quarterdeck from the aft starboard gun section, where he had been observing. He knew that all was not well from the urgency in the captain's voice. The wind had died down to no more than ripples of air, and the ship had all but lost steerage way, her sails hanging limp. Powder smoke hung like patches of mist across the silent sea. In the ship, continued activity. Rennie endeavoured to display no more than bustling authority, and a calm face, but his heart was not calm.

'Boatswain!—Mr Tangible, when the guns are secured, we will stand by to hoist out the boats, and the attempt will be made to bring the ship to a breeze.—Ah, there you are, Storey.' Taking him aside. 'From this moment we will not load any more red cartridge.'

'No more red, sir? May I ask——'

'Another gun has burst, Mr Storey. Another grooved gun. We must not load any more of this confounded dangerous cylinder powder, d'y'have me? Seal off all red marked casks, and we will then remove the remaining grooved guns into the hold.—James, come with me now, will you?'

Mr Storey was left standing aghast, as Rennie went away with James to the burst gun.

'Should we not have asked Storey to go with us?' As they went.

'He may see the gun directly. His work is immediately to secure those damned red casks. What in Christ's name was Waterfield and that other fellow thinking when they concocted this devil's dust, hey?'

'Dearman, you mean, sir?'

Angled light pierced the smoke of the gun deck, the hanging smoke, and the blackened figures of the stricken number one gun's crew made some attempt to stand up when the captain approached. He looked anxiously at them, and saw that they were not smashed, or broken, or bleeding, only dazed. He said a reassuring word, then transferred his attention quickly to the gun. As Royce had said the metal had not completely burst.

The cascable was intact, but the first and second ringed reinforces and the chase had bulged and cracked. Jammed in the muzzle was the coned shot, the cone itself protruding with a dull gleam. There was some minor damage to the carriage, but no damage to the port cill, or the decking. The breeching rope and the tackles were singed, but otherwise intact. All round the gun—on the decking, deckhead, side timbers—was the black reeking soot of vented powder.

'Where is Mr Royce?'

'He has gone with Hamble to the surgeon——He is here, sir.'

'Mr Royce, with Mr Storey's help when he comes to you, you will arrange for the striking of this gun, and the other grooved guns, into the hold. Choose able men to assist you, and carry out your task with despatch, if you please. Before dusk, Mr Royce. Then you will report to me.'

'Very good, sir.'

'Mr Hayter, a word with you.' Taking his arm and walking aside with his first lieutenant. 'Please to make detailed observations as you did with the other burst gun, James, and write out all you discover. I am now very anxious about our guns—all of our guns. I don't want it known in the ship, however. We must show a cheerful face the next day or two, and make light of this second burst. I don't want the men to be disheartened, nor to be fearful at quarters of their guns if that frigate should return, and we are obliged to defend ourselves.'

'Very good, sir. I shall begin at once.'

'The grooved guns will never again be fired in my ship, and I hope to God never in any other ships in His Majesty's service. Rifled guns in ships, and coned shot? Christ in tears! They belong at the bottom of the sea, with that damned infernal cylinder powder. I would send them there, too, except we are duty bound to tell their Lordships all about them, when we return to England.—If we ever do return.' Grimly.

*

Later, much later, James took his written observations to the great cabin, and gave them to Rennie, who sat at his table in his shirt, writing his journal. Before the captain began reading:

'May I say something, sir?'

'Well?'

'None of the other guns—the smooth bored guns—none has burst, or shown any sign of injury, even with full allowance of red. We achieved remarkable accuracy with ball-shot and red.'

'You are going to suggest to me that we should continue to use it, hey? That devil's dust?'

'Well, sir——'

'The question don't arise. I have forbidden its use in my ship.'

'Very well, sir.—I merely wished to say that I had included a line in my account——'

'Good God, don't I make myself plain? I have forbidden its use!'

James was silent, his hat under his arm, very correct. Rennie read half a page, and sniffed. He rubbed his nose. He took a long draught of tea, and turned the page. He did not ask his lieutenant to sit down. James felt this slight, but he gave no sign that he felt it. He waited, and presently Rennie looked up.

'Well well, James, I bit off your head. You had better sit down, and drink some tea. Or wine, you prefer wine?'

'Thank you, sir. I must take my watch.' As he spoke eight bells sounded.

'Mr Royce may keep the deck a little while, we will send word you are detained. Sit sit, you need not be formal and stiff and so forth, it is too damned hot.'

James felt himself obliged to do as he was told, and he sat down. Rennie himself opened a bottle of wine, his steward having been sent to bed. He sent a message to Royce by the marine sentry. There was not a breath of wind, and the ship rode the nearly imperceptible swell with scarcely a murmur of her timbers. The sounds of the watch changing over diminished, and Rennie spoke quietly in the close quiet air of the cabin, with the slap of the sea under the counter, floating in at an opened gallery window, making his hushed voice almost conspiratorial as he leaned forward over the table.

'You write that the smooth bored guns are sound, and have not in any way been punished by the cylinder powder. It is only the grooved guns that was, you say.—You did not know it, but I talked to Storey again while you was writing this, after he had stowed the grooved guns in the hold. He gave me this intelligence: all of the guns—all, mark—are disposed to jump and quiver, after the first shot. Upon the second, and subsequent shots, they overheat, and are very hard on the breeching ropes. He thinks—Storey thinks—that the Waterfield pattern is too light. It is a powerful and accurate gun, but he fears that with repeated firing more guns will crack or burst, even loaded with standard grain. He has had his doubts about the pattern for some time, but did not like to condemn it too hasty, since Waterfield got him his warrant. Today, after what happened, he felt he must speak.—Our guns, in little, are a failure.'

'Then—then, how are we to——'

'Defend ourselves? Should we need to? We must rely on the carronades. Which we will load with standard cartridge, and grape.'

'Grape, sir? In carronades?'

'Indeed. You wish me to explain? Should we need to defend ourselves, I mean to rake my opponent's deck with grape, and kill as many men as I can. We carry swivels, not yet mounted, do we not?'

'About a dozen, I believe, sir. One-pound guns.'

'We will mount them. On the forecastle, and on the quarterdeck. They will be loaded with canister. Our only chance, should we be obliged to engage, is to kill men.—I don't like it. Killing men is a horrible business, unless you must do it boarding and it is hand to hand, yourself or the other fellow. However, we have no choice. As things are, with our broadsides lost to us, we must kill men.'

'I think the circumstances will not arise, sir. I think it very unlikely.'

'We are a man-of-war, James, don't forget that. Anything may happen at sea.'

'We must be prepared, I agree.—The people must be prepared.'

'We will muster the ship's company tomorrow. I will address them.'

'Very good, sir.—It was unfortunate for Royce, when he had changed sections with Makepeace after the first gun burst, that he should have had to see the second gun fail at close hand.'

'What makes you say that?'

'It was just in passing, sir. I thought he conducted himself very well today.'

'He is an officer in His Majesty's service. It is his duty to conduct himself well. I'm glad he has seen two guns burst. It will harden him, and show him what his trade is.'

'Trade?'

'His trade, James, and yours and mine. Our trade is to kill men, and take, sink, burn and destroy their ships—if needs must.'

'When we are at war.—We are not at war.'

'I hate it, to say the truth. Never think I will shirk my duty—but I hate to see men die.' He sighed, and sat back in his chair. 'Sometimes I think—I think that instead of lying on the beach all the time, all those years, I should have been infinitely better off to have resigned. Resigned, and become a merchant officer in the service of the Company.'

'So might I have resigned, but with respect, sir—we are neither of us made for Indiamen.'

'Why not, though? It is a perfectly respectable thing to command a merchant ship, and make money, and buy a house with a park, and take a wife, and give her a carriage, and raise a family. What is wrong with that, hey?'

James laughed. 'Nothing, nothing—for dull men. We are not dull men, I hope.'

Rennie sniffed in a great breath, and sighed. He stood up, and slapped his hands down on the table.

'You are right, you are right, we must not be dull. Forgive my rambling talk, it's too hot for such bloody nonsense, and there is much to do tomorrow. I must talk to the men, and hearten them. Then we must send out the boats again, and pray for wind. Good night, James. Thank you for your patience.'

'Good night, sir.'

⊷ ⧓ ⊶

Days of back-straining, arm-straining, exhausting work for the successive watches in the boats, rowing and towing the limp-sailed, sluggish ship. Astern a spreading greasy wake of galley slops, faeces, and deck detritus washed from the scuppers. The ship south of the equator now. Brief days of wind—a light, wafting breeze—had given them enough southing, with stunsails set high and low, to cross.

The crossing ceremony behind them. Mr Wing and Mr Dobie had been excused the ritual humiliations. Mr Royce had not:

'Look here, this is damned unfair.' Royce, in protest. 'Why am I to be singled out?'

'The doctor has his duty, and cannot be spared.'

'That is nonsense, bloody nonsense.' Growing vehement, and red in the face. 'I have my own duties, have I not? Why am I to be unspared? Hm? Why is Dobie spared? Leave aside Wing, forget Wing. Why d'y'mean to except Dobie, hey?'

'He is too frail, Royce, you know. He has been frail the whole commission.'

'Fucking hell! So I am to be the only gunroom sacrifice! I object! I protest and object! Fucking hell!'

'There is no use in cursing, you know, Royce. It sets a bad example to the mids. The thing is to submit, d'y'see? Submit in good part. Ain't it, Tom?'

'Oh, yes. Certainly. Submit, like a good fellow.'

'Hell and damnation to you all!'

And so Mr Royce had been subjected to the absurdities of the ceremony, perhaps practised upon him with more vigour than would otherwise have been applied had he not made himself foolish in protest beforehand. They coated him in slush, and applied feathers from the bird coops to the slush, and made him wear fantastical costumes of painted canvas, and then he was plunged in the canvas bath rigged in the waist, and had his skull shaved close. He was not alone. The mids were subjected to the same ritual, which was conducted by men in disguise, Neptune and his court, selected from the ship's complement in a curious relaxation of all the usual rules of position and discipline. Neptune had licence. He was a god.

'It is damned unfair,' Royce muttered afterward, in the gunroom. He ran his hand over his smooth head. 'It is damned unfair.'

'Shut up, Royce, will you, like a good fellow? The mids had the same treatment, and the other boys, and not one of them complained.'

'Yes, *boys*. It is very well to degrade and discomfit *boys*. I am not a boy, however. I am a man, and an officer.'

'Lord Neptune don't regard office, you know. He is quite undiscriminating.'

'Oh, what is the use in talking to any of you! I will challenge you, instead!—Well! Well! Is there no man among you that will accept!' Standing, quivering.

Several pairs of eyes turned on him, and regarded him with derision. He saw their contempt, and became rash:

'You are all cowards! Cowards and poltroons! Pffff! You are beneath notice!'

The heat, the windless, unrelenting, close, sweating, night-and-day, wearing heat, had its effect in the ship. The mildest and most reasonable of men, accidentally bumped as he swung from his hammock, or put down the kid on the mess table, or moved along the narrow gangway, might suddenly flare and snarl, as if the sun itself was in his head, and burned to get out. More hands were brought to book for punishment, and Rennie stopped grog, withdrew privileges, and grew vexed at the increasing list of misdemeanours. Not long after his outburst in the gunroom, his ignored outburst, the still embittered Royce made an error of omission in recording his observations of the watch, and failed—this was more serious—failed to bring the ship to a passing breeze, which might have given her steerage way, might have relieved the stagnancy of their progress. Rennie was angry, very angry, and he sent for Royce, kept him waiting, then demanded to know why Royce had not come at once.

'Sir, I have stood at your door nearly a whole glass——'

'Do not presume to excuse yourself, when you have been unpunctual.'

'Sir, I have *not* been unpunctual——'

'Be quiet. You failed to bring the ship to the wind, Mr Royce. A thing so fundamental, so rudimentary, I am left speechless. What am I to do, when the officer of the deck don't know what the wind is for?'

'Sir, that is most un——'

'Be quiet, sir! The truth is, you don't know a halyard from a backstay. You are less accomplished than the most wooden-headed midshipman in the service.'

'Sir, allow me to say that I do not need *lessons*. I am not a midshipman, nor am I a schoolboy.'

'No, and you are not at your leisure, neither. Make your back straight, sir!'

'Sir, I will be heard. I demand to be *heard.*'

'*Demand? Demand? You damned impertinent dolt! You may demand nothing!*'

Royce fell silent, flushed and trembling, near to weeping with rage and humiliation. Rennie saw his distress, was at first inclined to be even more severe—then something eased within him, and he saw a frightened, proud, inadequate and desperate young man, who could not help himself, and must be helped by an older and wiser man.

'Mr Royce,' he said quietly, almost gently, 'I have no wish to add to your distress. But it is a fact that you allow others to know how the ship is worked, while you can do nothing but pretend. I have no idea how you came by your commission, but it was not by merit. No, do not interrupt, if you please. I cannot have an officer in my ship that does not know his duty, does not know it in the humblest distinction. At Santa Cruz, had it not been for the timely intervention of the first lieutenant, we should have foundered, by your hand. Earlier, we lost an azimuth compass, which was damaged by your clumsiness—no, no, do not deny what is fact, Mr Royce, I know everything in my ship, and you had the deck when that damage was done. And now—now we have lost what might have been a relieving breeze, a saving wind. These are faults I cannot ignore.'

'You are very hard, sir, when I have done my best——'

'Hard? How may I put these things to you soft, Mr Royce? Hey?'

'I am at fault—I know it. I am less in sum than the others.— I am despised.' Wretchedly.

'Listen to me, Mr Royce. You are not despised. You are found wanting. You will, therefore, put yourself at the disposal of Mr Loftus. You will attend upon his every word, and every action. When he keeps the deck, you will keep the deck. Perhaps in a month you will contrive to know at least something of your duty as a sea officer.'

'Am I to take the watch, sir, in my turn?'

'Mr Symington will take your watches. I do not mean this as an humiliation to you, Mr Royce. I shall speak to Mr Loftus, and ask him to instruct you as discreetly as may be possible. The only thing that is of consequence to me, when all is added together, is the safe and efficient working of my ship. In one month, we will re-examine your position.'

'Sir, I——'

'There is nothing more to say.' Holding up a hand. 'One month, Mr Royce.' A nod of dismissal.

When Royce had gone Rennie found that his heart was quite emptied of dislike for his third lieutenant. He could not allow that he would ever warm to Royce, but it was a great relief that he was no longer burdened by the weight of hostility. His peace of mind did not last.

The day following, when the captain's admonitions should have been fresh in his head, Royce again brought himself to unfavourable notice.

A commotion on the larboard gangway, a brief whirling of arms, something fell, there were shouts, and a knot of men gathered in the waist, became a swarm—then Mr Symington came hurrying aft.

'What is it, Mr Symington?' James saw his serious face, and put down his notations by the binnacle compass.

'Mr Royce has—he has been struck, sir.'

'Struck! By whom?'

'If you please, sir—by one of the hands.'

James took his arm, and drew him briefly aside. Urgently: 'Now then. Did you see what happened, Mr Symington?' A glance forrard.

'I did not, sir. I was just come on deck. I neither saw him struck nor what went before, though Mr Royce says he was sneered at, then hit. The boatswain's mate has seized the man.'

'Where is Mr Royce, now? Is he hurt?'

'He has gone below with the doctor, sir. His face—his nose—was very bloody.'

'Very well. You will come with me to the captain. Mr Loftus!'

'Sir?'

'Take the conn, if you please.'

They went below.

When the senior midshipman had given his account, Rennie dismissed him, and required James to bring him a full report within one glass.

James returned as asked within thirty minutes, gave his report, and Rennie sighed, bumped the table-top gently with his clenched fists, once, twice, and sighed again.

'Why did not I put him on the beach at Santa Cruz? He cannot turn about, he cannot take breath, he cannot say a single word, without he bungles it. I have tried to be fair to him, but by God it is hard work. I am in no doubt he provoked this assault, James.'

'No one of the hands saw anything, as I've said, sir——'

'James, James, of course they did not, because they do not wish to see their shipmate hanged.'

'Hanged!'

'Indeed, hanged. To strike an officer is a capital offence, as you know very well.'

'But, surely, if no one saw Royce struck, then it is his word against'—glancing at his notes—'against Isaac Temple's.'

'Temple is under arrest? He is held?'

'Lieutenant Raker has him under marine guard.'

'Mr Royce has been knocked down, and bloodied, has he not? On the gangway?'

'That is so, sir.'

'He has told you that it was Temple?'

'He has, sir.'

'Christ's blood then, James, do not be obtuse. He is guilty. Under Article Twenty-Two he shall suffer death.' He pushed back his chair, and walked to the stern gallery window, his hands behind his back. 'It does not signify that Royce provoked him, don't y'see?' Turning. 'For all his many faults, Mr

Royce is a commissioned officer in His Majesty's service. He has been struck, unlawfully struck, by—how is Temple rated?'

'Ordinary seaman.'

'By an ordinary seaman. I have no choice, James.'

'But—how are we to convene a court martial in these waters, sir?'

'Eh?—Well well, it ain't possible, not a court martial, in whole.'

'Nor even in part, sir, surely?'

'No no, very well, very well. There can be no court martial, when there is no other post captains within a thousand mile. I expect I could try him myself.'

'For a capital offence, sir?'

'Damnation, James. Is it your purpose to obstruct me? I cannot allow a seaman to strike his superior and go unpunished in the ship! It *is* a hanging offence!'

'There is other punishments that may be considered, under the circumstances——'

'What? What?' Pacing, pausing, turning. 'You mean—simply have him flogged?'

'If you decide to convene a captain's hearing, sir, and Royce gave evidence against him, then Temple could be flogged at once, and the matter got out of the way.'

A sniff, a conceding sniff, then: 'Well well, perhaps we need not hang him, after all.'

'Hands to witness punishment!'

The marines formed up, the drummer's sticks poised. Officers in full dress attending, and the ship's complement assembled. Silence as the grating was stood up by the ladder, and Isaac Temple, stripped to the waist, was lashed up spreadeagled upon it, hands at the top corners, feet at the lower. The boatswain's mate who had arrested Temple— John Bedford—removed the cat from its bag, a bag tied up the whole commission until now. He gripped the thick rope handle, canvas-bound, to which were knotted three lesser lines, and three slim loglines to each of these, with their tight, careful knots. He swung it once or twice, stood at the right angle, and the right distance, and waited, waited as the drumroll rattled implacably across the deck.

'Three dozen lashes—commence!'

The sound of the nine tails, under the rattling of the drum, was not more than a whispering swish, and the effect of those knotted tails was not at first very marked on the flesh of his back. Then as each stroke was followed by the next, each wrapping, whispering stroke, another sound could be heard. A low, awful exhalation, from out of the depth and bottom of breath, a repeated, gusting groan.

'Is that the man?' Alan Dobie, horrified.

'Hush!' Lieutenant Makepeace.

'One dozen, sir!'

'Continue punishment!'

The drumroll, and the delicate thrash of the tails, and now the glistening traces of them were all across Temple's shoulders and spine. Blood welled from these smearing cuts, and dripped on the deck. The knots of the tails were red, the three upper strands, the handle itself. And the groaning sighs were clearer now, anguished, desperate, deep.

'Oh, God,' whispered Dobie, tears starting in his eyes. 'Oh, the poor man.' He turned away.

'We must all witness punishment,' murmured Makepeace, beside him. 'We may not turn our backs. Bear up, now. It will soon be done.'

'Two dozen, sir!'

'Continue!'

'Oh, I cannot see it——' Alan Dobie shut his eyes, felt the tears sliding on his cheeks, was ashamed of them, and ashamed of himself, ashamed of *Expedient* and her captain and everything the navy stood for—barbarous, brutal, cruel.

'Three dozen, sir!'

'Very well! Cut him down!'

Afterward, in the gunroom: 'No thank you, I am not hungry.'

'Come now, Dobie, you must not allow a simple flogging to upset your appetite.' Makepeace.

'After all, you know, it's far better that a man should be flogged for his offence at once, then it is all over and done.' James filled Dobie's glass. 'Drink some wine, it will make you feel better.'

'It would choke me.' He pushed the glass away.

'Ah, Royce, you are back among us! Your nose heals? You can breathe through it?'

'I am—I am quite well, thank you.' Royce sat down, touching at his swollen nose, and blackened eye. But Alan Dobie could not meet that eye, nor could he bring himself to eat or drink. He sat silent, enduring the meal as a matter of good manners, unable to understand the callous forgetfulness of those around him, who might never have been present at the wretched scene on deck, who clearly regarded such things with equanimity and easiness of mind. Dobie knew, as he believed they all knew, that Royce himself was to blame for what had happened, that he had provoked the assault by his intemperate, prickling arrogance—and that made Alan Dobie even more ashamed.

＊—━◆━—＊

At 23 degrees 10 minutes west, and 7 degrees 24 minutes south, the ship was once more becalmed. Where were the great south-easterlies, into which *Expedient* might beat, steady winds that would mean steady progress? Becalmed, and the boats out. All the fresh provisions taken in at Santa Cruz long since exhausted. An air of dejection in the ship, of staleness and fatigue and incipient resentment.

Since Rennie had ordered the reintroduction into the ship's diet of sauerkraut and portable soup, a quiet rebellion had been mounted on the lower deck, unofficially led by

Jacob Gurrall, captain of the maintop. Gurrall was a resource-ful, determined man, strong and well liked, and in other circumstances—of birth, education, advantage—he might have been an officer. Mr Loftus had said to him that at the end of this voyage Gurrall might be well placed to move up, and seek his master's warrant. He was already a petty officer; he knew more than enough of navigation and ship handling to conn the ship, if the necessity should ever arise; he was an intelligent and reliable man, and he deserved his chance. But as yet he was not minded to turn his back on his fellows. The lower deck was his home, and these men were his brothers. So long as the commission might last, so would his loyalty to his topmen, and to his mess. He had no qualms about leading the quiet revolt against the foul damned cattle fodder that was being forced upon them. He would not openly revolt, but he would lead from the shadows.

At those meals of which the sauerkraut and portable soup made a part a slop bucket was set aside at each mess table, and from each mess a man was selected to carry the bucket to the head, and dispose of the contents as waste. Rennie learned of it by chance. From his quarter gallery light he saw the vegetable matter co-mingling with the brown matter drifting slowly aft. He saw it, and was at once suspicious. He sent for his officers, including Mr Loftus.

'Mr Makepeace, what d'y'hear in your division about victuals?'

'Well, there is the usual grumbling about cheese.'

'Grumbling? You have heard grumbling?'

'That it is too ripe to eat. Certainly some of them like living cheese, but others don't. I am not unpartial to it myself, sir, to say——'

'Yes yes. I am not talking of cheese. What d'y'hear of sauerkraut?'

'Sauerkraut? Nothing, sir. It ain't a palatable thing, but they eat it.'

'Do they? Do they?—Mr Royce?'

'I agree with Lieutenant Makepeace, sir. Filthy stuff.'

'Yes, I don't want your cultivated opinion of the vegetable, thank you. I wish to know what the men of your division say to it.'

'I never hear anything about it, sir. It has not been mentioned.'

'Mm. Hm.—Mr Hayter?'

'Just as the other officers have said, sir. It is not remarked.'

A sigh, his brow wrinkled. 'Mr Loftus? You know what the lower deck likes, and does not like. What do you gather from the messes when their grog is issued?'

'The men are not unhappy, exact. I don't say they don't grumble—but that is usual in seamen. I would know if they was discontented.'

'What do they grumble of? I don't like this grumble, grumble. It speaks to mischief.'

'Well, sir, they may not like this sauerkraut, nor the glue— that is, the soup—but they eat it. They know they must, and so they eat it.'

'Hm. I am not persuaded.' And he told them what he believed he had seen in the water. He enjoined them all to be vigilant, and sent them away. He then sent for the surgeon.

'Doctor, I am going to ask you about sauerkraut, and portable soup. Has there been any sign—any sign whatsoever—of scurvy?'

'Ah. Yes.—That is, no. No sign, as yet.'

'Come come, Doctor. That is no answer at all. What does "Ah, yes" mean? Hey?'

'I fear the men don't like the anti-scorbutics, sir. They did not mind onions, and other fresh things, nor the lemon juice in their grog, since they could scarcely taste it under the rum. But I fear——'

'Yes, you fear? What d'y'fear?'

'I have no—no evidence.'

'Leave the evidence to me. Tell me what you think, what you *fear*.'

'There is a certain trust, Captain Rennie, which a medical person must establish with his patients. It is not a trust wrote out in words, on a paper. It is more—it is more a thing of look and look. You see it in his eye. Should that trust be broke, once broke, then it is not recoverable.'

Rennie looked at the surgeon, and was not angry with him. He might have been angry, because he was aware, now, that the surgeon must have known all along what was happening, or if he did not know exact, must have surmised.

'You have told me all I need to know, Doctor, thank you.'

'I have told you nothing, sir.' Dismayed.

'Certainly. Certainly. That trust of yours ain't in danger, Doctor. And now, I need not detain you.'

Rennie caused a watch to be kept on the heads, after meals. It was not a thing he relished; any man deserved privacy in his communication with nature, his arse bared above the sea; but he was sufficiently sure of the subversion of his orders about the anti-scorbutics to know that he must use such methods. There was too great a price to pay if the rebellion was not stopped. Scurvy was a dire, dreadful, and preventable curse upon a ship, and he meant to prevent it.

The midshipman who had been required to undertake this duty had been chosen by his size. Mr Rogers was small, he was agile, and he could easily conceal himself. He did so with very understandable repugnance and unwillingness, but his captain had given him a specific order, and he followed it. He brought the evidence of his eyes to the captain:

'They tip the sauerkraut down the head, sir. They bring it in buckets, and tip it down.'

'Yes, as I thought. Very good.—You was not observed?'

'No, sir. I watched as you asked of me, sir, but was not seen. I hid myself in mending canvas.'

'Well well, I see that you found this duty onerous. I would not in usual give it to anyone on my quarterdeck. It had to be undertaken, however, for their own well-being, d'y'see.'

'For the—well-being of the quarterdeck, sir?'

'No no, Mr Rogers.' A sharp glance. 'For the good of the people. We cannot have scurvy in the ship. You know what scurvy is, certainly?'

'It is a very terrible affliction, sir.'

'Just so.—Will you dine with me tomorrow, Mr Rogers? And bring your glass? I should like to compare it with my own. Yours is a very fine glass, I think. Your father gave it to you?'

'My brother, sir.'

'A Dollond, is it not?'

'Yes, sir.' Subdued.

Midshipman Rogers, as he quit the great cabin, did not feel mightily impressed by the captain's attempt to make himself agreeable and familiar and friendly. He thought that what the captain had required him to do was ignoble and debasing to them both, but he could not say so. Nor did he say anything about it in the midshipmen's berth. He was ashamed of himself, and ashamed of the captain.

At noon on the following day, Rennie had the hands assembled. The sun baked the deck, and the rigged awning seemed to increase the heat, trapping the oven breath of the sun under it, and making sweat pour from the brows of the waiting crew. Rennie stood in his undress coat, sweating beneath, but determined to show cold resolve. His hat sat firmly athwart his head. Away to the south, scarcely noticed, a darkness loomed along the horizon, a murky smudge.

'It has come to my notice that I have been disobeyed.' A glare. 'You have wilfully ignored my instructions as to sauerkraut, and portable soup. You know why I require these things to be a part of your diet, but you have thrown away this food, deliberately wasted it, in wicked stealth. Food provided to preserve your bodily strength and protect you from scurvy, and you throw it over the side.' A raking glance. 'I have the remedy. All grog is stopped for one week.'

A murmur.

'*Silence on deck!*'

The murmur died.

'Your grog is stopped, and each man will be required to eat his rations, entire, under supervision. Any man that refuses any part of his rations will be flogged.—Mr Hayter.'

'Sir?'

'Pass the book to me.'

As had been pre-arranged, James handed the captain the bound Articles of War.

Rennie read the Articles aloud at a measured pace, pausing at particular places—the more ferocious passages—to glare at the sweating men. James kept his face neutral, but felt, as he always felt when the Articles were read; that the entire performance was a waste of time. If it was meant to strike fear into the hearts of these tough, practical, hardy men, it did not succeed, thought James. They did not care about these threats. What they noticed, what made them attentive, was hearing that their grog was to be stopped. In James's experience that was a far more effective punishment than any other. Its effect was immediate, the men were absolutely deprived of their chief and most consistent comfort, and they felt it keenly. They were beginning to feel it now. A week without grog. A week of utter and pitiless sobriety, in the confinement of a ship far at sea, the only relief back-breaking work in the boats, in blistering heat.

James saw their faces, their sullen, resentful, dejected faces, and he wished to God that the captain would finish with the damned Articles, so that the hands could be released to eat their midday meal. Christ crucified, were they not suffering enough already?

'. . . not mentioned, shall be punished according to the Laws and Customs in such Cases used at sea.' Rennie closed the book, and looked at the massed sullen faces.

'Mr Tangible. You may pipe the hands to dinner.'

'Thank God,' murmured James under his breath.

*

'You have brought your glass I hope, Mr Rogers?'

'I—I could not find it, sir.'

'Could not find it? Is it lost?'

'Oh no, sir—I—I may have lent it to someone, very probably.'

'A Dollond long glass, Mr Rogers? And you cannot recall to whom you have loaned it?'

'Not at present, if you please, sir. I am very sorry.'

'Do not be sorry on my account, Mr Rogers. We may only hope for its safe return.'

The captain sat down, and his guests sat down. His guests, other than Mr Rogers, were Mr Dobie, the purser Mr Trent, Lieutenant Raker, and James. As their soup was served—here the soup was the same portable glue so detested on the lower deck, served to every man in the ship at the captain's insistence—as it was served the ship began to heel quite sharply to starboard, there was the sound of things falling, and a glass on the table fell and smashed on the deck. From the quarterdeck above the diners came Mr Loftus's voice, raised to a shout:

'Bring her to the wind!' Then further bellowed commands, the high wail of the calls, and running feet. 'All hands to reduce sail! Topmen aloft!'

The captain rose from his chair, steadied himself, and was nearly felled as the full force of the wind surged over the ship. Decanters, plates, spoons, jugs, and other things spilled and crashed from the table, chairs tipped, and a locker burst open in a tumble of bottles. James stumbled into the space where the starboard number thirteen grooved gun had once stood, his coat drenched in glue and wine, kept his feet by an effort of will, and saved Mr Dobie, who added the contents of his stomach to the saturation of James's clothing. The purser rolled across the squares of decking canvas, gasped, and struck his head. An ominous creaking became a terrible roar, then a savage rending as a sail was torn out of its bolt ropes. Blocks crashed to the deck, there was the sharp crack of a breaking spar, and the thudding heaviness of ropes and canvas falling in clumps. The wind moaned and roared, and the ship heeled, and heeled, and heeled, until the deck was at a terrible angle. All of them in the tilted great cabin thought that the ship might be thrown down in the sea, her decks at right angles to the water, and then slip beneath, drowning every man in her. Lieutenant Raker's eyes stared out of his head, out of his appalled white face, as he clung to a tackle ring.

'By God, she is lost!' he shrieked, too terrified to modify his anguish.

Rennie and James thought it too, for a moment, but neither said anything, nor did they cry out. They waited, clinging, and slowly, slowly with innumerable small shuddering doubts, *Expedient* righted herself, water flowing everywhere in her, and Rennie ran up the ladder.

On deck, with the sea sluicing over the decks, pouring into gratings, around the guns, and around the sagging remains of fallen rigging, swirling and sucking at it, on deck Rennie began shouting commands, the masts swaying above him, flying with a dangerous spread of canvas, and the sun burned out behind a mass of whirling vaporous cloud and deluging rain.

'Hands to the pumps! Aloft, there! Hand the courses! Cut away that fouled rigging on the lee, there! Mr Loftus! Where is Mr Loftus? Weather helm, how does she lie?'

'She's heavy, sir. I cannot bring her up!'

'Then we must run before, and save ourselves.' On the swaying spars above, the topmen were strung out on the footropes, desperately furling, and tying gaskets, the wind snatching at them and sending dangling blocks flying at their heads. Rennie bellowed further orders from the deck, calling for thrice-reefed topsails. He called for the carpenter, for the boatswain, for the gunner, and for the master. By now James was at his side.

'Mr Loftus was knocked off his feet when she heeled. He was thrown into the waist and knocked senseless.'

'Is he senseless still? Can he walk?'

'He is recovered, sir, but sore.'

The master appeared, limping, his wet hair dripping blood down his cheek. 'I will take my place, sir. I will take my place, certainly.'

'Very good, Mr Loftus. I need every man.' The wind began again to wail in the rigging. James glanced anxiously aloft as the ship heeled and wallowed, at the canvas still billowing and cracking. As she bowed her head the sea surged up and over the lee rail, swam heavily across the hammock nettings, and flooded heavily along and through. *Expedient* was struggling.

'I will see to the pumps, then look at the ship for damage, with your permission, sir.' Shouting.

'Very good, do so!' His hand cupped at his mouth, bellowing in reply. Turning: 'Mr Loftus! Will you go below, and look at the hold! Tell me at once if her ballast has shifted, or if our stores has shifted, will you!—Mr Adgett! Mr Adgett! I do not want our boats to be smashed! Where is Mr Storey! I want a report our guns are secured!'

James mustered a dozen bedraggled waisters at the pumps, and got them working, turn and turn about, as hard and fast as they could. 'We must pump the water out of her, or she will founder at the next heavy blast of wind!' And he took his place at one of the pumps himself.

With sail reduced to a minimum, Rennie allowed the ship to fall off, risking the long wallowing moments in a lull of the wind, and wore her to run before. Something like order and control had returned to *Expedient*, but she was not uninjured. She had lost her mizzen upper masts, and her spanker gaff, and a great deal of rigging had had to be cut away. The boats were all damaged to one degree or another, though none was absolutely smashed. Casks had broken loose in the hold, and provisions had been spoiled. The surgeon was a very busy man, with dozens of men hurt with cuts, bruises, and more serious injuries and wounds. Everything was very wet. The fire had gone out in the galley. But the ship was alive, with all her people in her. *Expedient* swam.

What Rennie did not know, and would not know for several days, was that some of the water pumped out of the ship had been fresh. In that first great heeling lurch, very heavy damage had been caused in the tiers. A great number of casks, a tremendous weight, had torn loose and been crushed together. Their water casks had been reduced by nearly half.

When he did learn it he began to doubt that he could follow his instructions, his clear instructions to double Cape Horn without making landfall. He began to fear the failure of the whole commission.

Rennie was dreaming, and in his dream the most piteous sound came to him, halfway between a cry and a whimper, a sound of pain and grief, of bitter loss. He woke, and was astonished to discover that the cry issued from his own throat, was ending in a moan of breath. What was more disturbing to him was that he had no notion of its cause, none at all. He pulled himself into a sitting position in his hanging cot, further dismayed to feel wet tears on his cheeks. What had he dreamed, and why? What dismal or desolating circumstance had he dreamed of to provoke such a cry of anguish? He knew that he *had* dreamed, and was obscurely ashamed of it. Again, why? If he did not know the content, or the reason, where was the offence? Even a dog was obliged by Nature sometimes to dream, to lie quivering and yipping at the hearth, his paws scrabbling and jumping with the unbidden chase in his head.

'Am I a dog, then?' he said aloud. 'A sad dog?'

He would drink something, and collect himself. He swung out of his cot and found the deck under his legs, and was now aware of a strange glow, a penetrating glow that was in the ship and yet outside it. He knew that it was not daylight; it was not like to daylight but to a light that has banished darkness. He frowned, and sniffed, and scratched the side of his head and his stubbled cheek. Pulled off his nightshirt and pulled on his britches, and a shirt, and opened the door of his sleeping cabin. Light suffused every part of the great cabin.

'What the devil is it?' Good God, was it fire? Was the ship on fire?

He ran up the companion ladder. Mr Loftus stood by the wheel and with him was Lieutenant Makepeace. They were both staring aloft. The helmsman, also.

'Are we on fire?'

'No, sir. Unless the sea itself is on fire.' Lieutenant Makepeace, turning.

'Eh?'

'The light is in the water, sir, all around us.'

Rennie walked to the lee rail, and looked. The ship was cutting through the water at better than eight knots, and all around her the sea was ablaze with light. Fire leapt back from the bows, flickered hissing along the wales, and was borne flaring astern into the liquid coals of the wake. The line of the wake burned straight and far, receding into the distance. Rennie walked to the weather rail, utterly bemused. It was as if a huge volcano had erupted directly beneath the ship, with no concomitant violence. There was a swell, and the wind by which the ship so briskly progressed chopped and whipped at the wavetops, but the usual appearance of a wind-stirred sea at night—of heaving and tumbling blackness, scattered with whitecaps, streaked with fleeting luminescence—was here wholly dazzled away. The ship's sails, lit from beneath, had the strange, unsettling appearance of being upside down, and filled by an opposite wind. The sun's light had been reversed, and was now the great sun of the deep, shining upward, making shadows from below, turning the natural order of things on its head.

'What is it?' Rennie muttered to himself. 'What danger is this?'

'It is thought that it is a very small creature,' said a voice at his side, 'a tiny creature, swimming in his tens of millions through the sea and lighting our way.'

Rennie turned and found Mr Dobie at his side. 'Eh, Mr Dobie? Eh?—I am not in the mood for jesting, it is the middle of the night.'

'I do not jest, sir, I assure you. The light is emitted by a diminutive animal. We are in his territory. As he illuminates his own nocturnal world, he incidentally irradiates ours.'

Seamen of the watch had climbed into the rigging to look at the sails close to, to reassure themselves that they had not contrarily filled. The gangways and the forecastle were crammed now with astonished faces, some looking down-ward into the magical effulgence, others looking up at the glorious underlit spread of sail. Rennie returned his gaze there, to the bright lofting towers, and was moved by their beauty. He felt tears running on his cheeks, and saw the glory of the sails blur and dissolve, and he did not care that he might be seen thus unmanned. He was swept up, as if his feet were hovering above the deck, supported by nothing but the spell-binding power of the moment.

'You are moved, sir,' said Dobie quietly by his side. 'We are all moved, I think, for it is something rare we see tonight, rare and wonderful and grand.'

'Is it not, though?'

'We must count ourselves fortunate, do not you think?'

'Just so—indeed so.'

Rennie returned to his cot with all thought of his dream gone from his mind, his heart gladdened and his thoughts at ease.

When he woke again at dawn he was no longer easy. The anxieties of the past weeks crowded in upon him. Water. Victuals. A persistent and fretful leak deep in the forward hold, needing the pumps a good part of each watch. Growing restlessness in the lower deck. The sense that soon the commission would miscarry—would miscarry because it had been ill-conceived. The brief encounter with myriad glowing sea creatures, an hour or two of respite from the monotony of southing in the endless Atlantic, had done nothing to dispel his slowly deepening, slowly burgeoning disquiet.

'I cannot fail,' he said aloud.—'I may not fail.—I must not fail.'

'There ain't no sail, sir,' said his steward, pushing back-first into the sleeping cabin with a tray. 'It is only your tea. Hot and wet and flavourful.'

For once the tea did not revive him as it nearly infallibly did, for once his several cups of strong morning brew left him as flat as the moment of waking, and when he had shaved— cutting himself—and washed, and dressed, he wished for something foolish. He wished that he was not the captain of a frigate, that he was not a sea officer at all, but a dull, prosperous fellow in an office ashore, counting up columns of money.

Later, when he had reviewed the purser's books, and inspected the ship, and written in his journal that the leak was still unplaced and troublesome, he conferred with his first lieutenant.

'Surely we shall be obliged to make landfall, sir? Our water is getting very low.'

'My orders is plain. I may not do so.'

'Yes, the orders.—Written by men that are not here. Men that do not face thirst and starvation on the open sea. Could we not make for Tristan da Cunha?'

'It is too far out of our way, James. Thousands of miles.'

'The Falkland Isles, then?'

'Listen, while the ship is sound, and we have enough to eat and drink, I cannot entertain such notions. We must make all due speed, double Cape Horn, and sail into the Pacifick.'

'Sir, forgive me, but how and where are we to find water, wood, food, where are we to discover these essential things in the Pacifick?'

'Our commission is to discover islands, James.'

James allowed himself impatiently to sigh, saw Rennie's

answering, warning glare, and soon after excused himself to
go on deck. As James came up the ladder the lookout called:

'Sail of ship, on the starboard quarter! Three masts, hull
down!'

James jumped into the mizzen shrouds, and ran up to the
top, then up into the crosstrees. He focused his glass, his arm
hooked round a stay to steady himself. The ship, her hull just
now emerging from the wrinkled sea, was certainly not the
Larkspur, but almost certainly the unidentified frigate, her
sail a near replication of *Expedient*'s set. James stowed the
glass in his coat, steadied himself, swung out and curled a leg
round the t'gan backstay, and slid in a clinging plunge to the
deck. Rennie met him there.

'Well?'

'The frigate, I think. No colours.'

'Damn the fellow's impudence.' Mildly. 'We cannot outrun him, as we have learned already. Well, well, we'll allow
him to catch us up.'

'To speak?'

'Aye, and then perhaps we shall discover his purpose. His
very peculiar purpose in running ahead, doubling widely
back, and resuming the chase.'

'You think that it's the result of those despatches, in
Larkspur, sir?'

'I do not know. I do not know. Possibly. Again, there may
be an explanation quite separate, as you was at pains to point
out to me, James, on an earlier occasion.'

'I was, sir, but now—well, I think I was mistaken, sir.'

'You do? Hm. Hm. Yes.—However, I am not inclined to
neglect my duty as captain of a man-of-war at sea. When the
frigate is nearer, I will like to beat to quarters.'

'Clear for action, sir? Surely—surely there can be no doubt
that she is an English ship?'

Suddenly harsh: 'There is doubts about everything to do
with this commission, Mr. Hayter. I will like to allow the
fellow to catch me up, but by God he had better beware if he

thinks I am a lax, soft, unheeding and inconsiderable water-fly, that basks upon the surface only to be gobbled up. He will get a fright if he thinks that, Mr Hayter.'

Expedient reduced sail, and lost a little of her steerage way. Soon the other frigate was gaining on her, as Rennie intended. High above *Expedient* long white tails of cloud hung motionless in the pale blue of the ocean sky. At her cutwater spray and foam welled and spilled, and were rushed in heaving, curling lace aft along the wales. The ensign snapped and rippled on the taut gaff halyard. Though she was slowly losing way everything was taut, and sheeted home, not a block dangling, nor a roband loose. Feet braced apart on his quarterdeck, long glass under his arm, Rennie called:

'Clear the decks for action!'

And later, when every man was in his place: 'Mr Hayter! We will worm our carronades, and reload with red cartridge!'

'*Red*, sir?'

'Aye, red. You heard me right. We have no broadsides, save our fat fellows. They must do our smashing for us, if needs be, at maximum blast. Red, then. Red, and roundshot.'

'Very good, sir.'

'We will load with grape our second fire—if needs be. If we need to kill men.'

'Very good.' Grave and subdued, more than a little uneasy, James went below to inform the gunner himself, unwilling to entrust such a message to a ship's boy, given its import. In half a glass the new cartridge has been ladled and filled, and the carronades wormed and reloaded. Mr Storey had been reluctant, very reluctant, to have anything further to do with the red casks, and James had had to become insistent.

'Be it on your head, then,' Storey had said, with his face long. James had made no reply.

And now the moment was drawing near when the two ships would meet. James stood with Rennie on the quarter-deck, having inspected the full number of carronades with him, fourteen squat cannon on the forecastle and quarterdeck, seven a side, sitting on their heavy transverse trucked carriages. Because the twenty-six long guns on the gundeck were not in use, Rennie had ordered some of the guncrews into the tops with muskets, and others to man the small swivels, one-pound guns slotted into the rails fore and aft. These guns were little more than heavy muskets, and would be employed in a similar role—if needs be—to cut down men.

The mood in *Expedient*, from one of expectation and energy when the other frigate had first been sighted, had grown subdued now as the other ship gradually closed upon them. The captain's untrusting, grim mood had infected them. Everyone in *Expedient* knew they were outgunned, and knew that in all probability they could and would be outmanoeuvred by a faster and handier ship, if it came to serious business.

'Well, Mr Pankridge,' Rennie said to the signals midshipman. 'This would be your first sea action, hey?'

'Yes, sir.'

'Are you fearful?'

'Oh, no, sir!'

'We are all fearful, a little, Mr Pankridge.' Kindly. 'No shame attaches to it. Only a damned fool has no fear at such a moment. You apprehend me?'

'I—I think so, sir.'

'We overcome that fear by doing our duty, by thinking of nothing but our duty.'

'Yes, sir.'

'Very good.—Mr Hayter. When he is one mile off, we will make a signal for him to show his colours.'

'Very good, sir.'

Expedient ran on, and a deathly quiet now descended over her. Midshipman Pankridge did his level best to concentrate upon his book, and the halyards, and the flag locker, but in his heart now, and all through him, was palpitating fright. The captain's kind attempt to reassure him had had the opposite effect. His hand shook, his head felt cold, his heart itself seemed to shudder within him. Please God, let me not make a mistake, he prayed silently. Let me not fail. Let me be brave.

'Make the signal!'

And as soon as he was properly busy, the boy did begin to feel better. The flags fluttered aloft.

'Hold her steady!—Does he respond to my signal, James?'

'No, sir,' His glass raised.

'Very well, we must make the first move. Mr Loftus! We will heave to, if you please.'

The orders given, the calls sounded. *Expedient* came off the wind, put her maintopsail aback, and hove to, her forecourse in the brails. The other frigate lost way in an exactly similar fashion, and hove to half a mile away. No colours. No flag of any kind.

'Well, he clearly does not wish to fight us, sir.' James, with considerable relief.

'His guns are run out. You noticed that?'

'So are ours.'

'Indeed, indeed.'

'May I hoist out a boat, sir?'

'The bloody fellow does not respond to anything else, James. He will not answer signals, he don't want to show his colours. Yes, very well, you had better take the small cutter. We cannot lie here all day, rolling our masts out on the swell. It is time we had an answer from him, as to what the devil he wants.'

James gave the order for the small cutter.

'Mr Dobie!' The captain waited impatiently for Dobie to appear at his side. 'I will like to send a letter by your hand, James, to her captain. Ah, Dobie, you are there. You have got your pen? Paper?'

The captain dictated his letter, Dobie wrote it out in his careful hand, in black ink, Rennie put his name to it, it was sealed, and James put it inside his coat.

'Pray ask him to dine with us, will you, James? I forgot to put that in my letter.'

The cutter, lowered from the stern davits, settled under his weight, and the weight of the small crew. The mast was quickly stepped, sail quickly set, and the cutter quickly traversed the swell between the two ships, dipping and running, dipping and running. James sat in the stern with the captain's coxswain Randall South at the tiller. As they ran in under her lee a figure appeared at the frigate's hammock nettings with a musket.

'I carry a message from Captain Rennie of His Majesty's frigate *Expedient* for the captain of your ship,' called James. 'May I come aboard?'

A second figure joined the first. It was in a plain blue coat, not naval uniform exact, but it had the look of an officer. James saw the face, and was startled.

'Good God.—Are you Lieutenant Whatmore?'

The face was startled in turn, then opened in a smile of recognition. 'By God, you are Hayter! James Hayter, of *Persistence!*'

'Well, *Expedient* now, you know. What ship are you, Scud? Are you first in her, or perhaps you are her captain?'

This friendly exchange might have continued, and been fruitful as well as pleasant. However, another face appeared, older and more authoritative, beside Mr Whatmore, and an arm thrust him aside, and back. This man, this officer, also wore a plain blue coat, and a plain hat athwart his head. Again not naval dress exact, but his clothes had a naval look all the same.

'You may talk to me, sir, and to me alone.'

'Are you—are you the captain, sir?' James tried to peer past him, but Whatmore had disappeared. 'May I know the name of your ship?'

'You may not, sir. You may return to your ship, Lieutenant, and tell your commanding officer that I pose no threat to him, no threat to *Expedient*. We are by chance in the same waters, upon a private venture, that is all.'

'Will you not tell me what ship you are, sir? Did you

receive despatches from *Larkspur*? His Majesty's hired vessel *Larkspur*, sixteen.'

'Lieutenant, you try my patience, sir. My owners will not permit me to divulge anything of my business, at sea or anywhere. Good day to you.'

'Captain, with your permission, I should like to come aboard.' Politely, and firmly. 'Captain Rennie has asked me particularly to convey his written message to you, in person.' He held up Rennie's sealed letter. 'He also wishes to extend an invitation to you, sir, to dine with him in *Expedient*.'

'That I regret I cannot do. All I may tell you is that we are an English ship, and mean you no harm. You must excuse me, now.' He retreated from the rail, but James called after him, more forcefully than he had intended.

'If you are an English ship, then where are your colours?'

The officer re-appeared, stern-faced. 'My business is private, and confidential. Kindly stand off, now, will you?'

'Sir, I must insist——'

'Damn your confounded impertinence! Do as you're told, sir!' There was no mistaking the authority and certainty of this tone. The man at the rail above James's head was a post captain RN. His anger, however, quickly turned to perplexity. He had betrayed himself by this snappish display of naval ire, and at once regretted it.

'I—I beg your pardon, Lieutenant. Pray tell your captain—Captain Rennie—pray thank him for his kind invitation, and say that I wish him nothing but good fortune, and fair wind, and that I will take care in future to keep my distance, and leave him alone. Will you tell him that?'

'Very good, sir.' James took off his hat, bowed and sat down. Twenty minutes later he was in *Expedient*'s great cabin, hurried there by Rennie, who now held his elbow in agitation.

'Well? Well? What ship is she? Who is her captain? Does he come to dine with us? What is his home port? What is his purpose in pursuing us?'

'I could discover none of those things, sir, I fear—except that he will not dine with us.'

'What! None! Christ in tears, James. I was most particular. Pfff, I knew that I should have gone in the boat myself. He would not have dared to deny me——'

'Sir, if you please, she is a naval ship, I would wager my life on it. Her captain has an unmistakable manner.'

'Eh?'

'He is a post captain RN. He wears no uniform, but he looks it, and sounds it. And here is another thing. I recognized one of his officers. He was first in *Persistence*, when I was third in her. Scud Whatmore.'

'You spoke to him?' Urgently.

'Well, briefly, you know. But then the captain——'

'Good heaven, James!' Exasperated. 'You saw a man known to you, an officer, and yet did not find out anything? Why not? Why not?'

'I was refused permission to go aboard, sir. My way was blocked by a seaman with a musket, and then the captain ordered me to stand off.'

'But, good God, you are an officer in one of His Majesty's men of war! Where is your fortitude? Why did you not bloody well *insist*? We have been pestered, and harassed, and unpardonably dogged, and you allow him to dismiss you like a, like a, like a damned servant girl!'

'Perhaps, as you say, it would have been better for you to have gone yourself, sir.' Stiffly.

'What? What?'

'Since I had not sufficient authority to take a post captain to task.'

'But you don't know that he *is* a damned post! You *think* it, that is all! Good God, James.'

'I am very sorry indeed, sir.' With icy deference.

'Captain, sir! She is bearing away to the north, sir, under full canvas!' Midshipman Rogers.

'Very good, I shall come on deck.' And without further

word to James, Rennie went up the ladder, leaving his first lieutenant to follow.

The frigate was already nearly half a league off, with the wind on her quarter, and she made a pretty sight, her lines clean and graceful, her spread of canvas—royals setting— gleaming in the sun. Rennie looked at her in his glass. James stood silent and angry behind him, his anger bound tight in his breast, and found himself ignored when the captain turned to give the orders for *Expedient* to get under way.

◦—•—✦—•—◦

Forty-six degrees 28 minutes south, 33 degrees 16 minutes west. The air still mild, but not nearly so warm as in the lower latitudes. Two and a half foot of water persistently in the well, rising to three foot if the pumps were not worked each watch, and the leak not stoppable until they might reach a suitable anchorage and repair the ship. Long weeks of sun and sea had done their work. Paint had blistered, and peeled, Stockholm tar had melted, and the rigging had suffered. Her timbers were sound, but everywhere in the ship was evidence of material fatigue. The boats were towed to keep their timbers from drying out and opening. Rennie's careful routine of washing and smoking had continued, but the provisions that had spoiled when the ship was all but knocked down had not been wholly recovered, and in spite of the rate of leaking, and pumping out, everything in the hold now stank. Rennie had sworn before they put to sea that *Expedient* would never stink while she was under him, and he was sad now that he could not keep that promise. The hands, already hard pressed at the pumps, and their rations reduced, cared little about the smell; they craved only respite.

Relations between Rennie and his first lieutenant remained, like the ship, under strain. Their easeful conversations in the great cabin at night had ceased. Rennie had stopped calling him by his Christian name. The estrangement was noticed by the other officers—indeed by the ship entire—and remarked on, but never in the presence of either man. It was felt— generally felt—that this was just one more minus mark against the commission. The mood in the lower deck was downcast. The mood in the gunroom was low. Only in the midshipmen's berth could the atmosphere be described as more buoyant than elsewhere, but that was from the natural exuberance of youth, and in these weary days was far less spirited than at the beginning.

South-south-west and the endless sea. Birds hung by the ship, and on one day a great pod of whales kept the ship company, blowing tall spouts of breath, heaving and rolling and diving deep, their flukes flashing wide and dark as they went down. Rennie stood alone on the quarterdeck, watching the creatures by the hour. On the following day the whales had gone, and there was a storm of rain, thick heavy drenching rain, ice-cold. Water casks were hoisted up, and canvas troughs rigged, and tons of fresh water was collected. The ship got very wet between, but that was of small significance when they had so amply replenished their water supply. Rennie was quite lifted up, and asked James to eat supper with him. James was inclined to refuse the invitation, but felt that to do so would be seen as a deliberate insult by an officer to his superior, rather than as a simple dis- inclination to be placated. He went.

'Ah, James, come in and sit down, will you? Steward! I fear we shall not be swooning with delight over what we are to be given to eat, but at least we have plenty of wine left, and now plenty of water. Sit, sit, my dear fellow, there is no need to be formal and correct and so forth, hey?'

'Thank you, sir.' James removed his hat and sat down.

'Well, well, we make good time I think.'

'Indeed, sir.'

'Very fair time. I think we may hope to double in a fortnight, if our wind holds steady. The Horn ain't always a hostile place, by no means. It can be gentle as a cat.'

'Indeed.'

'A cat has claws, certainly. We must not forget that.'

'No, sir.'

'The whole ship has been elevated by the rain. Everything feels fresher and—and—and better altogether. Hey?'

'It would seem so.'

'Hm, James, yes.' A frowning smile, then raised eyebrows and a wrinkled forehead. 'Yes, I had hoped that this very modest occasion might settle any—any unsubstantial disagreement, any little rift that might exist, might have existed, between us. Hm?'

'Yes, sir?'

'These things happen in the course of a long commission. Take an example, now: that frigate. It was a very little irritation, in the setting of the whole cruise, a very small inconsiderable thing. As you wrote in your account, exact.'

'Did I write that, sir? Exactly that?'

'More and less, more and less. It is of no matter. The frigate has gone. Her captain said that he would leave us alone, and so he has.'

'With respect, sir, I think I wrote that I took him for a sea officer in His Majesty's service, did I not? And that his ship, and his actions in pursuing us, was a very considerable mystery. Did I not say that, sir? Exact?'

'You may have done, James, you may have done. It don't signify, now, d'y'see? Not now, when we approach our most consequential task.'

'Very good, sir.'

'Dear heaven, James, you make friendship a very hard thing to offer. Must I write it out in ink, upon a card?'

James relented. To have stayed aloof in the saddle of his high horse, petulant and disdaining and aloof, when Rennie so evidently wished to make amends, would have been foolish and ungentlemanlike. He shook his head, and smiled.

'No, indeed. No, indeed. I value friendship above all things.'

'A glass of wine, then?'

'Very happy, sir. Very happy indeed.'

They drank together, and swallowed their repellent portable soup without minding it, and ate their sauerkraut too,
and the other very dull things the cook had sought to make
palatable, and sat long over their cheese. Rennie opened the
last bottle of Admiral Hollister's port.

'You will have noticed, I expect, that in certain households
there is always an atmosphere of quiet and calm and pleasant
order, while in others there is an atmosphere of hectic upset
from morning to night: muffled voices raised, the banging of
furniture and the clattering of plates, doors slammed and girls
in tears. Yet both these establishments will profess themselves a happy home.'

'I have known both kinds.'

'Just so. For myself, I would prefer to live in the former,
but if put to it I could manage to live in the latter. A ship is
like a home. I do not care which kind of happy home it is, so
long as it is one or the other. What I do not care for, and will
not bear, is an unhappy ship.'

'You think *Expedient* an unhappy ship, sir?'

'I think she is in danger of becoming one. The hands are
resentful because I have reduced their rations, and I have
heard there is to be a group representing them, with spokes-
men, to complain, and make demands.'

'Heard, sir? I have heard nothing.'

'In divisions you would not necessarily hear of such things.
I have—other sources.'

'Ah.'

'I don't like having to use such methods, James. It don't sit
right with me. But how am I to deal with this sort of thing,
else? I know the ringleader is Gurrall. He is a very sound man
in all other distinction, an admirable captain of the top, a
right seaman. But he has sought to undermine me in this. It
was all his doing about the anti-scorbutics, you know. And
now he seeks to make trouble for me about quantity. I have

had no choice, God knows, but to reduce rations. We all eat less. Our very miserable supper, here, this evening, was only made tolerable by wine, hm? If we are to do our duty, and sail into the Pacifick, we must husband resources.'

'I will certainly urge the officers to emphasize that, in divisions.'

'Thank you, James. It will not be sufficient, however. It will not answer, while Gurrall holds them in his hand. I ought to have him flogged, in truth.'

'Flogged, d'y'think?' Doubtfully. 'He is much liked, and admired.'

'I have an obligation to flog him. It is my duty to flog him, the fellow. I could, under the Articles, have him very severely punished, and confined.'

'Is that your intention, sir?' Looking at him over the rim of his glass.

'No, James, no no.—I could, under both Nineteen and Twenty-one. I could, and would be entirely justified, by God. But I will not, I will not, because if I did we should be even more an unhappy ship than we are at present, with even greater resentment and ill-will.'

'I think that is wise.' Putting down his glass in relief.

'A ship is home to two hundred and fifty men; a whole village of men, in a home little bigger than a village inn, from which—unlike to a village inn—there is no escape into the adjoining field, or across the hill, or away to any private place. When it grows unhappy all manner of grudges simmer, and fester, and make a bilge of each man's guts. In an unhappy ship men ain't willing. They do not jump, nor work with a will at any task. They do as they are told with utmost reluctance—clumsy, indolent, shrugging reluctance. They slouch, and spit, and turn their backs. They grow deaf and blind.—No no, I cannot flog him.' A long sigh.

After a moment: 'May I make a suggestion, sir?'

'By all means, James. I will gladly hear it.'

'Bring him here, into the great cabin—alone. Speak to him

as one man to another, and appeal to his good sense. Say that you know his good qualities, and value them. Say that we are all in this together, and that we must all help each other.—Say that we are all Expedients.'

'You mean—say nothing of his rebelliousness?'

'Nothing at all. The opposite, in fact. Appeal to him as the natural centre of admiration and respect in the lower deck, whom the men will naturally follow.'

'Surely he will look through me like a window pane, and find out my motive.'

'Flattery—when it is sincere—flattery is a very powerful thing, is it not?'

'You think I could say those things to him sincerely, James?'

'He is a damned good seaman. One day he will tread a quarterdeck, I am in no doubt. If he is not a fool—and I don't think he is—he will listen to what you say, and take it to heart.'

Another sigh. A long silence. Then Rennie slapped his hand on the table, picked up the bottle and refilled their glasses.

'I believe you are right, James. I will do as you suggest.' He raised his glass. 'To a happy ship.'

'To *Expedient*.'

———※◈※———

In the lull before the inevitable storm and struggle—what most men in the ship saw as inevitable—*Expedient* sailed steadily south, the Falkland Isles to her west, making for Cape Horn. Perhaps in anticipation of the coming difficulty, the coming days of heavy weather and continual battering wind, the gunroom gave a dinner. In the circumstances it was a generous dinner, and in honour of the occasion Lieutenant Makepeace revealed to the table an entirely unexpected part of himself. His fellow officers had always thought him a

thoroughly reliable, level-minded, pleasant, decent young
fellow, but a fellow—if not dull, exact—of no great wit or
sparkling conversation, nor elegance of phrase. Now, as they
pushed away their plates and refilled their glasses, he gave
them this glimpse of another part of himself, altogether
deeper and more contemplative.

'May I dedicate a poem to you?' he asked, and when given
laughing—even ribald—consent, he gave them, in a quiet,
modulated tone:

> 'Fondly I remember them
> Magical afternoons
> Drinking tinto with companions
> The trees whispering
> The last of summer
> Round the garden table
> The talk all slight and easy
> Never recondite
> And the slow sun brushed
> Across our faces, thus
> Bright with easy dreams.
> A fountain over there in shade
> Sipping at the edges of our glade
> Cools all the world
> And we would nothing ask but this
> Who sit and tell ourselves
> Our telling fictions
> In the settling air.'

A silence. Then heartfelt applause.
'I would wish to have put my feelings so, Makepeace!'
'So would I, Tom. Well done.'
'Indeed, excellently put. Very—very——'
'Very apt,' said Royce, lifting his glass. 'Very apt, indeed.'
'It is a new form,' said Makepeace, flushed with their
praise. 'It is not quite verse. It is—new.'

'Very new,' said Royce, swallowing wine. '*Very* new. And splendid.'

'Is there not a difficulty of tense?' asked Mr Dobie timidly. 'In the last lines? It is a very slight difficulty,' he added when the others began to shout him down. 'I did not mean to adopt a critical tone, not at all.'

'It is new,' said Makepeace. 'I am happy that you liked it.'

'Have you any more such pieces, Tom?'

'Oh, lots, you know. But I keep them to myself, in usual.'

'Nonsense, you must let us hear them. Hey? Should he not give them to us?'

'Yes!'

'Let's hear them, by all means!'

But Lieutenant Makepeace could not be prevailed upon, on that occasion, to perform farther, and the table fell to talking of other things.

'How do you survive the schoolroom, Mr Dobie?' James asked politely, since Dobie had sat quiet after being shouted down, and now looked in need of rescue from his own thoughts. 'You don't allow the mids to bully you, I hope?'

'Oh, no. No, I find them entirely conversible young men. They and I have reached an understanding. If they will allow me to instruct them half an hour a day, I will not hinder them further, nor curb their other enthusiasms in any degree.'

'Other enthusiasms?'

'Oh, well—before we made this bargain, they had used to rush away during my instructing them, leap into the rigging, and fly away aloft, so that I could not follow them, nor admonish them, nor bring them back to their proper work of study. I—I do not venture aloft, Lieutenant.'

'No. No. Hm. You should have mentioned this to me, you know. I would have admonished them, right enough.'

'Well, yes, you would—and that is why I did not. And because I did not cause them to be punished, we have our present understanding, and I believe they really do learn something.'

'You think so? Very good, then. I will not seek to interfere.'

'Will you tell me something, Mr Hayter? How does any of these young gentlemen become a midshipman? I have tried to inquire of them, once or twice, but they told me such wild tales I could not believe a word they said. They were bastard sons of dukes, one of them said, and thus entitled to go to sea. Another told me they were all orphans, found in swaddling clothes upon the steps of parish churches, for whom the Royal Navy made special provision.'

'The truth is more mundane, I fear. Such a boy may come from anywhere, but in usual he comes from a family with naval connection. Such a boy cannot be rated mid until he has served three years at sea. It is true that many sons of naval fathers are put on a ship's books years before they do ever go to sea, to give them a place in the midshipmen's berth straight-way when they do at last come aboard. However, they must all spend years at middy's rating before they may move up.'

'Move up? You mean, into the rigging?'

'Good heaven, no. He must do that more and less at once. No, before he may ask for his Board.'

'You mean, the money to pay for his lodgings in the ship?'

'No no.' Laughing. 'No, his Board of Examination. Three senior posts, on a cold Wednesday morning, asking him the worst possible questions, the most horrible questions, for an hour or more, and then if he answers well enough, and don't drive himself in on a lee shore, and they are pleased to find him an officerlike fellow, they pass him, and he may look for a commission.'

'Look for it? Surely, if he has passed his Board, surely then he has gained his commission?'

'Not at all. A commission, d'y'see, is for a ship—a particular ship. He may wait a year, or two years, or even longer in the peace, and get nothing. Passing your Board is no guarantee of anything at all. That is, without interest.'

'Ahh. Ohh. The interest paid on a sum of money, hm?'

'What say?'

'Capital, in the funds. The interest upon it, set aside, with which he buys his commission.'

'Now you are confusing me. It has nothing to do with money, you know. It has everything to do with his connections, his friends. His father, or his mother, has a brother—or a cousin—who is let us say an admiral, or a commodore, or a senior post—or they know someone that is, you know, a friend. Or better yet a senior officer under whom he has already served, who wishes to see him moved up. Letters are wrote, a word is said in the right ear, and so forth, and the thing is done. Young Johnny Stoutfellow gets his commission. It is all managed by interest.—Now d'y'see?'

'Yes, I see now.—Now, I do.'

But he didn't. He was more than ever muddled.

'I am surprised your friend Royce did not tell you all about it. He must have been through it himself, has he not? Did not Lord Gillingford intercede in his behalf?'

'Lord Gillingham, yes. However, Lieutenant Royce and I do not—do not often communicate.'

'Is he not your friend, Dobie?'

'Yes and no. Yes and no. I—I can say no more.'

There was something very definitely odd about these two, thought James, but he said nothing to Dobie. He had really done remarkably well, had he not? James, the captain, all the officers had despaired of Alan Dobie in those first few days at sea between the Nore and Spithead, and on several occasions since. This frail, uncertain, clerkish young man, for whom a ship was at first so alien a home, had survived, had taken his place in the gunroom, had reached an accommodation with those ferocious young beasts in the midshipmen's berth, had even contrived to become useful to the captain. In truth it was Dobie, and not his supposed chum Royce, who had made a better fist of the commission, and was better tolerated in the ship.

—►—■◆■—►—

Expedient in the high fifties of latitude, and approaching Cape Horn; Staten Island, whitecapped, already left far to the northeast. Rennie knew that the currents immediately at the Cape could be very strong, and that the wind could blow with insane strength. He went south, and south, to avoid the fury of the sea there, in the hope that he would find more moderate conditions. He kept the deck long hours, and watched everything with sharp attention, noting the slightest change in the wind and sky, and in the washing of the sea all about the ship. He saw high streaks of cloud, long feathery tails of cloud, which heralded wind in the high clear blue of this southern sky. For now the sea was almost calm, the breeze moderate, and they began to make west—west towards the Pacifick.

'Mr Makepeace.'

'Sir?'

'We will wash and smoke between. To reward them for this added work I will like the hands to be permitted to be given a double allowance of grog, and full rations of meat, when it is done. Say so to Mr Loftus.'

'Very good, sir.'

'It is well to get these things done while we can. We may not have further opportunity for some time to come.'

'Very good, sir.'

'On t'other hand we may well double without trouble, hey?'

'We must hope so, sir.'

'Double, double *without* toil and trouble. Hey, Mr Makepeace?'

But neither the clear weather, nor Captain Rennie's sunny mood, were to last. Thick cloud came out of the west and rolled over the ship, and overcast conditions remained the whole day. The wind gradually died away to nothing, and *Expedient* rode a slow, slight, but perceptible swell. A clammy, dank, oppressive feeling came down on them, and as night fell fog enveloped the ship, chill and echoing round like a great empty hall.

Rennie kept the deck, wrapped now in his cloak, and James came to stand his watch. As a precaution Rennie had taken in sail, and ordered the remaining square sails reefed.

'We may get a sudden blow, James. I don't mind reduced steerage way, if we are ready for a blow.'

'We had better post men in the chains, and lookouts forrard too, I think.'

'Yes, yes, all precautions, James. There may be ice. We are nearly blind, but we must be vigilant. Mr Loftus?' Mr Loftus was on hand, standing near the wheel. 'Mr Loftus, in your experience, will the mist rise on a clear sky tomorrow? Or may we expect fiercer weather?'

'I will speak plain, sir. There will be a storm of wind.'

'You are definite?'

'I am, sir.'

'Then the ship must be further secured.'

'Everything has been done, sir, these three watches past.'

'Yes, yes, but I want it doubly checked. We cannot have guns getting loose in a storm, nor hatch covers whipped off by the wind and sea, nor stays damaged and the like. Everything is to be checked.'

Everything was checked, necessitating considerable upheaval in the ship, and the dank fog lay over her as she slipped through the riding sea, lay over her like a pall of disquiet.

At dawn the fog lifted, there was a brief, bright calm, then the wind struck. It struck with such utter ferocity of force that the ship reared up like a terrified animal, and was pushed back on her haunches. Horizontal rain smashed across the deck like liquid shot. The ship heeled, reared, clawed her way to the top of a huge sea, hung a moment, then rushed headlong into the trough.

Rennie, his voice torn from him, barely audible in the fury of the tempest, ordered the sails close reefed. By good luck the ship kept her head up, and was able to beat to windward, but she was now making so much leeway that it was impossible to tack. They wore, and beat helplessly on the starboard tack, wore again and beat fruitlessly on the larboard tack. As the ship crested each massive sea the wind flung itself at her, holding her there on the crest with trails of spray whipping into the faces of the half-drowned watch, so that they had to turn their backs to breathe. Then she plunged, surfing heavily down into the deep deep trough, the wind cut off a moment, and the bowsprit, spritsail yard, forecastle and rigging were flooded over and submerged.

'We are lost,' murmured James, again and again, as the whole ship, from the gammoning to the waist, and aft to the quarterdeck, lay under the boiling sea. Each man clung as he could to the lifelines rigged fore and aft, and felt himself bodily lifted, bodily dragged and towed under the heaving weight of water. And each time the ship, like an animal lifting itself from slumber, rose blearily and found her feet, and shook herself free, and water poured from her, poured from the scuppers, from the rails, from the waist and stern as she lifted her head to the next onslaught.

Mr Dobie, believing himself to be dying, came on deck to vomit away the last of his life where the air was at least fresh. The wind blasted him in the face, rain and spray blasted at him, and when he was able to open his eyes, he saw the wave ahead. It rose and rose, black and glistening, rose like a towering black wall, and Dobie was momentarily transfixed.

'God in heaven,' he whispered in utter shock, turned and fled below to vomit once more in his piss-pot. But when he leaned over it, clutching it in both hands, bracing himself against the plunging movements of the ship, he found that all compulsion to retch had vanished. In those moments of profound fear he had just then experienced, his belly had become with the rest of him intent only upon survival.

The ship survived with him. For a week she battled to make westing, and was defeated, and driven back. The wind screamed and raged, tearing at the rigging and the few scraps of canvas that kept her head up, and the ship alive. Rennie kept the deck for twenty-four hours at a time, fell below to his cabin and slept through a watch, then again came on deck to stand by the wheel with the helmsman. The fire went out in the galley, but Rennie saw that it was re-lit, and that the hands were served with hot food, and double issue of spirits. Those who wished it were given the rum unwatered.

Sightings could not be taken, and they had no real idea of their position until the seventh day, when the wind abated, the sun shone, and the sea, lately so violent, was a long, rolling swell. At noon they established the ship's position, and it was found to be far to the east of Cape Horn. The wind now came from the east, and Rennie ordered the topmen aloft, and all sail set, so that *Expedient* might run free. However, he did not sail west, but south-west, into even higher latitudes.

'We must outwit the next storm of wind by going as near as we dare to the frozen wastes,' he declared. 'I will run with this easterly south-west, then go north-west when we are clear of any land; north-west, into the Pacifick.'

But the easterly wind did not blow long. It fell off, and became a lull, and into that lull came the renewed tyranny of the westerly, shrieking in over the ship, blowing out the foretopsail, and carrying away the weather stunsail booms, and a tangle of running rigging. Desperately Rennie reduced all sail. The topmen, swaying on the footropes and handing the canvas into the yards, were in fear of their lives; and it took four men to hold the wheel. Rain-squalls followed, then a tremendous electrical storm, with rain so heavy the sky seemed linked to the waves in one continuous deluge of water. There was no hope here of getting water casks up, and Rennie made no attempt to collect any of the rain. The sky darkened to near nightlike black, and was lit by great flickering flashes of lightning which illuminated the ship and the sea all around, her masts and rigging outlined starkly against the huge waves and the streaming rain. The ship lurched and shuddered, buried her head, and her body, rose sluicing and trembling and rode to the crest of another wave, and somehow stayed afloat. The leak had got worse, and now the pumps had to be manned all the time. The hands were already very tired, and soon they would begin to be exhausted.

'As soon as there is any lull, any respite of any kind, we must fother that leak with a sail!' shouted Rennie in James's ear. James did not hear a single word.

At supper Mr Dobie crept from his cabin, and sat at table, not because he wished to eat, but because he wished to be with other human beings. They were not many at table, and there was not much to eat in any case, but Mr Makepeace, seeing Dobie's distress, attempted light-heartedly to relieve it by poetic language:

'What sky-splitting light and thudding concussion, what roar and whip and scud of wind, what slide and sluice of water along the deck, and sudden shivering lurch; what is it that first makes a man afraid for his life in the midst of the sea?'

'Wh-what? What?'

'And when? When is he first afraid? Oh, he will know the moment, yes. Sooner or later he will know it, and from it learn where his heart is. Safe at home, or flying with the dolphins at the spritsail yard!'

'Dolphins? In a storm?'

'Well, you know, that was just a poetical flourish, so to say.'

'Ah. Ah. I may tell you candidly, Mr Makepeace, that I have been afraid—ohhh God!' The ship rolled horribly, all her timbers groaning and protesting, and seemed about to be swallowed whole. Everything on the table had tumbled and spilled. Dobie clung to the edge of the table in grim silence as *Expedient* lifted herself at last, and righted herself. 'I have been afraid nearly all the time for many days together,' he continued. 'However—however, I am no longer afraid.'

'No longer afraid?'

'No—I am terrified.'

'Ha-ha-ha. That is a capital joke, Dobie. Ha-ha-ha— terrified—ha-ha-ha. No longer afraid—hhhh—terrified— ha-ha-ha!'

*

Early in the morning of the following day, under a clearer sky, one of the lookouts sighted a ship to the north. Both Rennie and James came on deck, each with his glass, and tried to sight her themselves. The sea was yet very rough, and the wind veering from west to south, and back, with unpredictable, vexatious abandon. The heaving deck and the weather rail did nothing for the ocular facility of either man, but in a few minutes they saw her. She rose sluggishly on a huge sea, half a league distant to the north, on their starboard beam. They saw her, and knew at once who she was.

'That damned frigate!' shouted Rennie.

'She certainly is damned, sir, by the look.' James brought up his glass again, and on the lift caught the frigate in the lens and held her there a moment. Her mizzenmast had gone by the board, trailing sails and rigging over the larboard quarter. She was by the head, and looked to be helpless, her boats smashed in the waist, and her rudder broken. Tattered sails streamed at her fore and main, the yards unbraced. A sea anchor had been lowered, and had torn away, the hawser dragging. On her deck there were tiny figures, clinging for dear life.

'She is adrift, sir.'

'Yes. Yes. She is adrift.—Well well, there is nothing to be done.' Lowering his own glass. 'We cannot reach her in these seas. A boat would not answer. A boat would be swamped at once, and the crew drowned. Nor can I wear to reach her.'

'No, sir.'

'Even if I could reach her, she would likely fall on board us, and cripple us.'

But something about the frigate fascinated them, and they watched her for minutes together, their glasses trained. There was nothing they could do, but her plight gripped them. Presently the stricken ship rose from a trough, her masts appearing first as she rode heavily up. Rode up a tremendous sea, was turned slowly and slowly by the sea and with horrible certainty tipped on her beam. Her masts were foreshortened as her deck came at right angles, then as she slipped down the glistening mass of the wave, she turned right over, her copper gleamed briefly, and she was overwhelmed.

'Oh, Christ,' said Rennie, bringing his glass quickly down. 'Oh, God help those poor men.'

'Can we do nothing for them? Nothing at all?' Distressed.

Expedient herself now climbed a huge sea, tottered and staggered up the quivering glassy slope, and was struck at the crest by a blast of wind. She shivered, every rope of her rigging whistling and howling, and in that heaving moment James had his answer.

'We must fother that damned leak,' said Rennie, and cleared his throat. 'As soon as we are able we must do so, and save ourselves.' As the ship began the slide into the trough.

'We cannot attempt it in these seas, surely?' James, steadying himself.

'No no, but we must think of it, for God's sake.' Harshly. 'My only thought is for my own ship, and my own people.'

'Very good, sir. I will take my turn at the pumps, sir, if you please.'

'Do so, do so, Mr Hayter. We must all do so, by God.— *Expedient* is everything, against the monstrous nothing, the unbearable nothing.'

⸺⸺⸻

The ship in the calmer waters of the sixties, calmer and much colder, at the very edge of the ice. Calmer now for several days, and the leak stopped three days since by a square of number one canvas, thrummed and smeared thick with animal dung, tar and fat, and slung under the ship, and there drawn in at the sucking place of the leak, thus sealing it. The ship pumped dry, and the pumps at last left idle for whole watches at a time. By Rennie's orders every man properly fed, with full rations of meat from their dwindling stores, and

double spirits against the cold. Damage to the ship assessed—
by Mr Adgett, Mr Tangible, Mr Loftus and the lieutenants—
and where practicable repaired. An overall assessment of the
ship's condition made by Rennie—repair, water, wood,
victuals. And now they lay at the very top of the Antarctic
Peninsula, at the edge of the frozen wastes, as far south and
farther than any man in her had ever sailed before.

In the great cabin Rennie and James had sat long over their
dinner, frugal as it was, and they drank deep, each deep in his
own thoughts, until:

'Was Mr Watson a particular friend of yours, James?'

'Eh? Watson?—Oh, you mean Scud Whatmore? No, not
a particular friend. On a long commission, however, the
gunroom mess all get to know each other and rub along
together, and I liked Whatmore well enough.—It was a hard
thing to see, very hard, but if you mean: will I miss him, or
mourn him, then the answer I fear must be no.'

'It was a hard thing to see. But sea officers must be hard in
turn. We witness such things, and they strike us at the heart
for a moment—then we turn our minds to other things, and
our hearts follow. Hm?'

'I fear that is true. We are hard-hearted fellows, we must be
that, or go mad else.'

'Just so.' Quietly, reflectively. 'Just so.' He sighed, wiped
his lips and got up. 'Let us go on deck and get some cold
reviving air in our lungs.'

Rennie stood with James at the bowsprit; both of them were
slightly drunk.

'We have come through much these last weeks, James.'

'We have, sir. And I think no man in the ship has been
found wanting.'

'Not even Mr Royce, hey?' He turned, one hand on a jib
guy, and stared ahead. 'Look where we lie, now. Look at this
vast, immense place, white and white, and indigo shadow of
white.' He paused a moment, then, quietly; 'At such a

moment as this, all that is past in a man's life may be forgiven, or forgotten, or made little, in the icy flood of the infinite. Here a man might ask himself: where are we come from, and where do we wish to go?'

'Where are we come from, sir? Where do we go? North, we wish——'

'Hush!' Rennie's voice descending to a whisper. 'Hush, for the sake of your soul—and behold.'

Entranced they stood at the prow of their ship. The sky held them, a great wreathing mantle of light, and at that moment, in the euphoria of wine and silence, they felt themselves part of something marvellous, something utter and glorious, without price.

At last Rennie said: 'This is where a man might find himself, do not you think? It is the last great mystery glimpsed. Did your Greeks know such mysteries, James?'

'I think they did, sir. The poetry of the infinite.'

'Then they was fortunate men. And so are we.'

'And so are we.'

*   *   *

Forty-two degrees 28 minutes south, 91 degrees 7 minutes west. Nearly a month later, and the ship now desperately short of everything—water, victuals, the wood to cook them. The hands had resorted to shooting seabirds, and fishing over the side. The seabirds had proved stringy and unpalatable, and inadequate to feed more than a few men. The fish, in this broadest of oceans, had proved elusive. In the forecastle it was suggested:

'We could shoot dolphins, could we not? Dolphins is meat, ain't they?'

An attempt had been made to shoot dolphins as they leapt and cavorted at the bow, and had failed, all shots going wide of their mark.

'Bad luck to shoot dolphins.'

'Aye, bad luck to shoot them. The dolphins has saved many a seaman from drowning.'

'I'll lay odds that's why the other ship sank. They tried to shoot their dolphins.'

The attempt to shoot dolphins for their meat was not repeated. The anti-scorbutics, both sauerkraut and portable soup, already much depleted before the ship had come into the Pacifick, were now utterly gone, and not much lamented. Mr Wing waited anxiously, and soon his direst fear was confirmed—the first signs of scurvy began to appear. Seamen appeared at his surgery in the orlop complaining of shortness of breath. Their short breath stank, their gums were swollen, and all past injuries of the flesh, from the tiniest cut to greater wounds such as gashes, all these scars opened, and festered, and would not respond to ointment, or salve, or bandage.

'Do you suffer lethargy, Samuel Mayleaf?'

'No I do not, doctor, no. I am short of breath when I go aloft, like. But I ain't got no leprosy. I am no leper.' Indignant, and alarmed.

'I did not say that you was a leper, Sam. Certainly not. Lethargy is, it means—are you chronically tired?'

'Oh, *tired*. Am I *tired*? Well, we is all of us tired, Doctor. We is tired from our heavy duties these last many weeks, in't we?'

'Yes, we are all tired in the ship.—What I mean is, are you tired even when you wake from long sleep?'

'I am wore out, yes. I will confess that. I am mortal wore out damn near all the time.'

Much of a tier of salted pork was found to have spoiled, and should have been condemned, but was not. Several hands became ill when they ate it. Rats became bolder and bolder in the lower decks. Ship's biscuit crumbled to masonry dust, or was so filled with weevil it was more wriggling flesh than bread. Rations grew shorter and shorter. It did not rain again, and the water in the casks fell lower and lower. Rennie, to show that he was not favoured above any man in the ship, forswore his generous twice-daily brews of tea, and restricted himself to a meagre cup or two in the morning.

The leak had again sprung, in spite of the fothering sail, and the pumps had had to be re-manned, and worked steadily. The hands were disaffected, exhausted, and if not disobedient they were reluctant to respond to commands. The ship sailed north, and sometimes west, then east, then north again, glass upon glass, watch upon watch, day after day. And everything in her, every man in her, the ship herself, fell into lowness of purpose, and struggled to keep going.

'I don't know what to do, James,' Rennie admitted as they drank a glass of grog late one night. 'If we don't make landfall soon we will not be able to work the ship. I should have gone due north for the ice, north to Valparaiso. There is nothing here. There are no islands here.'

'Have you broke the seal on the second packet of instructions?'

'What? No.'

'Perhaps, was you to do so, you might discover they contain further direction, and further information. Surely their Lordships could not have sent us all the way to the Pacifick on a wild-goose chase? It cannot all be port and scheming, and naught else.'

'I should have set a course for Valparaiso. The instructions make no difference now, d'y'see? It is our immediate plight I must consider. I thought we must have made landfall long before this. That we must have sighted an island, a whole group, an archipelago of islands, in this vast remoteness of the sea. I was a fool to think it. A damned fool. Nothing is charted, and for why? Because there is nothing to chart! The ocean here is empty!—I should have sailed to Valparaiso, north along the coast.'

'Those was not our orders, sir.'

'Damnation to the orders. I must think of my ship, and my people.—Are you a devout man, James?'

'Devout? In candour, I am not.'

'Not?' Surprised. 'You are not? I thought you had told me once that you considered becoming a clergyman?'

'I was brought up to go to Church, and indeed at one time began to read for Orders. However, I reached the early conclusion that I should have been a very great failure as a priest.'

'Should you? I see, your faith was not great enough. Yes, I see.'

'In truth, it did not exist at all, as I soon came to understand. My notions of Orders had been purely romantic, a sort of young man's fairytale of bucolic happiness, tending the docile flock, and so forth. So, if you had thought of asking me to join you in prayer, to save the ship—well, I could not do so, in all conscience.'

'I had entertained no such idea,' said Rennie, who had, and was quite put out to have been detected.

'How many country parsons are truly seized of the divinity of Christ?' asked James, warming to his theme, and failing to notice Rennie's dismayed frown. 'Do not they play a comfortable role, in their comfortable livings, preach comfort and ease of mind, and eat, drink, and ride to hounds in comfort? They cannot admit these things to themselves, in course, else be made most uncomfortable. And that is how they proceed, with full bellies and empty heads.'

'Mm. Mm.'

'I do not mean that the Church has done me injury, or that I bear it any ill-will. I can stand silent with the ship's company when we are rigged for Church on a Sunday, and bow my head at the required intervals, you know, and mutter my responses. Yet in candour it means no more to me than how-d'y'-do. It is a polite, a politic, exercising of the neck and tongue.'

'Mm.—You never pray? Never at *all*?'

'I should regard it as a waste of time.'

Rennie was profoundly shocked. He tried not to show it, he tried to assimilate James's casually blasphemous revelations with equanimity, but his rooted silence betrayed him.

'I hope that I haven't offended you, sir,' said James, seeing his captain's face, 'I thought, as we are accustomed to be frank one with the other, that I might speak freely on this, or any subject.'

'No, no, you have the right to speak plain to me. We are—we are friends, after all. If you have no belief, then you could not honourably say that you had. I would ask only one thing, James. That you should not make it known among the ship's complement. It might—it might unsettle them, to think that their lieutenant was an—that he did not conform to their convictions.'

'Certainly I should not think of saying anything to the hands, it is a private matter. But I think you are mistaken if you reckon them religious, you know.'

'Eh?'

'There is not one in a dozen of them that is in the least religious.'

'No, no, you are quite wrong, James. Seaman are—many of them are privately pious.'

'I must not quarrel with you, sir. I must respect your view of them.' Keeping a straight face.

'But you do not share it? Well well, if you do not, you do not.—Mm. Mm.'

Injudiciously, James made a further point to support his first. 'A better example is the Articles.'

'Eh?'

'The assembled hands do not listen to one word of them in a hundred, and yet the Navy persists in requiring them to be read aloud by commanding officers, in pious tones. Yes, I think I may say without offence: pious tones.'

'Pious? That is the word you would choose?'

'Well then, sanctimonious. It is not the fault of commanding officers. You are obliged to do so. You are obliged to read them, and to sound solemn and fierce, and so forth, but in truth we both know it is hellfire and brimstone and little else.'

'Do we, by God?' Ominously.

'Surely, you cannot mean to say that you find the Articles of War in any way sensible? Most of them is broad nonsense, in the narrowest terms. "Shall suffer death" is cant.'

'I think we had better not discuss it any more.'

'Were each piddling offence in a ship punished according to the Articles, good God, we——'

'Did you not hear me? I said that we had better not discuss it.'

'Oh, very well. Just as you like.'

'Just as I like! Just as I like! Do not take that petulant tone with me, sir! I will not hear the King's service made the subject of your raillery and contempt!'

'I—if I have given offence, I——'

'Go on deck and take your watch, sir!'

'Very good, sir.' Rising, shocked and aggrieved.

Afterwards, as he puzzled over what had made Rennie so angry, James was forced to admit to himself that he had been less than honourable in some of his pronouncements. He had maligned—not by name, but by profession and calling—he had maligned the Reverend Dr Armitage. He had called country parsons comfortable and empty-headed. Dr Armitage was the least empty-headed of men. He was a scholar of considerable distinction, and in most things not in the least complacent or self-approving. He was a kind, tolerant and sensible man, devoted to his daughter, and to his parish.

'I am ashamed,' said James to himself. 'I am ashamed.'

But he could not understand what had caused the captain to fly into so snappish a rage. He had not maligned the captain, nor had he sought in any way to belittle him, or undermine him. He had merely, in the spirit of civilized conversation, expressed a perfectly rational view. Could not two friends exchange views? Without rancour, exchange views?—Well, perhaps he ought not to have said the word "sanctimonious", about the Articles of War. But, good heaven, why not? He and Rennie were both adult human beings. Neither was a fool. A robust polemic ought—as a matter of course ought—to be possible between two intelligent friends, surely?

'I don't understand him at all,' said James.

'Beg pardon, sir?' said the helmsman. 'I might bring her a point closer, without luffing, if you would like.'

'No, no, I said nothing. Nothing at all.—Mr Rogers, we will find out the speed of the ship.'

The sound of the chain pumps sucking water up from the bilges into the cisterns, and sluicing it thence through the dales into the scuppers. The sound of the sea, the eternal, restless sea, and the sighing of the wind in the shrouds and stays. The logline run off the spindle, the half-minute glass tipped, the knotted line read in the lantern-light.

'Six knots, sir.'

'Very good.'

Mr Loftus appeared, looking weary and concerned. 'I don't like the way she lies, to say the truth. I have attempted to say so to the captain, but he don't want to listen to me.' Drawing James out of earshot of the helmsman. 'I thought if I said it to you, Mr Hayter, that you might be able to convey my concerns to him.'

'Certainly, I shall. I don't know that he will listen to me, neither. But I shall repeat what you tell me, Mr Loftus.'

'She is by the head. Should we get a blow, or even a sudden squall, well—well, I could not answer for the safety of the ship.'

James stepped to the wheel, nodded to the helmsman, and took the living creature in his hands. Looked aloft, and stood with his felt slightly apart. He eased the helm a fraction, then brought her up, and felt the ship slightly sluggish, very slightly sluggish in response.

'Aye, you feel it, Mr Hayter, do you not? She is by the

head, and the pumps are not quite coping with that. The leak gains a little on them each watch.'

'I will speak to the captain directly.'

'There is another thing.' Lowering his voice as they stepped away from the wheel. 'More men come down with the scurvy each day. A man weakened by the scurvy cannot take his turn at the pumps.—You see?'

'With great clarity, Mr Loftus. The ship will sink if the wind rises, and she will sink if we do not make landfall soon.'

'Very soon. Very soon.—Two days, or three.'

'The captain thinks we should have made for Valparaiso from the ice.'

'No doubt, no doubt—but we did not, and we are here, not there.'

'And so, therefore, what is your suggestion?'

'We must throw the guns overboard, and our shot and powder—anything that we do not need for survival absolute. The spoiled pork, that Mr Trent would not permit to be condemned.'

'Mr Trent? I had thought that was the captain's order, to save the pork.'

'Encouraged by Trent, then. It don't matter which of them, don't you see? It is extra weight in her, that is what counts against us at present.'

'I will speak to the captain as soon as I am relieved. Rest assured.'

'Listen, I will take the conn if you will speak to him now, this minute. Go below and knock at his door.'

'You really think it is so urgent?'

'I do, as God is my witness.'

'Very well—very well.' He gave the course of the ship, and her speed, and Mr Loftus took the conn. James went below, nodded to the marine sentry, and knocked at Rennie's door. Rennie appeared in this nightcap, peering at his first lieutenant.

'Yes, what is it? Is it land?' Eyebrows raised.

'No, sir. Mr Loftus and I have had an urgent consultation about the safety of the ship. He thinks, and I am inclined to agree, that—that we should throw the guns over the side, sir.'

'Throw the guns——What bloody nonsense is this? Hey?'

'The ship is by the head, sir. She is slowly sinking. The guns weigh us down.'

'Sinking? Sinking? The ship ain't sinking, Mr Hayter. She is not awash. I can feel her under me, heeling a little with the wind. The pumps keep——'

'Sir, with respect, the pumps cannot keep up with the leak. She is by the head. I took the wheel myself just now, and I could feel her lying sluggish.'

'What does Mr Adgett say? What depth of water is in the well?'

James had not thought to rouse the carpenter and ask him, so he improvised, and guessed: 'Nearly five foot, sir.'

'Five foot? Five? That is bad. Very well, Mr Hayter, I will come on deck directly.'

James returned to the quarterdeck, and presently Rennie appeared there, wrapped in an old cloak, his hat square on his head.

'I will take her, if you please.' The helmsman touched his forehead, and stepped aside. Rennie took his place and gripped the wheel, glanced up at the mizzen to'gan'sail, and eased her off. Then brought her up. He frowned as the ship was reluctant under his certain hand, reluctant and sluggish. He shuffled his feet, bracing them, and glanced again aloft. He repeated the manoeuvre.

'Mm. Mm. She don't respond immediate, that is true.' A pause, a sniff, a slight shake of the head. He beckoned the helmsman back to his place, and: 'Very well. Mr Hayter, you will come with me. Mr Loftus, you will keep the deck. Mr Rogers, pass the word for Mr Adgett to meet us in the forrard orlop. Jump, now.—Lanterns. We must have lanterns.'

In twenty minutes he had made up his mind. With a lip-puffing sigh: 'Very well. We must have the great guns out of her. First light, so that we may see what we are doing, God help us.'

'The carronades too, sir?'

'Every gun in her, Mr Hayter. Belay that. We will keep half a dozen swivels, which ain't great guns by weight. We may need them to defend ourselves from savages, should we ever find an island, which I——' He broke off, glanced round him, and sniffed in a large breath. 'Enough of gloomy talk, hey? When the weight of the guns is gone, and she is relieved, the pumps may gain.—First light!'

However, at first light the lookout called from the mast-head:

'Deck! Land!'

'Where away!'

'Three points on the larboard bow! Land!'

Rennie came running up the ladder with his glass, jumped without thinking into the mizzen shrouds, focused his lens, and found the land. Bumps of hills, and the dark shadow of vegetation. No other features discernible, but an island clearly of some size. With vegetation. Which in turn meant water, and very possibly fruits, and other foods—wildfowl, possibly, and game. He lowered the glass, his heart lifting. And descending to the deck:

'Belay that order, Mr Symington.'

Mr Symington, as master's mate, had the watch. 'Order, sir? I do not——'

'Was you not informed, when you came on watch, about the guns? We will not do it, now. We do not need to, now.'

'Did you mean to exercise the great guns, sir? At first light?'

'No no no, good heaven, boy. *We will not throw them over the side!*'

At nearly exactly noon, *Expedient* glided into the mouth of the lagoon, as the seaman sounding in the chains called:

'Five!—And five!—Five fathom and a half!'

At a few minutes after noon she let go her best bower, and rode at anchor in one of the most beautiful places James had ever seen.

PART THREE: THE ISLAND

The island of Nagu lay at 33 degrees and 15 minutes south, 93 degrees 26 minutes west. The lagoon at the eastern end, into which *Expedient* had ventured, was a wide three-quarter circle, made nearly a full circle on the north by a long sandbar. Sandy beaches lay all round, fringed by palms, and a kind of dense tea tree. Inland lay other vegetation—trees and flowering shrubs—and a line of green hills. The highest of these hills was about six hundred foot. On the south-western side of the lagoon the beach gave way to mud and mangroves.

The water of the lagoon was remarkably tranquil and limpid. Fish of all colours and dimensions darted and flashed over the white sandy bottom, thirty foot down. There appeared to be no coral, only occasional dark clumps of rock. The air was warm, not quite tropical in these latitudes, but warm and pleasant. James focused his glass and surveyed the shoreline. There was no sign of human life. He could see birds flying above the trees inland. What were they? Sea-birds, or wild fowl? He could not tell.

'Mr Hayter.'

'Sir?' Turning, lowering his glass.

'You will take the pinnace ashore. Mr Raker will go with you, and a small party of marines. You may take two swivels, loaded with canister.'

'Very good, sir. There don't look to be any sign of life.'

'There may be no savages, but I do not care to take chances. The ship is leaking, and in great need of all manner of repair. Not to say water, food, and wood. I do not care to lose a valuable boat, and valuable men, on the first expedition, should the place be swarming with savages that have hid themselves the better to attack us. Any sign of belligerent life, Mr Hayter, is to be met with a smashing show of force. Belay that. I don't want show—I want force pure and simple. Fire, then shove off as quick as you like, and the ship's guns will be brought to bear.'

'Very good, sir. Shall we take water casks?'

'Not in the first instance. You will make a brief foray. Examine the foreshore, and a little way inland, see what you can discover as to water, food, and so forth, then return and report to me.'

James removed his hat, and replaced it.

The boat ran in on the fine white sand with a subdued grating hiss, and the seamen in the bow jumped out and dragged it a little way farther. The marines and their officer came ashore, followed by James and several seamen armed with muskets.

'You stay with the boat, Randall South, will you?' he said to the captain's coxswain. 'Hail us if anything should happen, and we will return at once.'

'Should we man them swivels, sir?'

'Only if you are attacked direct. You have me?'

'Aye, sir.'

The combined party of marines and seamen was about to make its way across and up the beach when one of the marines spied a wild pig at the line of the trees, some sixty yards from the water's edge, to the right.

'Permission to shoot the hog, sir?' To Lieutenant Raker.

'Eh? Oh, the pig. Is that agreeable to you, Hayter?'

James had agreed with Rennie that any game they might see could and should be shot. Only concentrated fire from the boat would signal an attack upon the party, and cause the ship's carronades and swivels to be brought to bear.

'Shoot, by all means,' said James, and the marine raised his musket, aimed as the pig snuffled at something in the earth under the trees, and fired. The report sent birds exploding in alarm from the trees, shrieking and cackling. The pig was knocked down dead.

'Good shot, Joe!'

'Aye, pork for supper!'

Another sound came from beyond the trees, and Lieutenant Raker held up a hand. 'Silence, there!' He turned to James, raising his eyebrows. James had heard the sound, and nodded. A child's cry.

'I can see no one,' he said quietly, shading his eyes.

'Nor can I. But that was a child, or I am not standing here.'

James cupped his hands at his mouth: 'In the trees, there! Come out and show yourselves! We will not harm you!'

There was no response, save the chattering of birds.

'Might it have been a monkey?' suggested James. 'An ape's infant?'

'I do not think so.'

'Let us discover one way or t'other. If you will take your marines to the right, I will bear left.'

'Very good.'

The seamen under James moved away from the beached boat, up the bright white sand towards the trees at an angle of forty-five degrees, their sea muskets at the ready. Raker and his marines advanced to the right. Randall South and an ordinary seaman remained with the pinnace.

'Lovely place it is, this. I am right glad we found it.' Randall South filled his pipe.

'Alls I can think of is that pig,' said the seaman. 'Cooking in its own fat, crackling and sizzling. Christ, I am hungry.'

'Belay that, mate. You will set my guts grumbling. Have a smoke.'

As the two parties reached the trees, a hundred yards apart, the two officers paused and raised a hand to each other, then led their men inland.

The lines of palms immediately gave way to thick tea tree

and shrubs, some with large red and white flowers, and the sand gave way to rich dark earth. Birds flapped and gave harsh echoing shrieks high overhead. They appeared, as James gazed up at them briefly, to be a species of large red and green parrot.

Two more pigs were seen, fleeing through the shrubs, and one of them fell to a seaman's ball. The sound of the shot was tremendous in the sunny quiet, and sent the birds into further paroxysms of shrieking rage and fright. Presently the party crossed what could only be a path, the first clear sign of human habitation. It was bedded with crushed shells, beaten flat by countless passing feet, and led away in a long curving line towards the hills, and was lost in the trees.

'Should we follow it, sir?'

'Not yet, not now. I must return to the ship and tell the captain that the island is certainly home to human beings. We will go back at once to the beach.'

At the beach they waited for Raker and his party of marines, having called them several times, and presently the party appeared, carrying their pig to add to the second.

'You did not follow the path?' Rennie, sharply.

'Well, no, I did not. Your instructions was plain. Venture a little way inland, then report to you.'

'Did you find water, a stream of any kind?'

'Lieutenant Raker's party found a freshet on the far side, which runs down into the lagoon on the north.'

'Enough to fill our casks.'

'The stream runs clear, he says, plenty for our needs.'

'Thank God for that.—So, you did not follow the path, and you saw no person upon it?'

'As I explained, sir, we heard what we thought was a child's cry. We saw no one, neither then nor when we found the path. No doubt it leads to a village, or settlement of some kind, inland. Bearing in mind your exhortation not to risk valuable men, I——'

'Yes, yes, very well, James. You did right. Never think caution ashore is a vice. You was only a small party, and we do not know how many the savages are. We must find that out.'

'I should like to take a larger party, sir, better armed, and find the village.'

'We must find it, certainly, but not yet. Not yet, James. My immediate concern is for the ship. Food, water, and repair. You may take two boats, and fill casks, as first priority. I must consult with Mr Adgett and learn from him whether or no he can stop our leak, and repair it, while we swim; we may need to careen, if so. Other wise, we may have to ground her on the sand, and repair there, and warp her off afterward. Tangible must look to the rigging. When you have filled casks, we will look for fruit, and game, and there is multitudes of fish in the lagoon waters. As we repair, we must also provision.'

'Should we not begin to chart the island, sir?'

'All in good time, James. On second thought, Makepeace may take the boats. You will help me greatly by instigating all necessary repairs aboard—Boy!—Find the carpenter and the boatswain both, and ask them to come and see me.—Before we begin work in earnest, James, let us drink a glass of wine together.'

'Gladly, sir.'

'Our luck has turned, hey?'

'Indeed.'

'Turned just in time, thank God.'

———✦———

The notion of careening her made *Expedient*'s carpenter very agitated.

'Captain Rennie, sir, I must tell you that—I must insist that to careen a ship is a very entirely bothersome process, a very troublesome thing.'

'That is of no consequence to me, Mr Adgett. We must

stop that damned leak, however troublesome the method may be.'

'Yes sir, we must. And now that we are in a safe, calm, docile place, there is no need of careening. I and my mates will effect the repair whilst the ship is heeled, sir, heeled.'

'Surely that is an even more dangerous exercise. We must get water into the ship. Look what happened at Tenerife, nearly. No no, Mr Adgett, I am all in favour of careening——'

'With your permission, sir, allow me to undelude you. Heeling ain't more dangerous than careening, it is less—far less. Careening means taking a purchase on the masts, a very strong purchase, and heaving her down by that purchase on one side to expose her copper on t'other. The masts are at once at risk, very terrible risk. The entire ship is at risk. A stopped port may spring, as an instance. All her stores must come out of her, and much of her ballast, and her guns. Everything taken out of the ship. For a simple leak!—Asking your pardon, sir, but it just *don't answer*.'

'Kindly do not raise your voice to me, Mr Adgett.'

'Beg pardon, sir. I was—I was upset.'

'We are all upset, I dare say. It has been a long ordeal before we came here, and we are all of us worn down, and out of temper. However, the leak must be stopped, and repaired. That cannot wait.—Very well, Mr Adgett, if you think we will be better served by heeling her to do it, then we shall heel her.'

'Thank you, sir.' With a relieved bowing of his head.

'And we had better not take the water into the ground tier beforehand, neither. That was the first lieutenant's idea, you know. I shall have to dissuade him.'

The ship was heeled, her starboard guns run out and the crews standing by to run them in again should any danger to the ship—a sudden gust of wind—should any such peril threaten her. Mr Adgett and his crew, their boat moored to the lower stunsail boom, removed the now useless fothering sail, and went to work. The copper was again prised up, and the planking beneath examined. Then the carpenter's mate went into the hold with a light. The leaking place was discovered at last, and a secretive length of rotten planking removed from the covering of the foreframe, from a strake under the wales, and replaced, caulked &c., and the copper reaffixed and nailed tight. The guns were run in, and the ship righted herself, and she was again pumped dry. Rennie required that the level of water in the well be measured each glass for the remainder of the watch. At the end of the watch Mr Adgett was able to report: 'Near to dry, sir. Not even an inch of water, as I say.'

'Very well, thank you, Mr Adgett—Mr Makepeace, you may now bring your boats alongside with our water casks. Belay that. It is getting dark. I do not want any man out of the ship after dark in this unfamiliar place. We will bring into the ship a cask or two for our immediate needs, and the—'

Across the calm water of the lagoon, from deep in the trees to the west, a long wailing cry sounded, so mournful and penetrating and unearthly that it stopped Rennie dead, and chilled every man on board.

'Jesu Christ,' said Mr Adgett and he pulled off his hat.

'What the devil was it?' Rennie strode to the rail and peered across the darkening glassiness of the lagoon. A slow ripple spread away from the ship, and widened. Silence.— And silence. The boats rode behind the ship, and a rope slapped now, slapped and lifted dripping, and another ripple went away.

'Well well, it was nothing,' decided Rennie. 'Mr Tangible, we are very late, and the hands are hungry. We will pipe them to supper.'

The water party had shot further pigs ashore, near the freshet, and gathered quantities of fruit. For the first time in many weeks there was something like a feast in *Expedient*, and the horrible wailing cry was for the moment forgotten.

*

Mr Tangible completed his thorough survey of the ship's rigging in the morning, and was suitably grave when he made his report.

'There is a great deal of work must be done, sir. Both standing and running rigging. Stays, shrouds, ratlines. Braces. We must look to the parrels on the fore and the main. It is a very great deal of work, and much of it worm, parcel and serve. Time is required. Time.'

'We have adequate stores of cordage for three and four strand hawser laid, have we not?' said Rennie when he had heard everything. 'Swedes tar? Twine?'

'Yes, sir. It ain't the quantity that concerns me—it is the time available to carry the work through.'

'That is twice you have mentioned time. Well?' A side-cocked head.

'Yes, sir.—Well, I hear—that is, there is word in the ship that we are to bugger off right quick from here, because of the, the——'

'The what, Mr Tangible?'

'The demons.'

'What the devil d'y'mean, *demons*? *What* demons?'

'Ashore, sir.' A jerk of his head. 'That howls in the night. That could eat a shore party entire, sir.'

'Mr Tangible,' sadly, shaking his head, 'I gave you credit for more common sense. Good heaven, man—*demons*? There is no such thing on earth.'

'We all heard them, sir, last night.'

'Yes yes, no no, what you *heard* was the cry of a frightened animal, a wild creature of some kind, I am in no doubt. Like a, like a, —well, like an *owl*.' A vigorous confirming nod.

'A *owl*, sir? Forgive my speaking plain, but that wasn't no owl—and I think you know it, too.'

'Well well, it may not have been an owl, exact. I said an owl only because they do moan and screech and so forth, in the night, very ghostly. Hey?'

'With respect, sir, asking your leave—but you accused me of lacking sense just now. Where is the sense, might I ask, in saying a thing is a owl when what we all heard had the voice of a *demon?*'

Rennie sighed, scratched his ear, pulled his nose, and held his temper bowsed tight in his breast. He nodded rapidly several times, and sniffed.

'Yes.—Yes.—Well.—There is no point in arguing and disputing back and forth, like two midshipmen squabbling over the butter, Mr Tangible. It ain't dignified in grown men in the service of the King. You may take my word on it that there will be plenty of time to carry out all your repairs to the ship's rigging. Do you need extra hands? You have only to ask. I am at your service as to extra hands, since the ship's complement has nothing else to do.'

'I am obliged, sir.'

'I will say a word to Mr Hayter.'

'Much obliged.' His hat on, and he turned to the door.

'And, Mr Tangible?'

'Sir?'

'Please not to talk of demons aloud. Hm?' A lift of the eyebrows, and he sat down.

In the afternoon James was allowed his wish, and took a large party ashore, of marines and armed seamen—armed with muskets, pistols and cutlasses—found the crushed shell path, and followed it through the trees and undergrowth inland. Overhead the red and green parrot birds marked their progress with rasping, echoing cries of warning. The air was humid under the foliage, and insects flew round their faces, and quivered in little swarms ahead of them. The forest smelt of exotic flowers, and rich earth, and of the succulent green of massed plants.

'Whom do those damned birds warn?' muttered James to himself. 'What manner of people shall we find?'

Sensing his unease, Lieutenant Raker contrived to make

cheerful small talk, until James quite sharply required him to be silent.

'In the interests of our safety, you know,' he added, regretting his sharpness.

'Very well, just as you say,' murmured Raker sullenly. 'You there, Hill, keep station. We are not strolling in the twilight.'

'You could of deceived me,' said a voice in the ranks, and James had to bite his lip to keep his face stern.

They pushed on, and came into a sun-dappled clearing. Planted across the ground, in tidy long rows, was a crop of something very like maize.

'Good God,' said Raker, 'they are peasant farmers. That means they are not savages, surely.'

The men began to talk amongst themselves, and laugh at little jokes, and relax.

'Silence, there!' James, holding up a hand. 'Stand in close order, and hold your weapons at the ready. For all we know they may be watching us at this moment.'

The marines had unbuttoned their scarlet coats in the humid air, but those coats made the whole party a very obvious target for arrows, spears, stones, or waddies, thought James as they trod across the clearing through the rows of corn. Perhaps he should have suggested to Raker that the marines removed their coats, before the party had set off. Now it was too late.

'Looks like a village ahead.' Raker, pointing. James looked, and saw neat palm-thatched dwellings, with earthen walls. There was a pile of coconuts outside one of these houses, and other foodstuffs. Pigs ran through the settlement, squealing in alarm, and disappeared.

'There ain't no people,' said a marine.

'No children.'

'And no dogs, neither. There is always dogs about, in a village.'

'There may be no dogs upon this island,' said James. 'The

people must rely on the birds to screech and warn them. We will advance at a steady pace, muskets at the ready. Be vigilant, now.'

They advanced through the trees, away from the little plantation, and came into the village, into utter stillness. No man said so, but each privately felt that here he was an intruder, that they had blundered into a peaceful, blameless place, and so dismayed the inhabitants with this display of red coats, and muskets, and bayonets, and cutlasses, that the poor wretches had all fled.

James said what every man in the party thought: 'They fear us.'

'We found evidence of domestic life, such as this,' said James, and he put down on the table a carved wooden bowl. 'They grow crops, and live in small dwellings. We left two strings of beads and some nails in one of their dwellings, to show that we wished to be their friends.'

'What?—Beads?'

'As trade goods, you know.'

'Ah, yes. Yes. Trade goods. Just so.' Rennie stared at him distractedly a moment, then returned his gaze to the papers before him on the table, and the canvas packet from which they had come.

'Mr Hayter—James—do you perceive me a fool?'

'Eh? Indeed, no.'

'You do not see before you a perfectly artificed blockhead?'

'I do not, sir. What——'

'Then your eyes do not inform you. I am. You ought.'

'Will I ask Mr Wing to attend you?' Peering at him.

'The doctor? No, no thank you. I am quite well. But I am, too, a complete muddleskull and ten times a dismal fool.' He picked up the papers and held them out. 'Here, look these through, and tell me that I am not.'

James took the documents, saw the seal and the signatures, and the broken seal on the canvas-bound packet, and knew what these things meant: the second set of Admiralty instructions, at long last opened.

'Sit, sit,' urged Rennie. 'You will need to, by God. I did.'

James sat down, and began to read. In a few minutes he said: 'They did not trust us until we were far away.'

'Just so. I don't know what to feel—elated or wretched.'

'Oh, elated, sir, surely?'

'A thing of this magnitude tells me so. But, you know, I had grown accustomed to the notion of *Expedient* as a commission of exploration, finding just such places as this uncharted island. Of ourselves as explorers, and, and——'

'Heroes?'

'Something like, I expect, something like. And now I don't know what I feel.—Damn their Lordships' deviousness and knavery! Damn them for blindfolding us, and duping us, and treating us as stupid boys! Damn them! Damn them!'

James was quiet. He was feeling enormously excited, not at all put upon, or deflated, or cheated by the Admiralty. Yet he knew how proud Rennie was, deep within him, of this commission, of having been chosen to command a great voyage of experiment and exploration; of how he had wished for the recognition it might bring, even the glory. And so James stayed silent as he saw the tears start in his captain's eyes, and drip down his cheeks. The moment passed, and Rennie recovered. 'I did not make those remarks just now.' He blew his nose forcefully. 'I did not make them, and you will oblige me, James, by never recollecting them. A sea officer does his duty. I shall do mine.'

'You have my word, sir.' James returned his attention to the documents, and read:

Whereas during the late American War, Colonel Banning Draycott, representing the Loyalist Cause, came from New York to London and interviewed Lord Germain, Secretary of State for the North American Colonies, and requested further Assistance in fighting the Rebels (France having lately entered the War as the ally of the Rebels); Col. Draycott very urgently insisted, & was corroborated by Intelligence from other Sources in His Majesty's service, that the Revolutionary Army was badly weakened in the Northern Highlands; that a Push by Loyalist Forces, greatly enhanced by Recruitment and Supply, might destroy the Revolution, & lead to the dissolution of the illegal Congress, & restoration of His Majesty's Writ. Lord North, in consultation with Ld Germain & Others, including Lord Sandwich, First Lord of the Admiralty, caused a Fund to be raised in support of said Loyalists by HM Government & by various Persons in the City of London, acting for & under the Auspices of HM Govt, in the sum of Seven Hundred & Fifty Thousand Pound Sterling of Money, in Specie. The whole of the Specie to be transported to New York, with all possible Despatch.

Spies of the Rebels & of France combined was said to have been in London, & other Ports; in order to circumvent these Enemies a Diversionary Squadron under the command of Rear-Admiral Sir Jendex Lyle sailed from Portsmouth, discreet Information having been caused to be communicated in certain Places that the Squadron carried important Documents to New York. This Squadron comprised HM ship *Argus* 74 flag; HM ship *Mesopotamia* 60; HM *Marguerite* frigate 36; HM *Vaporous* frigate 36; & HM *Tyne* frigate 32. Departed August 28th, 1779.

However, the Specie was not in any of these Ships, but in HM armed vessel *Perseus*, Captain Geo. Mallard RN; sailed for New York out of Portsmouth Sept. 2nd, 1779. When in subsequent time this Ship did not arrive at New York, after several weeks, she was thought to have been Lost in a Storm in the Atlantick Ocean during 17th & 18th September, the same Storm which overtook Admiral Lyle's Squadron, & caused the Loss of HM *Vaporous* frigate with all hands, & great damage to the other Ships. The entire Sum of £750,000 was thus thought to have been absolutely & irretrievably Lost.

And whereas subsequent to these Events one Nathaniel Combes presented himself in London to an Official of the Admiralty, & implored & conjoined said Official to convey him to their Lordships thereof, that they might hear his Account of the above mentioned Voyage of HM *Perseus*, a Board in Camera was thereafter convened by the Secretary, of the First Lord & three of the Lords Commissioners, & other Interested Persons, who shall of Necessity of Confidence remain unnamed herein;

Which said Board heard the Evidence upon Oath of Nathl Combes, in the Month of October 1785, to wit that:

Following upon the Storm in which HM *Perseus* was thought & Deemed to have been Lost, the Facts was to the Contrary. During the night of Sept. 17th, 1779, a fierce Storm having overtaken *Perseus*, the wind from the West, the Ship was knocked down in the Sea, her foretopmast and maintopmast going by the board, & all Hands believed themselves lost. In the tempest and the accident to the Ship, Captain Mallard sustained a blow to the head which rendered him senseless upon the quarterdeck.

Officers and People did their utmost in all particulars to save the Ship, and by dint of supreme Effort repaired and rigged her such that she was able to be brought to the wind, and subsequent to this the Ship did withstand the onslaughts of the night, and swam on the morrow. However, Capt. Mallard died in the forenoon watch, of his injury, and Lt. Jno. Fisk RN assumed Command of the ship. A great number of the People being injured incapacitated & rendered unfit for their Duty Lt. Fisk determined, in consultation with his subordinate Officers, that the attempt should be made to sail the Ship to England rather than to New York, given the greater distance of the latter place from the position of the Ship in the Atlantick Ocean. The ship's complement having been assembled, they was informed of this Decision; a Dispute then arose, as to the efficacy of the Plan, the Command of the Ship was mutinously overborne, and Mr Fisk and his fellow Officers imprisoned in the orlop.

HM *Perseus*, under the mutinous command of various persons not Commissioned in His Majesty's Service, but of inferior rank, proceeded South in the Atlantick Ocean, at great Peril to the Ship & every one in her, passing by places of refuge such as might have afforded them comfort, repair, water & victuals, proceeded South, across the Equator, then South West to a place upon the coast of Brasil, South of Rio de Janeiro, where extensive repair was done to the ship, of a temporary kind, and water, wood and victuals taken into her, such as was available at that place.

The Ship was then sailed South into the high Latitudes, and she was attempted to be brought to a point where she might double Cape Horn. A very terrible ordeal was then experienced, lasting some three weeks, when such attempt was made to sail the Ship into the Pacifick Ocean, and was foiled time and again by the ferocious weather of that Region, the terrible Winds, Storms, Tempests &c., which nearly defeated the attempt. However, upon the passage of three weeks HM *Perseus* was brought into the Pacifick Ocean, her rigging, canvas, masts and all her timbers very gravely damaged, and the Ship leaking. The intention of the mutineers was then to sail North to Valparaiso. However, further setback circumvented this intention; HM *Perseus* was driven farther West into the vastness of the sea, and made landfall upon an uncharted island, very barren & inhospitable, which they named without irony: Despairing Island.

All remaining Stores was taken out of the Ship, and the Specie brought ashore for safe keeping, the intention of the mutineers having been to Repair the ship, and make a second attempt to sail her to Valparaiso, far to the East. However, this was made impossible by the further misfortune for these wretched mutineers, that their bower anchors dragged in the night, when a Storm blew up, and the Ship drifted on to rocks, and was Lost.

The condition of the mutineers was now very desperate. The weather cleared sufficient that Bearings was able to be determined, and the position of the island established, which Nathl Combes later—all instruments, recorded Bearings, &c. having been subsequently Lost—recalled from memory.

The Ship's complement then took a vote as to how to proceed, and it was decided that all of the people should go into the two remaining boats, with such stores, provisions & water as they had been able to bring out of the Ship, and set sail from Despairing Island, making East in the vain attempt to reach Valparaiso, above a thousand mile distant from that place.

Further squalls and foul weather swept over the two boats, and they were driven off their course. During a lull, as the weather briefly cleared, what was thought to be an island was sighted to the South. This second island—of a much greater size then the miserable rock upon which they had made landfall—seemed to offer the mutineers hope in all particulars necessary to them—water, food, timber, &c. It was determined that the two boats should make sail for that place, where the higher slopes was altogether clothed in mist or cloud. However, the weather was against them. A further squall rushed over them, and became a fierce Storm, and they ran all the day before the wind, a Westerly wind, which drove them to the East. As night fell and the Storm blew itself out, leaving a clear sky, no further sign of the island could be seen, and the current bore them farther East. Nathl Combes gave it as his opinion that very probably this island was an Illusion, an imaginary place, which they had sighted out of wishing to be safe, and recovered from their plight.

A very dreadful Voyage was then endured, when the two boats became separated. Lt. Fisk & his fellow Officers occupied the second boat, & nine other Hands. The first boat, in which Combes was coxswain, never did sight the other boat afterward. In a desperate Passage of seven weeks, no other vessel was sighted. Their food & water ran low, then was exhausted, and of the eleven men in the boat, all but two of them had perished. Combes made the admission—and broke down into tears as he did so—that during the last weeks some portions of the flesh of the dead was eaten, when attempts to catch seabirds & fishes had failed. Such was the extremity of wretchedness and depravity to which these surviving mutinous men had been driven by their overwhelming and ravening hunger.

After seven weeks, & only two men of eleven left alive in the boat, Combes and Arthur Clinton, rated able; the merchant vessel *Ariadne* 800 tons, bound for Valparaiso from Cadiz, sighted the boat, and took the exhausted men aboard.

Subsequent to the arrival of *Ariadne* at Valparaiso, and the two men from the boat put ashore, Clinton died, and Combes lay at the infirmary many weeks, & very slowly regained his strength.

By a very circuitous route, and during the passage of several years—partly spent in whaling Ships—Nathaniel Combes came to London at last, & determined to tell

his history, and the history of HM *Perseus*. As described
to this Board, his reasons for delaying his Confession
was chiefly Fear of Prosecution for Mutiny & Treason,
which would result in his Execution. The Board accepts
that this was very cogent and rational in Mr Combes,
since it was merely the Truth.

However, the enormous sum of money involved, and
the fact of its preservation entire upon Despairing
Island, these facts having been considered by the Board,
it was thought advisable that an Exception should be
make in the case of Combes, in particular because he
felt obliged to offer his services in finding the island
again, and in finding the place wherein the Specie is
buried upon that island. Accordingly the decision was
made by the Board, in view of Nathaniel Combes's
contrition, and the great assistance he could render to
us in the recovery of the Money, that he should be
spared any further suffering & torment, and Pardoned.
Regrettably Mr Combes did not long survive the period
of inquiry by the Board, but was soon after taken ill of
the Consumption, from which he had suffered without
revealing it, & he perished——

James looked up from the document as there was a shout
from the deck, and running feet.

'Captain, sir. A canoe! There is a canoe put off from the
shore!'

Rennie went on deck, and James put down the document,
reluctantly put it down, and followed him there. The canoe
that now approached the ship was long and narrow, paddled
strongly by six or seven men sitting one abaft the other, and
a lone figure seated apart in the stern. This man was covered
in a great drapery of shells, across his chest, and at his neck
and wrists, and he wore a head-dress of a curious rounded
shape, a kind of bonnet.

'That is their chieftain, no doubt,' muttered Rennie.

'James, will you keep the deck a moment? I must throw off these clothes and put on my dress coat. These savages must see that I represent the King.'

James did not say that it might be advisable for them both to put on their dress coats, but he felt it all the same. His plain coat was dusty, and his britches and shoes dusty from his shore expedition. He brushed himself down, and tidied his appearance as best he could. The canoe approached the ship, the paddles were taken inboard, and the little vessel glided to where *Expedient* darkened the water under her lee, lying tethered north and south, and came alongside. There had been very little time to prepare, but quick-thinking seamen had rigged side ropes for the ladder, and now the chieftain climbed nimbly from his canoe and up into the ship. He had hesitated only very slightly before doing so, had conquered his fear, and come, and now he stood on the quarterdeck looking at James as the lieutenant took off his hat and bowed. The chieftain's face was lined, but he was straight-backed and muscular. His skin—like the skin of all the men in the canoe—was light brown, nearer to olive than dark, his eyes were dark, with bloodshot whites. His grizzled hair was long, tied back and loosely braided, with decorations of shells. All about him were shells strung together, of various sizes and shapes, chinking richly as he moved. His bonnet, of shark's skin, was decorated with roundels of carved mother-of-pearl. He was not armed, none of them appeared to be armed. He wore a loin apron of shells, as did the others, although his was more elaborate, and finer. Otherwise they were naked. The men in the canoe made to follow their chief, but he said something to them, and they remained there.

Rennie now appeared at the companion, in his dress coat and cockaded hat, his sword buckled. The chieftain stared at him a moment as he approached, and appeared instinctively to understand that here was a fellow chief. Rennie removed his hat, and bowed.

'May I welcome you to my ship, in the name of His Majesty King George?' said Rennie. 'My Symington!'

The chieftain flinched, but instantly disguised his alarm by laughing, and taking off his hat in imitation of Rennie. Mr Symington appeared, carrying a hatchet, a mirror, and a bolt of red cloth. Rennie nodded at him, and the midshipman loosed the cloth with a flourish on the deck. Scarlet billows unfolded round the chieftain's feet, and he gasped in surprise, then laughed in delight. The midshipman removed his own hat, and presented the artifacts, the hatchet and the mirror. The chieftain stared at them in bewilderment, and dropped the hatchet on the deck.

'If Your—Your Excellency will allow me to demonstrate?' Rennie gently took the mirror, and made a show of staring into it, smiling and nodding at his reflection, then he handed it back.

The chieftain held the mirror up, and looked into it. Again he gasped, recognized himself, and laughed in astonishment. Rennie and James, and Mr Symington, waited politely as the chieftain continued to stare at his image, and laugh. At length he lowered the mirror, and taking up a position directly in front of Rennie he made a speech. It was a long speech, accompanied by gestures, and there was much pointing at the shore, and out to sea. Not a word of it was understood, and the curious high-pitched sounds, linked by rhythmic fricatives, and clickings of the tongue, were unlike any language Rennie or James had ever heard.

'Your—Your Excellency is very kind,' said Rennie, when it was apparent that the chieftain had concluded his remarks. 'May I assure you that the King is in all respects mindful of Your Excellency's most gracious welcome to your very— your very beautiful land. What the devil am I to say next, James? I must make a speech at least as long as his, hey? Other wise he will think I slight him.'

'Make frequent mention of the King, and bow frequently, sir—I should,' murmured James.

'Indeed, indeed, just so.' He bowed. 'His Majesty King George has asked me to convey to you his thanks for—for allowing us to to avail ourselves aboard His Majesty's frigate *Expedient* of your very excellent game, which we have enjoyed eating, hard pressed as we have been these many weeks for anything but the humblest foodstuffs. His Majesty hopes, and indeed trusts, that his officers in the ship may again take game from the bountiful stocks you have in your beautiful island.' He bowed. 'With Your Excellency's indulgence, His Majesty's officers will like to make—to make various observations, and so forth, upon your island, which will be of great interest to His Majesty, and to all those who serve him.' He gestured round the lagoon, and inland, and included the whole of the surrounds in a general, generous flourish of his hands. 'His Majesty King George is most grateful for your kindness, and hospitality, in welcoming his serving officers, and granting them your kind permission to do all that they ask, in the name of His Majesty King George. Good God, James, I am near exhausted. Is that enough, d'y'think?' And he bowed again, and smiled very graciously, his hat in his hand. The chieftain reached forward, and took it.

'Eh?' said Rennie, startled and disconcerted. He began to reach out his hand for the return of his hat, thought better of it, and smiled. 'Yes, by all means. Think of it as a gift, by all means. A gift from His Majesty King George.' And bowed again. 'My back will presently spring, James, and I shall be bent over like an old man.'

The chieftain watched him with keen interest, laughing a great deal, and clearly very pleased with his new hat, which he turned over and over in his hands. However, he made no effort to present his own hat to Rennie.

Mr Dobie appeared at the break of the quarterdeck, and caught James's eye. James in turn drew the captain's attention to the presence of his clerk.

'What is it, Mr Dobie?'

'I should like to try to speak to him, sir, if I may.' Indicating the chieftain.

'Speak to him? How, pray? Surely you cannot talk in his tongue?'

'Well, sir—I have a book by me, which I brought with me when I knew that I might go to sea. It is the language, or part of several languages, of the Pacifick Islands, compiled by earlier mariners. I admit, not the languages specific to this region, but I should like to make the attempt, sir, if you will permit it.'

'By all means, Mr Dobie. If you can make yourself understood, and in turn understand, that will greatly assist us. Proceed.'

Mr Dobie faced the chieftain, and made a show of obeisance, bowing down before him, then lying full length on the deck.

'Mr Dobie!' began the captain, but James touched his arm, and when Rennie turned shook his head.

The chieftain appeared to be both intrigued and pleased by Mr Dobie's supine posture. And now Dobie rose, and began saying something to the chieftain in a language unknown to the officers, not wholly unlike the language in which the chieftain had spoken, but by no means exactly similar. The chieftain gave no sign that he understood any word that Dobie spoke. He frowned, he looked puzzled, and then he laughed, as much to reassure himself as to reassure his interlocutor.

'Well, Mr Dobie? What do you say to him? Does he apprehend you?'

'I fear not, sir. The dialect I used—imperfectly used—is from the Sandwich Islands. He—he does not understand me.'

'Very well, Mr Dobie, thank you. You have done your best.' He smiled and bowed again to the chieftain. 'I did not approve of your prostrating antics, before a damned savage, but if it had assisted me in retrieving my hat I should not object. However, I do not complain in any case, since you did your best. What is his name? Can you discover it?'

Again Dobie attempted to make conversation with the chieftain; again without result.

'Never mind, Mr Dobie.' The captain smiled again at the chieftain, and by considerable effort of gesture, and more smiling, urged him to go below to the great cabin. The chieftain glanced once over the side, to make certain of his waiting canoe, then acquiesced, and went down the companion ladder.

In the great cabin the chieftain stared about him in fascination, looking at everything. When he was asked to sit down, and shown a chair, he did not know what it was until Rennie and James sat down. He laughed, and put on Rennie's hat, over his own bonnet, and stared about him again. He was given something to eat, hurriedly concocted by the steward. Cold pork, which he declined; fruit, which he ate; ship's biscuit, which puzzled him; and wine, of which he took a great draught, then clutched at his throat, his eyes starting, and coughed in a near paroxysm of fear. Rennie and James hastily took up their own glasses and drank them off with a show of satisfaction. This reassured the chieftain, he forgot his fear of being poisoned, and again fell to examining the cabin and everything in it. He rose, and moved about, looked at the glass of the gallery windows, looked through at the lagoon, and was delighted. He picked up the captain's long glass, he took up a pair of dividers, he took up a silver flask, another hat, a book, and from a rack the captain's pistol case. He piled these things on the table, and made another lengthy speech.

'I rather think he means to accept these things as gifts,' said James.

'Hah, does he? Then he may think again.'

'Are you sure that is wise, sir? To offend him by refusal?'

Rennie looked sharply at James, then at the chieftain. 'Wise? Wise? Good heaven, I cannot let the fellow walk off the ship with these valuable things. With anything he likes.'

The chieftain looked at them, at their anxious faces, smiled and laughed, then with supreme confidence and satisfaction gathered the objects on the table into his arms.

'He may take the book,' said Rennie. 'I do not value the book. Sermons, you know. Dull. However, he may not take anything else. I do not permit it. I will not.' He smiled beneficently at the chieftain, and bowed his head.

'Sir, you indicate by your expression and gesture that you approve. If you relieve him of these gifts now, it will appear a very great contradiction, a vexing insult.'

'Damnation, I have not approved of anything. I did *not* make presents of these valuables. Sentry!'

The marine sentry appeared at the door. The chieftain saw him, and was distracted.

'Sir, I think that you make a mistake if you——'

'I do not ask for your opinion, James.' He stood up, and firmly removed from the chieftain's grasp all but the leatherbound volume of sermons. He put the objects back in their places, one by one, with emphatic care. 'There, d'y'see? My things. My goods. Hey?'

The chieftain stared at him in astonishment, then he began to tremble. His eyes widened. He glanced in fear at the sentry. He pulled off Rennie's hat, and proffered it.

'No, no, Your Excellency. No, you may keep the hat, it is a gift from His Majesty King George. That, and those damned sermons, you know.'

When they went on deck with the chieftain a few minutes afterward, Rennie and James found the crew wrestling with the men from the canoe, who were removing anything they could lay their hands on: belaying pins, marlin spikes, oars, nails, rope, a knife, &c. One had tried to snatch a musket from the hands of a marine, and had been knocked down on the deck with the butt. A mêlée had erupted around this incident.

'Silence, there!' bellowed Rennie. 'I will have order on my deck!'

The fighting ceased, and the tangle of bodies and flailing arms became individual men. The islander who had been hit by the butt of the marine's musket lay senseless on the forecastle. A pool of blood had formed round his head.

'Mr Rogers. Fetch the doctor, if you please.'

Mr Wing examined the fallen man, and pronounced him gravely ill. His skull was fractured. It was unlikely, in his opinion, that the man would recover.

'I had better have him taken below, sir, into the orlop, where I will do what I can for him over four-and-twenty hours.'

However, when it was proposed, by sign language, that the patient should be kept in the ship, his companions, and their chieftain, made such a display of reluctance, lamenting and grimacing reluctance, that Rennie was obliged to allow them to take him away, limp and head lolling, into their canoe.

'What the devil happened?' demanded Rennie, as the canoe was paddled vigorously away from the ship. 'How came he to be injured?'

'He tried to steal my musket, sir,' said the marine. 'He was very impudent. They was all very impudent, stealing all manner of things without shame, in front of us. I had to strike him, else lose my weapon.'

'Aye.'

'They was stealing, aye.'

'They would not desist.'

The seamen, some with bloodied faces, backed him up.

'Very well. Mr Raker!'

'Sir?' Appearing.

'You will take a statement from your man, and have it written out and brought to me. I have no doubt he did right, but it must be entered in the log, and in your journal and mine, and made official.'

'Very good, sir.'

'Mr Hayter. We will worm all our carronades, and our swivels, and reload with canister. Should any assault be attempted to be made on the ship, I will like to see all canoes, rafts and other craft they may possess blown to splinters, and every man in them killed. You have me?'

'Very good, sir.—May I ask——'

'Yes? What?'

'It is nothing, sir. I will see to our guns at once.'

James went about his work with great reluctance. He felt sure that the islanders had meant them no harm, and that the officers and crew of *Expedient* had got off on the wrong foot with them. Supposing that they returned, a large party returned, in several canoes, and that Rennie ordered the guns turned on them, and fired? Fired without any sort of rapprochement being attempted? Such a thing would be very wrong, murderously and barbarously wrong. Would it not? And later he said so to Rennie in the great cabin.

'No it would not, James. Sit down like a good fellow, will you, and dismiss that sombre look from your face? Very likely the savages will return, and we must be ready for them, in case they should try to take the ship, or damage her. My first responsibility is to my ship and my people. Then to their Lordships and the King.' He held up the documents James had been reading earlier. 'Did you finish looking these through?'

'I did not, sir, no. With your indulgence?' He reached for the papers, and Rennie pushed them across the table.

'A glass of wine?'

'Thank you, sir, I dined in the gunroom.'

'That chieftain fellow'—as James sat down—'that I called your Excellency because I couldn't think of anything better, certainly not your Majesty; well, you know, he took away my best hat. My best hat, and a leatherbound book, a bolt of red cloth, a hatchet, and a mirror. Immense riches in a remote and isolated place like this. I don't suppose they ever saw a white man before this.'

'I expect you are right, sir.'

'They are only primitives. Primitives. You cannot tell

what they may think, or what they may do, from one hour to the next, whether they are piled with gifts, or no. They cannot tell what they may do themselves, since they do not know, neither. My responsibility is to repair my ship, without interference, and then search for that island— Despairing Island.'

James found his place in the documents, and read on:

And whereas the circumstances of Nathl Combes's untimely death presented the Board with a difficulty, namely that he could no longer act as Guide; and the further difficulty that his memory of these Events may have been imperfect; nevertheless it was deemed of eminent and profound Importance that the attempt should be made to locate the island wherein the Money lies, & to discover the Money. Subsequently, to bring the Money to England with the utmost Despatch.

You *Captain William Rennie RN*, in command of His Majesty's *Expedient* frigate, are therefore required by us the Board to follow these Further Instructions:

All previous, other & various Instructions, Duties & Commands to you, as to your Present Commission, are hereby Revoked. You are to Proceed, from the moment of your breaking the Seal hereto Attached, to seek and discover the said Despairing Island; & to Recover the said sum of Money, the property of His Majesty's Government, & to Carry that Money to England, and there Deliver it Entire into our hands.

The Document attached hereto shall be your Bearings, as given to us the Board by Nathl Combes, as nearly as his memory served him.

James turned over the document, and looked for the attached bearings. He could not see them. They were not attached. He felt his heart beating.

'Are the bearings not with the instructions, sir?'

'I have them by me.' Rennie held up a small square of cartographer's paper.

'May I know them, sir?'

Rennie pulled at his nose, and took a long sniffing breath. 'James, I must ask you something. You have not said any-thing—anything at all—about these new instructions, to any one in the ship?'

'I have not.'

'Very good. You understand, it isn't the kind of thing I would in usual ask a fellow officer. But this—these,' he held up the square of paper, 'are of such grave importance, the sum involved so stupendous, that I am obliged to ask.'

'Certainly. I understand.'

'Very well.' And he gave the paper to James across the table. James read:

32 degrees *south* × *94* degrees *west*

Despairing Isle: about 1 mile long E—W by ¾ mile wide,
& not more than 30 foot at the highest place;
rocky & barren.

He looked up. 'Do two things about this strike you, sir?' His earlier excitement much reduced.

'If you mean that firstly, the bearings is too imprecise for comfort, and second, that we are now in that very approxi-mate region ourselves, then yes, my answer is in the affirmative.'

'I meant that the island is very small, sir, and very low. It will mean quartering the ocean to the limits of these bearings, will it not?'

'Yes, I see. We might search for it a long time—and never find it, hey?'

'To find it—well, it will require the most extraordinary good fortune.'

'Indeed, James, indeed.' He filled two wine glasses. 'In Despairing may we find success.'

James allowed himself to smile, and raised his glass.

'And now, James, we must make a plan. We must repair in two weeks, and weigh. I don't mean to stay here a minute longer than I must.'

'Two weeks, sir? Surely, nearer a month? There is a long sick list, don't forget. We must be a seaworthy ship, and an healthy one, before we begin the search.'

'By God, James, what is the matter? You talk as if you did not want to find the money.'

'On the contrary, sir. You misapprehend me. It is because I do so very profoundly wish——'

'You must not allow the earlier experience of the commission to colour your thoughts. We was misled. Hoodwinked, and misled. Doubts lingered at all points of the compass. The scientificals bamboozled us, deliberate. We took in guns that patently did not suit, and dangerous powder. We was subjected to fantastical intrigue, and conspiracy. Sir Robert Greer, the fellow. A very sinister, dark, piratical, troublesome, secretive scoundrel, the fellow. I am bound to say, now, that he was certainly behind those two ships, James. He sent them both, I am in no doubt.'

'I am inclined to agree with you, sir. His purpose was to——'

'To prevent our running away with the money! That is his cast of mind! To trick, and deceive, and conspire, and then to cover everything in a cloak of mistrust! He is unable—his kind of man is unable—to conceive of the simple notion of duty! Of the honour of sea officers, and their duty to the King's service! He thinks we are *all* pirates, the damned wretch!'

'Yes, I think you are right, he does. Because of what happened in *Perseus*, he does.'

'At any rate, we are no longer troubled by *Larkspur*, nor by the other ship. In spite of his best scheming we are rid of that damned nuisance, in least.'

James was silent, and Rennie checked himself, and inwardly cursed.

'James, I should not have said such a heartless thing. Your friend was in her, Watkins, and you saw him drown.'

'Whatmore, sir.'

'Indeed, Whatmore—It was a very heartless thing to've said, and I—am sorry for it.'

'I felt heartsick for them all, so many men drowned.'

'I did myself. It was a very shocking thing. I should not have said what I did.—It is all the fault of that bloody bugger Greer. He made me immoderate, the fellow. Sending men to their deaths, the unfeeling villain!'

'He can hardly be blamed for the weather at Cape Horn——'

'I do blame him, by God! I have it in my mind to flay the skin off his back, if ever I set eyes on him again!'

'Tie him to a grating?'

'Aye, and—well well, I must not use such violent language, it don't become a serving officer. Fellows like that must face their Maker, and take the consequence, at the end. I say no more.'

⋯≍⋯

While the ship was repairing, Lieutenant Makepeace and Mr Symington, with Mr Dobie, and a small crew, sailed the cutter round the island. They came back with detailed and enthusiastic reports, and many bearings, soundings, and sketches. Rennie listened on the quarterdeck.

'The island is nine mile long, sir, and three mile wide. The highest point is near to the western end, and on the north, near cliffs, there is a spectacular bay, about two mile round the point to the north-west of us. The scenery is very grand, cliffs on the west, and south of them a large settlement, and many canoes. The people—the men—swarmed out to meet us in their canoes, and were very amiable. More than amiable, positively adoring, I should say.'

'Was their chieftain among those who greeted you? The savage who came aboard the ship?'

'Indeed, sir, but he is not the most important man in the island, by no means. He is merely a secondary figure, I should say.'

'Certainly, he is,' nodded Dobie.

'The great man is the king. We saw him, in his large canoe, with outrigged booms and a second hull that is not occupied. He wore a prodigious quantity of shells, and was draped about with our red cloth, and carried our hatchet, and he was wearing your hat, sir.'

Rennie glanced at James. 'Was he? Was he? And it was all very friendly and so forth, you say?'

'Oh, indeed, sir. They treated us like visiting royalty ourselves, almost with reverence.'

'We saw also the man who was injured aboard the ship,' said Dobie. 'He was on his legs, walking about, with a kind of coating of mud on his head, thick dried mud.'

'Good heaven.' Rennie, mildly. 'There was no sign of ill-will, because of this injury to him?'

'None, sir. He was cheerful, and pleased to see us.'

'The king took us to his village, that is, the king's followers took us there. It is a large settlement, above an hundred dwellings, I should say,' estimated Makepeace.

'We learned the name of the island, I think,' said Dobie. 'It is Nagu, I believe, and the king is called Naa Maa.'

'How d'y'know that, Mr Dobie?'

'I was able to listen to their patterns of speech, and to pick up words and phrases here and there. I believe I might learn enough to ask simple questions in a week or two.'

'Then by all means do so, Mr Dobie. We must maintain friendly dealings with them while we are here, and use our trade goods for the food and livestock we shall need. If you can talk to them, and they to you, so much the better. Mr Makepeace, I will like to see your notes and soundings and sketches, and so forth.'

'There was a most wonderful thing when we went ashore,' continued Makepeace, as Rennie examined his notations in the great cabin. From the deck overhead came the clatter of a serving mallet dropped. Makepeace checked himself, and was silent.

'What? What say?' Looking up, frowning.

'It is of no consequence, sir.'

'No, no, Mr Makepeace. Never think I am undisposed to listen to my officers. Say on.'

'Well, sir, there is a clear pool, a tidal pool under the cliffs, which the people showed us. It is filled with fishes, darting and dashing, and flashing to the surface, making great ripples across the water. When we ventured into the pool barefoot, and bare-legged, the fish swirled all about us, gliding against us, against our flesh, like caresses. It was the most entrancing event, and we would all hope to repeat it.'

'Indeed?—All?'

'Mr Symington and myself, sir, and Mr Dobie. And the crew. We all walked among the fishes.'

'You describe the experience with feeling, Mr Makepeace, and that does you credit. We are not always mere obedient cyphers in the King's service—we have hearts, and souls.'

'Oh, yes, sir.'

'Perhaps you will write it down for me, will you?'

'I should like to very much, sir.'

'Your drawings and observations also do you credit, Mr Makepeace. Should you like to make the detailed survey of the island's coast?'

'I should like that more than anything.'

'Then you may do so. You will begin in earnest tomorrow. Mr Hayter will explore the interior, with a larger party.'

But on the morrow, early, the king came to visit *Expedient*. He came by his regal outrigger canoe, with a platform amidships on which he sat in his swathes of shining and chinking shells, and his red cloth finery, and Captain Rennie's best cockaded hat. His canoe was accompanied by a large flotilla of smaller canoes, like the one that had first come to the ship with the lesser chieftain. They all came round the point to the north, and paddled into the lagoon, and they sang rhythmically as they dug their paddles into the sun-dazzled water:

'Naa Maa! Naa Maa! Teh-oo aa Naa Ga Neh rangeh Yan!'

'What a horrible great din they make,' said Lieutenant Royce.

'It is a powerful, surging, heartfelt song though, do not you find?'

'Eh?'

'Never mind,' said Lieutenant Makepeace.

The flotilla surrounded the ship, and having been observed for some time from the masthead and the deck, they were welcomed with what ceremony the ship could muster. Ropes were rigged, and ship's boys in clean britches posted. Captain Rennie and his officers stood on the quarterdeck in dress coats. The ship had been hastily and partially dressed in what bunting could be found in the sail lockers. The rigging was in a fairly lamentable condition, in repair, but the decks had been washed, and the ship was—if not at her best—then at least clean. Mr Tangible and his mates exercised their calls very sweetly, and the king came up the side and into the ship, accompanied by the chieftain the Expedients had seen on his earlier visit, and several other men similarly decorated with shells, and sharkskin bonnets. The king was taller than any of them, and his skin a shade lighter, or perhaps that was merely the effect of the light glowing and reflecting in the hundreds of strung shells festooning every part of him.

'Your Majesty,' said Rennie, and took off his hat; he bowed.

The king looked at him, stared at him, in something like wonder. He did not lose his pride of bearing, nor was he in any way diminished, but he stared at Rennie with wonder and reverence.

'Naa Ga Neh,' he said softly, then louder: 'Naa Ga Neh.'

Rennie ushered him below, where he was offered breakfast. The king ate nothing but fruit, and did not care for tea.

Without embarrassment he spat a mouthful on the decking canvas, and laughed. Rennie smiled, and endeavoured to be polite, and accommodating, and hospitable. But his quarters were now filled with the king's followers, who stood and squatted in every available place, and when the king rose and began examining the furniture and instruments in the cabin they made way for him, and in imitation began to pick things up and handle them. The king took Rennie's pocket watch, which the captain had not had the presence of mind to keep in his pocket; he took a handkerchief, and an inkpot, two pens, and Rennie's personal seal, with a stick of wax. His followers began to appropriate other things, and Rennie became increasingly anxious lest his ship be stripped of all valuable and essential items.

'We must reach an understanding with the fellow,' he muttered to James, whom he had asked to join the party for breakfast.

'I should advise Mr Dobie's presence here.'

The schoolmaster was sent for, and had to push his way through the assembled throng of shell-chinking bodies to the table.

'You sent for me, Captain Rennie?'

'Ah, Dobie, yes. Listen now, can you get this fellow—the king, to understand you? Can you understand anything he says, in turn?'

'I—I will try, sir.'

'What I want you to do is convey to him, with my respects, that he cannot steal my property.'

'Steal, sir?'

'Yes, yes, steal. Look, they are stealing everything in the cabin, for God's sake, look around you.'

Mr Dobie made every effort to converse with the king, and made some little progress. At last, after several minutes of awkward interchange, he turned to Rennie and said:

'Sir, I believe King Naa Maa—I believe he thinks you are his ancestor spirit.'

'That I am what?' Astonished, looking from Dobie to the king, and back. 'What?'

'Yes, sir, I conjecture, since communication is very slight, and impeded by my ineptitude, but the iteration, and reverential nature of it, I am sure mean something of that kind. You are his ancestor spirit Naa Ga Neh, and the ship, all of us in the ship, are come from across the immensity, from Yan.'

'Naa Ga Neh,' said the king, regarding Rennie gravely. Abruptly he crouched down on the deck, and bowed his head, and all his followers did the same. 'Naa Ga Neh. Naa Maa teh-oo aa Naa Ga Neh rangeh Yan.'

'I see,' said Rennie. 'Well well—what am I to do, Mr Dobie, hey?'

'I think that—that if you want your property back, sir, it will be as well to acknowledge that you are indeed from far away, across the universe—Yan.'

'Very well. It is great nonsense, Mr Dobie, but very well. Say so to him. Say that I am that person, will you? That I am Yan, and wish him to return my watch, and so forth.'

On deck a different and potentially more disastrous confrontation was happening. Other followers of the king, coming up the sides of the ship, now swarmed all over her. The marines, formed up with their muskets, were the chief objects of interest, both for their scarlet coats and their muskets. Islanders approached them, touched their coats, and peered into their faces. Two or three of the islanders became more insistent, and tried to wrest muskets from the grasp of marines, and their sergeant turned in agitation to Lieutenant Raker.

'Whatever happens, Sergeant Miller no man is to give up his musket,' said Raker, and to a ship's boy at the ladder: 'My compliments to the first lieutenant, and he must come on deck directly. Jump, now!'

James came within a few moments, took in the scene at

once, and said: 'The king himself must deal with this, other
wise we shall have bloodshed. Stand fast, Mr Raker.' And he
left the lieutenant standing there with his nervous marines
before an increasingly agitated group of a hundred muscular
and determined islanders. A musket fell with a clatter on the
deck as the marine who had dropped it wrestled with an
islander. White piping clay from the marine's crossbelt came
off on the islander's skin, on his hands and arms, and he was
momentarily surprised. And now Raker called firmly:

'Fix bayonets!'

and cocked his sea pistol.

And at that instant, as the menacing multiple clicking of
metal on metal sounded, King Naa Maa appeared. He said
something in a high, harsh, rasping tone, and all of the
islanders, on the deck fell back, and crouched down.

Behind the king Rennie now caused to be brought on deck
a large chest, which was opened with some show of care by
two white-gloved ship's boys. Inside it were trade goods:
hatchets, glass baubles and trinkets, hand mirrors and tray
upon tray of nails. There were also several dozen bracelets
made from copper.

'Mr Dobie!'

'Yes, Captain?'

'You will convey to our guests that I wish to make them a
present of these—these delightful things. Each savage is to
have a nail for himself, and one other trinket. The king may
take the hatchets, and looking glasses, and the bracelets, and
distribute them as he sees fit.'

'I will do my best, sir.'

'That is all any of us may do, Mr Dobie. I must do so
myself, presently, when I fear I am to be obliged to go
ashore.'

'You will remember, will you not, sir, that you are Naa Ga
Neh—and not Yan?'

●━━━ ⊫◇⊨ ━━●

King Naa Maa spat fermented coconut juice upon the swept earthen floor of his large dwelling, and Rennie, seated opposite him on the woven matting, sensed that this was part of a ritual which he too must observe, and reluctantly spat juice on the floor himself. The king laughed joyously, and gave Rennie to understand, by proffering a carved wooden bowl of roasted meats, that he should eat still more.

Captain Rennie returned bloated and queasy to the ship in the launch, and sent for Mr Wing. With him in the launch, and in three following canoes, came an immense quantity of foodstuffs, and live hogs, which were now being hoisted into the ship by the anchor watch, attended by the men from the canoes, who were fascinated by rope work, but of little use in applying it.

'Mr Wing, I have ate a very great deal of—of I don't know what, except that it was cooked after a fashion in a very large pit in the earth, covered in leaves and stones. Meat, certainly, and vegetables, certainly, and a kind of pudding, and a kind of liquor. My head aches, my guts cramp and stab, and I am very uncomfortable. Is there anything you can do to relieve me?'

'There are two things, Captain Rennie.' He hesitated.

'Well? What are they, in God's name?'

'Not in the Almighty's name, no. In the name of medical science they are, firstly, to induce vomiting, and secondly to induce defecation. Either, or both, in distressing volume.'

'Puke or shit, hey?'

'Put succinct, yes.'

'And if I don't care for neither the one nor t'other? Is there no potion, no pill, no medicine that will stop the burning and the bloating?' He farted heavily, and winced.

'There is pills and potions, yes. However, they will produce one or other of the effects I have just now described. Or you could—you could merely let nature take her course.'

'Eh?'

'By communing with her, sir, upon the humblest throne, peacefully, without taking anything.'

'Ah. Ah. Yes.' Farting again. 'Perhaps you are right. That will be best, perhaps, after all. Thank you, Doctor.'

'That, and sleep.'

'Sleep, hm. Very good.'

'And tea upon waking.'

When James came to the captain's cabin at dusk, having been asked to do so, he found Rennie drinking tea and studying charts.

'Will you drink tea, James?'

'Thank you, sir, I have already dined.'

'A glass of something, then?—No?'

'Nothing, thank you, sir.'

'Very wise in you, very wise. We eat far too much at sea, you know. Eat too much, and drink too much.'

'Surely, we have had very little to eat, until we came here?'

'Yes, what I meant was that whenever the opportunity shows itself, we eat more than is good for us. At any rate, it is charts I am concentrated upon.' Tapping the charts on his table. 'This island, where we are anchored now, which they call Nagu, is not charted, and the island we seek is not charted. The bearings from the sealed instructions place it anywhere within this broad region.' His finger circled and circled a place on one of the charts. The ship carried official Admiralty charts, but those for this region were, Rennie suspected, not wholly accurate. He pulled another chart to him, and spread it, weighting it with leads.

'There is Easter Island, far away west-by-north-west, and even farther away on this chart is a very small island called— what is it called?' A finger, tracing the cartographer's paper. 'Yes, here it is. Pitcairn. Even farther away.' The finger, tracing back. 'Our own bearings put us—here. We have checked them against the chronometers, and with good noonday sightings.' James nodded. 'And the charts show nothing at all, for near a thousand mile until San Fernandez to the south-east. Hm. Hm. Cook traversed the region, but could find no land here. Nor has any other mariner found land.' He sniffed, and pulled his nose. 'It ain't a cheerful thing, looking at these charts, hey? Thank God we have a good ship under our legs, or we should be hopelessly marooned.'

'Indeed, yes. Shall you wish to proceed, while we are anchored here, with the charting of this island, sir?'

'Aye, we must, for good reason. I have assigned the task to Mr Makepeace, James. What I——'

'To Lieutenant Makepeace, sir?' James found himself very slightly put out.

'Indeed, to Lieutenant Makepeace. He is a splendid draughtsman, and it will aid me to have his soundings and observations accurately charted.'

'Of course, sir. I will gladly lend him assistance, if you wish it.'

'No no, James. I have something far more important for you to do. Any competent sea officer may make charts, good heaven. No, what I will like you to undertake is a thorough exploration of the interior of the island. The vegetation, and so forth. The flora and fauna, to use the scientifical language. Birds, animals, plants, James. The lie of the land, hills, mountains, plains. A thorough investigation, with sketches, measurements with the, the——'

'Theodolite?'

'Theodolite. Just so. Such examples of plants as you may gather, and so forth, and so forth. An expedition that will enable us to hold up our heads at the Royal Society, should Banks ask for us upon our return.'

'I should think the only men who will ask for us upon our return will be led by Sir Robert Greer.'

Rennie sighed, and straightened from the charts, and stretched his back.

'We shall be here repairing for two weeks. We cannot look for, nor find, Despairing Island before that time has passed. It will be as well for us to busy ourselves during that fortnight, James, with some worthwhile occupations that may be of some use to their Lordships, or the members of the Royal Society, in years to come.'

'Certainly, you are quite right, sir. I did not mean to contradict you. I will prepare the expedition, and get the theodolite up from the hold.'

'Beside that, James, you and I are the only men in the ship who know *why* we are in the Pacifick Ocean. The others—all of them—think that we are here to conduct just such work as I have assigned to you, and to Mr Makepeace. Hey?'

'I see what you mean, sir.'

'Take a large party, James. Be thorough.'

'Good night, sir.'

'Before you go to bed, James, I wonder if you have noticed a very peculiar thing about this island?'

'Sir?'

'We have seen no women.'

'Oh, that. Yes, I had noticed that, all right. I expect every man in the ship has noticed it.'

'Well?'

'Well, certainly there are women here. There is no such thing as a race of men entire.'

'So, James. Why have they hidden them? Are we such monsters that we cannot be trusted?'

'I—I expect there is something in that. From their point of view, you know.'

'What? Good heaven, I have been invited to the most lavish feast. The king could not have been more obliging. My guts will remind me for days to come of his generosity. Not to notice the vast quantities of food he sent back with me to the ship. He cannot think me a rapacious scoundrel, ready to ravish any or all of his wives and daughters, when he treats me so well at his table, surely?'

James did not go early to bed, but sat up in the gunroom, reading by the light hanging from the deckhead. It was less stuffy in the gunroom than in his cabin, and he could stretch out his legs in a sprawl under the table. The light was not very good, but in any case his eyes soon strayed from the page, from Alexander Pope, and focused distantly elsewhere, in reverie. Rennie's aggrieved remarks about the women of the island had brought thoughts of Catherine into James's head, thoughts long banished—not from indifference, but from self-protection. Doubting thoughts, jealous thoughts, unhappy ones. Thinking of her made him unhappy; sometimes even wretched. Catherine was beautiful, and she was alone. The comparative remoteness of her life in Dorset, behind the rectory wall, could not protect her always and always from the eyes of other young men, and from their ardent wishes. Sooner or later she would feel those eyes upon her as she went about the town, or dined at a neighbouring house with her father, or attended a dance—Dr Armitage was not a confining or containing or censorious father, with thoughts constantly in his head about his daughter's chastity. And so therefore, sooner or later, Catherine would meet another young fellow, another young blood, who would be struck by her looks, and dark gaze, her intelligence and engaging good humour, and would fall under her spell. Damn him! Damn him! Even if *Expedient* should find this island, Despairing Island, even if the great sum of money thought to be there should be recovered, and he got his share of any reward, would it not be too late, by the time he returned with his newly acquired riches? That was supposing *Expedient*'s officers were to be allowed to share anything. Rennie had made no mention of reward, should the money be found. Had he? He had not.

Royce now came into the gunroom, evidently looking for James, and having found him interrupted his thoughts.

'I must ask you, Hayter, whether or not you was aware what has been going on?'

'Mm? Going on?'

'Yes, yes. That my facilities are being used, behind my back.'

'Facilities, Royce?' Looking at him, and frowning.

'Yes, they do. Repeatedly.'

'Who, pray? Do what?'

'The mess servants!'

'I am at a loss. What d'y——'

'My chamber-pot! They make use of it! In my cabin!'

James closed his book, and sighed.

'I don't know which one is the culprit. I'll pin back his ears for him, by God.'

'Will not that present a difficulty?' An edge on his voice. He stood.

'What?'

'If you do not know which one it is?' He pushed in his chair.

'I'll catch him, and pin back his ears for him!'

'Yes. Yes. I should, if I was you.'

'The damned presumption of it!'

'Indeed.' A glare at him.

'The squalid damned presumption!'

'Mr Royce!'

'Eh?—Yes?'

'I am not the mess secretary. Kindly take the matter up with him. For Christ's sake.' And he banged out of the gunroom, and went on deck for a breath of sanity.

There was a moon, reflected in a long lazy wipe of light on the glassy mirror of the lagoon. The air was slightly cooler here, and he could smell the forest ashore, the flowery, earthy perfumes floating across the quiet water. James put the book in his pocket, and leaned on the rail, and stared at the pale glimmering sand of the distant beach in the moonlight. He sighed, and wished that Catherine was by his side, now, closely leaning there at his hip, her head leaning in on his shoulder, and her arm round his waist. He felt his heart beating, and the pricking burn of tears.

From across the calm water now, from the deep silence of the forest, came the long unearthly cry, mournful and echoing, and as chilling as when he had first heard it. More chilling. He shivered, and tried not to let fear creep into his heart, to join sorrow there.

The interior of Nagu was, at the western end of the island, steep and difficult as the terrain rose from the little bay, noted earlier by Lieutenant Makepeace in his brief circum-navigation. James had landed in the little bay in the launch, and assembled his party and their equipment on the beach. James had brought with him two midshipmen, Mr Pankridge and Mr Rogers, and Lieutenant Royce. He was not fond of Royce, and had thought to exclude him from the party, then had had to bow to the captain's wish that his junior officer should be given something useful to do.

'He will fret if he is not occupied. Mr Makepeace don't want him, I know that. Likely he would drop a glass, or an Hadley's, or lose the boat anchor, or something like that. So you must take him, James, and make sure that he is not fretful.'

'Very well, sir, if you insist. I will take him, and a dozen handkerchiefs, in case he should graze his knee, or stub his toe, and fall to weeping.'

'Sarcasm, James, sarcasm. We shall make an officer of Mr Royce this commission, James, without sarcasm.'

'Very good, sir.'

His party was quite large—a dozen seamen, half a dozen marines under Sergeant Miller, the two middies, and Royce and himself. Now as they climbed up from the white sand, into the thick vegetation, James hoped that they might find a path. They spent half an hour hacking through the under-growth with cutlasses before they were forced to turn back, their way absolutely blocked by rearing rock. From the beach they turned a little further east, and this time they did find a path.

As they climbed, the marines sweating in their scarlet coats, and the seamen sweating under the burden of the equipment—the theodolite, the reflecting telescope, the anemometer, all of which the captain had insisted should be taken, taken and carried—James wondered at the elaborate extent of this deception. For that was what it was, after all, a deception. Need Rennie have made it so damned arduous? he asked himself. He paused to mop his face and neck, under the shading trees beside the path.

'Mr Royce.'

Puffing up beside him, and leaning forward, his hands on his knees. 'Yes? God, this is hot work.'

'Yes, well, we all feel it. Are you noting the vegetation? And the animal life? The birds?'

'I cannot very easily notice anything, you know, nor write it down, when we are climbing and climbing all the while, Hayter.'

'Pause then, as we are paused now, and make your notations, and catch us up.'

'Good God, I should become lost at once. No, I shall make my notes when we stop to refresh ourselves, with your permission.'

'Very well.'

James had decided to make his own observations, notes and sketches, so that there would be at least a reasonably accurate record of what they saw; but he must keep up the pretence that Royce had a particular part to play in the expedition, an important role as scientifical observer. The red and green parrot birds were again overhead, screeching and cackling and following the progress of the climbing men like aerial sentinels. James had glimpsed warblers on the forest floor, and silky white tropic birds, with their long red spiny tails, half-hidden in the trees. The trees here were tall hardwoods, with distinctive red flowers. Perhaps—almost certainly— they would make good timber trees. Something worth reporting. Even here, high in the hills, pigs scurried and snuffled in the undergrowth; they were everywhere in the island.

The party followed the path for three-quarters of an hour,

and reached a fork beneath a clump of trees. The air here was slightly cooler, and there was a light breeze from the west, which cooled the sweat on them, a grateful relief. The left-hand path climbed narrowly and steeply away into the north, the right-hand path levelled out, and led into a clearing not far ahead, to the east.

'We will tack to starboard,' announced James. 'Sergeant Miller.'

'Sir?'

'Your marines may remove their coats, I think. His Majesty's scarlet is all very well, when we are rigged for Church, or welcoming the island king aboard, but here in the forest it don't signify. Only the birds notice, hey?'

'Thank you, sir. Very welcome, thank you.' And he gave the order, and removed his own coat.

In the clearing, from which there was clear viewing at all points of the compass, James instigated various observations—of the highest hills to the west, and to the east; of the speed of the wind; of the sun. He made himself busy, and the party busy, and Royce sat down and began to make his notes. The party was industrious, and absorbed, and the clearing around them was peaceful, when they heard the sound again.

From deep in the slopes below them, deep in the dense forest, a wailing call, rising to a near scream, then falling off to a chilling moan. James felt a chill from the base of his skull, where the hairs stood on his neck, to the base of his spine.

'Fucking hell,' said one of the marines.

'I—I don't like the sound of that,' said Royce, clearing his throat. He stood up, his neckerchief undone, and his heat-reddened face now became pale. 'It sounded awful near.'

'It's the same sound we heard in the night, ain't it, sir?' Sergeant Miller.

'Possibly, possibly,' said James. 'However, we need never be fearful of a wild creature's call. It wishes to attract a mate, or repel a rival, or somesuch. Take no notice. We have work to do.'

The sound came again, and James had to admit that it did sound nearer, this time. The party was growing fearful. Men edged together, and the anemometer was left unattended where it stood on a flat rock. James saw that the creature must be discovered, and if necessary shot, to dispel what was quickly becoming unreasoning terror.

'Very well, it grows impertinent. As a precaution, Sergeant Miller, you will fix bayonets, and stand guard over the equipment. Lieutenant Royce, and Mr Pankridge and Mr Rogers, will remain here with you. I shall proceed to the east, with my own party. Gurrall, Torrence, Sams, Mayleaf, Blithe, Stock, bring your muskets, and follow me.'

'I will not face no ban-shee,' said Stock, a broad, muscular man, whose face, in usual ruddy, was now like Royce's waxen pale.

'Now, Reliant Stock, do not be foolish,' said James. 'We are men, armed men in His Majesty's service. That is a wild creature, an animal. We will chase it off, and if necessary——'

The cry came again, and cut across James's reasoned tones with unreasoning utterness.

'That is a ban-shee, a demon,' said Stock. 'Roman Tangible says so, and I says so. It is a demon. Shore parties ain't obliged to face no fucking demons.'

'You do not refuse to obey me, do you?'

'I—I do not mean to disobey you, sir.' His pale sweaty face very sullen.

'Then take up your musket, and file along.'

'Come on, mate,' whispered Gurrall. 'It is mutiny if you don't.'

'Silence, there!—Well, Stock?'

'Aye, sir. I am coming.' And under his breath, as he took up his musket: 'Shitting and passing water, but I am with you.'

The party moved off down the hill from the clearing, into the trees at the top of a steep draw. They could hear a stream far below, the rush of water through rocks. They descended with care and presently came, to the sound of a stone as it fell with an echoing crack, to an outcrop of rocks above a great drop. The shoulders of the rocks were covered in green and white lichen and furry green moss. Trees towered up the slope behind them. Here the air was damp and shadowy, and struck through with shafts of sunlight over the dark drop.

The sound came again, almost directly upon them, a terrible racking cry. It rose to a scream, a death-fearing scream, and ended in a moan. Every man froze where he stood. A musket fell, and clattered on the rocks.

'Stand fast, now,' said James in a low, confident voice, as confident as he could make it. He drew his sword, the blade ringing in the scabbard, and held it pointed.

'*Ahoy, there!*' he bellowed. '*Show yourself, or know the consequence!*' Steel gleamed in the shadowy light.

It was entirely absurd, entirely theatrical, and it had its effect. It cheered the men, who knew it was absurd, and it made them braver at the same moment, so that some of them even smiled. They did not smile long. From above them, pittering through the leaves, came streams of liquid, and the party was liberally and pungently splashed.

'Jesus, we are being pissed upon!'

They moved away from the rocks, and a man raised his musket, raised it without an order given, and fired high into the trees.

'Avast, there! Cease firing!' shouted James. He stared up through the ballooning mist of powder smoke, and could see nothing but foliage. 'Do not fire unless you are ordered to do so, d'you hear me?'

'Yes, sir.'

'Yes, sir.'

'Even was we to be attacked, sir?' Gurrall.

'Being pissed upon don't count as attack, Jacob Gurrall. Who fired, now? Was it you, Mayleaf?'

'Aye, sir.'

'Then you may reload, as quick as you like.'

'No powder, sir, no ball.'

'Christ in tears! Who has ammunition? Have we no pouches?'

'I have a pouch, sir,' said Gurrall. 'Brought with me at the last moment, as a precaution against the demons.'

'Very good. Give it to Mayleaf. We will fan out a little, every man at the ready, and make a search back up the slope. Do not fire unless you are directly threatened, d'y'have me?'

Cautiously, glancing frequently above them, the little group moved apart and ventured up the slope, James slightly ahead of them, his sword in his hand. A dilemma faced him: if they did not find the creature, if his men were not reassured, and their confidence restored, how could he ask them to pass the night on the island? They had stores enough, and sailcloth with the equipment to rig tents, but how could he persuade these fearful, superstitious men, unhappy ashore unless it was within easy reach of taverns, and whores, how could he persuade them to continue with this expedition for the next day or two, if they would not spend the nights in the forest? It may be that they would have to return to the beach, to the small bay in the west, and camp at the boat.

In the wider bay on the north-east of the island, Mr Dobie was landing in the small cutter, brought there by a midshipman and a small boat's crew with the captain's approval. Dobie had applied to go with Lieutenant Makepeace in his boat, on charting duty, but Rennie had said:

'You will not become fluent in the savages' tongue while you are afloat, Mr Dobie. You must go ashore, if you please, and talk to the king, or to his close advisors—princes, or whatever they are pleased to call themselves. Learn their tongue sufficient to discover certain facts.'

'Facts, Captain?'

'Indeed, facts. Have they ever before seen white men, in a

ship? And where do they conceal their womenfolk, and children? Make it plain we are no threat to their women. None at all.'

'You are sure, sir?'

'What the devil d'y'mean, Mr Dobie?'

'You are—you are sure that is what you wish me to ask the king? You are Naa Ga Neh, so far as I can understand a kind of god spirit. I am—I am merely a kind of underling. Perhaps the king may decided to behead me, in wrath, if I ask him about the women.'

'Nonsense, Mr Dobie, damned nonsense. You ask it in my name, and he will do no such thing. If he did, he would have me to answer to, you may be sure of that.'

'However, that would be of no benefit to myself, by then.'

'You are insolent, Mr Dobie!'

'I beg your pardon, Captain, but—it is my head, after all.'

'Oh, very well. You are not properly a man-of-war's man, are you, Dobie? Not a right seaman, in any sense. You are merely accustomed to pen and ink, and book, and such polite maidenly things, and I must not tax you with a task that is beyond your fortitude.'

Dobie was stung. By now he knew something of the status of men in a ship, and the captain's scathing remarks stung him.

'With respect, Captain Rennie, I am in least a member of the gunroom mess, and entitled——'

'Entitled, sir?' Sharply. 'You are rated, in a ship, and nothing above.' Then, seeing Dobie's deep wound, and knowing that he must rely on him for communication with the island's king and his people, he softened.

'I did not mean to insult you, Mr Dobie. If I did—I beg your pardon.'

Mr Dobie bowed.

'Pray ask the king only whether or no he has seen white men before this. Will you?'

'I will, sir.'

'Very good, Mr Dobie. And——'

'Sir?'

'And I will like to keep a journal of all your experiences in the island. Such a document may well be of great use to their Lordships, you know, and very likely to the Royal Society. All your observations, and experience, and a record of the island tongue, such as it is.'

'I had already begun to take notes, sir. I shall now expand, and amplify, with that in mind.'

He landed on the beach, steeped neatly on the sand, and went up towards the king's house. How his life had changed since he came aboard *Expedient* months since, unconfident, dropping his hat, knowing nothing of ships, or the sea, or the Royal Navy. How it had changed from those first miserable days of seasickness, and despair, when he had been unable to believe that he would ever belong in a ship, that he would not shortly die. No, he was not yet a seaman, would probably never make a seaman, but he belonged in the ship. The midshipmen liked him, the seamen tolerated him, amiably tolerated him, and he felt that in the gunroom he was now wholly accepted. Except by Royce. He knew that Royce would never acknowledge him, never accept him, never treat him as anything other than a damned shameful nuisance. He did not know how Rennie thought of him, or what he thought of him. On occasion the captain was jovial and pleasant, and treated him almost as an officer; on other occasions Rennie was dismissive, and brusque, and treated him as if he were no more than a steward, or a ship's boy.

'However, I am stronger in every way than I have ever been before, and I have found a home better than any other I have ever had, and I regret nothing.'

———— ✠ ————

James and his party of seamen did not find the creature they sought, and after an hour they returned to the clearing.

'The brute micturated upon us, but we could neither see it nor hear it, afterward,' he told Lieutenant Royce, who was not listening.

'There is a village, another village. Young Pankridge slipped away, you know, bored, and he found it. It is full of women.'

'Eh? So that's——'

'Women and children. Hordes of them, so——'

'How far to the east? Mr Pankridge?'

'Less than a mile, sir. It is perfectly hidden, in a hollow, a kind of natural mountainous hollow. I was not observed, myself, neither. There is a stream nearby.'

'Yes, we saw the stream, or heard it, farther down. Very well, thank you, Mr Pankridge. You will lead the way there, if you please.'

'Oh, but look here, Hayter. Shouldn't I go with you.' demanded Royce.

'No, I will like you to remain here, as before, and guard the equipment. I will take my party, with Mr Pankridge, and return in—what shall we say? One hour? If for any reason we should not return in that time, you had better return to the beach, and stay there with the boat, if necessary overnight.'

'With all of the equipment, d'y'mean?'

'Of course, with the equipment. You have a dozen men, with the marines. You must manage, somehow.'

'But, good heaven, how shall I know the way?'

'I promise you, Mr Royce, that I shall make every effort to wear and return within the hour,' James called as he and Pankridge, followed by Gurrall and the other seamen, set off through the trees to the east.

When the hour had elapsed, and there was no sign of them, Lieutenant Royce began to fret.

'Sergeant Miller?'

'Sir?' Knocking out his pipe.

'I should like you to fire two shots, close together, as a signal to Mr Hayter's party.'

'Aye, sir. With your——'

'And then we will listen, with the closest attention, for an answering pair.'

'Yes, sir. With your permission, I will fire three shots, sir. Then there can be no mistake.'

'Is that usual? Oh, very well. Three, then.'

The three musket shots were fired, and as the racketing echo died away, Royce and his party listened, hands cupped to their ears. There were no shots in reply. Only the sounds of birds and insects in the tranquil forest.

'That is damned odd, ain't it?' said Royce uneasily. 'We had better repeat the signal, Sergeant Miller.'

The exercise was repeated, with the same negative result.

'I could jump along and find them, sir, if you like,' said the second midshipman now. 'I'm sure they cannot be far away. If Pankridge could find the village, I know that I could——'

'That will do, Mr Rogers, thank you,' said Royce curtly. He was damned if he was going to be pre-empted in his duty by a choirboy midshipman. He glanced round in what he hoped was an authoritative manner. 'We had better make for the beach, I expect. I think we may leave the heavier equipment behind us, since we shall not need it before tomorrow.'

'Oh, but, sir. Surely the first lieutenant required us to take it all with us?'

'That will *do*, thank you. Sergeant Miller, coats on. The rest of you, take up your weapons, and the tents and so forth, and we shall proceed as far by the path as we can, towards the beach.'

And he strode out along the path with what he hoped was every appearance of confidence, and fortitude, befitting an officer in command.

⊷ ⸺⬥⸻ ⊶

Captain Rennie, with all his commissioned officers out of the ship, completed a thorough inspection of her with his warrant officers. With Mr Loftus, and Mr Trent, he assessed stores, and the storing of the hold. With the carpenter, and the boatswain, he looked at the ship's timbers, and at her rigging. He was satisfied as to the soundness of her timbers, and at the progress being made in caulking and in repairing spars. He was less than content with the progress of repairs to her rigging. The parrals, as an instance. Yards could not be sent up when the parrals were repairing. The ship was half-naked.

'It is time, sir. I did say that particular, if you will recall. We do require more time than a fortnight. Two weeks ain't enough.'

'Thank you, Mr Tangible,' as they passed along the larboard gangway. 'It is my place, I think, to decide these things in the ship, and I have allowed you a fortnight.'

'I do not follow you, sir.' Following him along the gangway. 'Why is there need for rush, for haste? Lieutenant Makepeace is charting the island. Lieutenant Hayter is exploring. We are carrying out our work according to our instructions from the Admiralty, are we not, sir?'

'You will allow me to know what my instructions are, Mr Tangible. We have lost a great deal of time as it is.'

'That's as may be, sir. Other ships might lose time, in our circumstances. And regarding as we have come here, and how fortunate we have been in finding such a place——'

'I do not release you from your commitment to complete your repairs, to both standing and running rigging, within the two weeks I have allowed you. Do you have me, Mr Tangible?'

They stood on the forecastle, so that Rennie might make an overall assessment as to the condition of his ship, a quick by-the-eye assessment, looking aft, and the water-reflected sun briefly dazzled him, glancing and dappling across his face. He raised a hand to shade his eyes. Perhaps the boatswain took this as a sign of wavering resolve.

'I understand you, sir. However, I must again declare——'

'Only a commanding officer may declare, Mr Tangible. That is all, thank you.'

Rennie returned to the great cabin, and drank a pot of tea. The brew soothed him a little, and he fell to contemplation, his eyes lighting on various places in the cabin—lockers, charts, the deckhead lantern, the quarterlights through the door ajar, a gleam of sun on his pocket watch as the ship eased herself almost imperceptibly at her tetherings.

'Far from home,' he murmured to himself. 'Far from home, William Rennie—yet fretful still.'

He thought of his life before the commission, of the long period ashore after *Mystic* was paid off. He thought of Admiral Bailey at Deal, of how they had strolled together in the afternoons. The admiral lived in rooms above a millner's shop in the town, and Rennie had lived in rooms—a room, one room—above the saloon of a public house that was pleased to call itself an hotel. The two sea officers had often walked together along the front, one or both with a glass under his arm, and looked at the sea, and talked. The admiral had not always been merely jaunty:

'Had I any influence at all, you know, I should long since have put your name forward.'

'That is kind in you, sir. Do not concern yourself.'

'But I do, my dear fellow. A sea officer don't belong on the beach, in a place like this. Not that Deal is unkind to us, mark you. Deal on the whole answers tolerable well. I have my duty, and must not complain, but you . . . A sea officer that has seen action, real fighting action at the Saints, and is still young—well, he don't belong ashore, sir. He wants a ship under his legs.'

'He does. You are right, sir.'

A judicious, sniffing breath. 'There is no disgrace, you know, in serving John Company. Had you thought of it? You would in least be at sea, with your own command—I am in no doubt you would get a command.'

'Admiral Bailey, I am astonished.'

'Eh?'

'You know very well how their Lordships look upon a sea officer that wishes to move up, should he be so unwise as to go into the merchant service while he waits.'

'Post captains, they do not countenance. Posts should not do so. But you ain't a post.'

'No, sir. However, I wish to be made post. Going into the merchant service—well I fear it would not enhance me in their Lordships' eyes. You see?'

And the elderly admiral had placed a hand on Rennie's shoulder, briefly placed it there.

'The navy can appear to be a damned rum thing. You never know what it may do, nor why. What I do know—know with utmost conviction—is that His Majesty's service always wants good men. Good seamen, good sea officers. You are such a man. Never forget that, and never despair. Hey?'

'Never despair,' murmured Rennie now. 'I have no damned right to do anything but rejoice. Then why do I fret? Why do I push Tangible, and tax him? It is a mystery.'

He heard a boat come alongside. Presently Mr Dobie came to his door, and asked to see him.

'What is it, Mr Dobie? Did the king try to cut off your head?'

Mr Dobie was hot and tired, and splashed with sea water from his brief journey in the jollyboat. He was disinclined to be frivolous.

'No, sir, he did not. However, he may plan something more serious for yourself, Captain, I fear.'

'More serious than beheading? I cannot conceive of it, I confess. Will you drink tea?'

'Thank you, sir, I am thirsty.' And he gulped down a cup of Rennie's brew, and sat down.

'Now, Mr Dobie. What has the king done, and what are his schemes?' Rennie took up a pencil, and made a note on one of his charts. He was still inclined to smile.

'He means to abduct you.'

Rennie looked up from his chart. Dobie's face was earnest in expression, so earnest that the captain lost his smile and was bemused.

'Abduct me? Abduct the captain of one of His Majesty's ships? The notion is fantastic.'

'No, sir, I do not think so. You are aware of King Naa Maa's belief, that you are their spiritual ancestor, the deity of his people, Naa Ga Neh. Such a belief lies at the very heart of their lives.'

'Yes, well, so it may, but they are primitives. Christian teaching is unknown to them. To them our ship is a magical vessel, and all her complement magical figures, in a magic lantern show. We must not expect from them the learning, nor the perception, of men such as ourselves. They have not the power of reason, you know.'

'It is not a question of reason, Captain, with respect. It is a question of *belief.*'

'Yes, yes, but your conclusion that they would try to abduct me is fanciful, Dobie. They would not dare. You are mistaken, I think.'

'Sir, I fear that I am not. I am not.' Leaning forward.

'But, good heaven, Mr Dobie,' impatiently, 'you have only just begun to unpick their tongue. You said yourself it would take weeks to understand, to begin to talk freely, and so forth. Do you say, *can* you say, with absolute certainty, that their king means to kidnap me? Hey?'

'You are right to suggest that my grasp of their tongue is very imperfect. However, the king iterated his meaning by gesture, by sign. In my opinion, sir, there can be no doubt about his intent. You, Naa Ga Neh, have returned. He means to keep you here, at Nagu, forever.'

'It is nonsensical. The whole thing is entirely fantastic.' Rennie stared out at the lagoon through the stern gallery windows, then turned again to Dobie. 'At any rate, let us put that aside for the moment. What did the king say in answer to your question?'

'My question, sir?'
'Has he seen white men before this?'
'Oh, yes.—No.'
'Well, which is it, Mr Dobie? Yes, or no?'
'He has never seen *anyone* before. The Naguans believe that they are the human race entire.'

⊷ ⧓ ⊷

James woke with a feeling of being chilled to the bone. His neck was stiff, and his back ached. He was lying on a hard, gritty surface, in darkness. He could smell damp, damp earth, damp rock. Near him in the darkness was heavy, snoring breath. Where the devil was he? What was this place? He sat up, and felt about him for his sword. Clearly he heard, echoing in a great tall empty space somewhere beyond, the trickling of water. And now it came to him—they were in a cave, had taken refuge there, late in the afternoon of yesterday, and had lain here all night. He was hungry. They had gone to sleep supperless. A faint glimmering of light away to his left told him that day had dawned. He stretched, and got to his feet at a crouch, anxious not to strike his head on hard rock, and made his way carefully, treading with infinite caution, towards the light.

They had taken refuge there, he and his party, yesterday, when they had seen a great party of island men enter the village below, just as James and his party had been about to go down there, into the hollow. The men had painted faces, and had decorated their hair, and their upper arms, with red flowers and white feathers. They carried long spears, and what looked like rocks tied in little woven baskets, which swung at the ends of woven ropes.

'Certainly, they are warriors,' James had muttered. 'They outnumber us forty to one. We will remain here, for the moment.' And they had stayed in the trees above the village, concealed there. The island men had gathered all the women and children together in the open spaces between the circled thatched dwellings, and performed a kind of ritual. The women wore no decorative shells, no decoration of any kind, nor did the children—all of them were entirely naked, so far as James could make out with the unaided eye. He had left his long glass behind with the other equipment.

The ritual dance, the ceremony, continued long. There was no music, no clapping or chanting, only silent, slow and graceful movements of the feet and hands, as if this mass of people moved as one, floating and undulating like kelp on the ocean swell.

'What is it? A mating dance?' Gurrall, wonderingly.

The ceremony had come to an end as quickly as it had been begun, the women and children returned to the houses, and the men began to leave the village, coming up by a path directly towards James and his party in their hiding-place. And so they had fled—literally fled—fearful of being discovered, overwhelmed, and beaten to death with the basketed rocks. And had found themselves at the entrance to caves, higher up, had run in there, had heard the throng of island men outside, and briefly despaired. The men had massed at the entrance to the cave, and begun a low, humming song, accompanied by a strange whirring boom, endlessly repeated.

'Christ, they are going to slaughter us,' said Mayleaf. 'Come in here after us, and cut us to pieces. That is their fucking death chant.'

'Silence, there,' said James. 'Stand fast.'

And they had stood fast, and waited, muskets cocked, sweating with fear in the chill damp of the cave. And after a long time—perhaps an hour—the humming song had ceased, and the relentless whirring boom, and there was silence.

'They have gone,' said James.

Darkness came on, and the decision soon had to be made: would they, should they, spend the night in the cave, or return to the clearing where the rest of the shore party waited?

'I think we had better wait here,' James decided. 'In darkness we cannot find our way back. In any case, Lieutenant Royce has instructions to return to the beach. We had better stay here.'

'All night, sir?'

'We are safer here than in the open. We do not know what those warriors may be up to, nor where they may be waiting in the darkness.'

'But—we has no victuals, sir.'

'Nor nothing to drink.'

'Now, we are all in the same condition,' said James, without raising his voice, but with authority. 'I go hungry with you, and thirsty. But which is better—hunger and thirst, for a watch or two, or become supper ourselves for those heathens without? Hey?'

This dire suggestion had its effect, and James felt slightly ashamed of himself for making cannibals out of the Naguans, when they had given no such indication of themselves. And so they had spent the night in the cave, uncomfortable, damp and chill, without sustenance, or light, or fire. Now as day dawned, and James made his cautious way to the cave mouth, he saw no sign of the massed warriors. All he saw were trees, rocks, and the path leading away down the slope, and an overcast sky. The air today was cooler, but still very humid. Birdcalls sounded in the trees, echoing across the forest in the hanging hush of early morning. James stretched, stretched again, and began to feel very hungry. Perhaps, in the forest, there were fruits—berries, or plums, or even grapes. He ventured from the cave-mouth, and glanced up the steep slope behind. He saw only rock, and clinging scrub, and mist. No good. Instead he turned and went down the path a little way, keeping a watchful eye, his hand on his sword. Presently he turned off the path down a gentler slope, with ferny undergrowth and wider-spaced trees. Halfway across, in the still indistinct light, he was aware of a shadowy figure ahead of him, between tree trunks. Was it a man?

James stopped dead, his heart thudding in his chest. Was it one of the warriors? Had they been watching him, following him, waiting to pounce and capture him? But the figure too had frozen, was poised there, half-turned towards him. Was it a man?

And now James became aware of a sharp odour, a strange pungent smell drifting on the air, like the reek of a hidden fox, or a goat penned in a foetid barn. Yet even more distinct, somehow, like a—like a—yes, like the itinerant man he had once found in a ditch in Dorset, who had fallen there drunk, and slept overnight, and when James found him had glared red-eyed and bellicose with hangover, and his huff of toxic breath and foul, months-unwashed smell had made James turn away in dismay and disgust. That sort of smell, near exact.

'Who are you?' said James sharply. 'Come out of that, now, and show yourself.'

The figure did not move for a moment, then with a bounding movement leapt from between the trees and disappeared away down the slope. James heard the snapping of twigs, and the crash of a dislodged rock, then nothing.

When he returned empty-handed to the cave, the men had built a fire, and were waiting for him.

'There is peculiar things in this cave, sir,' reported Gurrall. 'Hanging rocks, and spires of rock, and paintings on the walls—and there is bats, I fear.'

James accompanied him deep into the cave, and Stock came with them; evidently none of the others wished to leave the fire. James and the two seamen carried brands from the fire to light their way. Beyond a fissure, through which each man had to squeeze braced round, the cave opened and deepened, and was adorned with long pointed stalactites, and rearing minaret stalagmites, which cast great shadows on the walls in the flickering light. On the end wall, a broad space, were dozens of charcoal drawings, and paintings done with clay pigments, or possibly with vegetable dyes, James could not tell. They depicted birds, animals, and fishes. There were several depictions of what looked like eagles, or kites; parrots; tropic birds; terns. There were many fish, including primitive but fierce-looking sharks. There were dolphins. And a strange apelike creature, with a black face and white circled eyes. On a separate part of the wall were pictures of canoes, and warriors in head-dress and shells, under the fiery glow of sun. The warriors appeared to be greeting a lone figure in an enormous canoe, coming from the sun, from the sun far away across the sea.

'I think it is very possible that this is a sacred cave,' mused James, holding up his brand to look at the lone figure. 'Those fellows outside last night may not have been aware of our presence. They may possibly have been performing some kind of religious ritual, a ceremony of some sort, at the cave mouth.'

'It is like a cathedral church, so it is,' said Stock, removing his hat. 'Builded all of beautiful carved stone.'

'Well, not quite built, you know,' said James. 'Those pillars are stalactites, that depend, and stalagmites, that rise. I have never before seen them, only heard of them.'

'No, sir, surely they is artificed?'

'Indeed, no, I assure you not. Over time—centuries, I expect—water drips from the roof of the cave to the floor, carrying sediment in solution in each drop, which produces the pillars, both above and below. They are prodigious in size, and beauty, but they was not sculpted by a man.'

'Then it is God's work,' murmured Stock, turning and holding his brand high. 'That is the Almighty's hand there, so it is.'

Their brands burned down, and began to smoke, and James led the way back to the fire. 'We must return to the beach, lads. I am famished, as I expect so are all of you. We will douse this fire, if you please, and leave the cave as we found it.'

They found Lieutenant Royce waiting disconsolately upon

the beach, where he and his party had spent the night, some under the upturned boat, others under makeshift tents of sailcloth.

'I should have thought you must have heard our signals,' he said rather petulantly to James. 'I caused three shots to be fired, twice. You did not hear them?'

'We had to listen to a great deal of singing,' said James. 'I expect it was impossible for us to hear anything but that, you know.'

'Singing?'

'A kind of chanting. And a sort of drumbeat, too. Very loud. Now, where is our stores? We are very hungry, since we had no supper, and then no breakfast.'

'Ah. Stores. Yes.—The fact is, we could not carry everything last evening, and I—that is we left them hidden, under bushes, at the clearing. We brought only such things as we should need overnight, you see.'

'But I required you——' James took Royce's arm and drew him away towards the water's edge. 'I required you to bring everything here, to the beach. Why did not you do so?'

'Well, it was simply impracticable. Without your own men, I mean, there was too much to carry. In any case, if we are to proceed with the exploration, what is the point in constantly carrying all these things back and forth?'

'Very well. What you say has some merit, I expect. However, the equipment should never have been left unguarded, nor our stores. I put you in charge of the scientifical instruments, and of a party of men, because you are an officer, and must be expected to undertake responsibilities on such a venture as this. The captain was most particular about it. After all, this is our first landfall since Tenerife, and our first uncharted island. We are not here to amuse ourselves, and do as we please, at our own convenience. We are here to do an important job of work. What I require of you now is that you take a party sufficient to bring down from the clearing all that has—do *not* interrupt me—all that has been left there, to the beach. We will then embark, make sail, and return east to the lagoon.'

'The lagoon?'

'Indeed, the lagoon. I must make a report to the captain, and consult him.'

'Well, I must say, it seems a complete waste of time to——'

'Christ's blood, will you do as you are told!' And James strode angrily back to the upturned boat, leaving Royce to follow.

He was hungry, thirsty, and more than a little worried. There had been something unsettling about the chanting ceremony at the cave, which he could not quite define. Although they had not been attacked, although their contacts with the islanders at the lagoon, and at the large bay in the east, had been friendly enough, James had an underlying sense of disquiet. Well, it might have been the strange creature they had tried to pursue in the forest, and its disconcerting screams; it might have been the chill of the cave, and the strange paintings and drawings there; it might simply be the fact that his belly was empty and his spirit low; a blend perhaps of all these things; he did not know. What he did know, what he felt, was that this island was not a gentle place. For all its beauty and serenity of appearance, its sandy beaches and limpid waters, there hovered over Nagu another kind of calm: the brooding calm of menace.

——⚔——

'Pfff, I don't know what is the matter with everybody in my ship,' said Rennie. 'First, Mr Dobie rushes back from the primitives' king to tell me some utterly fantastic story of plots, and silly schemes, and kidnapping. Now you make it your business to interrupt your survey, and to return to the ship, to tell me that some damned cave dwelling has given you the vapours. Good heaven, James.'

'It is not a dwelling, sir, as I was at some trouble to explain. It is a place of worship, or a shrine of some kind. It was the paintings deep within, and the chanting ceremony without, that gave me a very chilling sensation, an icy foreboding.'

'Yes, there you are. Chilling. Foreboding. What febrile words are these from an officer?'

'Then there is the wild forest beast. There is a painting in the cave of a large animal, like an ape, but with white rings at the eyes. I have never seen anything like it. Possibly that is the creature of the forest, that we have all heard screaming. I thought I saw it myself, this morning, however, it fled before I could properly approach. I am almost certain it holds significant meaning for the——'

'James, James, I am having difficulty enough in the ship as it is, with Tangible and his damned slow rigging work, without the additional burden of delirium among my officers ashore. Kindly——'

'Sir, you said that Mr Dobie warned you of kidnapping. May I ask: what did he say, exact?'

'Oh, good God, good God. It is nonsense. He thinks the king wants to seize me, and hold me in the island, because I am a kind of god to them.'

'Naa Ga Neh.'

'Something of the sort. It is nonsense. They are primitives. We cannot allow this sort of thing——'

'It would explain the other ceremony we witnessed,' said James. He glanced at the captain, then around the great cabin, as he remembered the scene. 'The women and children——'

'You saw women? You saw children? Where? Why did you not tell me this at once? That was a mystery I wished to solve. Why they had hidden them.'

'It was a silent ceremony, like an intricate dance, swaying and—and beckoning, drawing in. Now I perceive what it was. A ceremony of welcome.' He looked at Rennie again. 'Have you heard anything from Mr Makepeace?'

'No, I have not. He is busy charting the island. I do not

expect him back for several days. I did not expect *you* back for several days, James.'

'With your permission, sir, I should like to sail to the north of the island, find Lieutenant Makepeace and warn him.'

'Warn him? Warn him? What on earth d'y'mean "Warn him"? He is not in danger. None of us is. The king is well disposed to us. He has already *welcomed* us. He has been aboard the ship, has been laden with gifts, and has in return given me a feast and has laden me with gifts.'

'Sir, with great respect—supposing Dobie is right? If these people do see you as their god, Naa Ga Neh, from across the universe, from Yan, as they call it—the infinite— it may be that they will do almost anything to achieve their objective of keeping you here for ever. It is there in the cave paintings.'

'What is? What is? Christ crucified, it is like listening to some damned play! In one of your damned books!' Rennie threw down his chart dividers on the table.

James felt himself growing angry, but was checked before he could make a furious rejoinder by the sounds of a boat approaching the ship: orders given, the bumping of the boat against the wales, footsteps up the side of the ship, and then Mr Makepeace's voice outside the great cabin.

'I must see the captain directly.'

Rennie strode to the door, and opened it. 'Mr Makepeace! Why the devil have you come back so soon, sir!'

Makepeace was taken aback by the captain's vehemence, and his ireful expression, but his news was too urgent to allow this to interrupt him: 'I have something most pressing to report, sir. Two things to report.'

'Your appearance is very reprehensible, Mr Makepeace. You are dirty, sir, and unshaven——'

'Sir, if you please.' In agitation. 'We was nearly upset by a great number of canoes. We had to fire into them, with our swivels.'

'Had to *fire*, Mr Makepeace? In God's name, why?'

'That is, one of my middies did, Mr Drummond. Thank God for those swivels, I very near did not ship them.'

'Yes, yes, *why* did he *fire*?'

'Because they wished to take the pinnace, sir. They wished to make us prisoners. I had gone ashore at the cliffs, on the northern side of the island, about two miles west of the bay. Mr Trembath came with me, and we scaled the cliffs, with ropes. We had reached the top, when we saw the massed canoes emerging from a hidden place further along the cliffs, a cove. They attempted to board the pinnace, and indeed had seized Welling, one of the crew, as he was shoving off. I descended at once with young Trembath, but we could not reach the pinnace, since the mêlée was now offshore a little. That was when Mr Drummond had the presence of mind to order the swivels trained, and then fired. This sank three or four of the canoes outright, and killed a great many savages. Canister load, horribly effective at close range, sir. The others then fled in terror, paddling away to the west as fast as they could. Mr Trembath and I then rejoined the boat, by swimming out to her. We had to leave our scaling ropes behind, I regret to say, and I lost my glass.'

'Never mind, never mind, Mr Makepeace. You are all safe? Every man?'

'We are, thank God.'

Rennie paced to the stern gallery windows, stared out unseeingly, and paced back past his table, sniffed twice, and rubbed his jaw.

'Hm. Hm.—You said you had two things to report to me, Mr Makepeace. What is the other?'

'Yes, sir. From the clifftop I saw in my glass what I believe is an island, far to the north. In the light haze it was very indistinct, but there is a rocky eminence there.'

'An island?' Distractedly. 'Yes, very good, thank you, Mr Makepeace. I shall note it in my journal. However, we must decide at once what is to be done about this change of temper among the primitives.' A pause. Another sniff. 'You are certain—quite certain—that their intentions was hostile? Mr Drummond could not have misunderstood an exuberant display of friendship?'

'Certainly not, sir. They meant us harm, I am in no doubt. They attempted to seize Welling by the throat. They swarmed about the pinnace. They had spears, and curious clubs, swinging them upon ropes.'

'I have seen such clubs myself,' nodded James.

'Very well, very well.' A sigh. 'It would appear that for reasons unknown to us, the primitives have decided to become murderously impudent. I must go ashore, and see the king.'

'Sir?'

'I must make clear to him that to incur my wrath will be very unwise in him, and in his people.'

'Sir, you cannot seriously mean to put yourself at such terrible risk.' James stared at him.

'It will not be such a risk, I assure you. Lieutenant Raker and his marines will accompany me, with orders to shoot any person who should be stupid enough to make any violent attempt upon me, or even a show of violence.'

'But, sir, they outnumber us. Muskets are all very fine, but they must be reloaded. Supposing several hundred warriors attacked? You might kill thirty or forty——'

'And the others would break and run in terror, pursued by bayonets, Mr Hayter. Fixed bayonets. Sea pistols will be issued, also. These creatures, as I have remarked, are primitive savages. They cannot reason, nor make adequate strategies of battle. I mean them no harm, but if I am attacked, or any of my boats or people, I will defend myself with severe consequence to those who would presume to assault His Majesty's service.'

'Very good, sir.' With a heavy and fearful heart.

'With your leave, sir,' said Makepeace, 'I shall go and clean myself up, and make a written report for your perusal.'

'Yes, by all means, Mr Makepeace.' And as Makepeace

departed the great cabin Rennie called after him: 'You did right, Mr Drummond did right to fire.'

James felt he should make a last attempt to dissuade his captain from a course of action that would almost certainly result in disaster, but before he could speak:

'I know what you are going to say, James. You are going to tell me that Cook was killed in just such circumstances as these, are you not? Hey?'

'I believe he was, sir.'

'You feel it is your duty as my second-in-command to point out to me the sheer folly of my proposal, I expect.'

'Well, sir, what has happened to Lieutenant Makepeace would rather support what Mr Dobie said, would it not?'

'I do not know that, I do not see that at all. Why attack Makepeace's boat, if they mean to capture me? Wrong boat, wrong man, hey? No no, I shall go to the king, with a show of pomp and finery and so forth, and with a heavily armed escort. The king cannot fail to be impressed, and very probably over-awed. Dobie will accompany the party, and convey to the king my very great vexation. Convey to him that if there is any more such barbarous conduct, a great many more of his followers will be killed. That cannot fail to impress him.'

During the forenoon watch of the following day—a humid, hazy day, with diffused sunlight glancing off the calm waters of the lagoon—preparations for Rennie's visit to the king were made. Two boats, the launch and the pinnace, were made ready, both equipped with swivel guns, and supplies of cartridge and shot. Lieutenant Raker and a contingent of marines were to accompany Rennie in the launch. The pinnace was to follow with more marines under Sergeant Miller, and armed seamen under Mr Symington. Lieutenant Royce was included in the captain's party, against James's dismayed objection.

'Sir, is it wise to include as your aide-de-camp a man in whom you place such small faith?'

'Who says that? I had no high regard for my junior lieutenant at the beginning of the commission, but now I believe he has improved. He went with you in your shore party. He did not fail, did he?'

James was silent.

'So, you see, he has improved, by your own admission.'

'Improved, sir? In what distinction?'

'James, do not attempt to obstruct me, if you please. Lieutenant Royce needs to see what the authority of His Majesty's service may achieve. He needs to be party to a show of force, and discipline. In little, he needs to understand something of his responsibilities as a representative of his own King, before a primitive monarch and his primitive followers. You have me?'

'It must be your decision, sir.'

'Indeed, it must. You will remain in the ship, and interview Tangible in my absence. See if you cannot obtain from him greater co-operation in his schedule of work. You have a knack in these things, James. Tangible is determined to delay me, as things stand. I do not wish to be delayed in this island a moment longer than is necessary—for reasons you well know.'

'Very good, sir.'

'Mr Makepeace may busy himself with the sick lists, and obtain from Mr Wing an estimate as to when we may expect a full complement of hands to work and fight the ship.'

'Fight it, sir?'

'Yes. Yes. We must be prepared for anything.'

And so Rennie had set off in his two boats, rowing across the lagoon to round the point and make west to the bay on the north. He was in his dress coat, and his boat's crew wore ribbons in their round hats. The marines were very conspicuous in their red coats, their crossbelts freshly whitened. Mr Dobie sat stiffly, palely, in his green coat, beside Lieutenant Royce.

James watched as the boats were rowed into the distance,

towards the sandbar. Vexed terns circled and dived there. 'It is utter damned foolishness,' muttered James to himself.

'Eh?' Makepeace, at his elbow, the sick lists in his hand.

'Nothing, Tom, nothing. What does Wing say?'

There is still several dozens of men unfit for duty. Scurvy is not a thing cured in five minutes.'

'I know it, I know it. Tangible is short-handed, which is why he is delayed, in turn.'

'James, why does the captain press the boatswain? He must know the number of sick. And yet he seems to blame Tangible for being lax, when it ain't his fault.'

'The captain is an impatient man.'

———— ✤ ————

It was Mr Dobie who brought the news. He hailed the ship from the lagoon shore, waving his arms and shouting as he waded out chest-deep—he could not swim—and constantly glanced over his shoulder. James heard his shouts, looked at him in his glass, and sent the jollyboat with a midshipman to fetch him.

He came aboard a few minutes later, helped by the boat's crew, his face deathly white. He was trembling and dripping, and at first could scarcely speak.

'I—nearly drowned—nearly drowned.' He sat down shakily on a carronade.

'Take a moment, Dobie, get your breath. Mr Trembath, fetch the doctor, jump now!'

'You must hurry—hurry——'

'It's all right, Dobie, take a moment.'

'No—no—it is not all right. I have only just escaped with my life. The captain has been taken.'

'Taken?'

'As I feared, he has been taken by the king, and his followers.'

'What happened? Continue, continue, when you are able.'

'I am able. The king's warriors surrounded us, very menacing. Lieutenant Raker ordered his marines to present their muskets, so they might fire, but the warriors overwhelmed us, and began swinging their clubs. I fell, hit on the shoulder, and crawled away on the ground. Shots were fired, but they had little effect I think Lieutenant Royce was killed the first moment, by a spear in his throat. God—oh God—I can scarce believe that I am alive.' He leaned away and was sick on the deck.

'Where the devil is Mr Wing! Ah, there you are, Doctor. Look after Mr Dobie, now, will you? Mr Makepeace! Mr Tangible!' Leaning down to Dobie again. 'What happened to the boats? Do you know what became of the boats?'

'I—I ran through the forest. I never saw the boats again after we left them at the beach.'

'You must leave him to me, now, if you please,' said Mr Wing firmly, interposing his small person between James and Dobie.

'Yes, very good. Thank you, Dobie, you have done well to get back to us.' To Makepeace, now beside him: 'Tom, we are in dire trouble. The captain is taken, and his party. Probably the boats, in addition. We must make a plan of action, right quick.'

<hr />

The great cabin, at the table; a rough chart of the island, drawn by Lieutenant Makepeace, spread out. James pointed to the lagoon.

'I will go ashore tonight, with a small party, and send the boat back to the ship. Overland, from the lagoon shore to the village, is not more than a mile and a half. We must get into the village, sneak in, with blackened faces, and discover where the captain is held.'

'I will issue arms and powder.'

'No, Tom. No firearms. Cutlasses only, then there can be

no chance of giving ourselves away by someone firing a shot
in error.'

'You, in least, will take a sea pistol?'

'I will not. I am not immune to mistakes; I am a man
like any other. Now. When the boat has returned, you are
then to weigh, take the ship out of the lagoon, and stand
off.'

'Weigh? Stand off?—Are you mad?'

'I was never more in possession of my senses. The captain
has been foolish. I mean to be cunning, and I will not risk the
ship before it is necessary to do so. Here, in the lagoon, she is
vulnerable to night attack. Warriors might easily swim out,
swarm aboard before they could be repelled, and——'

'I doubt that they could do that, you know. They are
primitives, and lack——'

'Do not make the same mistake as the captain.' Sharply.
'These people are anything but primitive, in these circumstances. They are formidable, and determined, and at
present——'

'But so are we! We are better armed, and better disciplined, too——'

'Christ's blood, Tom! They have took the captain, and
killed I don't know how many of his party! They damn near
took you! They hold the upper hand!'

'I repeat, however, that——'

'Did not you hear what Dobie said?'

'Well, yes, but——'

'The captain is their spiritual ancestor, returned from the
infinite. Naa Ga Neh. We, you and I and the crew, are merely
his underlings, that have brought him here. We are dis-
pensable. To be discarded or killed.—They cannot *reason*?
They cannot make *stratagems*? Well, by God, they have
outwitted us comprehensive, up to the present!'

'All right, James, all right—we are both on the same side,
you know.'

'Very well. Then you understand what I am commanding

you to do? Once I am put ashore, and the boat returned, you are to weigh, take her out, and stand off?'

'Very good.'

'Mr Loftus had better take her out. He is a better pilot than any of us.'

'Very good.—What will become of you, marooned ashore, while we stand off?'

'I shall not be marooned long, Tom. We now come to the second part of my plan. I go ashore at the beginning of the middle watch. Allow half the watch, then at four bells you are to make for the bay on the north, and anchor there.'

'Beyond the narrow coastal shelf is bottomless depth. There is rocks on the west of the bay. We are in darkness.'

'Anchor within the shelf. I know I said that I would not risk the ship unnecessary, but this is a vital part of our stratagem. Mr Loftus must bring her in as close as he dares, to within half a mile of the shore. There is just enough of a moon.'

'Very well—and then?'

'You are to set the ship on fire.'

'Eh?' Startled.

'Aye, and then, quite soon—her powder will begin to explode.' James nodded. 'Bang!'

Makepeace stared at him in growing unease.

'Ah, I see. You think I really have gone off my head.'

'Is it not—is it not a little extreme?'

'Extreme? Yes. Yes. It is extreme. That is the point, entire.'

＊＊＊

James ashore, with three picked men—Gurrall, Mayleaf, and Welling. All strong and resilient, their faces blackened, like James's, with charcoal. They made their way cautiously from the beach inland to the north, crossed the freshet, and struck north-west, as near as they could judge their direction in the spectral dimness of the half-moon. The screeching parrots of the day were silent. Nor, mercifully, did they hear the mournful screams of the forest ape; they were all of them enough on edge as it was. They came upon a path, which appeared to lead in the right direction, towards the large settlement, and they followed it, treading as silently on the crushed shells as they could, and keeping low.

'Jacob Gurrall.' Softly.

'Sir?'

'When we reach the village, we will go first to the king's dwelling. I know roughly where it is, from Mr Dobie's description, and it is very large. There may be sentries—we must assume so. D'you know how to kill a man without making any noise?'

'You mean, cut his throat?'

'No. No, you must snap his neck in one swift movement. I will show you. Mayleaf, Welling, attend closely.' He moved behind Gurrall, hooked his right arm quickly round his neck, under his chin, and with his left hand pushed the seaman's head partway forward. 'You understand?' Letting him go. 'The left hand must move forward at the same instant you grip him with your right, in a jerk.'

'I understand, sir. Christ, where did you learn such a murderous trick as that, sir?'

'Oh, when I was briefly reading for Holy Orders, you know, I visited prisons. A man in prison showed me.'

'You a priest, sir?' Astonished.

'Quiet, now. We are not far away from the settlement. I smell woodsmoke.'

And they crept forward.

The village was asleep, and it appeared to the four stealthy intruders that there were no sentries, after all. James held the small party back in the shadows under the trees, for several minutes, during which he twice threw a stone into the wide compound.

Nothing stirred.

The smell of woodsmoke was here aromatic and strong, drifting from a cooking-pit in the centre of the compound. A dozen dwellings lay round this compound; the king's on the far side was two or three times the size of the largest of the others. Farther back lay more dwellings, dozens of them in spreading groups under the trees. Earthen walls, thatched roofs, silence.

'What is our duty, sir?' whispered Gurrall.

'We wait. Quietly wait here.'

'The captain is in the great long house?'

'I expect so. But we must wait to discover that. We must be patient.'

'For how long, sir?' Mayleaf.

'Another glass, perhaps two. Then we shall see what the king and his followers make of our little entertainment in the bay.'

The quiet of the village, unchanged over an entire glass, began to weigh on James and his companions. It grew oppressive. In a village of hundreds of people, with the smoke of a cooking fire hanging on the air, there should have been sounds—small sounds, subdued, but distinctly apparent—a child's cry, a cough, a snore, the patter of feet as someone rose to obey a call of nature. There was nothing. No sound of any kind came from within the village.

From the east now a glow appeared over the trees, a glow which grew and became fierce, and was accompanied by a series of thudding detonations. Birds burst from the trees in squawking alarm.

'Will they not come out of their cottages now?' wondered Mayleaf.

They waited a moment longer, as it came in upon them all that the reason for the eerie and oppressive silence was that there was no one in the village except themselves.

'We have waited in vain,' said James. He stood in the open. 'We will just make sure that the houses are empty.'

'Aye, they're empty all right,' said Gurrall. 'They has found the wind, and flown, and left us becalmed.'

Five minutes of cursory looking showed them the accuracy

of this observation. The village was deserted. James led his party through the trees to the bay, to the sight of leaping and roaring fire out upon the water. On both sides of *Expedient* makeshift rafts burned furiously, covered in pitch and sprinkled gunpowder. From the deck cartridge was occasionally thrown into the flames. The conflagration gave *Expedient* the appearance of a ship burning from stern to stern, each new explosion bringing her closer to ruin and doom. Sparks streamed upward into the night sky, and the smoke against the moon was blood red. In the glow James saw the two ship's boats lying in the shallows at the water's edge. He ran across the beach to the water, followed by the others.

The boats were undamaged, but in one—the launch—there were bloodstains on the thwarts.

James hailed the ship, they all hailed her, waving and shouting over the crackling din of the fires, and presently Lieutenant Makepeace sent the jollyboat.

The two ship's boats were recovered, and the burning rafts sent drifting into the shore, where they grounded and broke up into sizzling embers among the rocks under the western cliffs. James held a council of war: Lieutenant Makepeace, Mr Loftus, Mr Tangible, and the gunner Mr Storey. Mr Dobie, recovered from his brush with death, attended as an advisor on the behaviour of the king, and his followers. He was recovered, but still very pale.

'I am not in possession of many facts,' he told James. 'I must say that with emphasis, since I do not wish to give the impression that I know the king's mind, except in one thing. He is determined to hold the captain, and keep him here. Other wise, I know nothing.'

'You are above us in knowledge, Mr Dobie,' James assured him, 'since you was there when the captain was took, and we was not. You saw what happened.'

'I saw little that was not confusing, confusing and terrible. A great noise, of chanting, and a whirring, roaring sound. They swing above their heads a hollow piece of wood, and the air passing through makes the sound. They also swung clubs made with woven rope, and bound rocks. I was struck by such an instrument, and felled.' He touched his shoulder, and winced.

'What did the king say? Could you understand anything that was said, or shouted out?'

'I could not, since at the time I was concerned to preserve my own life—shameful as that may be for a man to admit.'

'Indeed, no. There is nothing shameful in seeking to survive, when you could do nothing to prevent what happened. You did not hear the king, nor any of his followers, say where they might wish to take the captain, in the island?'

'I did not, I fear.'

'How many of the captain's party was killed?'

'I do not know that, for certain. Lieutenant Royce was killed right in front of my eyes. I think Lieutenant Raker went down, I did not see him after the first mêlée. I did not really see anything. They attacked the marines very savage, I remember that, red coats going down under a rain of blows, and muskets being fired. But after the first surge of the assault, I crawled away.'

'But you saw them seize the captain?'

'Yes, he was seized at once.'

'I am sorry to press you, Dobie, when I know that you are not well——'

'I am all right. I will answer any question as honestly as I can.'

'Did you hear Captain Rennie say anything? Did he call out?'

'I—I think he may have said "the impudent villains", or something like. "The impudent damned villains!" Yes, he said that, as he was seized.'

'And he was certainly taken alive? They did not attempt to injure him?'

'No. No. They—they seized him, and then they bore him

away, carried high. Yes. Now I do recall that. Carried high, but I do not know where.'

'Very well, thank you, Dobie. I am obliged to you.'

James laid out his plan of action before them, using Makepeace's chart. They gathered round the table as he spoke, and listened in silence.

'We will take the ship west along the northern coast, double the western end, and anchor off this small bay on the south, which I already know. A large shore party, commanded by myself, will land, assemble upon the beach, and move inland—here—to the village near the cave. I believe that is where the captain and his party are being held. From a position above the village we will mount an assault upon it, and rescue them, and return to the beach.'

When he had finished there was a brief continued hush, then Mr Tangible cleared his throat:

'Asking your pardon, sir, but I am afraid this is a damnfool idea, when we cannot sail the ship any distance in her present condition, sir.'

'What the devil d'y'mean, Mr Tangible? The ship has been brought without difficulty from the lagoon to her present position.'

'She is only part-rigged. We had to bring her to this bay jury-rigged, under very unsatisfactory canvas, as it is. What will happen if the wind should rise, I do not——'

'Then we will harness that wind like right seamen, Mr Tangible. It is not a great distance, not more than two or three leagues, at most.'

'I do not like it, I must declare. Mr Adgett will not like it, neither——'

'Mr Loftus, what d'you'say? Are we able to make this little cruise, or no?'

'It is not ideal, but we are able, certainly.'

'Very good. Then we shall manage not to founder, Tangible.' Curtly, turning away. 'Now, Mr Storey, I will like to carry a gun ashore, at the beach, and bring it to a position above the village, with a supply of cartridge, and grape-shot.'

'Take a gun ashore, sir? A carronade, you mean?'

'Yes, indeed, a carronade. We could not hope to bring a long gun out of the ship, and into a boat, and carry it up to the village, without great trouble. Nor could we rely upon it to fire without bursting in our faces, should we get it into that position. But a carronade we may manage, I think. It is only a third of the weight of one of our long guns.'

'Howsomever, sir, that is nearly eleven hundredweight. It will be difficult to rig tackles when the upper——'

'God damn this pusillanimous litany of complaint and defeat!' erupted James, banging his fist on the table. 'We are a man-of-war in the service of the King! Our captain has been taken by the enemy, an act of war!'

'Act of war?' Makepeace raised his eyebrows.

'I say so, by God! I say it *is* and act of war! We must rescue our commanding officer and our shipmates! What in the name of Christ would we look like, sitting with our thumbs up our arses aboard *Expedient*, hoping for the best, allowing our shipmates to suffer at the hands of heathen savages! We would look like fucking poltroons! Poltroons and water lilies! I will not countenance any more of these damned womanish objections while I have the ship, d'y'hear me!' He glared round the table. His language was intemperate, very intemperate, but in the circumstances he felt that it was justified. It had its effect.

'Very good, sir.'

'Aye, sir.'

'You are right, certainly.' Makepeace, a little shame-faced.

＊━◄◆►━＊

As *Expedient* limped along the northern coast of Nagu, making very little steerage way into a mild westerly breeze under headsails and staysails, and standing well off the coastal shelf and the tall cliffs, James examined Lieutenant Royce's——

the late Lieutenant Royce's—meagre notes from their earlier foray into the western interior of the island. In his curiously ill-formed hand he had written:

Hybiscis: a large wide shrub above three foot tall
                       having a red or perple coloured flour
Another plant:
                   of great leaves, near conceals the flours
                   within, which I do not know

Gooseberrie:
                   or very similar, however larger & softer
& other Berries of Various distinction, or Species also
a Species of Plantan fruit upon the lower Slopes
Palm trees & tee trees at the coast
An hard wood tree, or red wood, with bright red flours
(tall)
Upon the rocks at an height: lickchen of two Kinds

James sighed. Lieutenant Royce had never managed to make himself a real Expedient. He was in truth an immature boy when he joined her, and had remained a boy. Beside his notes he had made some crudely inept drawings. James compared these scribbled and scrawled observations with those of Lieutenant Makepeace, on his first circumnavigation of the island. In a neat hand:

Birds are v numerous:

A large red & green Parrot bird, with a screeching
cry
A silky white bird with a long twin red tail, & black
feet, which is I believe the Tropick Bird
Brown speckled Warblers, which are almost tame

Along the cliffs, & at the sandy beaches:

> Puffin Birds
> Terns—vexatious upon being disturbed
> & at a distance out to Sea Albatross glide low over the
> water

> Fishes are abundant. We have caught over the side
> Cod, & Mackerel, and there are numerous Sharks
> which circle in a place at the Western tip of the island.

> In the lagoon are myriad fishes—rainbow coloured &
> we also noticed a large Ray, which came up beneath the
> boat from the sandy bottom, so near we thought it
> would upset us, but did not.

His accompanying drawings, beside those of Royce, were
neat, well executed, deft.

A knock at the door of the great cabin, which James was for
the moment using as his own, while he was in command, and
the captain out of the ship. Mr Dobie came in.

'I wished to see you alone, Mr Hayter.'

'Well, here I am alone. What is it? Come in, Dobie, do not
hang back.'

Entering: 'I should like to come with you in the shore party.'

'That will not be necessary, you know. You have risked
your life more than enough. I will like you to remain on
board, if you please.'

'It isn't only a question of risk, d'y'see? Any man must take
risks, at sea. It is the nature of ships, and the sea, that any
voyage is a matter of some risk.'

'Well—yes, I suppose so. What point do you wish to
make?'

'I should like to come with you in the shore party, because
I wish to make reparation for—for having run away when the
captain was taken.'

'No, no, Dobie. Look, there is no need to feel that you was cowardly. I have already said so. You could do nothing. You was unarmed, and you saved your own life, as any man would.'

'Very well then, I must tell you—there is another reason. To avenge my brother's death.'

'Eh? Did you say your *brother's* death?'

'I did. I did. Lieutenant Royce was my brother—well, my half-brother. We had the same mother.'

'I see. I had no idea.'

'No one had, in the ship. We kept it quiet. We did not— we did not see eye to eye, exact.'

'No, well, I had noticed that, in least. I am very sorry you have lost your brother, Dobie, but I think that is not a good reason to lose your own life, you know. What will your mother say, if you are both killed? Think of her.'

'My mother is dead. Perhaps if I might explain my position?'

'Very well, if it will ease your mind. A glass of wine?'

'No, thank you. But I will sit down, if you will permit it.'

'Yes, yes, by all means sit down.'

Dobie sat down, studied his hands a moment, then: 'My mother was a maidservant at Lord Gillingham's house in Norfolk, Burndale Hall. She had been married very young, to a shopkeeper in one of the estate villages, who was my father. He died, and his debts left my mother destitute, and she was obliged to go into service. She was—she was a very pretty woman, I might almost say beautiful. Lord Gillingham—well, he found her to his liking, and when she had been about a year at Burndale, she was delivered of a son. It was kept a secret, for—for reasons you will understand. The confinement took place out of the house, and her son—my half-brother—was at once taken from her, and given into the charge of a Mr Royce, who was in Lord Gillingham's employ as a man of business. Mrs Royce was unable to have children of her own. He was given every advantage. Lord Gillingham saw to that.'

'I can understand that you might feel bitter——'

'Oh, I was not bitter. I was too young to know anything about it. I felt the loss of my mother very deeply—she died when I was eight years old—but I knew nothing of my half-brother until much later on. My uncle, who was also a shopkeeper, took me into his house. I was given an education, paid for by my uncle, who in turn was paid—as I later learned—by Lord Gillingham. I did not enjoy the sort of education that my brother had—he was sent away to school, to Winchester—but I was properly taught at a local grammar school. It was only when my brother——'

'Will you not call him by name?'

'Charles. His name was Charles. I scarcely knew him before we came into the ship. When he had got his commission, Lord Gillingham sent for me, and told me everything. He said that he would write a letter to the captain of my broth——to Charles's captain. He introduced us to each other, and I must say that Charles at first was very condescending, very high. He thought himself my superior in every way. Nor did he like the idea of serving in the same ship with me. However, Lord Gillingham wished to do something for me, and wrote the letter, and that is how I came to be here, in *Expedient*.'

'I see, yes. Forgive me, Dobie, but if you did not love your brother, why do you wish to avenge his death?'

'Because I did not honour him in life.'

'But he did not honour you. Did he? When you fell ill, he did not go near to you, nor ask after you. He was pleased to ignore you in the gunroom. He behaved towards you as if you did not merit notice as an human being, leave alone as a brother.'

'We shared the same mother. She was good and kind, it was not her fault that my brother was less than he might have been. For her sake I should have honoured him more, in spite of his dislike for me.'

'It is a matter for you, Dobie, certainly. It is a personal

matter, and I must not interfere with your feelings, nor condemn them.'

'Thank you.'

'However, that don't mean I am going to allow you to throw your life away out of a misplaced sense of guilt.'

'Misplaced! You have just said it is my business!'

'Aye, privately it is. Privately, you mourn your brother. But private things, private feelings, can have no place in an action. An action is too absolute a business, and only those fitted to battle may take part. Others such as yourself—and I fear I must be plain—others merely get in the way.'

'Do you say that I lack courage!' Dobie was pale and trembling. He had risen from his chair.

'I do not, sir. You have shown already that you are a brave man. But bravery, and skill in arms, is not the same thing. What we attempt, when we attack that village, requires not only courage, but something else entire: the willingness to kill. And not only the willingness, but the strength and skill to do it.'

'I am willing.'

James sighed, and stood up. He took from a rack a plain naval sword, the captain's spare blade. From the back of his chair he took his own sword belt. He pushed the captain's sword across the table to Dobie. He drew his own sword from the scabbard.

'You are a damned fool, Dobie. A damned fool, and a nuisance, and a proud, vain, irksome fellow in the bargain. If you are not, prove me wrong.'

'What? What?'

'Take up your sword, sir! And prove me wrong!'

Dobie snatched up the captain's sword, and stood clear of the table. They faced each other, James calmly, Dobie pale and furious. Dobie ran at him, lunging, and James made a feinting movement, then a deadly flicker, and Dobie's blade spun across the cabin and fell with a ringing clatter against the lockers.

'Very well—very well,' said Dobie after a moment. 'I have not your skill.'

James sheathed his sword, and hung it back on the chair. He held out his hand to Dobie.

'I will like to shake your hand, Alan. May I call you Alan?'

'I—if you wish.' Awkwardly. He took James's hand, and shook it.

'I did not mean those things I said just now, Alan. I said them only——'

'You said them to provoke me, in order to demonstrate something to me that I was entirely too obtuse to see for myself. I must thank you, and beg your pardon. I am in your debt.'

'Then will you repay it by calling me James?'

'That is generous in you, Hayter. James.'

'Very good. I must go on deck, and see Mr Loftus.' And he went up the ladder.

Dobie picked up the captain's fallen sword, and replaced it in the rack, his anger quite dissipated, and his honour—his determination to honour his mother's memory—if not entirely satisfied, then at least assuaged. He returned to his cabin, and took up his notes on the Naguan language.

⊷═◈═⊶

The ship rounding the western tip of the island, off the highest cliffs, which dropped black to a jaw of sharp-toothed rocks jutting out to the edge of the coastal shelf. There, in a slow pool of the current, circled a dozen large sharks, their dorsal fins cleaving the water, then sinking beneath it, circling and circling in the sly, sucking current, and rising again to cleave it smoothly further round, in a perpetual slow sinister glide.

'They give me an icy spine, to say the truth,' said Mr Loftus, looking at the sharks over the larboard rail. 'In all my years at sea, I could never look at sharks without fear.'

'Then you had better not go swimming,' said James mildly. 'We will wear, if you please, and make east for the bay.'

'Stand by to wear ship!' The calls.

Sunset as they approached the mouth of the little bay. Just outside the bay the current was stronger than at the other end of the island.

'Six!' called the seaman with the lead, standing in the chains. 'And six! Five fathom and a half!'

'We will anchor in the mouth, out of the current,' decided James.

'In the mouth, d'y'think?' Mr Loftus looked worried, shading his eyes against the glare of the sinking sun.

'Indeed, in the bay. I want to be able to get my party off the beach as quick as lightning, when we have completed our mission ashore, and back aboard. Mr Storey!'

'Sir?'

'We will prepare to swing out our number three larboard carronade and lower it into the launch. You have loaded cartridge?'

'I have, sir. Six, and another for luck. And seven rounds of grape.'

'Very good.—Red powder?'

'As you ordered, sir. Red.'

'Excellent. Thank you, Mr Storey. Mr Tangible!' Turning. 'Boatswain, are we ready to hoist out our boats?'

'Very nearly, sir.'

'God damn very nearly, Mr Tangible! I required you to be ready the instant we let go! We must hoist out the gun into the launch, for Christ's sake!'

Lieutenant Makepeace came on to the quarterdeck, and approached. 'Mr Hayter. Lieutenant. Sir.' Not knowing which form of address to use, now that James was in command.

'What is it?' Curtly, not wishing to be interrupted.

'If I may——' He walked to the rail, and James went with him. 'If I may suggest? That is, ask? How are we to get the gun out of the boat, on the beach?'

'Good God, Tom, does no one hear what I say in the ship? The boat will carry the gun to the shore, beach, and there be hauled up on the sand. The gun will be taken out of the boat by hoisting. It will be hoisted out.'

'Half a ton of dead weight, James? It ain't like getting water casks in and out of a boat, you know. This will need tackles.'

'Yes. Yes. Tangible has arranged something of the kind, I am in no doubt.'

'With Mr Storey?'

'Storey will remain in the ship. He will not go ashore.'

'I am sorry to press you, but if this carronade is to be of any use to us, it must first be got out of our launch, and then taken up the hill to the village. How will that be accomplished?'

'How will *what* be accomplished? I have just explained. *Tackles* will be employed. Good heaven!'

'But if the village is nearly two mile inland, uphill, from the bay—that is a formidable task, is it not?'

'We will manage to do it. It will be managed. We are English seamen, after all, very stout-hearted, very capable, very determined. We will manage it.'

But it was not managed.

The carronade was hoisted out by tackles, and lowered into the launch, with powder and shot, and was rowed in towards the beach, but at a distance off the beach of about three chains, in three fathom of water, the launch began to list to starboard, then abruptly tipped, water came in over the gunnel, and she foundered, leaving her crew in the water. Three of them drowned at once. The others, shouting and thrashing in fear, clung to floating oars, and a cask or two, and were presently rescued. The carronade, half in and half out of the launch, had fractured her timbers as she plunged on the bottom, and both gun and boat were utterly lost.

'My stratagem is thrown out,' said James. 'The whole of my plan hinged upon that damned carronade. And now it is all gone. To say nothing of the drowned men, and the loss of a valuable boat—an *in*valuable boat. Adgett could never build another to replace it.'

Lieutenant Makepeace resolved to do his best to encourage the temporary commander. 'You know the way to this village. Why not take a small party, and reconnoitre? Discover where the captain is held, and the others—then make a considered plan upon your return.'

'If I do as you suggest, I will not return myself, but send a good runner, a midshipman. Rogers is nimble, he might carry such a message.'

'It had better be written then. A middy don't have a brain big enough to remember much, and run as well.' Makepeace laughed, and straightened up from the table in the great cabin, over which they were bending under the deckhead light. James did not laugh, or even smile.

'Yes, very well, a written message. Certainly. To be delivered into your hand, on the beach. You will then bring the attacking force, and meet me at the cave—here.' Pointing on the chart. 'Every man to be armed with cutlass and sea pistol, or musket, the marines to have charge of the powder and ball for re-loading. You must carry with you also red powder in cartridge. I mean to make those savages pay for what they have done.'

'Cartridge alone will not damage them, surely? Without shot, what use is large grain powder? Without great guns, what use is it?'

'They will pay in fear. I mean to frighten away their wits, so they piss down their legs like infants.'

'Who will go with you in your party?'

'Two or three only. Gurráll, I want. Rogers, to carry the message.'

'Dobie?'

'Eh? Good heaven no, he is a schoolmaster, not a man of action.'

'But he understands some part of their language, does he

not? He may be able to hear, or overhear, where they are holding the captain.'

'No, no. I have already said to him that he might not come.'

'He asked to go with you?'

'Yes, he wished—well, no matter, I dissuaded him.'

'But if he went with you as a spy, would he not be useful? To creep down into the village, and listen? That is what I mean.'

'Tom, Tom, he is a clerk. Look at him, for Christ's sake. Skin and bone, and a pen.'

'He don't lack courage.'

'No, you are right. I must not talk ill of him behind his back, when he—no matter. We will make a new list of the attacking force, from the quarter bills, if you please. I will want every man on the list ashore by midnight.'

———— ✠ ————

As they climbed through the steep darkness, the trees looming and towering above them, James thought of what had befallen them, thought of the drowned men, and of the captain and the surviving members of his party, and what they might be suffering; he thought of how harsh he had become—had had to become—in assuming command in these perilous circumstances. What would become of the commission, and the new instructions which now governed it, if the attack failed, and he lost more men? What would he do if the captain, God forbid, should himself perish in the attempt to save him? What would he do then? He thought of Catherine, saw her sitting with a book, raising her eyes from the page, and looking out of the rectory window, lost in thought. Was she thinking of him? Was she wondering if he was safe, thinking of his return, and their life beyond it? What life, if he failed? His breath caught in his throat, and he clenched his fists as a wave of something very like despair washed over him.

'I must not allow myself such thoughts,' he muttered.

He had paused without knowing that he had, and Jacob Gurrall now bumped into him in the darkness, and mumbled an apology. The moon rode clear of cloud and shone down through a gap in the trees, illuminating the narrow path for a moment. Alan Dobie caught them up, and got his breath.

'Where the devil is Rogers?' James peered round.

'I am here, sir.' Midshipman Rogers emerged from the gloom farther up the slope. 'I ventured ahead a little, sir.'

'Did you see anything?'

'I—I did not, sir.'

'No, and you might have got your head cut off, in the bargain. Stay with the party, Mr Rogers, if you please.'

In the dim luminescence, filtered through the trees, they went on up the path in single file, and came to the clearing. James held them back under the trees until he was certain there was nothing amiss, then they came cautiously into the open.

'From here to the village is about one mile. We will rest here a moment, then proceed.' Speaking in a low voice in the hush of the clearing. 'Your pistols are loaded, Jacob Gurrall?'

'Aye, sir.' He tapped the butts of both sea pistols at his belt.

'Mr Rogers, you have my pocket pistol?'

'Yes, sir.'

'Alan, you refused a pistol; will you not take one of mine, now?'

'No, thank you. I am not a combatant.'

'But you do not even carry a knive——'

'I am content, thank you. My work is to move stealthy, and listen. Weapons cannot aid me in these things.'

James smiled. 'Well, that is true, I expect. I meant only— should you by ill luck be discovered, it might be as well to carry something to protect yourself.'

'I mean to avoid discovery, thank you.'

'Very well. I must iterate, before we move off, that pistols should be fired only in the direst difficulty, should you fear for your life, and need to shoot to defend it. Only then, d'y'have me?'

'Aye, sir.'

'Yes, sir.'

'Silence. Stealth. Vigilance. These are our watchwords.'

They moved quietly and quickly across the clearing, and took the path to the east, towards the village. James found as they marched that all his feelings of despair, of being cast down, and fearful, had vanished. His heart beat strong within his breast, and he feared nothing, and no one. The only doubt that niggled—it did not assail him—was whether or not he should have allowed Dobie to come. In the end it had been the matter of language that had persuaded him. That, and his feeling that he had been too hard on Dobie in challenging him, and then humiliating him with a fundamental trick of swordplay. He had thought afterward that Dobie did deserve his chance to be of service, and so had let him come. James would have preferred Midshipman Pankridge to young Rogers as his messenger, since Pankridge had been with them on the first foray to the village, and in the cave. But Pankridge had gone in the second boat with the captain's party, and was now either a prisoner, or dead.

—◦≡◦≡◦—

On the beach Lieutenant Makepeace waited with his assembled assault party, of armed seamen and a platoon of the remaining marines. By the first lieutenant's order they had all blackened their faces, and the marines wore ordinary dark clothing, their scarlet coats and white crossbelts having been adjudged too conspicuous.

That Makepeace no longer had the carronade at his disposal was both a relief and a handicap. A fat cannon, capable of throwing out a formidable weight of grape-shot to a distance of several hundred feet, and killing large numbers of the enemy, would have been an asset—idle to deny it. Yet to have carried the thing beyond the beach would have presented him with appalling difficulty. The path was narrow, and steep, and even with moonlight in the forest was all but non-existent. He must content himself with the red powder cartridges Storey had made up with canister shot enclosed, and fuses. The canister had been James's last-minute idea.

'These must be handled with great care,' the gunner had said, as the cartridges were brought up from the magazine. 'Two pound of red powder, and a pound of canister mixed, is—well, I will not say madness, but it ain't quite sound thinking, in my view, even with double linen bags. Look, this is the fuse. Never light it—I nearly said never light it at all, I am so fearful that something may go wrong. Howsomever, never light it *until* the moment you wish to throw it. Then throw it, *heave* it, with all the force in your arm, or the man you have assigned.'

'Throw him, too?' Makepeace had asked, mildly.

The cartridges now lay in a box on the beach, in the charge of the marine corporal. Makepeace stood up, and paced the sand. He looked towards the ship, and sighed, and wished they were at sea. How they had wished for this landfall. How they had sighed with relief when they dropped anchor in the lagoon. What a paradise the island had seemed, so short a time since.

'I hate waiting,' he muttered under his breath. 'And I hate this damned place.'

In the darkness above the hill village, James's little party waited. The moonlight was just sufficient to enable them to make out the circles of houses, and the great open space in the centre of the settlement.

Nothing stirred.

As they crouched at their vantage point among the rocks, James was struck by this silence—the same unbroken silence that they had found at the king's village in the east, on the night before. It was unnerving, and he found himself holding his breath. Then came a tiny sound, drifting up from below, the sound of a baby's mewling cry, quieted at once as its mouth was brought to its mother's breast.

'Thank God,' murmured James. 'I thought for a moment they had outfoxed us again.'

'I will go down, now,' said Dobie.

'Wait, wait.' James held his arm. 'Let us be sure there is no sentry post, nor watch-dogs.'

'There's no dogs in all the island,' said Dobie. 'I am quite sure.'

'Aye, but we don't know that about sentries.' Then, after a moment: 'I had better come with you, Alan.'

'No. No. No.' A vehement whisper. 'I am light on my feet, and quick. We agreed the plan. I to go down alone, and you to create a diversion, whilst I discover where the captain is hid.'

'Very well.' Reluctantly. James was having severe second thoughts, very profound doubts indeed, but Dobie had already crept away down the slope, moving between rocks, before James could express them, or act upon them. Christ crucified, what had possessed him to allow a frail Norfolk schoolmaster to embark on such a hazardous undertaking? Embark alone, and unarmed? To listen to an alien tongue, at the wall of a hut, in the hope of overhearing—what? A snippet of jabbering talk? Or even to chance upon the very hut in which the captain and his party were held, perhaps to hear them whispering fearfully among themselves? Fanciful nonsense. Folly! He should never have let Dobie go.

However. However. It was now too late. He was gone, out of reach, doomed or otherwise.

'He wished us to give him half a glass.' James turned to Gurrall in the gloom behind the rocks. 'We will do so, then begin our diversionary stratagem.'

After a quarter of an hour, James, Gurrall, and Midshipman Rogers spread out along the rocks, and began imitating the shrieks of the forest ape. Since each man had his own idea of how the creature gave its cries, the horrible noises that echoed over the village below were widely disparate, not only in location but in tone and timbre. In other circumstances James would have found these moaning shrieks funny and absurd, the exaggerated caterwauling of a schoolboy prank. Now he had never felt less like laughing in his life.

The village below was shaken into life. People hurried from inside the huts. Voices were raised. Children cried. Pigs woke, and ran squealing.

On the far side of the village, Dobie had discovered the largest house, in a semicircle of half a dozen houses, set back from the central space. He crouched behind this house, under the overhanging thatch of the roof, between heaps of maize and coconuts stacked against the mud wall. The fearful wailing of his shipmates high above the village had as yet provoked no sounds from within this house, no voices, no movements. A great crowd was gathering in the centre of the village. He could hear the whirring din of air sticks, and the clatter of spears.

He waited, crouching in the husks, then cautiously made his way to the front of the house. Fire brands were waving in the air as a large party of warriors gathered in the centre of the village. Keeping low, his face blackened, Dobie crept to the wide entrance, and called:

'Captain Rennie—Captain Rennie, are you within, sir?'

Behind him the noise of the assembling war party was rising in a crescendo. Flames flickered. In the dancing light Dobie caught a glimpse of the interior of the house. Woven mats lay on the floor. A large timber throne was draped with ropes of flowers and the red cloth which had come from *Expedient*. But neither the king, nor the captain, occupied the house. It was empty. Dobie waited a moment, then made his way, keeping low, along to the rear of the other houses. Several times, risking all by raising his voice, he called out:

'Captain Rennie—are you here?'

There was no response, and Dobie knew now that if he did not make his escape, he too would suffer capture, and perhaps death. The din of the war party rose and rose, the flames of the brands flickering across shell-strung torsos, and raised, waving arms. Dobie again waited a moment, then ran from the rear of the village in a wide circle through the forest and by sheer determination to save himself made his way—his stumbling, scratched, often thwarted way, in the near darkness—not by the path out of the village, but up through the rocks, using the same route he had used to come down, and at last scrambled breathlessly to the vantage point where the others waited, having regrouped.

'The captain is not there.' Getting his breath. 'Nor is the king, neither.'

'You are certain?'

'I found the king's house, with his throne in it, and the red cloth we gave him. I called out, and even crept inside, but there was no one there.'

'You are bleeding, Alan. Was you attacked?'

'Only by thorns, and branches. I am all right.' He mopped at his torn face with his neckcloth.

The massed warriors below began to ascend the path, carrying brands, spears, clubs, and the booming air sticks, which they whirled above their heads.

'Should we not retreat?' asked Dobie. 'We had better run, or be discovered and killed.'

'Not quite yet.' James crouched, and opened the heavy leather pouch he carried slung over his shoulder, and from it withdrew the linen bag of one of Mr Storey's cartridges. From his pocket he brought tinderbox, which he gave to Gurrall.

'Strike a light.'

'A light, sir? With them savages coming?'

'Strike it. Quick, now.'

Gurrall struck the light, saw the cartridge bomb in James's hands, and the fuse, and flinched.

'Come on, man, bring the light to the fuse!'

Gurrall did as he was told—fearfully brought the flame to the fuse—and leapt backward. James stood up, and flung the cartridge with all his strength up and out over the heads of the ascending warriors. He saw the fizzing spark of the fuse tumble in a high arc, then he ducked down behind the rocks.

The briefest lull, then a flash like a bolt of lightning, which lit the trees all around, and an immediate shattering bang. Canister-shot whizzed and sang through the air, spun whining off rocks, and produced below the most horrible shrieks and moans of agony.

'Canister,' muttered James. 'Terrible effective at close range.' He rose, and peered down the path. The progress of the warriors had been utterly halted, the survivors running for their lives back into the village, where there was a turmoil of rushing movement, wails and screams and confusion.

'What now, sir? Shall we return to the beach?' Gurrall.

'No, we will not,' said James. 'We will make our way, as quick as we can, to the cave. That is where the captain is held, I am in no doubt.'

'The cave?'

'We should have gone there at once, instead of wasting all our time here. Mr Rogers.'

'Sir?'

'We go to the cave, but you must find your way to the beach, and inform Mr Makepeace where we have gone. Can you find your way in the darkness?'

'Oh, yes, sir.'

'Very good. Then you may take this note. Strike that light again, Gurrall, will you?' he tore a sheet from his notebook, scribbled on it in pencil, and gave it to the midshipman.

'Jump, now!'

⋆——⊣◆⊢——⋆

Makepeace brought the assault party with him to the cave, following James's instructions to the letter, taking the larboard fork of the path up from the clearing, and causing his men to tread very quietly the last few hundred yards. James came to meet them, and they assembled below the cave. James outlined his new plan, keeping his voice above a whisper.

'We must draw out their captors from the cave, and seize them, and release the captain and his party before the warriors re-group at the village, and come here.' Makepeace had already been made aware by Midshipman Rogers of James's deployment of his bomb.

'D'y'think the king is in the cave with them?'

'I don't know that, Tom. I don't care, one way or t'other, so long as we release the captain. He may probably be suffering a great deal, bound up hand and foot.'

'Very good.—How are we to draw them out? Not with another bomb, surely?'

'I had thought of using the same trick we used at the village, or imitating the screams of the ape, but I do not think that will serve here. No, we must challenge them outright.'

'Come out and fight?'

'Aye, come out and fight. Mr Dobie?'

'I am here.'

'Are you able to make such a challenge, in their tongue?'

'No, I am not. I could call the king to come out, I expect, but that——'

'He may not be in there, however.'

'Indeed, he may not. What I was going to say: why not call out to the captain? If he is in there, even if he is bound up with ropes, he will surely answer a familiar voice, will he not? However, I don't think they will have tied him, d'y'see? He is their ancestor spirit, their god. He must be treated with reverence, and guarded, rather than held.'

These deliberations were now interrupted. From the direction of the village came the sounds of chanting, and the whirring boom of air sticks, and the clicking of spears. The warriors had re-grouped, and were approaching the cave.

'Damnation to subtle things!' announced James. 'We must act definite, and deliberate, and quick! Mr Makepeace, you will take the box of bombs, and deploy them in the path of the approaching army, and fire into their ranks if the bombs ain't sufficient. I will keep the marines here, and make an assault upon the cave. Jacob Gurrall, you will come with me. Mr Rogers, and Mr Dobie, you will take cover in the trees.'

'Oh, sir, may I not come with——'

'I will not take cover, like a girl in petticoats!'

'Silence, there! Corporal of marines! Form up your men! Fix bayonets!'

As Lieutenant Makepeace took his contingent to meet the massed warriors, James caused tar-soaked cloths, brought up from the beach and wrapped round staves, to be lit and carried to the cave mouth. Two of these torches were flung forward, deep into the cave, where they lay burning on the floor. The cave proved empty. The remains of the fire which James had lit with his earlier party, was the only evidence of recent human invasion.

'They must be in the great chamber at the rear,' he said. 'Follow me!'

James led the way forward, holding high a torch in one hand, and in his other hand a cocked pistol. He and Gurrall made their way through the narrow fissure—and found the pillared chamber empty. The light of their torches jumped and soared across the wall of paintings. James walked forward to look at the wall, and now became aware that the cave was not quite empty, after all. A black stream of life rushed in a writhing torrent from the high roof, and poured away towards the cave mouth.

'Jesus, it is bats!' said one of the marines behind, ducking his head. 'I hate the buggers!'

'Aye, they are the only occupants.' James, returning with Gurrall. He led the marines out of the cave. As he did so there were two flashes in the middle distance, and two thudding explosions, followed by screams and cries. The whirring boom of the air sticks ceased, and the rhythmic clicking of massed spears. Another explosion, and the rippling cracks of small-arms fire. More screams, and the baleful yells of men about to triumph over other men in combat.

'We will win the battle,' said James. 'We will not achieve our objective, however.'

'We will not rescue the captain.' Beside him Gurrall uncocked his pistol.

'Not this night, Jacob Gurrall. We must resume our search at daybreak. We must not give up.'

James felt a tug at his elbow, and turned to find Dobie. 'Will you lend me one of your pistols, now?'

'Now? What for?'

'You offered me one earlier. I refused it, but I have changed my mind. You have two sea pistols and two pocket pistols.'

'I gave one of my pocket pistols to young Rogers.'

'Will you give me the other?'

'Why, Alan? We are no longer in danger.'

'Well, that is not quite true, is it? We are all of us in danger upon this island, every moment. Yes, your men have defeated the Naguan warriors in one battle—an action, I think you call it? But they are a numerous race. If the captain is not here in the cave, and the king is not, we must assume—must we not?—that there is a great many other warriors accompanying them, wherever they may be.'

'Yes, I think that is an accurate assumption.'

'Then we shall have to fight again.'

'You will not. You are not obliged to.'

'Hayter, will you listen to me? James? These people, these Naguans, are used to the notion that they are the only human beings upon the earth. Nagu is their world, the sea all about them their universe. Captain Rennie is their spiritual father, the very core of their lives. The king and his warriors will fight to the death to claim and protect him. Do not, I beg you, think that tonight's battle, tonight's triumphant action, will make an end. Every man in the island will now seek to destroy us, and our boats, and the ship. The ship brought the captain here, therefore it could take him away again. They cannot allow that, d'y'see? They cannot begin to allow it!'

James raised his still burning torch and looked at him.

'I believe you are right, Alan. We must act.'

— • — ✠ ◊ ✠ — • —

The ship lying just off the island to the south, at noon. Every man fit for duty assembled in the waist. James addressed them from the break of the quarterdeck:

'Expedients! We must make the savages think that we are going away from their island, that we are going to sail away, and leave them alone, and never return. They must believe this absolutely. However, we will not go away! We will stand well off until nightfall, then return. We will never go away, never, until the captain is back aboard with us, and our shipmates with him! No! No! Do not cheer, if you please! Do not cheer!'

The cheer died in a hundred throats.

'We may cheer when it is done, but now I want you to chant something. It is the saddest sound in all the world, and I will ask you to give voice with feeling, with very considerable feeling, fit to make yourselves weep. We will sing the twenty-third psalm!'

And he opened his prayer book, and began to chant, in a loud, mournful drone, leading the combined voices of the men assembled before him. And so there drifted across the water, from the slowly riding ship, a dreadful sound, the sound of a hundred and more men singing, with heavy emphasis, the words that some clergymen feel are the most heart-feeling in the English tongue:

The Lord is my shepherd; I shall not want.

He maketh me to lie down in green pastures: he leadeth
me beside the still waters.

He restoreth my soul: he leadeth me in the paths of
righteousness for his name's sake.

Yea, though I walk through the valley of the
shadow of death, I will fear no evil: for thou art
with me; they rod and thy staff comfort me.

And James was gratified to see—as an unbeliever he was
glad—that as the psalm was concluded a number of men were
indeed in tears.

'It is moving, is it not?' said Dobie quietly.

'So long as it deceives those damned warriors, I am
pleased to find it so,' said James with a grim little smile. 'Mr
Loftus! We will make sail, and stand away to the south-
east!'

- ◆━✦━◆ -

Although James was using the great cabin as his centre of
command, he was not living there. He preferred to remain in
the gunroom mess, and to sleep in his own cabin. This
enabled him to retain the necessary balance between temporary command and his usual position in the ship. Captain
Rennie was alive, he was certain of that, and was therefore in
command, *in absentia* in command, and James was simply
representing his authority in the ship, and carrying out his
duties as Rennie himself would have done, were he able. In
this he was allowing himself great flexibility, great leeway. He
must preserve the ship and her people, and keep in his mind
the terms of the commission, the detailed instructions. But
his first duty, his paramount duty at present, was to rescue the
captain. His stratagems so far had failed, but his purpose was
by no means exhausted.

*

'There is an increase in the strength of the wind from the west,' Mr Loftus reported. 'If we are to return to the island by midnight, we must wear, and beat to windward.'

The wind was rising, but it was not a troublesome, variable, shifting wind, merely a fresh and steady breeze. The ship came about, and Mr Tangible remained in a condition of dismay. She was under staysails, many of the yards not yet sent up because of the condition of the parrals, and much of the rigging still in a parlous state. Mr Wing too was troubled, and came to James to complain that dozens of men still sick were unlikely to return to health if the ship was constantly in an upheaval of movement. Why sail away from the island at all, when the captain was still there? Why was he told nothing? Sick men needed rest, did they not? Why had they not remained at the lagoon? Had anything been achieved by sailing this way and that, dropping anchor, weighing, and haste, haste, haste?

'You are a good fellow, Wing, and a good doctor,' said James, 'but you must leave the handling of the ship to me, you know.'

'May I make a bargain with you, Mr Hayter? That you will inform me at once when these changes are to be made, so that I may prepare——'

'Changes, Doctor?' Growing testy, in spite of his intention to keep his temper. 'A man-of-war is accustomed to *changes*, as you call them, at all times, and at any moment. I must work the ship as I see fit, and sick men must make the best of it, since they lie idle below, and cannot do their duty.'

'Idle! Idle! A sick man is not idle, he is incapable! Cannot you see the distinction!' Thomas Wing, although very small, was formidable in defence of his professional judgement, and of his patients. James bit his tongue, and pressed down very firmly on the table with both hands.

'Thank you, Doctor. You make your point with force, and candour. Allow me to make one in return. My sole object, in everything I have done these last hours and days, was and is—

to save the captain's *life*. Just as it is your business to save life, so is it mine. We both have our duty, sir. *Let us do it.*'

—◦—≡◦≡—◦—

Expedient to the north-east of the island, under a waning moon, obscured by hazy cloud. James's objective: to find the cove on the north of the island, the cove of the canoes, and make a landing there by boat; to surprise and overwhelm the warriors there, and foray inland to where the captain might now be held. The wind had dropped, and the ship was making very little steerage way. James raised his glass once more, and peered at the coastal cliffs. He could see almost nothing. He lowered the glass, and sighed impatiently.

'Where is the damned cove, I cannot——'

'What the devil was that?' Lieutenant Makepeace stepped to the larboard rail. 'I saw a light, high above the cliffs.' Raising his borrowed glass. 'I could swear it was the muzzle flash of a gun. Look, there, again!'

'A gun? They have no guns.' James, joining him at the rail. 'Besides, there was no report.'

And now there sounded, not a report, but a deep, heavy rumbling, out over the quiet sea.

'What pattern is that?' wondered Makepeace aloud. 'If it is guns, there must be fifty or more.'

James stared in fascination at the sea. It was covered in fluttering ripples, as if a huge creature swam far beneath, its progress marked by vibrations all the way to the surface. The rumbling came again, deeper and longer, and edged with intermittent muffled detonations. Something splashed in the water a few yards off the larboard quarter. Another splash, farther away, then a fragment fell on the deck, by a rope fall, and lay there smouldering. An acrid smell, sulphurous and hot, filled the air. James and Makepeace exchanged a glance of alarm. A shudder ran through the sea, a tremendous jarring shock that they felt in the ship's timbers.

James felt his hair blown back off his forehead, and his shirt plucked at by rushing air, then the air itself seemed to shudder, and there was a prodigious boom, followed by another, and another, great thudding detonations. Burning fragments fell sizzling all round the ship, and rattled across the deck. Behind the cliffs inland a column of fire rose above the island, tall with sparks and shivering orange flashes. The undersides of low clouds were lit up, like curtains by glowing coals.

'The island is on fire!' said Makepeace. 'The forest is alight, from end to end!'

'Mr Loftus! We will wear, and make for the bay in the east!' To Makepeace: 'We must get ashore there, Tom, and see what may done to find the captain, before he is burned alive.'

But when they reached the bay, a terrible sight met their gaze. Trees burned in soaring brands on either side of a massive tongue of molten lava, which spread down across the beach and into the sea, where it roiled and hissed in gouting clouds of steam. Ash fell across the width of the bay, and far inland geysers of molten rock flung and spouted against the night sky. The waters of the bay had grown milky with ash and debris, and the surface seethed. The wind now fell off to a breath above nothing, and the ship lay nearly becalmed, her staystails limp, ash and smoke drifting slowly through the rigging. The rumbling and booming rose to a deafening roar.

'It is no good, Tom!' James shouted. 'We are damned to hell!—Mr Loftus!'

'Sir?'

'Have we enough wind to reach the other bay?'

'Maybe, if we stand off a little, and try to find a breath of wind to the south. One thing is certain, we cannot stay here.'

'We cannot. We will take fire, if we do, and the ship will burn down to the waterline, or blow up. Mr Tangible! Stand by to hoist out the boats! We must pull ourselves clear, or join Old Nick!'

'They cannot live, now,' whispered Makepeace, staring at the inferno ashore. 'We are too late. They are doomed.'

━ ═◆═ ━

At first light, as *Expedient* swung out of the current into the mouth of the small bay on the west, James saw that the beach was deserted. At this end of the island the booming roar of eruption was less fierce, and the forest had not yet begun to burn, but the curve of sand ahead was empty of life. The captain, wherever he was, had perished with the islanders inland, and now there was nothing to be done except to save the ship, and her people. He lowered his glass.

'I had thought—I had hoped—that the captain and his party might contrive to escape their captors in the confusion of the explosions, and make for the safety of this end of the island. It was a foolish hope.'

'Should not we send a party ashore, to make certain?'

'I will fire three rounds from the signal gun, at one-minute intervals. We will then wait one glass. If no one has appeared, we will then stand away and leave this place behind.'

'In one glass, I could take a small party ashore, in the jolly-boat, and venture up the path——'

'No! No! I will not risk any more of the officers and people! We have done our best, Tom, and we must face the truth. We have lost our commanding officer, and his entire party. The ship is not in a proper condition of repair, and we are short-handed both watches. But we cannot stay here. We must make for the open sea to save the ship, and ourselves.'

As he spoke further rumbling sounded, much closer to them than the concussions at the other end of the island. It came from the direction of the village and the cave up the hill. The waters of the little bay rippled and fluttered. Birds flew low overheard in a wide shrilling curve away from the island, and turned north far out over the sea.

'We cannot stay here,' repeated James.

Makepeace ordered the signal gun fired, and paced the deck all that glass, anxiously looking at the beach. The booming din increased, and fire and ash began to pour into the sky from the western hills, joining the great cloud that hung over the whole of the rest of the island. James went below to the great cabin to plot a course. He took Mr Loftus with him, and together they endeavoured to behave like level-headed, sensible men in His Majesty's service, with charts before them. Privately each was greatly dismayed by the nature of their predicament, but for disparate reasons. At last Mr Loftus voiced his own.

'In my estimation, sir, we should try for Valparaiso.'

'Valparaiso? We could never reach Valparaiso with the ship in its present condition. We must find another island, and complete our repairing.'

'Well, sir——' glancing up as Tom Makepeace joined them, 'I believe that Valparaiso, far as it is, very far—is in least there.'

'Eh?' Sharply.

'We know that it is there. We don't know any other islands.' His hand swept the chart. 'Where——'

'There is that island to the north,' said Makepeace now.

'What island?' James stared at him.

'We sighted it from the cliffs. It is very small, merely a rock, but it might——'

'Could we repair there? How far is it?'

Bernard Loftus frowned: 'With respect, with respect, gentlemen, it will not do. A rock will not do. Our timbers are sound, our rigging may be repaired as we go. We have food enough, if we take care, to reach Valparaiso. Water also, and wood. Was we to fart about—forgive me—was we to go tacking about the ocean, looking for a rock, when we could plot a course for——'

'For Valparaiso, yes. Thank you, Mr. Loftus.'

A cry from the deck, forrard. Running feet, and the cry

repeated, right overhead, from the companion: 'There is men on the beach!'

James jumped to the ladder, and as he climbed up a blast of wind struck the ship, and she heeled. A ticking moment. Then the full tremendous bang shook every nail in her, and deafened every man. As the ship righted itself in the aftershock of the blast, James came on deck. High above the hill molten rock fountained red against the smoke-dark sky. The air stank of sulphur and toxic gases. Trees along the hill had begun to burn, and smoke hung in a pall over the bay, but the figures on the beach were plainly visible—three figures frantically waving, and shouting. Burning fragments pocked and sizzled in the water all round *Expedient*, and dropped scattering and smouldering through her rigging and along the decks.

'I had better take the jollyboat,' said James, turning.

'I will go,' said Makepeace from the companion, and before James could demur began giving instructions for the lowering of the boat, and quickly chose his crew. As the jollyboat was rowed in towards the beach James raised his glass and tried to make out the figures. Was one of them Rennie? Smoke drifted across his line of sight, and he could not tell.

'Is it the captain?' Loftus, at his side.

'I don't know. I don't know.'

'They must hurry. The ship is defenceless against this rain of fire.'

James reached for his speaking trumpet, brought it to his mouth—and lowered it. 'Tom Makepeace don't need telling,' he muttered. 'He knows what to do well enough, and shouting at him will not aid us.'

The drifting smoke cleared a little, and from the quarter-deck they saw the boat approaching the ship. The trees were now burning right down the slope of the hill. Thunderous shocks were now nearly continuous, and men with buckets of water and sand ran about the deck dousing incipient fire as it fell from the air. The boat steadily nearer, through the smoke.

The boat alongside. Figures climbing up the tumblehome. A head at the gangway port.

'Mr Hayter!' The familiar voice. 'Mr Hayter, we will weigh at once, if y'please!'

⚫━━◆━━⚫

Three men only. Of the whole of the captain's ill-fated—ill-judged and ill-fated—shore party, a mere three men survived to come back into the ship. The captain himself, the master's mate Mr Symington, and the captain's coxswain Randall South. The captain alone retained his clothing, or the chief parts of it; the others were naked, their flesh much bruised and chafed. The captain refused the offers and efforts of Mr Wing to examine him, but allowed—indeed insisted—that his two companions should at once be given medical assistance.

Expedient beat slowly away to the west, then came about and sailed to the north. The whole of Nagu was now ablaze, and lay under a long cloud of smoke. The island was wracked by continuous detonations, and eruptions of glowing liquid rock, which spewed and ribboned down the folds of the interior hills like the death's blood of a huge supine dragon. *Expedient* was now beyond the falling ash, and the rain of hissing fragments, all smouldering remnants had been extinguished on the ship, and James began to feel that she was safe—that they were safe in her, at last. He was about to turn his attention elsewhere when he thought he saw something at the base of the black northern cliffs, a flicker of movement there. He lifted his glass, focused, and there was something. A gap in the fall of the cliffs, and from it came dozens of canoes, paddled at great speed into the open sea. At their head was the large canoe of the king. Was that the king aboard, was that a tiny flash of red cloth! James lowered his glass, and reluctantly sent word to the captain—reluctantly because Rennie was lying in his hanging cot, deep in exhausted sleep.

However, the captain came on deck. His receding hair was spiked and unruly, his eyes bleary, and his face still bore the curious yellow whorls and patterns James had noticed as Rennie had come up the ladder into the ship, evidence of his ordeal at the hands of the Naguans.

'Where away?' His voice gravelled with sleep.

'Due south, sir, coming away from the island.' He offered Rennie his glass. The captain took it with a nod, raised it, and:

'Ah, yes. That is the king's vessel, I believe. And above an hundred warriors. By God, the fellow must inspire loyalty, if he can muster an hundred men to his cause after all that has befallen that wretched place.' He lowered the glass, and turned to his first lieutenant. 'I believe they mean to try and catch us.'

'Can we not outrun them, sir?'

'I think not. We are slow, and they are determined. They mean to chase and catch us, and overwhelm us.' Returning the glass. 'How are the carronades loaded, Mr Hayter?'

'With grape, sir.'

'Very good. We will heave to, presently. I have something to conclude, this day.'

James raised the glass, and peered through it once more, and as he did so there was an orange flash at the top of the black line of cliffs, and then the cliffs themselves, the entire line of them above the flotilla of canoes, plunged in a mass into the sea. There was a rush of wind across the sea, and a frightful booming thud. As the ship steadied herself James saw in his lens that the canoes had disappeared, and that advancing towards the ship was an enormous rolling line of green water.

'It is a wave! A giant wave!'

'Lash the wheel!' shouted Rennie. 'Double-lash the wheel!'

As soon as it was done the wave was upon them, rising

astern in the hazy sun, the reflected light glossy and beautiful on this inexorable, rolling green mass, which lifted the ship with effortless and nearly silent ease, and flung her forward.

Flung her with appalling violence, which became a roaring, rushing slide of terror, the bow tilting and tilting, the masts canted forward and over, the stays stretched to the limits of their strength, every part of the ship groaning and creaking *in extremis*—and now as the vast mass of water passed beneath, sucking and seething, the ship was let fall. She fell back, and her bow lifted, up and up at a terrifying angle, the masts flung back on their clinging stays, and blocks dangling in the sky, ropes dangling, and men yelling in mortal fear. Water rode seething up over the stern, and buried the quarterdeck. James, a rope doubled round him, felt himself lifted weightlessly, and pulled, his breath pulled from his lungs, his clothing, his hair, his very skin sucked and dragged and pulled, as if the sea wished to suck out his life from him, and bury him forever in its limitless green depths.

'We are lost.'

Expedient, an oak-built, Chatham-built frigate, was not the kind of ship to allow herself to be lost to the impudence of a single wave, and she did not founder in the wallowing sea behind that passing wave; nor had she suffered grievously in the shocking transit; she had righted herself, water pouring from every part of her, and lay quietly in the seaweed clots and the floating ash that had been sucked along by the wave, and now lay drifting in its wake.

In fact no man had been lost. Those on deck had had time to secure themselves, and those below, while they had been flung about, tumbled upon, and bruised—in one or two instances knocked senseless, against a deckhead beam—had suffered little worse. Mr Wing had dropped an array of instruments spread upon a cloth, and banged his shoulder in trying to retrieve them. The cook had burned his hand in attempting to save the galley fire, which had been inundated, with the whole of the forecastle. Animal pens had been inundated, and several hapless pigs drowned. Water had flooded down through gratings, and entered the ship at every aperture and gap, and she was saturated everywhere, but she was afloat, buoyantly aswim, and no one was dead.

'Mr Adgett! Mr Tangible!'

Both men, bedraggled, attending.

'I shall want your assessment of damage to the ship, right quick. I want to get as far away as may be possible from this damned treacherous place. God knows what that bloody island has in store for us next. Beelzebub, I am in no doubt.'

' "Pandemonium", the high capital of Satan and his peers,' said James.

'What? What?'

'The island, sir. The trumpet call, to Satan's army—Milton.'

'Mm. Mm.' Turning away with an uncomprehending frown, then: 'Good God! Where is the jollyboat?'

The jollyboat had been torn from the stern davits, smashed and lost. A single block was all that remained, dangling down over the stern gallery window.

The wheel unlashed, and the rudder examined, and found to be secure. The ship running to the north, as extensive running repairs were commenced, according to lists brought to the great cabin. A sick list brought also. And the purser enjoined to make an accurate tally of stores, including the dead hogs, which the cook was required to bake before their meat spoiled.

'I don't wholly approve of drowned meat,' Mr Trent observed in the gunroom mess.

'Is it not simply meat slaughtered by another means?' inquired Makepeace.

'I don't see how waterlogging a beast is slaughtering it,

when no human hand has done the work. It ain't natural, Mr Makepeace.'

'To waterlog a fattened hog
Is not a natural thing
It speaks to mischief
Yea by God
And it will doubtless bring
Misfortune on our heads
As in our beds we lie

For having eaten drown-ed pig
We shall for certain die!'

'I shall not die in my bed, thank you. I shall eat no pork.'

'It is really very good, you know.' Makepeace, chewing heartily, and scooping gravy with his spoon.

'I never knew such a commission as this, in the peace, for upset and calamity. I shall not tempt Fate to visit further misadventure upon us. I shall eat no pork.'

James ate his supper in the great cabin with the captain. 'You do not find the pork to your taste, sir?' he asked. Rennie had not touched his plate.

'Mm?—No, I do not, in truth. One day, James, I may tell you what we suffered at the hands of Naa Maa. For now I must put it from my mind. We have lost—a great many men. I am not such an arrogant fool that I do not recognize my own fault in this. It was my fault, and I shall regret it the rest of my life.'

'Losing them—was not your doing, sir.' Gently.

'I risked the whole ship, and every man in her. I must write it all in my journal, each fact, everything.—In effect, I killed those men.'

'The king killed them, sir. The island did. And now the island itself is dying. You will recall that on such a remote and dangerous commission as this, Anson lost all but one of his ships. He lived to become First Lord.'

'Anson? I do not compare myself with Anson, good God. He came home with a great treasure. How are we to do that now. Hey?' His voice growing harsh. 'How am *I* to do it?' He threw Mr Adgett's list across the table. 'We are limping, James. Even if we find Mr Makepeace's rock to the north, and repair there, we will be hard pressed to reach Valparaiso. Perhaps there at Valparaiso we might refit sufficient to begin the search, but I cling to no foolish hopes.'

'Surely we could begin the search without having to sail to Valparaiso first, though? I know that is what Loftus would prefer, but he is ignorant of the search, he knows nothing of our sealed instructions. If we go to Valparaiso, likely we will never come back——'

'It is a hopeless search, James. You tried to show me that when we first came to Nagu, but I would not see it. Now I do see it. Good heaven, the bearings is so approximate we will never find anything. The commission is cursed, the whole thing is cursed and damned! What happened in the island——' Rennie sat slumped in his chair. He had washed and shaved, and changed into fresh clothes, and all trace of the Naguan markings had disappeared from his face, but his face looked older, the lines in his forehead and about his mouth were more pronounced, and those at the corners of his eyes. 'What happened there has left me much tormented——' He sighed, and pushed his plate away.

'Will it help you, sir, to unburden yourself?'

The ship rode the swell, her timbers creaking and ticking in the washing quiet. She was making very little steerage way, as the wind had fallen off steadily throughout the afternoon.

'Hm, unburden myself. You sound like a priest, James. Perhaps you have missed your calling, after all.'

'Forgive me, I did not mean to be impertinent.'

'No no, never think it is impertinent to offer me your friendship, my dear James. Mr Makepeace said something in the boat, as we came off the beach, about your efforts to rescue us. I am most grateful for all your endeavours. Some day, another day, we will tell each other all about our several experiences in that dreadful place.—I am tired, now.'

And James left the exhausted Rennie to his rest. Fruitless to pursue him when he was so near to complete bodily collapse—collapse in all senses.

———— ✦❖✦ ————

The small rocky island—first seen through his glass at great distance by Lieutenant Makepeace from the clifftops of Nagu—sighted to the north, through haze. *Expedient* approached the island in light airs, at hammocks up, and found a crescent of rock, not much above half a mile long, curved round a shallow cove on the east. Floating all round the little island were dead seabirds, their nesting colony devastated by the passage of the great wave, and everywhere was other evidence of that massive inundation. Clumps of seaweed clinging to the rock at the highest points of the island; and all the sand of the beach thrust as if by a giant scooping hand to the northern limit of the cove, and caught there by the rocky point jutting into the sea, the smooth heaped surface of the sand encrusted with shells. *Expedient* dropped anchor in the cove, and rode moored at the bow and stern in three fathom of water. Beyond the cove the sea darkened into fathomless depth.

'Sharks,' noted Mr Loftus, pointing.

'In the cove?' Rennie, peering. 'Ah, yes, I see them. Off the point.'

'May I take the pinnace round the isle, sir?' asked Makepeace.

'Yes, I don't see why not, Mr Makepeace. Make the usual observations and sketches, if you please. Mr Tangible! Pipe the hands to breakfast!'

Repairs begun in earnest, now; much to be done. And then Mr Adgett came to the great cabin—where Rennie was attempting to busy himself with his journal, and his charts—bringing grave news.

'Yes, Mr Adgett?'

'I fear——'

Looking up from his table, and waiting. 'What d'y'fear? It is unlike you to be at a loss for words.'

'Well, sir, as I say—it is the foremast.'

'Yes?'

'I fear it is sprung, sir.'

'Sprung? You mean, the foretopmast?'

'No, sir, I do not. I mean the mast itself, sir.'

Rennie was silent a moment, then: 'Very well, thank you, Mr Adgett. It is bad, very bad, but we must do what we can. Is it sprung the whole length?'

'No, sir, I think not. My crew has examined it thorough, and we think—that is, I think—that it is sound from the step through the partners, and above, and is sprung beneath the hounds, sir. I fear we must attempt to bind up the springing, since we have no replacement, and in any case could not rig sheers to step it in, even had we a new mast. Which we has not.'

'Very well.' Rennie sent for the armourer, Jubal Farthing.

'I wish to bind the upper part of the foremast in iron, hooped about it and bolted tight. It will be better to bind it in two places, I think. What say you, Mr Adgett?'

'I—as I say, I do not know that hoops of iron will answer, sir.' Dismayed by the suggestion.

'Lashing it with ropes will not do. Gammoning, so to say. We must bind it tighter than that, Mr Adgett. Iron is far stronger than cordage, and two hoops is better than one. Hey?'

'Well, sir——'

'Very good. You will make the hoops in your forge, Mr Farthing, right quick. Will it be more convenient to rig your forge upon the shore?'

'It is always more convenient to have room all about us, sir.'

'Then you may go ashore, and work there.'

Rennie sent for his first lieutenant, and told him of the sprung mast. In dealing with Adgett, and the armourer, he had been authoritative, and composed, and decisive. With James he allowed his true feelings to emerge, and James was dismayed to find them stronger than ever.

'It is yet another damned misfortune in the whole disaster of this commission. James, I have determined that the commission—everything in our instructions—cannot ever be realized. We have as little hope of recovering that specie as we have of taking wing, flying across the world to Windsor Castle, and joining the King at his breakfast. I have determined that we must abandon all further attempt to obey our instructions, since our circumstances have rendered them nullified, and nonsensical.'

'That is—that is a very grave step indeed, is it not, sir?'

'Our circumstances is grave, James. We are above a thousand mile from land, from the western coast of South America. With a sprung foremast we cannot risk sailing the ship except with the utmost caution towards the coast. Any sudden squall of wind, any storm, any adverse weather at all, could bring us to ruin.'

'Ruin, sir? Surely——'

'You think I exaggerate? That I speak too precipitate? That I am become febrile?'

'No, sir—but I——'

'You *do* think it. You *do* think it. You *see*?'

'See—what, sir?' Beginning to feel deep disquiet.

'You see what *I* face!'

'It is indeed daunting, sir, what we face—what we all face. However, we are sea officers in the service of the King. To face such things is our trade, our obligation—is it not?'

'To take unreasoning risk! To stare death in the face, and laugh! To sail deliberately on, under a full press, into oblivion! Christ's blood, that is reckless folly! Yes, we *are* sea officers, by God! And our obligation is to the ship, to the *ship*, and the people!' His voice had risen sharply, and was rasping, nearly shrill. James knew that to attempt to continue the exchange was unwise.

'I am thirsty, sir.'

'What? What?'

'I am uncommonly thirsty, from the sun on deck, sir. If you will permit it, I will ask your steward for some tea, a pot of tea.'

'Tea?' something like rational distinction emerging in the captain's gaze. 'Yes, tea. I—I am thirsty, myself. Pray order tea, will you, like a good fellow. I must just visit the quarter gallery——' He rose from his chair with apparent easy confidence, and at once fell to the deck in a dead faint.

'Boy! Fetch the doctor! Jump, now!'

Later, when Mr Wing had attended, and had given him something in a small glass, and had confined him to the hanging cot in his sleeping cabin, Rennie sent for James again.

'Bring that chair, and sit close by me, will you?'

James pulled the chair, and sat down.

'I must not talk too loud, else the hands will hear, and think I have gone mad. No no, James, there is no need to grimace, I am no more a madman than you are.' He paused, and settled his head against the pillow. 'However, I think you may well have been right, you know.'

'Right, sir?' Shifting in the chair.

'Aye, right. When you said that I needed to unburden myself, I brushed it aside. That was—it was unwise in me. On the island, in the king's village, and later in the uplands, where we was held, I saw dreadful things.' He coughed, and lay quiet a moment. 'Wing has given me a drug to make me docile. No doubt he thinks me mad, too. I do not wish to be entirely docile, James. I wish to tell you what happened.'

'If you would like, I will come back later, sir—when you are rested.'

'With your indulgence, my dear James, I should like to—

to unburden myself. Only that will allow me to rest, d'y'see?'

'I am here.'

'Young Royce was killed, deliberately slaughtered in front of me. He very bravely—very bravely attempted to intervene in my behalf, when it became clear that the king's intention was to separate me from the armed party. A warrior thrust a spear through his throat. It was very shocking. His blood stains my coat still. And indeed my soul.' A tear fell on the pillow.

'Sir, really, you should not——'

'Hush, James,' his hand on James's arm, 'be a good fellow, and hear me out. Will you?'

'I will.'

'It was my fault Royce was killed, and I feel it bitterly. I do not know what I shall say to his people, his family.'

'His family is on board, sir, and does not blame you for what happened.'

'Eh? You mean, his fellow officers? As family?'

'No, sir. I mean that Alan Dobie, our schoolmaster and your clerk, is his brother.'

'Good God. Then Dobie saw his own brother slain.' He was silent, looking up at the deckhead. A long moment, then: 'Raker was killed, too, and most of his marines, in that first rush to take me prisoner. I was seized, and did not see anything of the battle afterward. Randall South and Mr Symington I did not see until I was taken into the hills. They was both brought to the same place. They told me that all the seamen, and young Pankridge, had been killed also, some of them in the village, and some few at the boats on the beach. And I know that later—their flesh was eaten. There was a feast in the village, and a ceremony, at which the king——' He caught his breath, turned his face into the pillow, and wept.

'Sir, it is too much for you to——'

'Take my hand. Will you?'

James took his hand. Rennie's grip was very tight, very

hard. 'For Christ's sake, let me get it all out. Let me tell it all to you, and then I will never mention it again. We neither of us will. Do me this service.'

James said that he would, that he would hear him out as he had promised, and the captain continued:

'I could understand nothing of their tongue, save the one constant iteration: Naa Ga Neh, Naa Ga Neh. They painted my face, and brought young women to me. This was in the uplands, in a hollow basin there.'

'A village?'

'It was not a village, it was a very wide natural hollow in the rocks, high in the hills, evidently a place sacred to them, with boulders placed all around in a pattern. They carried me there insensible from the king's village below. I was given a potion of some kind, the king himself caused me to drink it, and I was then carried to the hills, I know not how. When I woke, they worshipped me, before a great fire. I was upon a large flat rock, and they bowed down before me, and chanted, and the king presented young women to me—above a dozen young women, naked. I was half-dazed with the filthy potion, and sick with fear. I—I could not respond to them. They danced naked, and I—I was unable to respond, I could not——' He coughed and spat phlegm, and took several long gasping breaths, gripping James's hand. 'A human head was brought from the fire—God save me from such a sight again—they brought a head, and the women, the young women ate the brains from it, from out of the skull. I fell into a stupor of terror. I wanted to vomit, but could not. I trembled so greatly I could scarce get breath in my lungs. I thought I was about to die, that I had failed as their god of manhood, and that having failed I was about to be sacrificed.'

He coughed again, and James saw with consternation that what he had thought was more copious tears was running sweat, pouring from the captain's forehead. He found a handkerchief, and mopped his brow for him. The captain appeared not to notice.

'At last, when they brought South, and young Symington, tied naked to a stave, I saw that the savages did not intend to sacrifice me, and eat my flesh. They intended to sacrifice my companions. But before they could, the ground beneath us became very hot, as if the earth was on fire. There was a sound like a broadside of guns, and all the savages fell back. The king prostrated himself at my feet. There was a terrible stench of fire and burning all around. I don't know what I did, or how. I think I cursed them all for fiends and monsters. I remember running. Running with Randall South at my side, and turning to see young Mr Symington. We were all running, the air was filled with fire, and the ground shook, as if in the din of battle.'

He had raised himself from his pillow, and now fell back, his face deathly pale and slippery with sweat, his thin hair stringy on his head.

'I don't know how we escaped. I don't know how we survived. How in God's name did we survive? How came we to live through it? I don't know, I don't know——'

James held his hand until his breathing calmed, and became even and regular as he drifted into sleep. He mopped the sweat from Rennie's forehead, and detached his hand from the captain's still clenching grip.

'Mr Wing, a word with you.' Calling on the doctor in his quarters.

'You look concerned, Mr Hayter.' A stopper into a bottle. The bottle racked.

'I am concerned. I wonder, is there anything you could give him, a potion, that would cause him to sleep a whole day, or two days?'

'I could dose him further and induce such a sleep, certainly. But natural sleep will be better for him. Does he sleep now?'

'He does, but his mind is greatly agitated. His experiences in the island were—they were profoundly shocking to him. I fear that if he does not sleep long, very long, these terrible thoughts will plague him and make him ill.'

'I have known this affliction in seamen, after a battle, or a shipwreck they have narrowly survived. They have seen things, known and felt things in moments of such utterness— literally flashes of time—that they cannot forget them for months afterward. Simply to close their eyes causes the scene vividly to appear in their heads, a kind of waking terror.'

'And what was your solution?'

'Solution?'

'How did you treat them?'

'As I would any man with a severe affliction. With kindness.'

'Yes yes, that is well, Doctor. We will take care to be kind to the captain. But that will not restore him to health, it will not make him well.'

Mr Wing rolled an array of instruments into a leather fold. 'There is no miracle in any medical treatment, Mr Hayter, no magical solution. Time. Rest. Kind attention. These are the healing things.' He put the instruments into the drawer of his chest. 'There are times, certainly, when kindness will not assist, and only swiftness will answer. Amputation is an instance. The limb must be cut——'

'Yes, yes,' hastily, 'thank you, Doctor. You are right, no doubt. Kindness.' And he retreated.

The pinnace had needed some few minor repairs before Lieutenant Makepeace could take the vessel on his little jaunt of observation round the island; accordingly he had decided not to embark until the morrow, and on the morrow, another calm, hazy morning, he was about to take his crew into the boat with the equipment when a deep rumbling filled the air. It came from the south, a deep rumbling shudder, followed half a minute later by a tremendous booming shock. Seabirds squalled in alarm above the ship, and as their cries died away out to sea an ominous quiet descended.

James came hurrying on deck. 'Hoist up your boat, Tom. Let's get the boat inboard right quick.'

'You think that——'

'I think that another wave will be upon us very soon. That was the sound of Nagu exploding, and we must prepare for the worst.'

'Very well. Mr Tangible!'

James consulted with Mr Loftus. Could they weigh in time, and stand off the island?

'How long have we got? Has the captain been informed?'

'A few minutes at the outside. The captain is unwell, and sleeping. I don't want him disturbed.'

'He will be disturbed by another wave, will he not?'

'We will all be disturbed, for Christ's sake.'

'We might weigh, but we could not hope to stand off, not in a few minutes.'

'Then we must stick, secure, and hope for the best.— Hatches, fore and aft!'

Ashore, Jubal Farthing was working at the forge with his mates, making up a second set of iron hoops for the foremast, the first set having proved too small for the width of the mast, and a third hoop having been bespoke as a precaution. The pinnace, which had taken them ashore, had returned to the ship for Makepeace's use, and now the armourer and his crew were marooned.

James saw them now, and knew that there was no time to help them.

'Could they swim out to us, sir?' Symington, the master's mate, shading his eyes, peering at the beach. 'Should we hail them, and tell them to swim?'

'There is not time for them to swim—even was they able. None of those men can swim. There is nothing to be done for them.'

'Oh, but, sir! Surely we cannot let them drown!'

'Be quiet, Mr Symington. You will assist in securing the ship.'

'But, sir! They——'

'Christ's blood, do as you are told, sir!'

Mr Loftus gripped the boy's shoulder, and said quietly to

him: 'Nothing to be done, lad. Do not think of it, now. We must save the ship.'

The wave came out of the south through the haze in a long, nearly even line, glistening and shivering along the crest. It rushed at the little island, the helpless men ashore, and the tethered ship, and in its massive unminding purpose rolled overwhelmingly over them, tearing the ship from its moorings and flinging it right over the point, the stern anchor dragging in the rocks and snapping its cable like a thread. Water, roaring water, the ship tipping and teetering like a toy boat going over a waterfall, then at the moment of plunging down released, spared, and sucked back into the wallowing water behind. The wave roared on, a vast ripple of destruction, and left *Expedient* afloat in its wake—stunned and bedraggled, trailing ropes, cables, and booms, but afloat.

Captain Rennie, tied in his hanging cot at James's instruction by his steward, woke as water surged through his quarters, and the door of his sleeping cabin swung open in a clicking tide of bottles from a locker in the cabin. Clattering and banging echoed throughout the ship, and the sound of plates smashing in the gunroom below. He attempted to lift himself up, and swing out of his cot, and found himself restrained.

'What has happened?' he called out, in a feeble voice. And hearing his feebleness he grew angry, and bellowed: 'Untie me at once, you mutinous villains! Every man will hang! D'y'hear me!'

Two days passed, days of recovery and then repair. No trace of Jubal Farthing and his two mates had been found. The sand of the beach had disappeared altogether, and there remained only a narrow rocky shelf along the shore of the cove. The ship's copper along her keel had been torn away as she was flung forward over the point. Jacob Gurrall, who could swim, dived down—when the ship had been brought back into the cove, and moored once more—he dived down to look at the damage, and gave his assessment to the captain.

'Part of the false keel has been tore off, sir, from the after keelpiece, and the copper with it, but the scarfs is sound. Part of the coppering on the very lowest strakes, below the bilges aft, is damaged, but all the rest of the staggered strakes that I could see is entirely sound. And remarkable little weed growth.'

'Excellent, Gurrall, thank you. You may tell Mr Loftus—belay that, I will tell him myself—that you are to have a double ration of rum.'

'Thank you, sir.' He touched his hand to his forehead, and went forrard. Rennie turned to the carpenter. 'I know what you are going to tell me, Mr Adgett. We must careen her.'

'I had no such intention, sir. As I say, the ship has seen enough battering and serving from the sea, without we push and pull and interfere with her ourself, more than is strictly needful. No, sir, no, I would not recommend no careening, sir.'

'What level of water is in the well?'

'Not above a few inches, sir, now that she has been pumped out, now that the ship is drying all through. She is sound enough, sir, in spite of what she has took.'

'Very well, thank you.—Mr Storey!—You there, find the gunner, and ask him to come and see me.'

'Sir?' Storey, climbing the ladder from the waist a few moments later.

'Can we rig another forge?'

'We lost the forge, if you will recall, sir.'

'Yes yes, I know that we lost it. Can you find material in the gunnery stores to rig another?'

'Well, sir—as you will recall, the armourer and his mates was drowned.'

'Good God, Mr Storey, I do not need such damned

mournful reminding at every glass! Is there means in the ship to rig a fucking forge!'

'I should not have lost my temper with the gunner,' said Rennie at night in the great cabin. 'He is an honourable man, who liked Farthing, and feels his loss. I should not have shouted at him like that. It was ungentlemanlike, and unfeeling.'

'Such things seem far away.'

'Far away, James? Good manners, d'y'mean?'

'Aye, all gentle and humane things. Everything pleasant, and caseful, and gratifying.'

'Well well, you have lost your books in the flood. That is vexing, no doubt——'

'I do not mean my books. What is a few dozen books when one's life has been spared? You have lost your store of wine.'

'Just so, but I do not mind grog. So long as we have something to drink, I do not mind.'

'What I meant, I expect, was that we have lost the habit of being ordinary men. I have tried to write everything down in my journal—I am obliged to do so by the regulations—and I find myself entirely at a loss for the congruous words. I catch myself staring at the deckhead like an imbecile child, pen in hand, the ink drying on the nib. On deck I look at the sea, and the sky, and the masts, the rigging, and at certain blanking moments I do not know what they are, or what I am about. I am become nothing, vacant, null.'

Rennie peered at him. James met his gaze, and smiled.

'Oh, it don't last. Never think I am a candidate for Bedlam, sir. I expect—I think it is because I cannot quite believe that we have lived. Sometimes, sometimes I feel that I am not awake. That everything is dreams. It is nonsense, I know. Here I am, drinking grog, and feeling its comfort.'

'I thought it was myself that was under the doctor's hand, James. For the vapours, and addled brains. Now I find that it was you, all the time.'

'Wing has enough to do, without I add to it with my childish fears.'

'Fears?—You fear for the ship, or for yourself?'

'Neither, sir, I was——'

'Musing aloud, hey?'

'I expect I was, yes. Take no notice of me.' He swallowed the last mouthful of his grog. 'I will bid you good night, sir, and make my way to what the gunroom servants are pleased to call my thorough washed cabin.'

'Thorough washed? Ha-ha-ha, that is very good, ha-ha-ha. We are all damned well washed between, if not smoked. Hey? Ha-ha-ha. Good night to you, James. Sweet dreams! Sweet and clean!'

But Lieutenant Hayter found sleep at first difficult, and at last impossible. His cabin smelled not sweet, but damp. Everything in it was damp. His books, his clothes, his bedding. His small writing case, wrapped in a tight canvas cover, had by good luck survived intact; even the ink bottles had not broken or spilled. All other personal belongings had been drenched, or swept away as water poured into *Expedient* through hatch covers torn loose and was flung surging through the ship by the blind force of the wave.

They had got the pinnace hoisted in and lashed with moments to spare. Some few of the instruments had been lost in the furious rush—a sextant, and one of the new sounding devices, which even Makepeace, practical and adept as he was, had been able to make little sense of. And now Makepeace wanted to complete his little survey of the island, in the pinnace, just as he had meant to do before the wave struck. Rennie had not yet given him permission.

'I will decide when all damage has been assessed,' he had said. 'Until such time no man, nor boat, is to leave the ship.'

Before they had settled to their grog in the great cabin, Rennie and James had reviewed those assessments, and Mr Trent's list of victualling stores. *Expedient* swam, but she was heavily impaired. Much of the rigging work and repair work that had been undertaken before the second giant wave had struck, had been undone. They had lost many men. They had lost half their boats. Her foremast was sprung. Her copper was damaged. There had not been time to kill and cure much of the livestock meat taken in at Nagu, and now the livestock was lost. They had taken in water, but in the rush and difficulty following the captain's disastrous shore party, very little wood had been brought into the ship. James knew that to begin—to continue—the search for Despairing Island was now an impossibility.

'We must set a course for Valparaiso, sir.' With great reluctance.

'Aye.' A sign of acknowledgement, of recognition of James's recognition. A glance, a nod.

James turned in his hanging cot, and kicked his foot clear of clammy bedding. They would be able to reach Valparaiso, he was confident of that. But would they be able to repair there? How long would that take? Could he send a letter home by an English ship? Even if *Expedient* could be repaired sufficient to be reckoned wholly seaworthy, and take in stores for long months at sea, would they return to the immensity of the Pacifick, to search? Or would Rennie conclude that the more sensible and responsible course of action, for a commander who had so nearly lost his ship, was to return to England, to set a course for home?

And then, when they returned, would Catherine be there, at home, waiting for him? Would she want him still, a penniless lieutenant, returned from a fruitless commission, and beached on half-pay? He had no doubt at all—none, *none*—that was *Expedient* to return thus, empty-handed, their Lordships would conclude that the officers to whom they had given such an important commission were unworthy, and worthless. 'Nor you, nor any of you, may fail.' Failure would not be forgiven. It would be the end for them all, for Rennie, for Makepeace, for himself.

'*Expedient?*' they would say, over their port. 'A fiasco, sir.

A piddling, limping, half-arsed, wretched failure of a commission, when there was every opportunity to shine. A sea officer don't lie down, sir. He prevails! What did Captain Rennie manage to do, the fellow? He lay down like a whipped dog. Well well, he shall return to his kennel, sir, at Deal, and be damned to him!'

James turned again in his cot, and wished that he had drunk more grog, so that he might fall into drunken insensibility. Tomorrow he would ask Wing for something, a draught; he would ask him for a bottle of the stuff, to keep in his cabin. If he could not sleep at night he could not face the world in daylight—the bleak, uncompromising, damned pitiless world.

* ⊨⊹⊨ *

The day following was a Sunday, and Rennie insisted that the awning for Church should be rigged, and the service read. He read the form of service for Thanksgiving after a Storm, with Psalm sixty-six, and his voice caught at the lines:

> Thou has caused men to ride over our heads:
> we went through fire and through water, but thou
> broughtest us out into a wealthy place.

James, whose eye had remained wholly dry on the day they sung the twenty-third Psalm, was moved by Rennie's evident emotion.

'The poor devil has been through a terrible ordeal,' he said to himself. 'In his place I should have faltered long since, and cracked.'

The final amen, and: 'Mr Hayter, we will inspect divisions, and then the ship.'

And afterward, when the hands had been piped to dinner, Rennie had given Lieutenant Makepeace leave to take the pinnace round the island.

'You mean—I may take the boat today, sir?' Pleased.

'Indeed you may, Mr Makepeace. Make the most of your island. It will be the last fragment of land you will see for some time.'

Makepeace departed from the cove immediately after dinner. He had confidently predicted that he would return before nightfall, having circumnavigated the island, sounding, observing, and sketching, and ready to write an extensive report. The island was little more than bare rock, denuded now of seabirds' nests, and what little scraps and tufts of vegetation had lodged in clefts and crevices at the higher places. At its highest point the island was no more than forty or fifty foot above the sea, but the pinnace soon disappeared round the western side, behind the rock, and was forgotten in the ship, where more pressing work was being undertaken. Mr Storey himself had contrived to rig a makeshift forge, and was permitted the remaining boat to carry it ashore; Rennie having demurred when it was suggested that it might be fired up and used in the forecastle.

'Never fear another wave, Mr Storey. You are quite safe ashore.'

The gunner was not entirely convinced, but he did as his captain asked of him, and with his own crew made the iron hoops, to newly taken measurements.

Mr Tangible supplied his ropemaker with extra hands to assist him, and the deck echoed to the clatter of serving mallets, fids and spikes, as tools were prepared and employed, and many yards of new hawser and shroud-laid rope were wormed. Mr Adgett, when he was not hunched over his bench, fussed about the ship, scattering shavings and disquiet, a pencil in his hand, another behind his ear, and long lists tucked under his arm.

'Caulking, sir,' he said to the captain, sucking in a breath. 'As I say, we must caulk like demons, else take in the sea like a sponge.'

'I thought you said she was sound, Mr Adgett?' Sharply.

'Ah, yes, *now*. *Now*, she is sound. But when we weigh, sir, and stand out to sea, well——'

'Well what, for God's sake?'

'The ship is a very long way from home, sir. And many of our shipmates is dead.'

'What the devil d'y'mean by that?'

'I—I that is, I was merely making an observing remark, sir. Far from home, short-handed, mindful of possible disaster, after what has already——'

'Keep your observations to yourself, Mr Adgett, will you? Get on with your work.'

Rennie's uncertain temper was felt throughout the ship. Among the hands there was the sense that the captain did not quite know his own mind. They did not so much resent Sunday work, when the ship so clearly needed urgent attention, but they did resent and fear a captain who was unsure. One moment he was appreciative of their efforts, nodding approvingly as he moved about the ship. Half a glass later he was scowling and silent, pacing the quarterdeck and hating everything in sight.

James saw Rennie's swerving moods, knew their cause, and knew also that he could do nothing except be on hand as dutiful support. If Randall South and young Symington had suffered at the hands of the Naguans, the captain suffered more—much more—because he felt himself to blame for their suffering, and for the loss of so many men. And he laboured under the added grave difficulty of having now to abandon the commission, to face failure in his heart, and in the eyes of the Admiralty.

'What is my plight, compared with his?' James said to himself. 'He alone will take the blame, God knows.'

As darkness fell, and Makepeace had not appeared from round the point in the pinnace, James began to be seriously concerned. He voiced his concern to Mr Loftus, who shared it, but was by no means certain that the captain would permit the use of the remaining boat, moored now to a stunsail boom, in a search for the pinnace at night.

'I must prevail upon him,' said James.

He did not need to. At that moment a light appeared at the farthest extreme of the rocks on the point, a lantern held and waved, and a few minutes later the pinnace came alongside, her lateen sail slipping down, and her oars boated. Makepeace came energetically up the ladder. James took his lantern.

'We had give you up for lost, Tom. We was about to come looking for you.'

'Listen, James, there is something I must tell the captain. He should know it tonight.'

'A wreck?'

'Yes, sir.' Makepeace came forward to the table. 'I have not yet had the opportunity to make accurate drawings, but the ship lies'—taking up a pencil, and making a rough map of the island—'immediately beyond the point, on the northern rocks, here.'

'You are certain it is a ship?'

'I am, sir. We came upon it just before the light began to fade. She is badly broken up, but the timbers are plainly visible beneath the water, on the rocks. There is part of a spar, jutting a little above the water, at an angle. She has foundered there, where she struck the rocks.'

'Is the wreck recent? Could the ship have foundered at the first great wave? Is there other wreckage? Casks? Rope?'

'No, sir. The timber is blackened, and there is marine growth.'

'Ah.—What size of ship? As large as a frigate, would you say?'

'Smaller, I should think. Possibly a merchant vessel, or a whaler.'

'Mm.—How deep does she lie?'

'About three fathom, sir, on her side, and a spar jutting. The bowsprit, I reckon.'

'Very good, thank you, Mr Makepeace. You have done

well. Tomorrow we will send a boat to examine your find.'

'Good night, sir.' Withdrawing.

'Good night to you—James, will you stay a moment?'

And when they were alone: 'What d'y'make of this, James?'

'Nothing, sir, until we may look at the wreck in daylight.'

'Just so. Just so.—A whaling ship, blown far off course, I am in no doubt.'

Because he could swim, and was a good deep diver, Jacob Gurrall was included in the party that visited the wreck in the forenoon watch. The pinnace was moored for convenience to the blackened jutting spar, and Gurrall was ordered to dive down on the wreck, with a rope, to which he might hitch anything that could easily be hauled to the surface.

On his third dive, he came to the surface clutching a broken china dish, much stained, and said that he had hitched his rope to what appeared to be a small swivel gun. The gun was hauled into the boat, and it proved to be a one-pounder, heavily encrusted with rust.

'I saw part of a name on the stern counter timbers, I believe.' Heaving himself into the boat.

'Did you, by God?'

'Aye, sir. It is nearly wore away, just the gold lettering very faint—part of the name.'

'You must tell the captain yourself,' said James, when Gurrall had spelled out the letters.

On the quarterdeck, Rennie peered down into the pinnace as James brought Gurrall aft from the waist port. 'I see you have brought me a gun from your wreck,' he said. 'A swivel, if I'm not deceived.'

'Yes, sir. Jacob Gurrall has something to tell you.'

'Eh? Well well, what is it?'

'Mr Hayter wished me—wished me to tell you myself, sir.' A glance at James. 'It is the name of the wrecked ship, sir.'

'Ah?'

'That is, part of it, sir.'

'Yes?' Glancing impatiently at each man in turn. 'For Christ's sake, now, *one* of you tell me, will you?'

'Aye, sir. The name begins P E R, sir. That is all I was able——'

'What? What did you say?'

'P E R, sir, in very faded gold——'

'By God, James! By God!'

'Yes, sir. My feelings, exact.'

'By God!' Rennie turned away a moment, and gripped the rail. He turned back to James. ' It must be the same, wouldn't you say? It can be no other, surely?'

'It is the ship, I am sure of it.'

'By God!'

Gurrall stared at them in bewilderment.

'The question is, sir,' said James, after a moment. 'The question is——'

'Yes, yes, yes, I know the question.—Is it here?'

'Indeed.'

'Should you like to see the swivel gun, sir?' Gurrall inquired.

'Eh? No, no, no, there is nothing in the wrecked ship of the slightest interest.'

'Beg pardon, sir.'

'Hoist it up, though, will you, Gurrall?' James said to him. 'And then wait in the pinnace. We shall need to go ashore directly.'

'Aye, sir.' Watching unenlightened as James and the captain went below to the great cabin.

In the cabin Rennie quickly found the second set of instructions, which with most of the charts had survived the flooding of the cabin intact. He glanced urgently through them, flicking the pages. 'Damnation. Nothing. Not a word as to where they concealed it. Brought ashore for "safe-keeping", is all that it says.'

A dismaying thought occurred to both men at the same moment.

'Could the wave——'

'The *two* waves——'

'No, no, I will not believe it. That quantity of specie must have been carried in chests. Stout, heavy chests. No wave, no tempest could conceivably wash away such things from under the earth. No, it is there ashore.'

'Then let us discover it, sir, without delay.'

'Without a moment's delay. Randall South! Where the devil is my coxswain when I want him!'

All of the shallow layer of sand and shingle had been carried away by the great waves, leaving bare rock in a curving shelf along the shore of the cove. Inland the rock rose in a low gradient of clifflets and scattered boulders to a slight eminence, about fifty foot high. Rennie and James, in two small parties, searched the entire area, beginning at opposite ends of the cove and working towards the highest point, gradually converging one party with the other.

Lieutenant Makepeace, to his puzzlement and increasing resentment, had been required to remain in the ship.

'What are they looking for?' said Mr Loftus, shading his eyes.

'It concerns that damned wreck. I know it concerns that wreck.'

'Then why do they not return there, to the wreck itself? Why do they clamber about ashore?'

At noon the combined shore parties had discovered nothing but rock, solid rock.

'Should we return to the ship for dinner, sir?'

'No, no. We will continue, if you please. Mr Makepeace knows what to do to in keeping the ship to regulations. We must search. I will proceed downhill to the south-west. You will go to the north. Randall South, you come with me.'

The search went on all through the afternoon watch, and into the first dogwatch, and nothing was found. James joined the captain on the low cliff to the south.

'The hands are hungry, sir. We brought no food ashore. Should we not——'

'Kindly permit me to know what is suitable for the people under my command. You have your duty to carry out, Mr Hayter. And I have mine.' He turned on his heel and walked away along the cliff. James sighed, shrugged, banged his hat against his leg, and returned to his men.

At dusk they returned to the ship.

'Mr Loftus!'

'Sir?' On the quarterdeck.

'All the hands in my boat, that have been ashore, are to have a double ration of spirits.'

'Very good, sir.'

'They may drink it unwatered, if they wish.'

'Very good—Did you find what you was looking for, sir?' Politely.

'Sarcasm will get you nowhere with me, Mr Loftus.' Banging aft to the companion.

'I meant nothing by the question,' said Loftus to James. 'I merely asked.'

'Better not,' was all James said.

All in the ship went to their beds either mystified, or bewildered, or uncontent.

In the morning James interrupted the captain at his breakfast. 'I am sorry to intrude, sir, but a thought came to me in the night. That is, I observed something yesterday, and took no particular note. Then I woke in the night, and I——'

'You thought of it again. Well?' Chewing, swallowing tea.

'On the far side of the island there are rockpools. Tidal rockpools. They are well protected from weather, heavy seas, and so forth. Since there was nowhere in the island the crew of *Perseus* might *bury* the specie—perhaps they *sunk* it, instead, in one of those pools.'

'Randall South!'

The pinnace was taken to the far side of the island, and

beached at a small inlet near the uneven line of rockpools, which stretched for two hundred yards along the shore. The rock there was glistening dark and nearly flat, and pocked by these watery indentations. For the third time Randall South prompted the captain, put knuckles to his forehead and prompted:

'If we was to know what we was looking *for*, sir, that would make our work——'

'You are to report anything unusual to me, as I have told you.'

'Aye, sir. Howsomever——'

'You do not apprehend me?'

'Yes, sir. But the men don't know just what "anything" might mean sir, you see.'

'You will know soon enough, all of you. Mr Hayter, you will take the first dozen pools on the north. I will examine those to the south.'

They found innumerable examples of marine life—limpets, mussels, crabs, sea anemones and the like—and nothing else. After an hour they gathered at the inlet, a dozen very wet seamen, and two wet sea officers.

'Well?'

'No, sir.'

'A word with you, James.' They walked a little way inland from the inlet out of earshot. 'We are the only two in the ship who know what this is all about. I have kept it so because it seemed the wise thing to do. However, I have decided that silence and secrecy will no longer do. Incentive, James, incentive.'

'Sir?'

'We must employ the entire ship's complement. Every man able to walk on his two legs must come ashore, and assist in this search. Every man must know what he searches for. Gold. A vast prize of gold. With ample reward.'

'Very good.—Perhaps this ain't the time to ask, but I wonder——'

'Yes?'

'Do we know the terms of that reward, sir? It cannot be the usual prize money terms, surely, given that this was government money, and remains so?'

'A seaman don't calculate beyond a few pound of money, James. Ten pound to a seaman, in his hand, is infinite wealth.'

'With respect, sir, I do not mean to contradict you, but this is such a prodigious sum in gold——'

'You fear mutiny?'

'I fear that ten pound per man, when hundreds of thousands of money lie in the hold, will not find much favour on the lower deck.'

'Hhhhh, well. You may be right. We will just say "ample reward", and leave it at that.'

The search—now involving the entire ship's company, down to the last boy—continued all that day, and most of the next, and still nothing was found. Rennie sent boatloads of men back to the ship in relays, and stood on the shore of the cove with his hat in his hand, his face grim with defeat in the glare of the setting sun.

'We must begin again tomorrow, sir, and comb the island once more, entire. The gold is here, it must be here——'

'There is no must, James. No certainty in anything, as we have learned this commission, again and again.'

James woke in his hanging cot, and sat up so violently that he nearly upset the cot and tipped himself out on the deck.

'It is near the wreck!' he said aloud. 'They did not come ashore in this cove. They anchored off the point, and hoisted the chests into the boats on that side, on the north! They hid them there! On that shore!'

He went to the great cabin, and roused Rennie from his bed. Rennie listened to him, sat silent a long moment, and shook his head.

'There is nowhere to conceal chests on that shore.'

'But we have not looked there, sir! I beg your pardon, I did not mean to raise my voice. We have not looked there. We looked at the wreck, and discovered the name of the ship, and did not believe the evidence of our own eyes.'

'Eh? What evidence?'

'Because we have anchored in this cove, does not mean that they did. D'y'see? How could the *Perseus* have dragged her bowers in the night, and foundered *beyond* the point? She foundered there because she was anchored there! She never was in this cove!'

'Can you be right, by God?'

'It is the only possible answer. It is the must.'

'Aye.—Well, further sleep is now impossible. We had better sit in the great cabin, and drink tea, and wait for the dawn.'

Both the ship's boats were taken round the point, and a large party put ashore on the rocks there, near the jutting black spar of the wreck.

'There is a hollow place here, sir,' called Jacob Gurrall. 'Like a shallow cave.'

James climbed along, his feet slipping on the tidal growth of the rocks, and came to the place. In under a low overhanging cliff was a long shallow space, with a floor of gritty sand. At the far end was a large heaped pile of rocks, packed high into the inner wall. The tidal smell was very strong—a fishy, saline, clammy reek. Gurrall and three other seamen had begun to pull rocks from the pile, and heave them down towards the water. James joined them.

At fifteen minutes before ten o'clock he was able to report to Rennie that four large oak chests, bound in brass, and covered in green mossy slime, had been uncovered.

'Thank God. Have you broke them open?'

'Not yet, sir. I wished to get your permission.'

By the beginning of the first dogwatch all of the chests had been taken out of the cave, with great difficulty hoisted into the boats, and brought to the ship, where they were hoisted aboard by heavy gun tackles, and there at last broken open with chisels. All four chests contained massed thousands of gold coins, which in the sinking sun seemed burnished with fire, reflected in the face of every man who stood there, hushed.

⊷ ⊱⊰ ⊶

EPILOGUE

'James, where do you go, so early on your first day at home? You arrived so late last night, and I have had so little time to bid you proper welcome.' Lady Hayter was mildly reproachful. 'You have not even had breakfast.'

'I am just going to hack over to the rectory, Mother, and pay my respects to Dr Armitage, and to Catherine.' James took up his riding crop, and kissed his mother briefly.

'Oh. Oh, James, of course you could not have known——' A hand to her mouth.

'Known what?' Staring at her, holding his crop.

'It happened months since, while you were away——'

'What happened?' Dreading the answer.

'The poor rector died. He fell from his horse at a culvert, and struck his head, and did not live the day through. It was very sad. We all felt so sorry for poor Cath——'

But James did not wait to hear any more. He ran out to the stable yard.

'Padding! Where are you, man!'

＊ ⚔ ＊

Leaves lay in heaps at the crossroads, and floated russet and sere from the trees in gardens and lanes, as James galloped through the morning air. Rain was coming in from the west, puffs of cold wind, the sky there piled tall and dark. James rode down the hill, sawing at Jaunter's bit as the animal skidded on the flinty road, and turned into the lane by the rectory. He dismounted at the gate as rain pattered across the cobbles. Tufts of grass pushed beneath the gate, and a branch hung down loose over the wall. He pushed open the gate, forcing it, and led his horse in. The stable doors stood open, the stalls empty. Mildewed hay lay scattered, and dried dung. The house had a gloomy, closed-in look. There was a green stain of damp from broken guttering; leaves lay in the gutters all along the line of the roof. The windows were shuttered on the inside. James felt his heart thudding in his chest.

'Catherine?' he said, as if to himself.

He hurried across the cobbles, and went in under the portico, and pulled the bell.

'Catherine!' he called. 'Cathy!'

Pulled the bell again, harder, and heard it echo dully deep in the house.

'Cathy! Are you here!'

No one answered.

⚓

'But where has she gone?' James demanded of his mother, his coat spattered with mud.

'James, please do not shout at me. Have you no feelings? When you have only just come——'

'Mother, please!'

'Catherine Armitage has had to leave the house, since it did not belong to her father. The——'

'Yes yes, but where is she now?'

'The house has been left empty, and the rector's duties assumed by the curate of Melton Abbas. Alas, Dr Armitage died rather in debt. He kept horses, you know, and a groom, and a gardener——'

'Yes yes, Mother, I do not care anything about the late rector's debts!'

'He lived just enough beyond his means to make his life

comfortable, and not enough to make his bankers uneasy. That is, until he departed so sudden. Then they did become un——'

'Mother, for God's sake!'

'You must not shout at me, James.' Letting her embroidery fall in her lap. 'I am trying to tell you everything, and you shout at me.'

'Yes yes, I am sorry. There, I have said so. Now. Where has Catherine gone to?'

'I understand that she has gone to Wells, to become a governess.'

'A governess! Cathy, a governess!'

'Really, James, what on earth is the matter? You upset me dreadfully, with your intemperate questions, and your unfeeling rush and haste——'

'She cannot become a governess, for God's sake!' And he dashed away again, leaving his mother much discomforted and vexed with her son.

'Where is James?' said his father, at luncheon. 'Does he not join us at table?'

'He has gone to Wells,' said Lady Hayter.

'Wells? His first full day at home, and he has gone to Wells?'

'My dear, please do not be violent. James has been violent, and now you are violent——'

'I am not violent! I beg your pardon, madam. What the devil does the boy mean by dashing off to Wells? Taking my best horse, I am in no doubt.'

James reached the house—a large house behind a wall, near the cathedral close—after nightfall, having ridden all day. He left Jaunter in the paved court, by the wall, and rang the bell. The cathedral clock chimed the half-hour as James waited, and he could hear voices lifted in a hymn. He was about to ring the bell again when the door was opened by a maid-servant.

'Does Cath——does Miss Armitage live here?'

'Miss Armitage does live here, sir. She is governess to——'

'May I see her?'

'She is at the cathedral, sir, at evensong.'

'Yes, of course. It is Sunday, I had quite forgot. Thank you, I will find her there.'

He walked across the close, feeling light-headed with fatigue, and saw a spill of people at the great door of the cathedral, the light behind them. He walked towards them, and among them. He could not see her. He went into the church, and glanced along the depth of the nave. He could not see her, and turned in disappointment to leave. A figure, carrying a book, emerged from behind a pillar. A young woman, all in black. She turned, her face catching the light—

'Catherine!'

—and was in his arms.

Badge of Glory

Douglas Reeman

It was an age of Empire, an age of contrast, and an age of dramatic change – and one which would determine the destinies of nations as well as of men.

Captain Philip Blackwood of the Royal Marines rejoins his ship, HMS *Audacious*, in the August of 1850, anxious to get back into action. Per Mare – Per Terram is the Marines' motto. In the torturous heat of Africa, where they are sent to stamp out the remaining strongholds of slavery, and later, in the bitter war of the Crimea, Philip Blackwood and his men learn to obey it without question.

This is the first novel in the Blackwood saga, spanning 150 years in the history of a great seafaring family and the tradition in which they served.

arrow books

ALSO AVAILABLE IN ARROW

Dust on the Sea

Douglas Reeman

It is 1943, and Captain Mike Blackwood, Royal Marine Commando, is a survivor. Young, toughened and tried in the hellish crucible of Burma, he labours, sometimes faltering, beneath the weight of tradition, the glorious heritage of his family, and the burden of his own self-doubt.

For Blackwood, the horizon is not the lip of the trench seen by men of the Corps in the previous war, but the ramp of a landing craft smashing down into the sea, and the fire of the enemy on a Sicilian beach.

Here, tradition is not enough, and Mike Blackwood must find within himself qualities of leadership which will inspire those Royal Marines who are once again the first to land, and among the first to die.

This is the fourth novel in the Blackwood saga, spanning 150 years in the history of a great seafaring family and the tradition in which they served.

arrow books

First to Land

Douglas Reeman

1899, China. The Mandarins are becoming troublesome again and there are rumours that attacks will soon begin on British trade missions and legations. Captain David Blackwood of the Royal Marines, received a VC in the bloody battle for Benin, Africa but is now being packed off to this apparent backwater.

But there are plenty of troubles in store for Blackwood in the shape of an errant nephew and a beautiful German Countess who insists he personally escort her up river on a small steamer into the heart of the country. China is a sleeping tiger that will soon awake when the Boxer Rebellion erupts into bloody war in 1900. True to their motto, the Royal Marines are the first to land – and the last to leave.

This is the second novel in the Blackwood saga, spanning 150 years in the history of a great seafaring family and the tradition in which they served.

arrow books